A Place to Call Home

BOOKS BY LIZZIE PAGE

She viewed them with looks of despair,
She said (and I'm sure it was true),
''Tis not for myself that I care,
But, my poor little children, for you.'

'Poverty', Jane Taylor

GOOD HOUSEKEEPING MAGAZINE
AUGUST 1949 QUIZ OF THE WEEK

What is your perfect home?

You have scored: Mostly D's:

You're a rare case: happiness for you is not living in a palace, a castle or a beachside villa. You can be content in a hut or an igloo! For you, home is all about being surrounded by the ones you love. Some people would say you're 'easily pleased', we would say it's because for you, 'home is where your heart is.'

1

SEPTEMBER 1949

Suffolk

On Wednesday morning, just as Clara was about to go to the market (Rita was desperate for radishes), a black Ford Anglia pulled up and Miss Bridges clambered out of the driver's seat. The usually impeccable children's services and part-time cemeteries officer looked like she'd been dragged through a hedge backwards. Her navy pillbox hat had slumped sideways and her blouse was untucked.

'We've been travelling since seven,' Miss Bridges said loudly, as though they'd come from the other side of the world. She shook her head at Clara and made help-me eyes, before whispering, 'You're going to have your hands full with these.'

'Better late than never, Miss Bridges!' Clara responded heartily. The three new children had been expected last Sunday. On Saturday, Clara had strung up so many brightly coloured banners and Union Jacks it looked like VE Day all over again. Fourteen-year-old Maureen, the oldest girl at the Grange, had been bribed to make a rhubarb crumble. Clara had practised saying, 'I'm your housemother', with a welcoming tilt of the head in the mirror. She had a speech in her head: 'I'm here to do the best for you'. She wanted to look like the women she'd seen at picture club: wholesome. Trustworthy. Judy Garland.

She had put a mattress in the girls' dorm, and a camp bed in the boys'. One of the girls would have Terry's old bed – it would have to do for now. Ten-year-old pianist Rita had offered to put her ancient Molly Mouse on the pillow because it looked rather sterile, but, impulsively, Clara had blown her budget on three hand-knitted bears – after all, some children came with nothing.

On Sunday morning, Clara had plaited the girls' hair and smoothed down the boys' with Brylcreem. She had made twelve-year-old Alex, the home's clever-clogs, wash behind his jug-ears. Little Peg, only eight years old, had drawn pictures of pigs with curly tails like telephone wires and Clara hung them up too and at the expected time of arrival she had made the children sit in the parlour, even the thirteen-year-old white-haired twins, Billy and Barry, who hated to sit still, except for eating – no, especially for eating.

And yet the new children hadn't turned up. They hadn't turned up on the Sunday and they hadn't turned up since.

Every day Clara had called the council children's services (she loved using the telephone in the hallway and using her sophisticated telephone voice – '0500, 434909 Lavenham') only to be told, 'Not today, Miss Newton.'

The rhubarb crumble had disappeared. The anticipation and the bunting had frayed, the curly-tailed pigs had come off the walls and the children no longer asked, 'Are they here yet?' every five minutes.

Only when the children were all at school, when Clara was

off to the market with a fistful of chores and a head full of worry, had they turned up.

'What was the hold-up?' she mouthed.

'Don't ask...' Miss Bridges was redder than ever. She fanned herself with her hands and Clara decided not to mention the ladder creeping up her stockings. Instead, she peeked into the car and saw two girls on the back seat. She retreated quickly.

'Only two?!'

Miss Bridges pursed her lips. She seemed in a frightful mood.

'Where's the boy?'

'There's been a change of plan,' Miss Bridges said, avoiding Clara's eyes and patting her hair into place.

'A change? Wh-yy?'

It took Miss Bridges a while to catch her breath. 'The council weren't sure if you could manage... He's been sent to a larger home.'

'Oh.' This was hurtful. Clara turned away from her and peered into the back of the car, for longer this time.

'Out you pop!' she said enthusiastically.

The girl who slipped across the leather seats looked hot and uncomfortable. She had a polka-dot bow in her curly hair and her cheeks were round, extending further forwards than her button nose. She looked like she wanted to hide her face in a jar of sweets. All the clothes Clara had set aside for her would be too small; she'd be better off in some of Maureen's old stuff. She looked about fourteen but couldn't have been. One of the only things Clara knew about her was that she would attend the local junior school.

'This is the thirtieth place I've been to,' she huffed as she jumped down. She was clutching a small bag. Someone had scrawled on it: 'Vee'.

Evelyn?

'Thirtieth?' Clara whispered to Miss Bridges, who was rummaging in the boot of the car.

'Not true. It's actually her ninth.'

Nine was better than thirty, but that was still an awful lot; and it probably *felt* like thirty to the poor thing.

'Welcome,' Clara announced, 'to your new home, Shilling Grange. I'm your housemother, Miss Newton.'

The girl looked her up and down.

'Is it even worth unpacking?'

The other girl folded her arms, crossed her legs and refused to get out of the car.

'I'll sit with her,' proposed Clara brightly. 'Miss Bridges, would you take Evelyn in to meet Stella, please.'

Miss Bridges looked relieved, although whether that was relieved to see the cat or to get away from them both, Clara couldn't say.

This one was a scrawny girl with severe features and brown hair as straight as pump water. Her skin was olive, almost yellowy-green in tone, and she had circles under her eyes as though someone had got carried away with pencil shading. She was playing with a piece of string wound so tightly round her thumb that the tip of it was as scarlet as the leather seats.

'I'm not coming out,' she warned Clara. 'No matter what you say.'

'Okay then,' said Clara, smiling, for she had anticipated resistance and she liked a girl with character. 'Mind if I sit here?' She felt her welcome speech 'You are home and safe,' would be too much at this point: still she was confident she could win the girl over.

'Put yourself in their shoes,' was a good guiding principle for a housemother. Clara had been given a second chance to be housemother at the Grange and she wasn't going to squander it. This was the year her charges would have an opportunity to blossom – the old ones and the new. There were housemothers who didn't care, who were indifferent, who were biding their time until retirement or marriage. Not Clara. *Not Clara any more.*

And Clara had a secret weapon – lemon sherbets, shiny nuggets of yellow with the white powdery stripe peeping through, sharp on the tongue. These were easier to get than before, but rare enough to produce a thrill.

Clara held out the bag. 'Do you like these?'

The girl had to admit that she did like them, and, grudgingly, she plucked one from the bag. Clara did too. Difficult to be annoyed with the world when you've a mouth full of lemon sherbet, Clara thought.

The last of the summer flies bashed themselves against the windscreen. The girl sighed. Clara realised that Miss Bridges had left her paperwork in a cardboard box on the passenger seat, under her driving gloves. 'Why don't you start by telling me your name?'

The girl's eyes darted to the files. 'It's all there, isn't it?'

If she were alone, Clara would have leaned over to have a rummage and a read. As it was, she sat there and waited. And waited. The girl pulled the string tighter. They watched her thumb grow redder like a glowing light.

'Pull that any tighter and we might have to chop your thumb off,' Clara observed.

It was time for a different strategy.

Clara talked about what had happened to her last month. She could talk about it now, without sounding too indignant. The council had asked her to leave the home and she explained she had had to appear in front of a panel – 'a tribunal, they call it, and they had to assess my fitness to stay.'

The girl raised one solitary eyebrow. She *was* interested, despite herself.

'And we put up a strong case, and the children all helped, and Iv—' *no, don't mention Ivor* – 'a neighbour did too and eventually I was allowed to stay. I was over the moon and I'm determined, absolutely determined, to do the best I can for you children.' Clara smiled, remembering. 'I'm fond of this place, although to be honest, I wasn't at first.'

Shilling Grange did look impressive in the sunlight. It was old and crumbling at the edges, but it never failed to make a good first impression.

What would the girl be thinking?

'It's run-down: the floors are uneven and the radiators leak. But it's lovely inside.' She checked the girl was listening as the sweet moved around her cheeks. 'You'll love the garden. There's no whipping or smacking or anything like that here. I prefer to negotiate. As Churchill says, jaw-jaw, not war-war.'

Clara remembered what Billy, the more outspoken twin, had revealed to her once about the brutal regime in place under her predecessor, the dreaded Sister Eunice: the locks on the doors, the regular whippings, the silent mealtimes, the public humiliations, being put in the cupboard without dinner. Being made to eat foods that made them sick. It had broken Clara's heart just to hear about it. How terrible it must have been for the children to go through it.

'I don't believe in punishments for bad behaviour. I believe in rewards for good.' *And it mostly works,* she thought. The girl was tying the string round the next finger along. She didn't appear to be listening, but...

'I like to be honest with you all. And anything you're interested in, from piano to comics, I'll do my best to support.' Clara considered. 'Since I've been here, I have grown to like poetry: my favourite poet, Jane Taylor, was actually from Lavenham! Do you know "Twinkle Twinkle, Little Star"?'

The string began to unravel. The girl looked up scornfully. 'You can tell all the sob stories you like, I don't care.'

Clara's blood pressure was rising. She wondered what Miss Bridges was doing with the other child and the cat. It was all very well being the 'character', but the compliant ones always had to wait around for you and didn't get the attention they deserved. How was this fair to Evelyn? And it was surprisingly chilly in the car. Clara wasn't wearing a coat or hat – she hadn't expected to be out for long.

'The other children are kind.' She paused. *Did that make them sound dull?*

'And fun. You'll meet them soon.'

Her speech didn't come out half so well as it had sounded when it was in her head.

'Whatever happens, you are here, you are safe.'

Finally, the girl unravelled her string before placing it in her lap like it was a precious gem.

'I want to go home.'

A breakthrough.

'Why don't you tell me about your home?' Clara's mouth was aching from the unnatural smiling.

Hesitantly, the girl began. 'We used to have buttered toast round the fire with Daddy after church and Daddy would sing "My Old Man's a Dustman"?'

Clara nodded. *Go on.*

'And then he'd tell us stories of the good old days in the RAF and we'd all laugh and laugh until our sides ached...' She looked up at Clara defiantly.

'Is this true?' asked Clara.

The girl laughed. It was not a sweet sound but a rat-a-tat-tat like machine gun in a war film. 'Ha, of course it's not true. What the heck would I be doing in this old dump with you if that was true?'

'Right, that's it!' Leaning across, Clara yanked open the car door and nudged the girl towards it. Instead of climbing out as she had expected, the girl dropped out and smacked down, palms flat, onto the pavement. Then, raising her head in shock, she let out an almighty shriek.

. . .

Half an hour later, the girl – her name was Joyce – was lying under a blanket on the sofa in the parlour, but she had at least stopped sobbing. Clara had tried stroking her hair but Joyce wasn't having any of it – she wouldn't let Clara anywhere near her. It was Miss Bridges who had half-carried, half-dragged her into the house and who applied ointment to her scraped hands and who pursed her lips sympathetically. Clara had been dispatched back to the car to fetch the beloved string.

The parlour was probably Clara's favourite room in the house. When Clara had arrived it was virtually unused, but now she took pride in its marble fireplace, the second-hand pictures from the market of windmills and bubbling brooks, the lamp with its exotic tassels, the cushions from Ivor, the blankets for winter evenings – also from Ivor. Joyce's feet stuck out over the end of the sofa, but when Clara made an attempt to take off her shoes – one had a large heel – she howled.

'I didn't mean to,' Clara said. 'I thought you'd just be more comfortable.'

'Don't ever touch me again.'

All the while this was going on, Evelyn played solitaire quietly on the carpet, as though she wanted everyone to forget she was there.

In the kitchen, Miss Bridges was making tea.

'You could have warned me Joyce had trouble with her legs.' If she could make Miss Bridges feel as bad as she herself did, Clara decided, it would help with her guilt. A guilt shared was a guilt halved.

'It's in the files.' Miss Bridges pointed at the paperwork that had been in the car.

'It might have been helpful to know in advance.'

Miss Bridges looked pained. 'I didn't have the files in advance.'

'Wouldn't that be an idea in future?' Clara asked, mindful that after her tribunal she had been asked about making improvements to the running of homes. This would go to the top of the list.

'You'll cope, Clara.'

'And if I can't?'

It's not like you can return children to a stall at the market.

Miss Bridges said there had been a radio documentary recently called *The Joys of Adoption,* with that lovely presenter Donald Burton waxing lyrically. The day after it was broadcast the children's department phone wouldn't stop ringing. Everyone wanted a cute child to adopt. The staff hadn't understood why the surge in interest at first.

'Are any of them likely to proceed?' Clara pondered.

Miss Bridges shrugged.

'I still don't understand why they didn't send the boy.'

Although, it was probably a blessing. Three difficult ones might have been too much.

'I know you don't understand...' Miss Bridges said, averting her eyes. 'That's the way it is.'

It seemed to Clara that Miss Bridges was backing away from her. She was usually so sympathetic (Clara didn't know what she would have done without her over the last year). Just as Clara was about to say something, Miss Bridges announced that she was handing responsibility for Shilling Grange to Miss Cooper, a colleague in children's services. Miss Bridges looked after cemeteries as well as children's services and she said cemeteries were taking up so much of her time nowadays that she had to step back from Shilling Grange. She explained that it wasn't quite her choice and she was still ready to help Clara, not in an official capacity perhaps, but as a friend and a shoulder to cry on. This – and the boy who had not turned up

– made Clara's senses tingle. It felt like she was being demoted.

She asked Miss Bridges if that was what it was but Miss Bridges adamantly denied it and said, 'I think highly of you. And you do *like* Miss Cooper, don't you?'

Miss Cooper lived in a shared house in Colchester. Sometimes Clara thought Miss Cooper lived how she herself might once have been on track to live – if the war hadn't knocked her off course. Miss Cooper was always going out dancing. Sometimes she pulled an 'all-nighter', which meant she'd be sat at her desk, gulping back cups of water and contacting prospective adopters with a head like a sore bear. Clara *did* like her but found her less *comforting* than Miss Bridges, who was usually quite motherly. But not today. Miss Bridges only had one cup of tea before she scraped back her chair. Miss Bridges was usually at least a two-or-three-cup person. Was this how it was now?

'That's me done.'

'Anything wrong?' Things really were changing.

Miss Bridges just gave her fairground Aunt Sally smile. 'Meetings.'

'What about?'

Miss Bridges pursed her lips. Clara bit hers. *Wasn't she supposed to even talk with Miss Bridges any more?*

Miss Bridges put on her coat and driving gloves before muttering, 'Just looking at different ways to save money. The usual.'

Money, money, money. Money was a constant fly in the ointment. Just when you thought you'd been squeezed enough, they came back and squeezed you some more.

'Who is it with this time?'

Miss Bridges obviously did not want to talk about it.

'Mr Horton...'

Mr Horton was the inspector for children's services. Clara couldn't recall Miss Bridges having meetings with him before, but she could recall that Miss Bridges enjoyed complaining about him. The way she said he liked bowls and lived with his mother, you'd think he was a war criminal.

'Oh, bad luck.' Clara grinned, hoping this would be something they might finally bond over. But Miss Bridges went an even deeper shade of pink. 'He's not going to make you play bowls, is he?' Clara went on.

Miss Bridges looked like she had been poked with a hatpin. Her mouth open and shut a few times like a goldfish, before she said, 'Clara – this is not the way to talk about a respected senior official.'

This was the same woman who had worn a tea cosy as a hat and sung, 'It's a Long Way to Mr Sommersby' (Mr Sommersby was the actual head of children's services!) at Clara's staying party just last month.

Now Miss Bridges clutched her files to her chest. 'I'll see myself out.'

The rest of the morning passed so slowly it was like a Sunday. Uneasily, Clara left the girls to it in the parlour while she did her chores. She couldn't help thinking about Miss Bridges' attitude towards her. Usually the other woman was warm and encouraging. She used to say they were a team, 'the two of them against the world'. Now it felt as though Miss Bridges had just changed team.

Oh well, Clara decided, maybe Miss Bridges was also upset about no longer being Clara's key contact. Perhaps the abruptness was her way of dealing with it.

When she returned to the parlour, Clara found the girls in the same positions: Evelyn cross-legged, dealing out cards, and Joyce under the blanket, scowling into nothingness. They couldn't have kept stiller if they were artist's models. In one way, it was admirable, but mostly Clara thought it was odd. The only sound in the room was the swish-swish of the cards being shuffled.

Maureen was the first to arrive home, at just after three. She swept past Clara, galloping upstairs two at a time with barely a pause for hello. Maureen had started working for Robinson, Browne and White a couple of weeks earlier. Just one hundred yards from the Grange, it was a law firm with Grecian arches and portraits of King George in every room. Maureen was their girl Friday, but she didn't just do Fridays, she did four 'til six every day after school.

Maureen loved the job; she especially loved getting paid. Clara had always imagined Maureen would go into domestic service because, although she hated needlework, she was an intuitive and resourceful cook – far better than Clara. However, she was now talking about secretarial college. At present, her main task at Robinson, Browne and White was to put files in alphabetical order. (Goodness knows how they used to keep them!) Clara had written the alphabet on a strip of paper that Maureen kept for reference in her pocket because she tended to get lost in the LMNOP section.

Within minutes, Maureen had changed from her school uniform and into a smart belted dress that Clara had worn – a billion years ago – in her office days and was dashing to the front door. She was always a whirlwind lately.

'Won't you say hello to the new—' Clara called, but Maureen had flown past, pretending not to hear.

'Did you get my radishes?' Rita said, scowling, as she and Peg arrived home. After Clara admitted that no, she had not, the mood seemed to go downhill – as it often did with Rita. She was a girl with a glass half-empty.

'You're the same age as the new girls, Rita!' Clara said brightly. 'I'm sure you'll get on wonderfully.'

As she looked at Rita's incredulous expression, Clara thought, *It is a nonsense that people the same age get on.* Clara was twenty-seven, the same age as Mrs Garrard the local florist, with whom she had a frosty relationship. Judy, her darling best friend, had been five years older than her.

'Anyway, just introduce yourselves!' Clara reset her sights, her smile a rictus.

The girls surveyed each other warily. Joyce, Evelyn and Rita mumbled greetings. Peg hovered, grinning like she had a twitch.

'What's the matter with her?' Joyce asked.

'Peg doesn't speak,' Clara explained, briskly. In fact, Peg had uttered one word – 'Cows!', at a timely moment – but rather than that uncorking her speech as Clara had hoped, she had returned to her old silent ways. Peg was a foundling and had been in care all her life. Her most treasured possession was the seashell she had been left with at the door of a church in Lincolnshire.

'Why?'

'Because...' said Clara, letting it hang there in the air. *Because I said so* was usually sufficient, but it didn't seem right now. 'She doesn't.'

'But why?'

Clara backed into the kitchen, where she grabbed the fruit cake she had been saving for the occasion. Hopefully, it would stop a 'why' or two.

Later, Billy and Barry raced in the back door and each grabbed slices of cake as Clara put the rest away in a tin.

'Sit down to eat, please...'

'We're going back up the pitch.'

'Big match next week. Didn't we tell you?'

Billy and Barry were benefitting from an enthusiastic PE teacher, which was a relief. There was only so much roaming in the fields they could do without the farmer coming at them with a shotgun. There was only so much knock-down-ginger they could play without a neighbour giving them a whack round the head. The downsides from all the sport were that they ate like carthorses, and it felt like washing was coming out of Clara's ears.

'What about the new children, boys?'

'Do they play?' Barry looked thrilled.

'I mean, would you go and introduce yourselves to them?'

Billy looked pained but Barry agreed, nudging his twin. 'If they're any good, they can go in goal.'

Maureen's boyfriend, sixteen-year-old Joe, was more helpful. Initially, Clara hadn't liked Joe – his cheek, his whistling, his sullen expressions – but as she got to know him, she had changed her mind. Joe couldn't do enough for them. He had taken in Alex's blazer, hemmed Rita's skirt and patched the twins' shorts – and for the past couple of days he had been weeding the garden. That afternoon, when he came in, he called, 'Who wants to see the hairiest spider in the world?' and Rita and Peg jumped up, Rita squealing, 'Has it caught any flies – or slugs?!'

The new girls frowned at each other. Clara said, 'Go on!' and Evelyn obediently rose, but Joyce pulled the blanket over her head and wouldn't move. *It's going to be like that, is it?* Clara thought. Nevertheless she admired Joyce's refusal to submit to authority. It was a behaviour Clara herself could never contemplate.

'It's a squash but it'll do for now,' Clara told the girls in their dorm after tea their first evening. They made a morose pair. It was normal, of course, it was probably overwhelming, but the occasional smile would have been helpful. So far, they had displayed no affinity with the other children and, perhaps more surprisingly, no affinity with each other either.

Clara noticed that Joyce's hand-knitted bear had rolled under the bed and Evelyn's was nowhere to be seen. *Not everyone is a cuddly-toy person,* Clara thought – she wasn't either – but she couldn't help feeling deflated.

In the boys' dorm, Billy and Barry had fallen asleep,

exhausted from their activities, their clothes spread on the floor. Fourteen-year-old Peter was reading a comic in the lamplight. He said, 'Goodnight, Miss Newton,' but his eyes never left the page. Clara smiled indulgently. There was little that lanky, freckly Peter could do to annoy her. Last year, Peter had been trouble. He wouldn't communicate, he wouldn't get out of bed. The only thing he was interested in was the *Dandy* or the *Beano*. Clara had eventually found out he was being abused by his uncle, who he had visited weekly – it was a devastating discovery and Clara hated that it had taken her so long to realise what was going on. In her head, she still went over the times she had encouraged the trips out, the stupid things she had said. She would never be so trusting again. Since it had come out and Peter had stopped seeing him, things were improving, little by little.

Alex had been quieter than usual since he'd got home; he had already intimated that his new school wasn't as stimulating as he'd hoped, so Clara wondered if that was it. Alex had just joined the Ipswich grammar school – he'd had to pass the eleven-plus entrance exam to get in. (He had achieved that with some of the highest marks the school had ever seen.)

'Can I ask you a question?' Alex whispered now.

Clara knelt at his side. His breath smelled milky. 'Anything.'

'How did Aunty Judy die?'

Anything but that, Clara thought. Unfortunately, smart Alex seemed to have a sixth sense about it. Alex and her best friend Judy had had such a bond that, before she died, Judy had wanted to adopt Alex.

Clara paused. *How could she say this?* 'She just did,' she said eventually. 'I don't know the details.'

True.

Clara deliberately did not know the exact details of how Arthur, Judy's husband, had killed her. It seemed he may have beaten her, thrown her down the stairs and then gone out, leaving her to suffer alone. Clara *kind of* knew Arthur had been violent, but Judy had insisted it had stopped and Clara had believed her. But one month on, it still hurt her heart just as much as it had when she first heard the dreadful news in a telegram from Judy's mother.

'I hate to think she was ill and we didn't know it,' Alex said softly. 'Or if we could have done something...'

'It wasn't, we couldn't,' Clara whispered back, her voice catching. *Oh, Alex.* 'Please don't worry, Judy wouldn't have wanted you to.'

Clara's bedroom was at the front of the house; a box-shaped room with faded flowery mustard wallpaper and thick brown curtains that were not aesthetically pleasing but kept out the light. (Ivor had promised to change them but hadn't got round to it.) That evening she read an article in *Woman's Own* – the magazines were borrowed from the library so they were always a little out of date – about a vitamin-rich brown bread she would probably never make and two lovely dresses from a ninepenny pattern that she would *definitely* never make. Just before she got into bed, she looked over to Ivor's workshop across the road. There were, as usual, no signs of life.

It would have been nice to feel a little less alone.

Clara's parents had moved to Africa when she was a girl, leaving her at boarding school. Her mother had passed away there and Clara no longer spoke to her father. When unexpectedly he had come back to England last year, she had left the family home in London, where she was living by herself, and got this job in Suffolk.

Her first love, American serviceman Captain Michael Adams, had been with the Eighth Air Force and based at Lavenham Cockfields, just down the road from the Grange.

They met in London in 1943, Michael pursued her, they had a wonderful time together. He had asked her to marry him and she had said yes. Now when she looked back, it felt like their time together had something magic, even unworldly about it; perhaps it was too good to be true. She had been happy though; it wasn't just her memory playing tricks – they were making plans for their lives together after the war was over.

Then Michael was killed in action over Christmas 1944 and Clara was devastated. She had thrown herself into the war effort – at the time she was working at Harris & Sons – while her friendship with Judy was probably the thing that saved her.

Clara didn't have much family to speak of, but it wasn't until she had come to Lavenham last year that she had realised how much she wanted one. Caring for the children at the Grange hadn't come easily to her – she suspected it never would – but she coped with the help of her friends. Between them – her oldest friend, teacher Judy, experienced childcare officer Miss Bridges and neighbour Ivor – a supportive triangle had formed around her. Now darling Judy was dead, Miss Bridges had been transferred (and seemed to be docilely accepting of that) and Ivor? Well, Ivor was gone too.

It had taken a community to keep the children safe and Clara didn't know if she was up to it on her own. At the same time, she knew she had to stand on her own two feet. It was long overdue.

She had learned many lessons last year; not to mention the dreadful abuse of Peter, she'd dealt with runaway cows, May Queens, eleven-pluses, nits and this year she'd hoped to be able to put everything she had learned into practice. Concentrate on keeping the home safe and happy for ALL the children. She could do it, she just had to have a little more faith in herself.

She tugged the curtains across firmly. Enough gazing into space, Ivor wasn't out there.

Clara didn't just miss Ivor as far as helping with the chil-

dren was concerned. She missed him in a deep, yearning kind of
way. For she had fallen for him. Unexpectedly and dramatically. She hadn't planned to; in fact, she'd disliked him at first –
although that was mostly because he'd disliked her. He thought
she was a pen-pusher, a jobsworth. Someone more concerned
with paperwork than people. He'd even called her the hokey-
cokey, implying she was half in and half out. Maybe she was.
But over the months, as she had grown to love the children, she
had come to rely on Ivor. Whenever she had worries – and she
had a lot of those – she would go and see him. He was always
her first port of call.

Which was wrong.

But it was what it was.

She remembered when Ivor had put his arm round her
waist once to steady her in the garden; it had felt like an electric
current had run through her. Another time, he had squeezed
her shoulder in the street and she remembered hoping nobody
would comment on her giveaway crimson cheeks. Mostly, she
remembered that fateful time in his workshop when they stood
close together, he was behind her as she looked through the telescope. How hot she had become, how every part of her seemed
to want to be close to every part of him. She could have stayed
there forever. He must have known. Now she wondered if the
telescope were still there. She might borrow the key to the workshop, Ivor's home, just to check everything was okay. (An unin-
habited building took on a smell...)

They had kissed once but not quite – or rather, not for long.
In the embrace – and oh! Clara could remember the feel of him,
the rise and fall of his chest, the way they locked together so
perfectly – she had whispered her ex-fiancé's name: 'Michael;'
she *had* said it, no use denying it, but she had been in shock. She
had just found out that Judy was dead. Not long after that, Ivor
had left.

If she had told Ivor she loved him then, maybe things would

be different. If she had *realised* she loved him sooner, then maybe things would be different.

And if he wasn't married to Ruby, a picture-postcard glamour girl, then maybe things would be different too...

When Clara had arrived in Lavenham last year, there was no Ruby. It wasn't that she had gone – it was like she had never existed. Clara had no idea there was someone missing. Gradually, the story had come out, as hidden stories are wont to do. Like Clara, Ruby had been seduced by an American serviceman during the war. Unlike Clara, Ruby's American beau had survived the war. Ruby had left Ivor – who had been fighting in France – and gone to live in America. Naturally, Clara had assumed Ruby was out of the picture since, frankly, there was no picture. Three years had passed; you would assume, wouldn't you?

Well, apparently, she wasn't.

On the day of the tribunal, the tribunal that saw Clara vindicated and her position at the Grange secured, Clara had come out of the council offices euphoric, only to have a different vision set in front of her, a vision she'd never forget: Ivor and Ruby entwined. Ruby and Ivor embracing. Ruby's hair, her delicate pale hands. Ivor gazing over her shoulder, looking – what was the right word? – petrified.

Ivor was really trying to work things out with his wife. Ruby may have been away for *over three years*, but Ivor had made a commitment to look after her forever – Ruby, like Ivor, was ex-Shilling Grange – and everyone said it, 'Shilling Grange children stick together'. Ivor, bless him, was standing not only by his wedding vows but by his childhood promises. Clara admired him for it. If there was someone who'd always try to do the right thing, it was Ivor. She knew that – it was one of the things she loved about him even though it was also the thing that was kicking her in the face. The day after Ruby came back, they'd disappeared off somewhere; Ivor hadn't told Clara where. His eyes had told her that he loved Clara. His mouth had told her it was something he had to do.

Whether he'd succeed or not was a different matter.

2

'I don't think I like the new children,' declared Rita the next day over breakfast. 'One of them snores like a trumpet.'

'That can't be helped,' Clara said, juggling toast and porridge. She had been woken by Rita – 'can't sleep' – and Peg two times each, but thankfully not by the new girls. She didn't think she could cope with more poor sleepers.

Peter was making tea and Peg was sweeping the floor because Evelyn had managed to drop a glass of milk, shards had scattered everywhere, and Peg was the only one with her shoes on. Evelyn had padded off crying and Clara had sent Alex to console her. Usually Maureen helped, but she had slept late and Clara had let her off.

'Stella doesn't like them either.'

'Stella is a cat,' Clara reminded her.

Clara remembered an old neighbour in London who thought he could read his cats' minds. The day war broke out, he took them outside and shot them, which was bad enough, but then he said, 'Tilly didn't mind but Leo was annoyed.'

'Have you fed her?'

'Stella is always hungry, Miss Newton.'

The cat made Clara sneezy and wheezy. The children adored her but Clara was the only one who attended to her needs, which wasn't how she had imagined it.

'Is Evelyn all right?' she checked with Alex, brushing the hair away from his forehead. She'd need to get out the pudding bowl soon for a cut.

'I was in the middle of explaining the French Revolution to her when she ran off.'

Sensible, thought Clara.

Joyce was complaining about school. She didn't want to go. Clara decided she was probably just nervous.

'You might enjoy it: the other children do.'

'No, we don't,' added Rita unhelpfully.

It was a beautiful autumn morning and Stella accompanied them some of the way to school. The sky was a stretch of uninterrupted blue and made a lovely backdrop to the Suffolk pink of the houses, and it was warmer than it had been in August. The hedgerows were teeming with life and the leaves were starting to turn. There were people to wave to, ladybirds to land on your sleeve and count their years.

Joyce was grumpy. 'How much further?' she said when they had only just left the Grange, and 'Miss Newton, my legs aren't strong like the others.'

One of the few things Joyce's notes had made clear was that she needed to exercise.

'You've got to keep going,' Clara insisted.

She sent the others ahead as Joyce walked slowly alongside her, dragging her bad leg, her face furious.

'I don't see why I have to go to school.'

'That's the rules,' said Clara brightly. 'I'll be waiting for you at home. And you are safe.' She smiled reassuringly.

'I am safe,' Joyce mouthed back, rolling her eyes. 'Yeah, right.'

At the school gates, Peg tugged Clara's sleeve, pointed at Joyce and made a face that suggested she was unimpressed.

'It takes time to settle in,' Clara whispered, surprised at the usually forgiving Peg. 'Be nice.'

Peg looked unconvinced.

'This is my twelfth school,' interrupted Evelyn, making puppy-dog eyes.

Clara wanted to give the new girls a profound message for their first day, a something to live by, but her tongue didn't seem to work and, for a moment, she understood how it might feel to be Peg.

'Work hard,' she eventually blurted out to their disappearing backs.

That first week, Joyce remained a thundercloud. She hated the walk to school and threatened several times not to go. Evelyn wasn't much better. Twice Clara caught her snaffling crackers, and twice Evelyn gazed at her as though she wasn't fully present. However, the sun kept shining, which helped keep Clara's spirits up. She loved Lavenham, with its medieval timber buildings and cobble-stone streets, and she bought cut-price pumpkins and berries from a stand at the side of the road. Maureen too was in a bouyant mood; she bounced out of the house to work and bounced back afterwards. It was obviously good for her. Alex grew happier at his new school (they were setting him lots of homework), the twins, Peg and Peter seemed fine, and one night as Clara tucked Rita into bed, Rita whispered something that made Clara's heart sing.

'Ivor said you have the kindest eyes of anyone he knows.'

'*Ivor* said that?'

Rita snuggled down. 'He *always* said that. I think he is in love with you, Miss Newton.'

She is ten years old, what does she know? Clara told herself. Still, although she wasn't someone who stared in the mirror a lot, she did take a long look at her eyes that evening. Perhaps she wasn't so bad. Perhaps Ivor would be back for those eyes soon.

At the weekend, the older boys wanted to build a wagon. Clara sent them to the grocer's and they came back with a soapbox, far larger than she had been expecting; then they went to see the postmistress – who was a terror for encouraging mad schemes – and she sent them to a junkyard, where they found old pram wheels and a stick for steering. Maureen didn't want to get involved at first, but Joe persuaded her. It was great to see the older ones laughing together.

'You're a great team,' Clara said encouragingly, bringing them out some squash. Then Maureen offered to help Clara make lunch – which was unusual since it wasn't her turn – and Clara was glad because she wanted to find out more about Maureen's work at Robinson, Browne and White – surely Maureen had put the files in alphabetical order by now? Side by side, they stood peeling and chopping potatoes and carrots.

'Are they kind to you?'

Julian White was very kind – until you disagreed with him. Then he could be cruel, enraged, vengeful. The thought of him displaying any of those qualities towards her Maureen made Clara feel breathless.

Clara had been engaged to Julian White last year – something that even Clara herself now found hard to believe. It seemed so unlikely. Julian had been generous and charming: a perfect distraction from everything going on at the Grange. He was also the most amoral person she knew and utterly unsuitable. Clara had broken it off last summer.

According to a quiz in *Woman* magazine, Julian was, mostly C's, an 'entertaining gentleman'. Clara should look for a more compatible 'homely chap' (mostly B's) in future. (Was Ivor homely? Quite possibly.)

'I hardly see Mr White,' Maureen replied, cheerfully.

'Really?' That was a relief, thought Clara.

'I'm in Mr Browne and Mr Robinson's room.'

At this Clara tensed, for she disliked Browne most of all. 'What are they like then?'

'Mr Robinson leaves at four fifteen most days so I don't see much of him either.'

'And Mr Browne?' Clara prompted. Maureen said he shared his packet of shortbread with her after she made them both tea.

'You make yourself tea?'

When Clara had worked at Harris & Sons, even the thought of sharing biscuits with the bosses would have made her blush. It would have been an overstepping of boundaries. But the world had changed since then. The War had given some women and some working-class people new roles and opportunities. The newspapers had declared the UK was entering an Age of Meritocracy. Still, a young orphan on breaking-biscuit terms with a head solicitor was big news.

Between this job and Joe's affection, Maureen's confidence was growing. Maureen had had a poor time at school, and she'd had a miscarriage last year, so it was positive to see her take off. Clara told herself she should be more supportive.

The older children worked on the wagon most of the afternoon. Just before tea-time, Peter called Joyce out to have a look.

'What do you think of that?' asked Barry proudly.

'Cool, isn't it?' prompted Billy.

'You can use it when your legs are tired,' Peter added gently.

28 LIZZIE PAGE

'We noticed. You can steer it, or we'll be able to pull you along to school.' He looked at Clara. 'That's why we made it.'

Clara, who had been an only child, plus a solitary child by circumstance, gulped back a sob. How she would have loved older brothers like this. She smiled at Joyce, who was staring at it, taking everything in.

'What do you say, Joyce?'

Joyce didn't say anything. She did a half-run half-limp back indoors.

Clara was hurt for the boys. She went after Joyce and found her under the blanket in the parlour again.

'Joyce, Joyce! They didn't mean any harm. What has upset you?'

'Nothing...' she grunted. 'I don't like it.'

'You don't like walking and you don't like the wagon?'

'Why would I want to go about on that? Stacked up like a loaf of bread?'

Clara sighed. And that was probably the moment she realised: settling in the new girls was going to be much more complicated than she had anticipated.

3

That evening, as Clara looked out of her bedroom window before drawing the curtains, she saw a light flicker on at the workshop across the way. Suddenly, for an instant, the place was bathed in gold. Then the light went off as quickly as it had come on.

Ivor was back?

She couldn't have been mistaken, could she?

Clara dressed quickly, mindful of the time. She was just about to tell Maureen where she was going, but changed her mind. Best not tell anyone yet. She could deal with it.

Ivor was back. Of course he was back. How long could he go away for? It was already nearly three weeks and he needed to work.

Clara went to the window at the front of the house to get another look.

Maybe she'd been mistaken. There had been no purring of a car, no sound of suitcases being pulled along, no Ruby clattering in her heels, patting those curled hair rolls more rigid than something from the Italian patisserie that Julian had delivered from Soho. Maybe they didn't want anyone to know they were back? That would be right; Ruby was probably someone who kept herself to herself.

The door was still padlocked. Should she wait until the morning? She missed him, though.

She had to know. *Didn't she have a right to know?*

They were friends. Even if that was it, even if it was never more than that, friends was a big word too. Friends had an obligation; friends had a responsibility.

Maybe he was alone. Maybe he'd come back for her. Maybe he was in love with her. Clara pushed her hair away from her face, glad she hadn't applied face cream tonight. She imagined an emotional reunion. How should she play it – scolding and frosty? Or worried and maternal? Or fall into his arms... *Ivor!*

She went round the back. Nothing gave. Still locked.

Oh, come on, Ivor. Don't be ridiculous. She knew she'd seen a light. She knew it. Tempting to kick at the door. Temptation resisted. If she *was* there, what would Ruby think?

It might be blacker than the blackout, but... Clara knocked again. There was movement.

'Ivor?' *Perhaps it wasn't Ivor?* 'If you don't come out now, I will call the police. I mean it.'

The back door slowly opened. A figure came out of the shadows. It wasn't Ivor. Or Ruby.

'What on earth – Joe?'

'Please don't tell anyone, Miss Newton, please.'

'What's going on?'

Joe stood by to let her in, but she would have pushed past him whether he wanted her to or not. Looking around the room, Clara saw blankets, a cushion and a paper sack stacked up in a corner – presumably his clothes. It was the evidence she needed.

Joe explained that last spring and summer, he and Maureen had been living from friend to friend, sofa to sofa; and now Maureen was back at the Grange, which was great for her – but he had no one here. He'd tried staying in the shed for a couple of days, but Rita, who used the shed the most out of all the children, wasn't happy about it and anyway, her constant piano-playing got on his nerves. He shuffled. And it was getting colder at nights. Winter was on its sure-footed way.

Would Ivor mind Joe staying in his workshop?, Clara wondered. He'd probably prefer it. You never knew who was hanging around.

Had Joe really nowhere else to go?

'I don't,' he admitted, his eyes cast down. And Clara remembered: he was too old to be in care – but let's face it, he was still too young to look after himself. Maybe if he had been better equipped, better educated – but of course, he had no money. No wonder he and Maureen were so close – they were like kindred spirits. Or two lost souls.

What would Ivor do? Having grown up in Shilling Grange himself, Clara thought, he'd always struggle to say no to Maureen – to any of the children.

'How long have you been here?'

'Since about a week after Ivor left.'

'I'm going to have to write to him,' Clara said before remembering Ivor hadn't even left her an address. How it hurt that he hadn't. What did he think she'd do? Send him purple prose and scented paper wrapped in ribbons to embarrass him in front of his wife? Did he not know her at all?

One of the children would have an address for him, surely...

'And if he says no, then you will have to go, Joe. No doubt about it.'

Joe shook his head seriously. He was still a child himself, deep down. Just a boy, beneath the errands and the bravado. How was it fair that he was supposed to fend for himself?

Clara sighed. 'I'll bring you over a cup of hot Bovril, shall I?'

For a moment, his eyes lost their frightened doe-like quality. He whispered, 'I'd love that.'

Later that night, after the lights were out, Peg charged into Clara's room for a cuddle, then Stella needed to be let out, and Alex dashed in, in a panic about some history homework; but they weren't the only reasons Clara had a broken night's sleep – she was worrying: Joe was over there, living alone in the workshop? He was only sixteen. She had to tell Ivor about Joe, but at the same time, she was embarrassed about initiating contact. It was the last thing she wanted. He might think she was making excuses to get in touch with him.

Was she making excuses to get in touch with him?

After school the next day, Peter had some comics to show Clara. The fact that Peter still cared about her opinion – after all he'd been through – made Clara's heart ache and she tried never to look at his work without taking the utmost care. The new children (and now Maureen and Joe) were taking up much of her mind – but she mustn't neglect the old ones. She was beginning to feel as stretched as the string wrapped round Joyce's fingers.

There were knights, bears and aliens racing across the comics' pages, but Peter never failed to have a human theme at the heart of his work. Clara often wished each one of the children could have a talent like Peter did. It must be a blessing to be good at something.

'Where *do* you get your ideas from?'

'Here and there,' Peter said modestly. 'Sometimes, when I'm falling asleep, I think what if this happened or that happened.'

'And so do you write it down?'

'No.' He smiled. 'If I remember it in the morning, it's a good idea. If it's gone, it's gone.'

At the door he hesitated. 'There was something else I wanted to show you.'

There always was with Peter. And it was usually delivered right *after* you thought the conversation was over.

We are looking for a super-dooper cartoonist/illustrator with all the ideas to take us forwards on a rollercoaster ride. No experience necessary. We are looking for you to create characters who zing off the page, tell us something about our lives, people who our readers can look up to, or look down on, or relate to, or even despise. As long as they feel something!

If you think it's a swell position for you, send us your best shot, and we'll see if you've got the potential to join us on a spiffing, London-based adventure, hold on to your hats!

A sudden melancholy overcame Clara. She felt as though she knew nothing about this 'super-dooper' world, this bish-bash-boom language. It was so lively, while she felt increasingly stolid and past-it. And yet she was not even thirty. She supposed there *had* been a new language when she was younger – they'd had words like Blitz, National Socialists, Auschwitz to learn – but those weren't sparky, colourful words, they were the dark language of war, death and trauma.

Sometimes she felt like her generation had lost a few years. Swallowed up in and by catastrophe. She supposed she was envious of the ones growing up now. To enter adulthood without rationing, without conscription, without fear – it must be amazing. But then she told herself off. She was being self-indulgent, for she'd managed to have happy times too, compared to many, she knew that; and it was only new words: the human condition underneath was surely the same.

'D.C. Thomson – the publishers behind the *Beano* and the

Dandy – are taking on cartoonists,' he said, translating the advert for her. 'As a full-time job.'

Clara paused. *A job? In London?* But Peter was so young!

'Is it okay if I apply? For when I've left school?'

He's only going to apply. That's all.

She forced herself to smile. 'It's a brilliant idea. How did you hear about it?'

'Oh.' He reddened. 'I just did.'

Clara felt nervous. She was nervous that Peter wouldn't get it and be demoralised; *and* she was nervous that he would get it. The home wouldn't be home without Peter.

It wasn't until later the next evening that Clara managed to get Maureen on her own to talk about Joe. Maureen fluttered into the kitchen, her skirt swirling around her knees. Julian was having a party next weekend. He'd said he wanted Maureen to be there to hand out the canapés. Maureen had never heard that word before. Was it something to do with trees? No? Then what the hell was it?

'Don't say hell,' said Clara. She usually skipped 'The Hostess with the Mostest' page in *Good Housekeeping* but she vaguely remembered something about them. 'They're kind of party snack-things.'

Maureen was pleased: Julian would give her money on top of her usual wage. And she would get to bring the left-over whatsits home for Clara and the children, she went on. It was hard to get a word in edgeways. Finally, Clara snapped.

'Maureen, what on earth is Joe doing at Ivor's?'

'Oh,' Maureen said flatly. 'Don't you like my Joe?'

'I do, as you know – that's not the point,' Clara said firmly. 'You've been sneaking around behind my back.'

Maureen took her sullen face and her plate over to the sink.

Even the tap water sounded resentful. 'He doesn't have anywhere else.'

'Then you should have said, I would have...' Clara tailed off. She wasn't sure what she would have done. 'It's a ridiculous arrangement. How long did you expect to get away with it?'

Maureen's expression suggested this wasn't a question that had occurred to either of them.

'I'm going to have to write to Ivor,' Clara said. 'Do you have an address for him?'

Maureen nodded mutinously. Of course she did. Clara's feelings of hurt were compounded.

Maureen washed her hands, more thoroughly than usual. She seemed reluctant to move away from the sink. Clara still felt tense. She hadn't got Maureen to admit that it was not appropriate.

'I heard something interesting at work today,' Maureen suddenly said brightly, now drying her hands as though she were on the stage. 'About us. Very interesting.'

'Oh, Maureen, don't try changing the subject.'

'I'm not.'

'So don't... don't keep secrets like that again. If Joe needs somewhere, I will do my best, but no more sneaking around, promise?'

'Promise.'

Clara looked at her puckered expression and felt a sudden empathy with her. She remembered the terrible things in her file. Maureen's father had murdered her mother and Maureen had been the one to find her – she hadn't had a good start in life, by any measure. That she was now on the straight and narrow was a remarkable accomplishment.

'What was it you were going to tell me?'

'It doesn't matter.'

Clara regretted her runaway mouth. She got up, put her hand on Maureen's shoulder.

'I apologise but finding out your boyfriend was illegally occupying my— Ivor's workshop put me in a bad mood.'

Maureen was unpinning her hair, her expression impassive. 'I *said* it doesn't matter. I'm going up to get changed, Miss Newton.'

4

The Jane Taylor Society was a quarterly meeting in Lavenham library, led by the librarian, Mr Dowsett, where they looked at the poems and the writings of local poet Jane and her sister, Ann. Mr Dowsett was a wise soul and the way he talked about both women made you fall in love with them even if you hadn't expected to. (Clara certainly hadn't!).

Clara had a stack of chores. However much she scrubbed them, Billy and Barry's once-white shorts remained as grey as the rain-filled sky; and she was worrying about Maureen. She blamed herself for the girl clamming up like an oyster last night. Still, when Anita Cardew, the Doctor's wife, called round to remind her to come to the meeting, Clara was delighted. Anita was such a strange, accomplished and beautiful woman that at times Clara wondered what she was doing in Lavenham. She had said that once to Ivor and he'd said, 'Where should she be?' and Clara had considered before eventually suggesting, 'Paris? Casablanca?' And Ivor had laughed. 'If the best people moved to Casablanca or Paris, then what would become of the rest of us?'

Anita was also, in her unique way, kind to the children at

the Grange, especially ex-resident little Terry – who last year
she had tutored for the eleven-plus exam – and Alex and Rita,
who she still taught piano; but Anita had never been as
immersed in the children's world as say, Judy or Miss Bridges,
and certainly not Ivor. Maybe now those other adults were no
longer involved, there was a gap she could fill?

Clara and Anita sat on wooden children's-sized chairs in the
library. Somehow Anita in her dogs-tooth check suit, pearl
choker and matching pearl earrings managed to make even that
look elegant.

There were more people at the meeting than usual, including, to Clara's surprise, Maureen's employers, Browne and
Robinson; but not Julian White, thank goodness. Julian was
probably too busy investigating party foods. Browne and Robinson, with their stiff suits and pompous chins, couldn't have
looked more out of place. Browne was staring around the library
as if he couldn't believe he was there.

The Garrards, who ran the flower shop were there with
their wee dog, Bertie. Mrs Garrard kissed the air alongside
Clara and then the postmistress came over and said she wanted
to know about the wagon.

Anita looked bewildered. 'What wagon?'

The postmistress explained enthusiastically, but Anita's lip
was curled. 'Who would go on that?'

'Not Joyce,' muttered Clara. 'Unfortunately.'

Mrs Garrard and the postmistress took seats in the row in
front, which pleased Clara; she always preferred to get Anita on
her own.

'Are you getting on with the cat with the silly name?'

Anita disapproved of the name Stella, which had been
decided upon by a democratic run-off between that and Mrs
Roosevelt.

'I'm allergic to her,' Clara admitted. Anita made an *I told
you so* expression, but then Anita was a rabbit-person.

Anita asked questions about the new children. Whatever Clara said left her looking dissatisfied, though, as if she believed Clara were keeping the interesting stuff from her. They were next to the shelves of contemporary literature and out of the corner of her eye, Clara kept getting tantalising glimpses of titles of the latest books, such as *The Pursuit of Love* and *Brideshead Revisited*. Recently, she hadn't had time to read full-length books – or rather, she only had the patience for short articles in magazines, or poems – which made her a little sad. It was natural perhaps; keeping up with the children was hard enough, never mind keeping up with the antics of people who weren't real.

'And Ivor,' hissed Anita. 'Have you heard from him?'

'Not *recently*,' said Clara, as though she'd been inundated with letters one month ago.

'You should have.'

What use was should? Clara *knew* she should have.

'He came to say goodbye,' she added quickly. Again, she could picture the agonised look in his eyes; he *hadn't* wanted to say goodbye, she was sure of it. 'It's not like he... he... didn't... explain.'

She always found herself standing up for him, even when, like now, she didn't want to. She was as annoyed with him as Anita was. More annoyed. Sometimes, she found it hard to think about anything else. Ivor. Ivor Delaney. The neighbour. The neighbour it took her a long time to decide she was in love with and—

'That's the least you should expect.'

'I *know*.'

Mr Dowsett the librarian finally reached his wonky music stand at the front. He cleared his throat for them to quieten down, but no one did until Anita let out one of her fierce shushes. Before the war, Anita was a teacher in Poland and her disapproving expression could sour milk.

'Today, I am going to talk about Jane Taylor and her social conscience,' Mr Dowsett announced.

The room started buzzing again – Jane Taylor's social conscience wasn't what they were here for – until Anita turned round and gave everyone her beady stare.

Mr Dowsett read a poem by Jane Taylor that Clara didn't know, called 'Poverty', and she shut her eyes, half to immerse herself in the poem and half to block out Anita, who for some reason had turned her beady eye on her. She would think about Ivor's non-communication later, when she was alone. Useless to try to explain it to Anita when she couldn't yet explain it to herself.

Mr Dowsett talked about Jane and Ann's lives. The Taylor family were not well-off and the daughters, including Jane and Ann, were taught engraving to support themselves financially. Even so, the women were always concerned with those more impoverished than themselves.

Someone asked Mr Dowsett if he expected that if Jane Taylor were around today, she would be one of those nasty socialists, and a kind of frisson went through the audience and Clara wasn't sure if it was agreement or not.

Mr Dowsett said that question was interesting but difficult. Who would dare transpose writers and thinkers from one epoch to another? Anita shot up her arm and agreed, saying that the values of yesteryear rarely could be accurately represented in a different era. Clara thought she was magnificent.

Mrs Garrard, who was a great film buff, asked who would play Jane Taylor if there were a film made about her and everyone laughed; there were some super suggestions, including Veronica Lake and Ingrid Bergman.

Much as she enjoyed the discussion, Clara hoped there wouldn't be any further questions, for – like a mermaid in the distance distracting the sailors – the wobbling tea trolley had caught her eye. Clara knew the biscuits on there – made by Mr

Dowsett's accomplished-baker wife – would be crumbly and melt-in-the-mouth; and she wasn't the only one who knew – they always disappeared fast. She would try to pocket one for Evelyn perhaps. The girl did love to eat.

When she saw Mr Browne's arm was up, Clara silently sighed. Typical of the man to make his presence felt. She had laughed about him with Ivor on more than one occasion. Ivor disapproved of 'toffs' like Browne.

'Is it true Jane Taylor lived in Lavenham?'

'Oh ye—'

'At the Grange?' Mr Browne persisted.

Clara swivelled round to look as though by looking she might understand more. *Shilling Grange? Her* Grange?

'That's right – granted, she spent a longer period at Colchester.'

Her hand half-raised, Clara stuttered, '*Shilling* Grange, you mean?'

'Absolutely...' Mr Dowsett beamed at her and Clara tried to ignore his misshapen teeth. 'I thought you knew, Miss Newton.'

The thought of Jane Taylor running up the stairs, tripping over the doorways, gazing out the windows of where she lived, was delightful. Clara had walked, eaten, slept even where her favourite poet had? Jane had been in her garden, in her kitchen, in her bedroom? There was something heart-warming about that. She wondered what the children would say; Rita and Alex would be delighted. They both had a sense of history. The others? She smiled to herself. Not so much.

'That's wonderful,' she said and Mr Dowsett responded, 'Isn't it!'

Mr Browne frowned. He pushed on: 'She wrote her most famous song there? The nursery rhyme?'

'We're not sure.' Mr Dowsett said, quieter in the face of the aggressive tone. 'Here or probably Colchester—'

'But you could say she did?'

Mr Dowsett chuckled; then, when he realised Mr Browne was asking in earnest, he said, 'The weight of evidence suggests she did not.'

'It's the orphanage now?'

Few people could raise their eyebrows as high as Anita Cardew could. She tapped Clara's knee.

Mr Dowsett pushed at the music stand until it collapsed. 'The Grange is currently a children's home, yes.'

'That's a waste, isn't it?'

'What's the matter with that man?' muttered Anita.

'Sssh.' But Clara was thinking the same. *What was Mr Browne trying to suggest?*

'Knowing what we do about Jane and Ann's care and affection for deprived children – both by poetry and their actions – it is fitting. I imagine Jane and Ann would have been glad at the thought.'

'A heritage centre being used by a bunch of ne'er-do-wells?'

Mr Dowsett grabbed his papers.

'Shall we help ourselves to some tea?' Everyone rose and obediently headed towards the trolley except for Mr Browne, who made for the door, followed by an apologetic-looking Mr Robinson. Clara scowled after them both.

She wanted to discuss the Jane Taylor connection some more over the biscuits – this really was lovely news – but Anita said she had something to tell her. Clara struggled to switch subject matters. She suspected that it had something to do with the Festival of Britain. The festival was to be a nationwide event designed to celebrate the nation's recovery after the darkness and deprivation of the war years. Clara couldn't help thinking exhibitions, parades and street parties were a dreadful waste of the nation's already limited funds and she hoped it wouldn't happen, but although it was more than a year and a half away, Anita was obsessed with it. She wanted the children of the Grange to perform at the Suffolk festival. 'Who,' Anita asked, although she didn't seem to want an answer, 'could resist a troop of singing orphans?'

Clara privately thought she, yes, she could resist.

Anita was gazing at her intently now. She had crumbs around her mouth and Clara was thinking that was unusual because Anita rarely ate in public when she said breathlessly, 'I'm having a baby, Clara. I imagine you guessed ages ago.'

Clara hadn't guessed. People talked about 'sensing' when a woman is pregnant, but that particular skill had passed Clara by. Anita had never mentioned that a baby was something she wanted so it was hard to believe this was intentional but Clara knew she couldn't ask if it was. Did Anita want to go through pregnancy and all the upheaval it entailed? Anita with her fitted outfits, her pearls and her self-discipline? Clara swallowed.

And it was selfish, but Clara couldn't help thinking: she *really* was on her own now. No one was going to rescue her. The absences she was feeling so keenly weren't going to be filled by Anita. She was by herself. Yet perhaps, she wondered, that was the way it should be? Time to grow up. Clara shoved these thoughts to the back of her mind and tried to think of something positive to say.

'How is Dr Cardew feeling?' she asked.

'Panicked.' Anita laughed.

She is happy, thought Clara suddenly. For the first time since she'd known Anita, she could see her friend really was happy.

At home that night, once the children were in bed and Stella had reluctantly gone out, Clara wrote her reports. She was a diligent note-keeper and being organised gave her pleasure. She didn't gaze out over to the other side of the street anymore because it was only poor Joe out there, not the person she most wanted to see. Clara wondered if she needed to worry about Mr Browne's declarations at the Jane Taylor Society – 'That's a waste, isn't it?' kept playing in her head – but she decided not to. She had far too many other things on her mind; and what could Mr Browne do, exactly?

CHILDREN'S REPORT 9
Evelyn Margaret Wyatt

Date of Birth:

5 December 1938

Family Background:

Evelyn was brought into care by a maternal grandparent when she was a few days old. Father unknown. She was moved around a lot during the war and since. Nine separate homes. The last foster placement broke down when the father lost his job, the one before that when it was discovered the family had not been feeding the children properly. The one before that broke down for reasons unknown.

Health/Appearance:

Evelyn has large brown eyes and a warm smile. She is heavier than the other girls but seems in excellent health. She says in all the schools she has been to, she has never taken a single day off.

Food:

Often asks for or takes seconds. She eats everything (except for semolina). Has no interest in cooking, but has uncanny timing when it comes to licking the bowl.

Hobbies:

She likes being at home, lying on the hammock, lying on the sofa.

Other:

A capable if disinterested student, Evelyn enjoys practical subjects such as domestic science and needlework. She has been to twelve different schools.

5

Peter's entry for the comic competition was coming along a treat. One of the strips was about twins – twins! One of them had strange superpowers, but Peter's story unexpectedly focused on the other one; it was beautifully done.

Alex had his nose in his books as usual. The new girls were very much on the periphery of his life. He was focused on school and his best friend, the impossibly tall and supremely brainy Bernard Braithwaite, and 'What did you think of the dissolution of the monasteries, Miss Newton?'

'I hadn't given them much thought, Alex.'

Rita wasn't interested in the new girls either but then that was Rita; she seemed to take pleasure in not getting on with people. She wouldn't even lend anyone her hairbrush – which Clara understood – but it was the *way* she went about things. Rita was a self-contained unit. The only human she needed was her mama, who had gone missing after a V2 attack towards the end of the war and who Rita refused to believe was dead. Rita was slightly better at sleeping than she used to be, but still. Rita also reacted furiously if she was kept from her piano practice. She did three or four hours every evening.

'I've got a difficult piece,' she wailed. 'Anita is stretching me again.'

Clara listened outside the door. She thought it sounded marvellous but every few minutes she would hear Rita huff and tut, and sometimes she would even scold herself, 'Do better' or 'That's not it.'

New girl Joyce remained sullen and resentful. She complained her leg hurt and she hated walking. She sometimes liked Peter's comics but showed no inclination to try drawing herself. Maureen said Joyce had a crush on Peter ever since he'd made her the wagon, but Maureen match-made everyone; it didn't mean it was true.

Clara tried not to let Joyce's attitude affect her mood, but it did somehow. Joyce was effective at making her presence felt. The only time she laughed was when another child was in trouble, and, because she was so sharp, she sometimes knew when someone was in trouble before they did. Her favourite thing seemed to be getting Rita told off.

Evelyn was also flat and disinterested, but unlike Joyce, she stayed in the background. She would sit in the kitchen, not listening to anyone, her eyes following the plates. Unlike Maureen, she had no inclination to bake. Unlike Barry and Billy, she didn't want to take sweets to school and sell them. But she ate anything and everything.

Clara brought up the matter with Anita one afternoon when she dropped Rita off for a lesson. Anita sighed and said, 'I was hungry for three years.' Anita never usually talked about the war but now she was starting to. Maybe being pregnant had unlocked something. Or maybe she had got to know Clara better. 'When the Russians liberated us, they tried to be kind, they shot a horse and cooked it on a fire. They fed us.'

'That must have been—'

'Some people ate and ate until they dropped dead.'

'Oh.'

'I didn't eat it – I was full on the crust they gave me. Even that made me feel bloated.'

What did this have to do with Evelyn?

'It's hunger. And it's not hunger. Do you see what I mean?'

Evelyn had been malnourished for some years. Some children it doesn't affect. Some it did. Evelyn was making sure it didn't happen again.

Evelyn occasionally sat in the garden, but even there she didn't read, draw or play marbles, but stared, wide-open eyes, into the dappled leaves. Clara privately dubbed it her 'hundred-yard stare'.

She came to the monthly Kids' Club at the cinema but didn't seem excited about going in the way the others were – even Joyce. The first film they watched was *Little Women* and afterwards, when everyone was debating which character they were most like, and wasn't Laurie a hunk?, Evelyn said, 'I don't get why everyone is making a fuss. I thought it was boring.'

'Only boring people get bored,' said Rita pompously. 'Isn't that right, Miss Newton?'

'We-ll.' Clara attempted diplomacy. 'I'm not sure that's always the case...'

'That's what you told me.'

'Maybe then.'

Rita kicked a stone in the road. Joyce grinned.

Later that evening in the kitchen, after watching Evelyn pick at everyone's leftovers like a crow, Clara suggested collecting foreign coins – Anita had some from America – or stamps (also Anita's), but Evelyn just stared at the biscuit tin.

'I wish you'd be interested in something,' Clara said. 'It's important that you have interests or skills.'

She meant it lightly, a throwaway remark, but Evelyn left the room immediately. Maureen looked up from stacking the

plates: 'Not everyone has to have a bloody hobby, Miss
Newton.'

'I know that,' Clara protested, 'and don't swear.' But in bed
later, she thought, Maureen didn't understand – sometimes, like
Jane and Ann Taylor, you had to do engraving even when you'd
rather watch the clouds go by.

~

One Saturday towards the end of September when the girls had
been at the Grange for just under four weeks, Clara was chatting with Joe in the garden about Stella; the cat was making her
sneeze. Secretly she regretted getting her. Rita adored her, true,
but she didn't take care of her.

Clara tried to involve Evelyn in the conversation, but she
was monosyllabic. She lay in her hammock, her legs spilling out
either side. Clara was going to say something about being more
graceful, but then stopped herself. *Be more ladylike* was something her father had said to her – and she felt a sudden flicker of
rage against him. Why shouldn't Evelyn sit how she liked? So
what if it offended anyone?

Suddenly Evelyn sat up, nearly tipping herself out. Since
she rarely acted with urgency, Clara was surprised.

'Everything alright?'

'Miss Newton, is it true the Grange is up for sale then?'

Joe pulled a puzzled face, while Clara barked a laugh.

'No-oo. Why do you ask?'

'So the rich lawyer man doesn't want to buy it then?' She
swung both legs to the front and jumped down.

'What?'

Evelyn ignored her and trudged towards the house. She had
had enough of the conversation. The hammock kept on
swinging.

'Evelyn – what? What were you saying?'

'The lawyer man from the house with the pillars. He's not buying it?'

For a moment, Clara was speechless. Joe wiped his hands on his trousers.

'Who on earth told you that?'

'Maureen did.'

'Maureen? Really?'

A thousand questions swarming. The Grange. Joe shrugged. He didn't know what she meant – which suggested to Clara that Evelyn was confused.

'I bet I'm going to have to move again,' she sighed. 'As always. I've moved sixteen times.'

Clara didn't think correcting her on this was helpful.

'Maureen's got it wrong, love,' she said instead. 'There's nothing... happening to the Grange. It's our home.'

She looked at the Grange gleaming in the autumn light, the kitchen door wide open. The soup in the saucepan on the stove. The girls' dorm window open, the boys' window shut (and the glass slightly cracked). In the girls' dorm, there would be Rita's hairbrush, Evelyn's pilfered food, Peg's shell collection. Stella might be in there, dozing on Rita's bed. In the boys' dorm, Peter's comics, Alex's workbooks, Billy and Barry's smelly socks would be all over the place.

Clara looked at Joe: 'You don't know what she's talking about?'

'Beats me,' said Joe, making another face, as he grabbed the watering can and went over to the tap.

The rest of the day thoughts of Mr Browne buying the Grange were the only thing on Clara's mind. *What was going on?* She thought about how hard she was trying to settle and encourage the children – Rita, Peter, the new ones, all of them. The council wouldn't pull the rug out from under them, would they?

More likely, Evelyn had got something wrong. Most likely, Maureen had something wrong.

The Grange *wasn't* for sale. There was no reason for it to be for sale. Then she remembered Maureen starting to tell her something important the other day. Perhaps that was it? No...

And Mr Browne at the meeting? No, it couldn't be.

Clara couldn't wait for Maureen to come home. She posted a letter to ex-resident Terry and one to the council and listened to the postmistress complain about her sore back. She washed the damp sheets of the bedwetters – and waited.

After tea, all hell broke loose. Barry and Billy were wrestling, the girls were screaming at each other, Peg was curled up under the kitchen table and Peter was running around, frantically.

'What on *earth* is going on?' Clara bellowed.

'My comic has gone!' wailed Peter.

There wasn't much time left until he had to send the comic to the contest – Peter, being a perfectionist, hadn't wanted to let his work go until the last minute – but now he couldn't find it. It wasn't in his bedside cupboard where he had left it.

'You've lost it?'

'No. It's gone. Someone's taken it.' Peter was panicking – unsurprisingly. He'd worked so hard on his comic and it was so accomplished too. 'Monday is the last day to send it.'

'We'll find it.' Clara sounded calmer than she felt. 'We will, Peter.'

Billy and Barry, self-proclaimed masters at finding things, had no luck and started arguing with Peter, who was near the end of his tether. Peg was crawling around on hands and knees, peering behind the dresser and under the rug.

Clara went out to the shed, where Rita was still 'stretching' herself with Tchaikovsky.

'Rita?'

But Rita ignored her. The shed was a mess. A jumper, a

half-eaten bun. Music books scattered. Clara picked up a few bits and found the comic under a coat of Peg's. She picked it up. It was torn and smeared and the back page was ruined, but the rest didn't look too bad.

'Rita, did you do this?'

Rita's hands sailed up and down the piano, her fingers roving on the keys, completely oblivious to Clara.

'RITA!!'

Rita turned, looked at her with disdain, then shook her head. She went back to her piece, the keys sinking and rising.

On her way back to the house, Clara tried to gather her thoughts. Joyce had a crush on Peter – but Peter had hardly noticed Joyce. A suspicion grew and by the time she reached the back door, she felt certain.

'Joyce!'

Joyce was polishing shoes. She looked up, wide-eyed, over-innocent, smears in stripes on the newspaper.

'What is it, Miss Newton?' she enquired in a sickly-sweet tone.

Clara showed her the comic, asked if she had anything to do with it. Joyce shook her head mutinously, but Clara knew, she just knew.

The other children were in bed when Maureen danced in, fluttery as a butterfly. Her face done out in cosmetics that Clara was sure she hadn't been wearing when she left the Grange.

'You needn't have waited up.' Maureen slipped off her shoes – shoes Clara didn't recognise either – and rolled down her stockings insouciantly.

'I... what's going on?'

'About what?'

'Evelyn seems to think the Grange is up for sale... She says you told her that.'

She was surprised when Maureen sat down, grinned and said, 'All right.'

She obviously *wanted* to let the cat out the bag.

'It's still hush-hush, but yes, Mr Browne *is* interested. He'll keep it as a children's home though, so there's nothing for us to worry about, Miss Newton, nothing is going to change.'

'How do you know this?'

'He told me.'

Clara narrowed her eyes. Maureen pinkened. She put her hands in her lap and straightened her back, chest forward.

'It won't make any difference to us.'

'What do you mean?' Clara felt discombobulated. It was like when her father first came back from Africa last year. She just sensed everything was going to change, whether she liked it or not.

'I mean, it won't be a *bad* difference, it might even make a good difference. He's got plenty of money, Miss Newton.' She smiled secretively. 'You have no idea.'

Clara didn't like this. It was Maureen who had no idea. She was a child involved with things beyond her control.

'He could fix the windows and the floor and everything. We could have better clothes.'

Better clothes?

If Clara said the wrong thing, she knew Maureen would clam up like an SOE agent. She'd enjoy it too, the not-telling, a spit in the face.

But Clara couldn't help asking: 'Why is Mr Browne telling *you* these things?'

In the dark kitchen, Maureen's eyes grew catlike: 'We get on.'

Clara couldn't contain herself. 'He's thirty years older than you, Maureen,' she burst out.

'I know.

'And married with children.'

'I know that. He wants me to take care of them sometimes. Anyway, I have Joe.'

'Yes, you have Joe. So-so-what is he doing telling you these things? You're the office help, not a...'

Not a what?

'I won't talk to anyone about it next time. I thought you'd be interested, that's all.'

6

'I'd be as outraged as you, Miss Newton!' Miss Cooper said. 'More so!'

As soon as the children were at school the next morning, Clara had called up the council: *Evelyn said this, and Maureen said that*; and it was an enormous relief that Miss Cooper didn't know what on earth she was talking about:

'The Grange is an historic building—'

Clara interrupted her. 'And also...'

'Your home, of course, you and the children. It has been for many years and I can assure you, I haven't heard anything about this. If something was going on, I would know. I'd be the first to know, in fact!'

Clara doubted this but she said, 'Yes, exactly!'

'So honestly, Clara, put your mind at rest. It is not an issue.'

Shilling Grange was run-down, it always had been, but now Clara wondered if run-down was turning into something else. Some windows wouldn't shut. The floorboards were loud. She wrote to the council regularly about dry rot and they wrote nothing back and nowadays they rarely supplied any of Clara's requests for paint, sheet music, buckets and sometimes even shoes, until she argued them round.

Clara said she would try to do exactly as Miss Cooper said, although it sounded like Miss Cooper was simply telling her to stop thinking about it. Which was probably sound advice too. There was nothing worse than overthinking. Clara knew she was just the type to add 2 and 2 and come up with 50. At Harris & Sons, during the war, that hadn't been a bad quality, but it was a hindrance now at the Grange.

As Miss Cooper continued her assurances, Clara thought about the *Woman's Own* quiz she had done. Which *Little Women* character are you most like? She had come back as B's and A's tied: Josephine and Meg March. Clara miserably supposed Miss Cooper would be 100 per cent Josephine.

Miss Cooper was saying some prospective adopters were coming at the weekend, one set to see Billy and Barry, and one for Evelyn.

'That is quick,' remarked Clara, immediately wondering if this was to do with this new rumour.

Miss Cooper did her tinkly little laugh. 'It's all relative.'

Clara wasn't sure if that was a joke or not.

'They need homes.'

'They don't just need homes, they need the *right* homes,' Clara said, toying with the hang-up button.

'Exactly,' said Miss Cooper forcefully and as though they were in disagreement.

Miss Cooper said she wanted to be there, desperately, she said, but, 'Unfortunately I have Labour Party socials, you know how it is.'

'Oh yes,' agreed Clara, even though she didn't. It was hard to remember having a social life. 'And you'll tell me if there's any news on the house...'

Who was more likely to be in the know, the stroppy fourteen-year-old or the children's services officer?

'I will, but there won't be. It's silly rumours – remember during the war, "careless talk costs lives"?'

Clara thought, *that's a strange thing to say,* but out loud she agreed.

The prospective adopters drove from Cardiff in a van. They wore matching overcoats and underneath their hats, they had matching short dark hair that was kind of hat-shaped too. The woman's lipstick was all over her teeth though and he had the beginnings of a dark beard. Something about the stilted way they talked to each other suggested to Clara they'd had a row. The man apologised loudly: he was hard of hearing, from the war.

'Good thing too,' the woman said unsmilingly. Then to Clara she muttered, 'He wouldn't want to know the half of it.'

Clara called the twins from the garden. Barry was making a poor job of hiding a slingshot underneath his jumper. If he so much as thought of firing it, he would be grounded for a week, Clara told herself. (Although that would be funny.)

After they were introduced, the woman said, 'Are you sure they're not girls? I was sure...'

'What?'

'They said they were twelve-year-old girls.'

'We do have three ten-year-olds,' Billy said. 'You can take them. What, Miss Newton?'

'It's London,' shouted the man. 'In London, the girl twins. This is the boy twins. You said boys were easier. They don't look easier.'

Billy and Barry scowled at them. Clara watched Barry put his hand up his sweater and quickly shuffled them out.

Joyce came in and threw herself on the sofa. She put her leg up on the table – even though she wasn't allowed – and didn't acknowledge the guests.

'This is Joyce,' Clara said. 'She's not a twin but she's lovely, aren't you, Joyce?'

'Evelyn called me a cripple again.'

'Oh dear, no.' Evelyn always adamantly denied this: in fact, she always cried. Clara thought Joyce was lying again but felt she couldn't challenge her in front of the guests. 'Let's talk about this later.'

Clara made an expression at the prospective parents that she hoped conveyed, 'Kids, eh?!' They stared blankly at her.

'Rita said I'm jealous of her. Why would I be jealous of that little squirt?'

'Alright – did you see we have people here, Joyce?'

'Stella threw up on the stairs. I hate her.'

'Get her into the garden then,' Clara snapped. 'And you... Out!'

As they went out to the van, the man shouted for the whole street to hear, 'I told you it would be a waste of time,' and the woman said, 'Did you hear the way she talked about the girl, Stella? I should report her.'

That evening, Clara was ironing and chatting to Peg when Peter came in, slamming the door behind him.

'Should I bother sending it?' He held out his revised comic like a dirty hanky. It was the last day he could send it in. Peg nodded enthusiastically and blew kisses at it.

'Of course, you must send it,' agreed Clara. 'You might be surprised.'

It wasn't half as well done as the original, even Clara had to admit. It was hurried, slightly crude. Even so, it was the story that stood out and Peter had replicated it perfectly. Clara still burned with annoyance at Joyce. Maybe the girl hadn't meant

to ruin it, maybe she had just been careless, but it was a deliberate carelessness, Clara thought. Joyce had hurt Peter and
anything or anyone that hurt him made Clara's blood boil.

It was difficult to know what to do with Joyce. Miss Bridges
was preoccupied with her new role and Miss Cooper did not
assist much on the behavioural side of things. Anita would *assist*
but her expectations of children came straight from the ark.
Judy would have known what to do. Ivor would have helped,
but he was occupied. Clara still needed a second opinion – and
she hated herself for it. Why *couldn't* she do this on her own?
What kind of housemother was she?

After she finished the ironing, Clara sat Joyce down in the
parlour. Joyce wouldn't meet her eyes. Clara spoke about
respecting people's property. Joyce wouldn't like it if someone
took her things, would she now? It was about *consideration*. It
was about being kind. Perhaps if Joyce had simply asked if she
might look at the comic, Peter would have said yes.

Clara thought it went well until Joyce pulled herself up and
screeched into her face, 'I didn't even take it. It wasn't me.'

The following day, the next set of potential adopters got the
train up from south Essex and were full of the details of their
journey. They could write a book on the Chelmsford line! They
were both lively and Clara's hopes rose.

Evelyn skulked into the kitchen. Clara had insisted she say,
'How do you do?' and she did so, with minimal feeling.

'I didn't realise she would be this dark.'

'That's fine though,' interjected the man timidly.

'What will people say?' the woman continued. 'I mean –
you won't have to deal with it, will you? There will be so many
questions.'

Clara carried on making the tea, saying nothing. The hairs

on her arms, standing to attention, were saying enough. The woman made her feel sick; singling out mild-mannered Evelyn in this way was horrible.

'Did *you* know she was this dark?' the woman demanded of Clara, who blinked at her.

What a ridiculous question!

'I suppose you did,' she went on. 'You live with her, don't you?'

Clara slammed the best cup and saucer down in front of her. Tea slopped over the side of the cup. The best saucer trembled. The chatty husband wouldn't look at her; he was pretending to be transfixed by something out of the window.

'What did they tell you then?' Clara asked.

'Nothing much.' The man laughed, then covered his bad teeth with his hand.

'Have you got any others? Ones with lighter skin?' asked his wife.

'I don't know what you mean...' Clara mumbled but the wife snapped back at her: 'White British, that's what I mean. I hope you haven't been wasting our time.'

Scowling, Clara called for Joyce and Rita. Only Joyce came. She staggered in, exaggerating her leg, Clara was sure of it.

'Rita said she wants to kill Anita,' Joyce said. 'She's evil.'

The couple stared at her. 'What's wrong with her leg?' the man eventually said.

'I don't think so,' the woman said, emphatically shaking her head. 'No, I don't.'

They only drank half their tea. They backed away to the door like they had seen a rhinoceros and were scared of being torn from limb to limb.

'It's the trains,' he said, apologetically. 'You don't want to miss the four oh nine or you'll be waiting for the four thirty-two.'

'Don't go on,' his wife told him. 'No one cares about your

stupid trains.' Then she pointed her finger at Clara. 'You got us here on false pretences.'

After they'd gone, Clara sat Joyce and Evelyn down and explained that these people were daft and nothing they said was real or kind or big-hearted and they mustn't worry. Most people were not like them. Most people *cared* about children like them, 'cared *more,* in fact,' she added, wondering if that was true. The girls squirmed disinterestedly.

'Any questions?'

Joyce had one: 'Evelyn said they're selling us to the rich lawyer man from the place with the pillars.'

Clara felt like she had been awoken with a jolt.

'I'm only saying what Maureen said,' protested Evelyn.

Clara sighed. 'They're not,' she said. 'I'd know...' she was subconsciously echoing Miss Cooper. But she felt herself grow nervous again. She wiped her palms on her skirt and decided to pursue Miss Bridges for answers instead. Surely she knew *something*?

Clara found herself hoping that one of the children would be poorly and she wouldn't have to attend Alex's harvest assembly. Two hours stuck in a draughty school hall, praying – something that always reminded her of her own parents – was not the most productive way to spend a morning. Especially when she had vegetables to chop, letters to write and a pile of washing as high as a kite. Just two more children and the load had increased exponentially. And she had been trying to call Miss Bridges for the last week. A more paranoid person than she might have imagined Miss Bridges was avoiding her.

For once though – wasn't it always the way? – the children scoffed down their porridge merrily and skipped out, complaint- and ailment-free, even Peg, even Evelyn, *even Joyce!*

Bernard's father, Mr Braithwaite, was driving Alex, Bernard and Clara to the school. He had a Ford Anglia, the same as Miss Bridge's but the passenger seat of his car was a mess of wrappers, papers and handkerchiefs. Mr Braithwaite was not a tidy man. Clara found her feet were resting on a copy of *The Social Contract* by Jean-Jacques Rousseau and she had to shove newspapers onto the floor before she could sit down. Bernard's father read the big newspapers; the ones that Julian took.

Clara wondered where Bernard's mother was – she had never even seen her. She wondered what Bernard's mother thought about a. the state of the car. And b. the fact that Clara was in the passenger seat sitting on a book about Hobbes and Locke.

On the way there, Mr Braithwaite fired general knowledge questions at the boys, who bounced in the back seats like puppies, puppies who had done this many times before. They listed the American states and the prime ministers of the nineteenth century.

'Join in,' he said, 'Don't be shy!' Clara didn't have the heart to tell him that she was joining in, she just didn't have any of the answers. She was weak on chemical symbols, although she wasn't bad at Second World War battles – Julian's favourite subject. She could however do the 'Common Sense' quizzes in *Woman*, *Woman's Own* or *Good Housekeeping* magazines with her eyes shut.

The hall wasn't draughty. It was wood-panelled and airtight; Clara felt like she was in a sardine can. On one panel was a long list of the old boys lost in the First World War and an even longer one from the Second World War. It was a painful reminder. The chair was too small for Bernard's father and he spilled over in every way possible, making Clara feel secretly proud of how compactly she fitted. Every child had to walk to the stage and hand in their item for 'the poor, the needy and the destitute'. Clara tried not to think of the irony of this and instead focused on the boys and their different gaits and variety of mannerisms. A serious Alex handed in a tin of golden syrup. He hadn't told Clara until that morning that donations were needed and she had gone in a tailspin, looking through the cupboards for something unopened.

The headmaster was a dry fossil, although less interesting

than a fossil. As he talked, about the importance of doing good, Clara drifted off, thinking about the new children and the old children and also homeless Joe, who wasn't her remit, and Ivor, who most definitely wasn't.

There were prizes in weird and wonderful subjects. Bernard was commended for geography. At this, Mr Braithwaite chuckled, then whispered, 'The boy can't find his way from my house to the car most days.'

Alex won a maths prize and was shortlisted for history and Latin. Clara would have stood up and clapped, only no one else did. Alex was another one whose start in life had been chequered – *chequered?* she thought, *that's just a euphemism for awful* – but here he was, getting exactly what was needed. It was satisfying to see. Less earnest once he was back in his row, he waved at her, her jug-eared boy. He was Going On to Great Things.

It was a very different school to the one Peter, Maureen, Billy and Barry attended. During 'All Things Bright and Beautiful' – who would have thought you could play that on the trumpet? – Bernard's father handed her a mint.

Clara wondered what the other parents thought of the pair of them. They probably thought that she was the stepmother and Bernard's father was 'the money'. She sneaked a sideways glance at him; he was sitting with his large hands clasped between his legs. He smiled nervously back at her, mussed hair falling across his eyes. No, he didn't look like 'the money'.

As they left the grandeur of the school, Clara braced herself for more general knowledge questions. She was surprised when instead Bernard's father asked gruffly, 'Shall we have a stroll along the seafront before we head back?'

Clara thought of the laundry mountain. She had to arrange meetings with the school about the new girls and Joyce needed an appointment with Doctor Cardew. Rita wanted radishes again. The council had sent some plimsolls that she had to collect from the post office and Peter had requested more drawing paper. Plus, there was the thrum of dread, a background fear about Mr Browne's plans. Only Miss Bridges would be able to put her mind at rest. But she found herself saying, 'I suppose I owe you an ice cream for driving us.'

They sat on a sandy bench looking out to the grey-blue sea. It was a long time since Clara had been to the coast. The last time had been with Judy just before her wedding, five years ago. Judy... She couldn't think about her now. She would only cry and Mr Braithwaite would think she was mad. Or he might take her in his arms, and the only arms she wanted to cry in were Ivor's.

She should bring the children here, she told herself. She should have thought of it before. Judy would have thought of it. Judy thought of everything like that.

Clara concentrated on the scene in front of her. You could hardly tell the sea from the sky. Morning mist – although you'd have thought it would have lifted by now. Clara liked the sound of the waves as they hit the sea wall, a bracing clatter. The ice-cream kiosk wasn't open, but they found a takeaway tea-van instead and declared that was just as good.

Bernard's father name was Victor Braithwaite, as in Victory, not Victor Frankenstein. He was born in October 1918, which meant he was only thirty years old, but he was definitely an old thirty, Clara thought. He was weathered and wheezy. That was what the war did. He had served in France.

'And what is it you do now – er – Victor?' she asked, trying out his name in her mouth. It was a noble name.

'I wonder can you guess?'

Victor liked newspapers, she knew that. He had a messy car, factual books in the footwell and a supply of Kendal mint cake that could probably see him through another war. She also knew, from seeing him at the summer fair, that he was accomplished at darts and liked the crooked house best.

Clara shook her head.

'I couldn't possibly—'

'I'm Professor of Politics and International Relations at Oxford.'

She thought he was joking. Not *The* Oxford. But his face convinced her he was not. He was proud of himself too, not in a pompous way, but in an *I'm happy with what I've achieved* way.

'Oxford?! You don't look...' Clara wasn't sure where she was going with this, 'old enough.'

Actually, he did. Victor's hair was grey and his was a heavy-set face, attractive in a carved-from-stone, sculptor-left-a-few-corners kind of way. Clara tried to work out who he reminded her of before remembering a bust of Beethoven that was on her music teacher's desk. She giggled to herself. He was less angry than that Beethoven though; he had an amiable, pleasant expression. If only she had someone to tell this to: Judy would have laughed. Miss Bridges didn't seem interested any more. And Anita would say, 'What? I don't get it, Clara.'

And Ivor? It probably wasn't an observation Ivor would be interested in.

He's a professor? she thought, and her mind leapt to Friedrich Bhaer – Josephine March's husband in *Little Women*. (That was definitely an observation Ivor wouldn't be interested in.)

'Bernard's mother couldn't come today?'

Victor explained that Bernard's mother, Iris, had died of cancer in 1944.

'I'm so sorry,' said Clara thinking, *same year as Michael.*

'Bernard was only eight.'

'That must have been hard.'

'I have to admit, Bernard kept me going. If it weren't for him...'

Clara used to wonder how things would have been if Michael had left her pregnant. To carry on something by him.

Her life would have been totally different. She wouldn't have come to Shilling Grange, for a start. She wouldn't have had this life. But was this life better? Sometimes she thought it was, but sometimes she thought it was lonely too. She wondered it less recently. She felt it was probably for the best it had not happened. She could no longer imagine herself with a baby – not Michael's, not anyone's.

'Eliza, my sister, lives with us.' He gave a sad chuckle. 'She had a rather torrid war. Her husband was held prisoner by the Japanese – Burma. Managed to survive three whole years only then to be executed just as the British were arriving. Pointless – it all is – but she still gets the occasional letter from him – they've taken all that time to get to us, can you imagine? I'm glad she's there, but sometimes, when it's just us three, rattling around the house, the sadness is overwhelming. It's palpable – you can feel it in the walls, in the wallpaper, in the furniture. Does that sound ridiculous?'

'No,' Clara said. She was used to sad tales – everyone was – but they never failed to move. Poor Victor. Poor Bernard. Poor his sister. She couldn't think of anything more to add, although she wanted to. But then Victor grinned at her suddenly.

'When Alex comes over, it's different, it's like a spark is lit. Bernard is happy and when Bernard is happy, I'm happy. They are wonderful friends – peas in a pod.'

'Long may it last,' said Clara, thinking that was a sweet thing for Victor to say. She had worried about Alex making friends at the grammar school. She knew some parents didn't like their children mixing with the Shilling Grange children. Some had screwed up their faces when they heard Rita was an orphanage kid – 'But she's so talented at the piano!' Betty Hanshawe had excluded the girls from a picnic. One mother rescinded a birthday party invitation for Joyce. The fact that Bernard and his father had been unfailingly welcoming felt special.

'To good friends,' he said. And he knocked his tin cup against hers. 'Cheers.'

Taken by surprise, Clara steadied her cup and laughed. 'Cheers!'

It took her a little while to realise he might be looking at her in a way she hadn't been looked at for some time. It was a boost to be admired. She felt like she was the view.

As they walked back to the car, Victor promised he would be in touch, 'very soon' and his voice was tremulous over the 'very'. Something inside Clara felt more adventurous than she had yesterday and it wasn't just from the sea air.

8

'They would have told me,' Miss Bridges said again irritably. 'And I would tell you, you know I would.' Clara had begged and begged until finally Miss Bridges had agreed to take her to the council so that she could hear everything directly from the horse's mouth – as it were.

Clara was going to make a joke about calling Mr Sommersby a horse, but Miss Bridges was not in a laughing mood today, thank you, Clara.

They couldn't park. Lips set, Miss Bridges circled the town until finally she found somewhere. The car came to a juddering halt, throwing Clara towards the windscreen.

'There are too many vehicles on the road nowadays,' snapped Miss Bridges. 'They need to put in restrictions or something.'

'I'm awfully glad you brought me along,' said Clara appeasingly.

Miss Bridges snapped off her gloves. She shook her head sympathetically or irritably or perhaps both. 'You know I miss Ivor...'

Clara gazed at her in surprise. *Miss Bridges missed Ivor?*

'He helped you keep things in perspective.'

In the reception of the council offices, there were three crying children with snotty noses and a man with a grey beard. The smallest of the children had a string tied round her wrist that tied her to the oldest child. The oldest child kept jerking it, making the tiny child bawl.

'I can't take them any more,' the man was saying.

The woman at the desk was repeatedly tapping a brass bell. 'But you can't just leave them here, Sir. Wait, please.'

Another two children stood in the corner facing the wall. Clara couldn't see who they were with. Not the couple there. The woman was knitting a hat, possibly, and the man was hiding his face in the newspaper. Clara read the front page. *From the cradle to the grave.*

Miss Bridges grimaced. 'It's all go.' She was annoyed that Clara had made her come and for the first time, Clara could appreciate why. She *was* bothering the council for no real reason when they had so much on. It was rumours, wishes and speculation when they were dealing with concrete urgent issues. And that bell ringing was enough to drive anyone doolally.

They walked into an office with a wide-open window, which made the room too cold and felt like the noisy street outside was right there with them. As soon as Clara sniffed, she could understand why; it was as though something was dead under the floorboards. She pretended she couldn't smell the foul thing, but it was eye-wateringly bad.

Mr Horton, children's homes inspector, looked done in. He was leaning back in his chair, his tie loosened, five o'clock shadow, and his shirt rumpled. He looked even less attractive than usual. His face lit up at Miss Bridges, then fell when he saw Clara behind her.

'What a morning!' He shook his head. 'We've had an adoption break down. A train crash, orphaned children. No money.

You name it, we've had it. And it's still –' he glared at his wrist-watch – 'before midday.'

Clara properly regretted the visit then. She was, as Miss Bridges insinuated, making a mountain out of a molehill. And after that jerky car journey, she needed the lav. Through the window, she could see a sign for the key-cutters opposite and a lamppost with a poster for a lost dog.

Timmy. Last seen on Tuesday. Please check your garages. Reward Offered.

Miss Bridges tugged at her jacket apologetically. Clara noticed for the first time the thick layer of foundation her face was covered in, down to her throat.

'Sorry to bother you, Mr Horton,' she said. She could be obsequious sometimes. 'I know how busy you are. It's just Miss Newton here has some questions.'

Clara jumped forward. This was her chance.

'You're not going to sell the Grange, are you?' The words tumbled out.

Mr Horton's cheek twitched. He started to say something, then changed his mind.

'How on earth did you hear that?'

'I just did.'

'I'm not at liberty to comment,' he said, which Clara thought gave away much more than he intended.

But then the actual head of children's services, Mr Sommersby, walked into the room. A tall man, comfortable in a suit, a man used to being in charge; he narrowed his eyes at them.

'What's going on now?'

'Sorry to bother you, Mr Sommersby,' said Miss Bridges, bowing her head.

'There's a rumour that a sale of the Grange is being planned,' said Clara, determined now.

'I've told her it's complete nonsense,' said Miss Bridges disloyally. 'But you know Miss Newton!'

Mr Sommersby walked over to the filing cabinet and opened the drawer marked A–C. He plucked a file from the drawer like he was tweezing a chin hair. Clara licked her lips and waited.

'What a week!' he said, echoing Mr Horton's words. 'Have. Not. Seen. Anything like it. Where were we? Right. Miss Newton, we meet again.' He was unhurried and smooth. 'Under better circumstances this time. Nothing to worry about, we're not decided either way.'

'What?' said Miss Bridges. Her mouth stayed open, her eyes narrowed. Mr Horton covered his face with his hand. Clara could see the sweat marks under his shirtsleeves.

'Whether to sell or not.' Mr Sommersby gazed around him as though surprised they didn't know. 'It's the property, you see. The Grange is a place of interest. If we sell it off, we'll be able to get somewhere more appropriate. You'll admit it's not ideal for children?'

'I... I think it's perfectly fine for children,' Clara responded tartly. She was taken aback; she had expected to have to do far more coaxing to get a straight answer.

'It's damp. You've said in the past you have problems with the windows and doors, no? Some dry rot?'

Clara blushed. Why, oh why, had she complained? She cleared her throat. 'That's not insurmountable.'

'The issue is the Grange is not value for money. You could say it's a white elephant.'

Clara thought of Peg's latest drawings of elephants'

bottoms. She thought of Alex once telling her about Hannibal crossing the Alps with elephants.

'It's a financial drain.' Mr Horton sighed.

Which was it? thought Clara. *An elephant or a drain?*

'We have to throw so much money at it, and you know, money doesn't—'

'Grow on trees?' Miss Bridges joined in helpfully. Clara felt like giving her a pinch.

Clara's mouth was dry. So this was it? Now it was coming to fruition she didn't know what to say, what to think.

'So you're saying you will sell?'

'Not at all, as I said we are undecided, but we are considering it.'

Miss Bridges had crossed her arms over her chest and was doing tiny head-shakes side to side. 'I seem to have been missed out of the loop.'

The two men stared at each other. Finally, Mr Horton, with his hands pressed together in prayer, said, 'Emily, there is no loop.'

Since when did he call her Emily?

Mr Sommersby said, 'Unless we can save money, then it looks like Shilling Grange is increasingly unviable.'

'I can do it.' Clara spoke up.

'Can what?'

'Save money – that's what I used to do, during the war. I was in charge of organisation, administration, budgets. I know I'll be able to.' She suddenly felt full of hope. It *wasn't* decided and she could prove her mettle. This was what she was made for. The men looked at each other. Miss Bridges was staring out of the window, an unhappy expression on her face. Mr Horton wouldn't look at her.

'The other thing is...'

'Yes?' Clara said eagerly.

'We're less likely to sell if it works.'

'Sorry?'

'If the children are thriving. If the children are seen to be thriving. If the location is deemed suitable. Those factors are also important. The children's well-being.'

'They are,' she said breathlessly, thrilled they had reached an understanding. She admired Mr Sommersby. 'It is. I can show you that they are.'

'For example, the little girl who doesn't speak?'

'Peg?'

'Perhaps if you could – do something about her?'

'I can't just make Peg speak.' Clara was again confused at what was required of her. She had thought she understood, but... 'We can't *force* her.'

'Oh, I see,' he said. 'Maybe not that then, something else, yes?'

'I... yes,' agreed Clara, mystified.

Outside, an ambulance went past, its siren howling. Two women chatted as they walked by, then there was a sound of something heavy being dragged along the pavement.

'Shall we say Christmas then?' Mr Sommersby said finally.

'Christmas?'

'That will give you nearly two months to prove to us that Shilling Grange is financially viable and works for the children.'

Mr Sommersby went to the metal cabinet nearest the door. Clara expected him to produce more files, accounts maybe, but instead he got out a glass ashtray and poured some sweets from it into a paper bag.

'Barley sugar.' He smiled. 'Take these for the little souls. Thank you for coming.'

Miss Bridges said tightly, 'You go ahead, Clara, I won't be a minute.'

Mr Horton still refused to meet her eye. Clara realised she disliked him intensely and she wasn't sure why.

. . .

In the car, Miss Bridges thumped the steering wheel, then stalled twice. They had only been on the road five minutes and she had sworn at three other drivers for the most minor of infractions. Clara's mind was leaping ahead. What Mr Sommersby had said about Peg made her feel uneasy, but he must understand that she couldn't just make her speak: that wasn't possible. She knew she could do numbers, but when they represented actual children's feet and children's food portions – *and* Stella's food portions – then would she be able to? She began calculating: she had been offered firewood and some other bits on the black market. She had an idea of where they might be able to make further cutbacks. It would be like during the war. She had brought enough clothes with her from London, she and Joe could turn them into clothes for the children. Shoes were more difficult. But perhaps she could take in washing? Maureen could contribute more – all the older ones could...

At least she knew, and knowing was better than not knowing. She would tell the children tonight, Clara decided, but she would play it down. She would gather them in the parlour and talk about lean times and money-saving schemes and the importance of being even more brilliant than usual. The children liked a mission. She was sure they'd oblige.

'You've got a job on your hands, that's for certain,' Miss Bridges said. She didn't take her eyes off the road.

CHILDRENS REPORT 10
Joyce Hall

Date of birth:

24 February 1938

Family Background:

Joyce comes from a large family. Five older brothers and two older sisters. She doesn't seem close to any of them. When she was diagnosed with polio, she was left at the hospital and the family refused to have her home.

Health/Appearance:

Joyce was poorly with polio and hospitalised for over eight months. One leg is weak, the other not too bad. She spends most of her time indoors and is pale/looks undernourished.

Food:

Despite appearances, Joyce has a healthy appetite. Enjoys a Sunday dinner. Anything sweet. Cakes. Dislikes wet food.

Hobbies:

She dislikes most games, playing, walking and all forms of sport. **She must exercise.**

Other:

Miss Fisher reports she would be a candidate for the eleven-plus, if she could be bothered. Joyce has since said she can't be bothered.

9

When Clara had imagined Marilyn Adams, the mother of her lost fiancé Michael, she had imagined a little old lady, like the grandmother in *Little House on the Prairie*. Or with long grey hair winding like the Mississippi River.

They had been writing, not a huge amount, but every six months or so; they seemed to instinctively tune in to each other and sometimes their letters would criss-cross over the ocean. When she had broken up with Julian, it was Marilyn who she had written to first, and it was Marilyn who had written the most satisfying of messages. This was strange – Marilyn was Michael's mother – but it had not *felt* strange at the time.

'You're worth five hundred times of him,' 'I bet he's kicking himself,' and 'There's no fool like an old fool.'

Even though probably only one of those – the last – was true, Marilyn's response had cheered Clara up no end. Marilyn sounded like a rocking-chair blanket, a cup of Bovril, a quilt by the fire on a frosty day.

Clara was certainly not expecting the 54-year-old blonde bombshell in fashionable wide-legged trousers and a figure-hugging jacket who turned up on the doorstep of Shilling

Grange one morning in late October, a few days after Clara's meeting at the council.

Marilyn hugged her. Clara stood poker-straight. This was a turn-up for the books. Marilyn held her at arm's length, then peered into her eyes. It felt oppressive. She said she wanted to get to know the daughter she had never met, and the daughter's children.

'They're not—'

'Oh, you know what I mean!' she said.

She pronounced herself an Anglophile. Clara wasn't sure what this meant either. She had a camera round her neck and high-heeled shoes with a bow. And a trunk. And a suitcase.

'How long did you say you are in England for?'

And a loud voice – half of the high road must have heard her.

Marilyn laughed. 'Don't look so horrified. I'll be staying up the block at the Shilling Arms Hotel.'

Clara laughed; she couldn't help it. Marilyn seemed bright-eyed and fun and goodness knows, they could do with some of that. The children had reacted well to the news about the Grange and the tighter budgets (she wasn't sure the younger ones had understood): 'as long as we're together,' she'd said; but still, insecure children and insecurity weren't the greatest combination.

When the children came home from school, they stared at Marilyn like she was Betty Grable herself. Marilyn played up to it: 'I wish I could put you in my pockets and take you back to the States.'

'I've always wanted to go up the Eiffel Tower!' said Barry. He was getting ready to go to football. Why his knees were bloodied *before* the match was anyone's guess.

'Honey, that's France,' explained Marilyn patiently. 'We have the Statue of Liberty in America.' She stood up, dramatically holding her glass of water in front of her. 'Give me your tired, your poor, your huddled masses yearning to breathe free.'

The children gazed in awe, everyone except for Evelyn, who crept to the back door.

'Hey there, little lady.'

Evelyn grunted.

'Evelyn, you're being talked to,' Clara said.

Sometimes the girl could be so frustrating.

Marilyn winked at Clara. 'Evelyn, is it? Now that is one of my favourite names.'

Finally, Evelyn looked up, her eyes glazed. 'Thank you.'

'What are you interested in?' It seemed Marilyn, like Clara, was a great believer in the restorative power of hobbies.

'Nothing.'

'Nothing? That can't be right!'

Evelyn puffed out her cheeks. For the first time, she said, 'Actually, I like babies.'

'Babies?' echoed Clara. In what way were babies a *hobby*? But she had to be encouraging. 'How interesting. I don't know if you can collect them, but we could certainly' – she couldn't think of anything to say. *What could they certainly do?* – 'count the babies we see in the street.'

Marilyn raised one beautifully pencilled eyebrow at Clara as if to say, 'You're going to have fun with this one.'

But Marilyn's eyes lit up like London in the Blitz at the sight of Peter. He came in, swiped a cracker and was about to make off upstairs but she grabbed his arm.

'He's going to break a few hearts.'

Peter blushed redder than a tomato.

'We-ell,' said Clara, aware that she might sound like a scold, 'Peter is a kind boy, I don't think he'd deliberately hurt anyone, so...'

Marilyn didn't notice. She had moved on to Rita.

'Who's this peach?'

Rita hated a nickname. 'My name is Rita. *You're* a peach!' She turned on her heels.

'Say that again and I'll spank you to kingdom come, little girl,' Marilyn said, laughing.

'Marilyn,' Clara warned.

Once the children had left the room, Clara cleared her throat. She didn't want to offend Marilyn. 'I know it was meant in jest but I don't think we should speak to the children like that.'

'Like what, honey?'

'Like spanking them,' said Clara, embarrassed. 'To kingdom come?'

How could she express what the children had been through? The thought of Barry being beaten until he was fainting. And little Peg locked in a dark cupboard, getting slippered, getting whipped. The last manager of the Grange had loved to dish out brutal punishments. Even her name, Sister Eunice, still struck fear into everyone's hearts. She had overseen a reign of terror and it had taken the children a long time to adjust to the fact that they weren't going to get beaten every time they took a wrong turn. The last thing they needed was more threats, however jokingly they were said.

Clara was so surprised that Marilyn listened to her explanation and then said, 'You're the expert' that she peered hard at her to see if there were signs of sarcasm: there didn't appear to be.

'I don't understand everything these children have been through,' Marilyn went on, 'but I want to try.'

Clara couldn't believe it. If she had pulled up her parents on anything, they would have fought her for days, even if they agreed with her; they didn't like ideas to have come from her.

'I'm here to help, girl,' Marilyn said cheerfully, 'not to make things worse. Don't forget that. Put me in my place if you need to.'

It would be easy to get attached to Marilyn. And if Clara had assumed that someone as glamorous as Marilyn would not be domesticated, she was wrong about that too. Now she sat sewing the hem of Rita's winter skirt, her cigarette smouldering on the ashtray beside her.

'Did Michael tell you about the time he got lost on the beach? He was about six. I found him with an ice cream, having a lovely time. That was my Michael.'

Clara laughed; she could just picture it. Michael *never* felt lost – that was another thing she had always admired about him.

After tea, Marilyn gathered the children round to show them something. She fussed with her handbag, but when she produced a photograph, they were disappointed – they always hoped for sweets.

'This is Miss Newton in 1943 – only six years ago. And this is my boy, my son, Michael.'

Clara and Michael were posing at the gates of Buckingham Palace, pretending they were royalty. Michael was such a tourist. He wanted to go to all the places he'd heard of. It was Clara who had resisted at first – *what's the point, we can't go inside?* – but she had never resisted anything he suggested for too long.

'I remember who took this.'

It was another couple, another American serviceman with another British girl. Clara could remember being embarrassed. She had felt so special sometimes, with Michael, and yet at moments like this, when she met another couple just like them, she felt so ordinary – as though her story, her *life,* was two-a-penny. She wondered what happened to these two. Had he too been killed, or had they hit the jackpot? Or had they – like Ruby and her American – lasted the war but fallen apart in the peace?

There he is: the proud fitted uniform, the short, short hair and that big grin. She once asked him, 'Do you always smile?'

'When I'm with a girl like you, you bet. Why wouldn't I?'

There she was: girl in a tight white sweater. How could she be so innocent? It seemed rotten how much she had changed. She remembered older women looking at her back then with a mixture of indulgence and – it wasn't envy, it was wistfulness. They were remembering their youth, they were remembering the calm before the storm.

Funny, it was like she was a different person, in a different life.

Before she left for the hotel that night, Marilyn grabbed Clara again for another of her long hugs. Then she held her away and smiled into her face. 'Look at you! I can see why Michael fell in love with you.'

Clara blushed.

'And he *was* so in love with you. The things he wrote, I remember them word for word. *"Ma, there is this English girl who makes my heart sing. We might be at war, but she makes me feel like a king."* Five years. Feels like both a lifetime and a blink of an eye.'

Her eyes filled with tears. Clara was so taken aback that for a moment, she couldn't speak.

'Thank you,' Marilyn said, 'for making my boy's last few months so precious. As a mother, that's all I could ask for.'

The next morning, Marilyn was knocking at the front door, dressed for a garden party. She twirled: 'Like Princess Elizabeth, huh?'

She looked nothing like her or any Englishwoman, but

Clara couldn't work out what it was that made her different: Was it her glow? Her glamour?

'Is it normal to have kippers in the morning? And while I knew you English liked tea, I had no idea it was an obsession!'

As they walked down the high road, Marilyn admiring everything, a drunk man was shouting outside the post office. Ungenerously, Clara couldn't help thinking he was blighting the otherwise attractive scene.

'I'll give him some cash,' said Marilyn. 'Let him buy a drink.'

'Noo,' said Clara embarrassed. 'Oh, perhaps you could buy him an Eccles cake or...' She had wanted to show Marilyn Lavenham at its best, and now here it was in its most unflattering light. Marilyn didn't seem worried though. She was easily pleased, thought Clara, but it was more than that. Like her son, she had a generous spirit.

They were just admiring the Tudor exterior of the Cloth Hall when Clara glimpsed Julian White out of the corner of her eye. Oh, no! He snaked his way to them and won over Marilyn instantly with his beautiful 'English' manners. It was like watching someone be hypnotised. They chatted about the Shilling Arms Hotel and then he leaned in conspiratorially:

'And what do you think of our Shilling Grange?'

Our?

'It's run-down, that's for sure. I can imagine if you spent some money on it as a hotel, the tourists would come. We Americans would be beside ourselves. It would need a huge investment though.'

'Don't think it hasn't been thought about!'

'By whom?' interrupted Clara, her ears pricking up. 'Who's thought about it?' *Browne,* she thought. The rich lawyer man in the house with the pillars. He was behind this.

Julian ignored her. 'I'm having a soirée next weekend. Won't you ladies join us?'

He'd never asked Clara before – at least not since they'd split up.

'I have the children,' said Clara.

As you know.

Marilyn said, 'Sorry, I'm not here for long – but I'll be back soon with my dancing shoes, so hold. that. thought!'

Julian promised he would. Jubilantly, he kissed the backs of Marilyn's hands – Clara kept hers resolutely in her pockets.

Even from behind, Julian looked smug, Clara thought resentfully as he made off down the road. *How could a walk look so privileged?* she wondered.

'Isn't he a charmer?' cooed Marilyn.

'That's Julian...' Clara cautioned. 'Remember, I wrote to you about him?'

Marilyn was shocked. 'The ex-fiancé? I should have known.'

Clara chewed her lip. It shouldn't annoy her that Marilyn hadn't figured it out but it did.

'You've met no one else since?'

That was another thing Clara was picking up about Marilyn: she was nosy, unstoppably so. She didn't seem to mind that Clara was moving on – and that Michael was stuck in 1944. No, Clara reconsidered, she probably did mind, but she accepted it. She was a realist.

'I thought I might have met someone,' Clara said cautiously. 'But he didn't get in touch.'

There had been no advance from Victor Braithwaite. She must have been wrong about the way he was looking at her. It wasn't admiration, it was manners. Or if it was admiration it was for the beach, not her. She had been so *sure* he would get in touch too. It irked her almost as much that she'd misjudged the situation as that he hadn't.

'Is he married?'

'I... no, his wife died.'

'Hmm,' Marilyn said. 'And in a letter, you mentioned a special neighbour? Ivan, was it? Ivan the terrible?'

'Oh, Ivor.' Clara pretended she didn't know who she meant. *Special neighbour?* That just about summed it up. 'Mm...'

'Is *he* married?'

'I suppose he is.'

'Forget about him.'

Marilyn didn't know the full story, but maybe the full story was just complications, obscurity and fudge. However you dressed it up, right now Ivor was with his wife.

'You will want children one day, I imagine?'

Clara didn't want children. The knowledge had grown gradually inside her, rather as she imagined a baby would. It had fused when Judy told her she wanted children and Clara had felt, yes, absolute compassion, but not understanding. She did not want a child of her own. People assumed she did – *she* had assumed she did but she was thinking more and more that she didn't. It was nothing to do with her relationships – It was nothing to do with Michael, Ivor, or the embarrassing rest of them. It was her.

She didn't want to do it.

She wanted what she had right now. *Other* people's children. Her job as a housemother.

Sometimes, she wondered if Mrs Garrard and Miss Cooper who were about the same age as her, felt the same: Miss Cooper was so bohemian, it would be just like her to have five children, yet it would also be just like her to have none.

'I'm not sure,' she lied. Marilyn smiled at her and Clara couldn't tell what the smile meant.

Marilyn walked like Michael, Clara thought. And the way she suddenly stopped slouching and stood upright was something Michael did too. It made her feel closer to Marilyn – and Michael.

· · ·

That evening, Clara told Marilyn that they might be moving. She explained that the council saw the Grange as a white elephant or a financial drain.

Marilyn rubbed her chin (like Michael would have) and said, 'What do you think about that?'

'I'm going to stop it happening,' Clara said resolutely. Somehow, Marilyn was a woman who inspired resolve. 'I don't think it's right and I'm going to prove it to them.'

Marilyn reached out and squeezed Clara's knee, creasing her nylons. 'There's another reason why Michael loved you, right there.'

Marilyn wasn't used to girls. 'I have more experience with boys,' she said. It was throwaway remarks like these that hinted at her deep well of grief and each time she said something like that, Clara got a lump in her throat.

On Saturday, Marilyn was at the back door while most of the children were eating breakfast, although Rita had already bolted hers down and was practising piano in the shed. Evelyn was eyeing up the leftovers.

'I need someone to take photographs for me. I want to go back to the States with some pictures of English life. You'll do.'

She pointed at Joyce, who seemed to shrink from her manicured finger.

'Not me, I can't.'

'Why? What's wrong with you?' Marilyn asked.

'I can hardly walk.' Joyce scowled.

'Best behaviour!' Clara mouthed at her.

'What happened?' Marilyn said.

Clara flushed on Joyce's behalf. Joyce didn't like talking about it.

'Polio.'

'Horrible disease,' Marilyn said. 'I remember when Michael was little – such a worry. You look strong now though, girl.'

'I'm not,' said Joyce. Her jaw moved from side to side, a tiny picture of mutiny.

Clara watched, interested to see how this would play out: two forces of nature up against each other.

'Can you or can't you?' persisted Marilyn.

'With the wagon or a stick, I can, I suppose.'

'Then, let's go.'

Joyce got up. Marilyn had won. Joyce clipped her callipers on, her hair swinging. Clara was surprised that she did it.

Only once Joyce was ready, her face timid and rat-like, did Marilyn soften. 'One thing I regret is that I don't have more photographs of my Michael...'

Marilyn and Joyce were out most of the afternoon. Clara went through her books. There were more savings to be made, she was sure of it. Peg sat under her desk playing marbles and was so silent, Clara clean forgot she was there. Occasionally, out of the front window, the Joyce-mobile wagon went past, Marilyn stoically pulling it, tottering on her heels, Joyce lying back, fiddling with the camera. Another time, when she was pinning up the washing at the back, she saw Joyce chasing after Marilyn, with her stick, the camera swinging round her neck, throwing her out of balance.

They didn't get back until the sky was darkening, by which time Clara was beginning to worry. Had Marilyn finally run out of steam? Had Joyce behaved terribly? But the pair returned cheerfully, chatting.

'How was it?'

'This one doesn't like taking photographs of flowers much.'

Joyce pulled her face that said 'boring'.

'Or buildings. Though we got a lovely one of the First World War memorial on the corner.

'Or cats. Although we got one of Mr White's dog. What was its name – Pirate?'

'Bandit.'

'We're going to try people next.'

'I'm a people person,' Joyce announced.

Clara decided not to even raise an eyebrow at that. If Joyce saw herself that way, then who was she to say otherwise?

The next morning, Clara was surprised to see Joyce was up and her callipers were on before Marilyn came over from the Shilling Arms. (Joyce was not usually an early riser.) They set up shots in the garden; they wanted to take a photograph of Clara hanging out sheets.

'Seriously?' Clara had been envisaging something more regal or dignified. A portrait of her sitting in the parlour like Princess Margaret perhaps.

'We want you to look natural,' called Marilyn. 'Just doing what you normally do. What do we call that?' she asked Joyce, who responded like she'd been drilled: 'Reportage style.'

'Ignore us,' added Joyce, which Clara thought was the opposite of her usual commands.

Natural!? Clara did tidy her hair and tied her apron extra-tight so she had a waist. She remembered going with her parents to a photo studio once, just before they left, although she never got to see the photographs they had so diligently posed for. It was a strange studio in Kilburn. An awkward fella hiding under a blanket. A boom. She remembered expecting something magic to happen.

'What do you do now?' Joyce asked, following her.

'Lay the table for lunch?' Clara suggested.

They trooped in after her, Marilyn making *I can't help it* faces.

There was some debate about the light and Clara had to pick up and put down the bowls three times. She wished she had some lipstick to put on.

'You'll be wanting one of me cleaning the bath next?'

Joyce burst into laughter. Fortunately, Billy and Barry had got up and were in full football regalia, so Marilyn said, 'Let's go outside and capture them.' She winked at Clara. 'Sports photography is a fabulous field to get into, Joyce.'

The next day, Clara was ironing when Joyce came in. The other children often popped in and out, but it was a first for Joyce. Her bottom lip was out like a crust of bread.

'Everyone I like goes away in the end.'

Clara had a tower of clothes to get through, but she stopped ironing.

'Is that how it feels, Joyce?'

She paused. 'That's how it *is*.'

Clara considered. It was gorgeous when people came to visit. But coming along, swooping into someone's life, was easy – it was the staying that was the important thing. Staying was what counted.

'Do you want a go with the iron?' Carefully, she passed it to the girl and showed her how to use it. They were on Maureen's cotton work blouse, one of Clara's old ones. It occurred to her that Joyce might burn it on purpose. No, Clara told herself, Joyce could be destructive, but she wouldn't do that.

'Like this?'

'I'm sorry you feel like that.'

'I bet as soon as I feel at home here, it will be over.'

'You're not going anywhere, sweetheart. Well, maybe if some appropriate adoptive parents come along.'

'No one is going to want me like this.' She pointed to her leg.

'Someone will care for you just as you are.' Clara added daringly, 'Like we do here. You can't get rid of all the creases.'

'I know that,' Joyce said.

She stayed ironing side by side with Clara until the pile was done.

On Marilyn's last morning, some of the children cried before they went to school, even to Clara it felt as though a holiday was coming to an end. Life was more enjoyable with a Marilyn in it. And Clara had some big issues to face. Marilyn's visit had distracted her from them, but they hadn't gone away.

'What are we going to do about you?' Marilyn said in the kitchen, tapping her hand with her large rings.

'How do you mean?'

'You're too young for the spinster life. You're not much older than some of the children.'

Clara squirmed. Was *this* what Marilyn had come here for?

'There's a whole world of lovely men out there...'

Clara screwed up her nose. It choked her to say: 'Michael was one of a kind.'

'That he was,' agreed Marilyn, wiping her eyes. 'I'm sorry you two didn't get to build a life together.'

Clara inhaled. Her life, the stages of her life, stolen from her by the war. It hit her again. Usually, she avoided thinking of it – if she had been blown off track, then what of those who had been so spectacularly wiped out?

Marilyn had brought up lots of the past, but you had to move on.

'Don't give up on love. It's no way to live,' she said as she hugged Clara again. She smelled wonderful. She had told

Clara, 'Every woman needs a signature scent,' and Clara had laughed and claimed hers was 'eau de porridge'.

'And don't give up on this place either. You *can* save the Grange, sweetheart.' She went out to her taxi, pulling her trunk behind her.

And although Clara felt like the lone adult again, she had the warm fuzzy feeling of it being a good trip. It wasn't just Joyce she had helped; Marilyn had worked wonders all round. Clara could do this. And she would do it by herself. She didn't need anyone.

10

The day after Marilyn left, a letter came from Ivor.

> Thank you for your concern. Yes, Joe has permission to stay
> in the workshop. All fine. Trust all is well with you and the
> children. Thank you, Clara.

Why did Ivor have to be so stilted? The note hurt more than
if he'd ignored her. As for the 'All fine' – this was deliberately
ambiguous. Did he mean 'we' or 'I'? And the no questions made
it evident: he might as well have written DO NOT REPLY.

Still, at least he'd got in touch – Victor hadn't. Victor had
left her high and dry – and the more he hadn't got in touch, the
more Clara wished he would. That would teach Ivor! She told
herself it was good he hadn't contacted her – she had so much
going on – but it was no use – she *was* disappointed. She coped
better with the children when she knew she had something to
look forward to. Clara reminded herself that she had made it
her mission to stand on her own two feet – she didn't need
anyone any more, even Ivor.

Since there was nothing private there, Clara showed

Maureen the letter. Maureen's eyes whipped across the page. 'I'll tell Joe!' She danced off. 'He'll be over the moon.'

Nothing to worry about, Clara told herself. Maureen knew which side her bread was buttered.

So that was one thing sorted. And maybe some other things too: Joe had got himself a job delivering papers. It was only a few hours a day, but he'd sorted it by himself and the pay was reasonable.

Joe told them about it: 'I have to deliver to most houses – some take two or, your mate Bernard,' he said to Alex, 'his father gets three!'

Joe got up at five and was done by seven except once a week, when he had to collect the money. That was the part he dreaded most, for the customers often weren't at home, or were rude, but he'd heard that at Christmas they gave generous tips.

The children wanted to go with him on his rounds.

'It's not exciting,' he protested, but the way he told it – a fierce dog who bares his teeth, a garden like a jungle you had to hack your way through and a lady who was only ever in her negligee – made them shriek.

'I'll give some of my wage to you,' he said shyly to Clara, 'for the food and you know, your budget...'

He was a thoughtful boy.

'I've had an idea,' Joe said a few days later.

'Well done, Joe!' Clara liked teasing Joe. He seemed happier since the permission had come from Ivor. It was legitimate now. Or maybe it was since he'd got the newspaper delivery job. He was less defensive than he had been. Joe thought the children might want to start up a newspaper of their own: 'I could get some paper free from work and some carbon-copy paper. They've already got some skills we could use: Peter could do cartoons and Joyce has her photos and...' He considered. 'You said that you wanted to turn us into an example of a brilliant home. And I thought it would be a way to showcase that and maybe raise some money too.'

'You're a genius, Joe!'

They held their first meeting in the shed. Everyone took or was allocated a job. Clara was invited, but told she wasn't 'to interfere'.

Billy and Barry decided they were sports correspondents, naturally. Anything to do with football, hopscotch, skipping would be down to them. They huddled together, scheming. 'Give us as many pages as possible,' they requested. Joe was editor and Alex designated himself as subeditor – everyone said that was great, although Barry whispered, 'Why does he get to be on the submarine?' Alex put on the reading glasses that Miss Bridges had left behind last visit and said that he would be strict on spelling but no one was to take it personally. Because Joe was involved, Maureen didn't have much choice but to get involved too. She said she'd write some recipes. She might even do can-o-pays. Joe also volunteered to write something on gardens. Or vegetables.

'We go together like fish and chips,' said Maureen, snuggling up to him and then making a point of meeting Clara's eyes.

All Peter had to do was an up-to-date and hilarious cartoon, featuring people they knew in Lavenham.

'You don't ask for much, do you?' he said grumpily, but Clara thought he was secretly pleased with his assignment. He was waiting for the letter from the comic-contest people. He told Clara he didn't mind either way, but he got up every morning to check the post – something he never used to do.

Joyce volunteered to be picture correspondent: 'Does it have to be a photo of you lot,' she asked, 'or could it be something interesting?'

Rita would write a piece on music or books. 'Or Mama,' she added.

Peg wrote down that she was going to do poems about fairies or dancing, then she spun round.

It took them a while to decide how often to produce the newspaper. They eventually settled on every two months. It took Clara a while longer to realise Evelyn had no role. She was cross-legged on the floor, puffy and sulky, pulling the petals off a daisy. No one else seemed to have noticed her either.

'Evelyn,' Clara nudged her, 'how are you going to contribute?'

Evelyn scowled, the stripped flower flopped in her palm.

'What would you like to write about?'

'Nothing.'

'What things are you into?' Joe asked.

She shrugged.

Clara remembered: 'You said you like babies.'

'Mm.'

'Thank goodness there are no babies here,' Rita said wearily. She found Evelyn tiresome, and she didn't care who knew it – but then Rita did love to have an enemy, so in that way, it made her happy.

'No, but she could write a nursery rhyme or something,' Clara suggested. 'Evelyn, you could choose one from my poetry book or make up one of your own?'

Evelyn wrinkled her nose. 'Suppose so.'

'Think what you can achieve when you work together.'

She had only meant to be in the shed a couple of minutes. Clara scuttled back to the kitchen, leaving them discussing how much to charge. They seemed to think their readers were millionaires. Clara laughed to herself. It would be fine. Her budgeting was paying off and, more importantly, the children had come a long way.

Joyce and Evelyn seemed to be getting along better since

Marilyn's visit. Alex was enjoying school and his friendship with Bernard protected him from bullies there. Peg and Rita were doing their usual Peg and Rita things. Maureen and Joe were love's young dream. When they kissed each other goodbye in the morning and the evening, Billy and Barry made smoochy noises and rubbed their hands on their own backs. And Peter was coming out of his shell like she'd always hoped he would.

As Clara was thinking this, scraping off the black bits of tomorrow's leek and potato pie, smelling of eau de burnt pudding, Alex came and stood in front of her, his head bowed.

'I'm sorry, I've done something bad.'

Alex had? Straight away, her mind jumped to Mr Sommersby and her task. What would he say? They mustn't give the council an inch, nor a centimetre.

'I should have given you this ages ago. I forgot...'

He handed Clara a crumpled note that had clearly spent some days or weeks nesting in the bottom of his schoolbag. There were crumbs, rips and creases but the message was just about legible. Clara laughed with relief. Nothing to worry about here.

What a lovely morning. I enjoyed our chat. If ever you want to see the university, I'd love to show you around. Or we could have another cup of tea. Here is my telephone number. Look forward to hearing from you,

Victor.

11

Victor said she wasn't too late to get in touch – good gracious, not at all.

They arranged to meet on a Tuesday morning, a time that seemed incongruous for a date, since surely everyone knew dates were Friday and Saturday nights? This was both a relief and a disappointment; it cemented them as just friends. Even less auspicious was the location: Bury St Edmunds, which was where she and Julian had gone for their first date. Yet although the exchange on the telephone was awkward, Clara was enthusiastic about seeing Victor again. She felt like she was stepping away from something, or had given up looking for something in one place and was trying another.

Ivor and his wife could go whistle.

She concentrated on what Marilyn had said about moving on: 'You're too young for the spinster life.'

At the station, Victor waved, then abruptly put down his arm as though someone had ordered him to stop. He looked shy, as though he was wrestling some demons himself, although that may just have been his messy hair. Clara thought about his resemblance to Beethoven; she had meant it as a compliment, but she did not know him well enough to say it out loud. He surely had a sense of humour but it was probably not the same as hers.

They went to the Lyons tea room, which, fortunately, was one of the few tea rooms she hadn't been to with Julian. She would only have one (the budget!), but Lyons was usually reasonably priced too.

Victor said, 'I do love a nice cup of tea,' as though it was something extraordinary. *Doesn't everyone?*, thought Clara, and then berated herself for being so picky. It wasn't fair. He was nervous and he was feeling inhibited. Nothing wrong with that. He couldn't help not being Ivor.

She sipped her tea and eyed him over the cup. Perhaps Ivor wasn't the only one to think she had kind eyes.

He said, 'So tell me about Miss Newton.'

That irritated her. Why speak about her in the third person? And then she realised she was deliberately letting herself be annoyed. What was it she liked to say to the children? 'Best behaviour' – well, it would do her good to apply it to herself too. And what *could* she tell him about Miss Newton? She was no longer anyone's daughter, not a sister, she was not a partner, nor a best friend, nor a mother – what was she?

She wasn't sure.

Tears came to her eyes.

And then she thought: *I don't have to be someone in relationship with other people; I am myself* – so she chatted about her interest in poetry, her friendship with the Cardews and the cinema trips she enjoyed. She said that she didn't like cooking, didn't know much about art or music, but liked listening to people, liked helping children. As she talked, she thought, *I'm not so boring.* It was all true, it was just she didn't usually hold herself up to this light.

He said, 'You're a champion of the underdog, aren't you?'

'That's the first time anyone's said that to me.'

He kept his gaze on her. 'It's a precious thing.'

He told her about himself too and as he was talking, Clara thought how, during the war, everything was fast; relationships sped up, an hour was a day – was it any wonder? They were like mice on a wheel. Slowly, slowly, she thought. Sometimes, when you went too quick, you ignored the glaring incompatibilities. *Look at Julian,* she told herself.

And the honest thing was, she still had this corner in her heart that was forever Ivor's.

There is nothing worse than a woman in love with a married man though. Her mother had left her with a few adages like that – a friend at the church had been overly friendly with the men and had been sent to Coventry – and there were those women in France who collaborated with the Nazis and had their heads shaved. (Funny how the men, who also collaborated and had the affairs, didn't seem to be considered bad people though.)

Clara shivered.

Anyway, she didn't feel like she was *that kind of woman,* for a zillion thoroughly legitimate reasons, but if you boiled the situation down to its essence – like a ham in a saucepan – that's what you'd be left with. *That kind of woman.* And if you heard 'her' story from a friend of a friend, that's what it would look like too.

Move on, she told herself. Ivor was not coming back. Or if he did, he wasn't coming back *for her.*

Sometimes you get a hold of someone by the way they talk about other people and it was as Victor talked about his sister, Eliza, that Clara got a better idea of him; the way he talked about her revealed he was sensitive and kind. And when he talked about Bernard, he seemed to take on a glow. 'He's wise beyond his years,' he said. 'Like his mother was – and so open-minded too.'

It was refreshing to hear how generously he spoke of his family. Julian used to be so negative, while Ivor hated to – what he called – gossip.

'I'm glad Alex and he are great friends. Alex is a wonderful boy.' And he didn't spoil it like so many did with a 'considering' or 'in spite of'. It was just a flat-out *Alex is a wonderful boy.* Clara's heart swelled.

'What's it like living at the Grange?' he asked suddenly. 'I've always wondered.'

'It's marvellous, but...' Clara looked up, at his open face. Should she say anything about the possible changes? She decided to give him a summary. 'The council are considering selling and I'm hoping to persuade them not to.'

'How are you doing that?'

'Well,' she began, 'they say it's too expensive, so we're saving money and if I can just show them that the children are in the right place, I'm hoping to prove them wrong. I've got until Christmas.'

'I have no doubts that you can do whatever you set your mind to.'

How lovely it was to speak to someone who was able to see things from her point of view. And not just her point of view. He extrapolated outwards – he was talking about how the children were the responsibility of *everyone.* He was a political man and after time with him, she felt like she was a political woman. Yes, care of unwanted children was a big issue, yes, she was making a big contribution. Yes, she was fired up, MORE needed to be done! And they had spent three whole hours chatting – having a jolly time – that was not to be sneezed at. And he did have attractive hands.

Victor was *not* married and he was actually here in front of her, and good grief, that had to count for something! She put a smile on her face.

'Let me pay for this,' he said.

~

One week later, they went out again. This time, mindful perhaps that Clara was trying to save money, Victor suggested a walk and had packed biscuits (made by his sister) and a flask of hot tea. He was a lovely *build*, she thought, like a brick wall. She wondered if they might sit closer together. Perhaps, under the pretext of being cold, she might suggest it.

He asked how she was doing. She told him she had cut her own hair following a guide in *Good Housekeeping* and that Joe had turned an old dress into a skirt and blouse for Rita. She said that she had run out of papers and pens, but Mr Dowsett the librarian had heard her explaining that to the children and had offered her some. She said maybe it was too hard – keeping the children at the Grange – and he said, 'I bet you can do it,' and it was lovely him having faith in her.

'So not a bad week all in all and I'm feeling better for seeing you,' she dared.

But Victor had bad news: he was going away on a research trip. He was writing a book – his third, in fact – and had to spend time in Germany, Poland and France. It was about the left-wing resistance to National Socialism.

Victor said that it was a tragic tale – one of the reasons fascism was able to grow in the 1930s was because the opposition – or oppositions – were so disunited. They spent more time arguing among themselves than they did with the fascists!

Clara felt they were spending more time arguing about fascists than they were planning some interesting dates. He would be away for eight weeks. 'What about Bernard?' she asked distractedly. Victor reminded her of his sister, the sweet-natured Eliza. That's how it was with men, Clara remembered; even when they were encumbered, they always seemed to wangle a way they could be unencumbered and that wangling always seemed to involve a little woman somewhere somehow.

'You won't be back until after Christmas?' she spluttered, then pretended that the tea had gone down the wrong way. Alone again. Abandoned again. Their connection was too fragile, like a spider's web, to withstand such a distance of time and space.

'I'd like to write to you if I may,' he said. 'And I won't send them through the Alex messenger service next time.'

'No, not through Alex,' she repeated dutifully, then told herself to laugh.

She thought Victor might kiss her, but he didn't. There wasn't much point, she supposed, if they weren't going to see each other for so long.

12

Joyce didn't want to go to see Dr Cardew – neither walking nor in her wagon – but a visit was long overdue and Clara was adamant they could not afford to have any marks against them.

'Best behaviour, everyone!'

'Best behaviour!' did not change Joyce's mind, but the prospect of meeting Billy and Barry 2, the goldfish the twins had won at the fair last year, did. In the waiting area, Joyce stared so intently at the fish swimming effortlessly around the glass tank that she went cross-eyed. Clara said she was just impressed the fish were still alive.

'They wouldn't have lasted this long at the Grange – especially not with Stella on the scene!'

'I don't think so either,' said Joyce flatly. She had an uncanny knack for turning everything into an insult.

It wasn't that Joyce was unhappy, just she wasn't happy. Clara had expected the new girls to fit in but there still seemed to be a line of demarcation around the old ones and the new arrivals, and she wondered if it was just a question of 'time' or if she had to do something else. Joyce had loved having Marilyn to stay and she had embraced the photography, but as time went on, she seemed as downbeat as she had ever been.

Joyce looked up at her. 'Rita called me a name yesterday,' she said.

'Oh dear,' said Clara, but she thought Joyce had what Miss Bridges used to call 'a distant relationship with the truth'.

'So did Peg.'

'Peg doesn't speak.'

'Still,' said Joyce, 'I knew what she was thinking.'

Clara was glad when they were called in. Dr Cardew examined Joyce and asked questions about her diet, her sleep and her pain level. Then he signed her off as fully fit.

'You're in fine fettle,' he said to Joyce. 'A credit to you, Miss Newton. But you do need to exercise that leg.' He addressed this last to them both.

'She's not keen, are you, Joyce?'

Joyce scowled.

Clara looked away from Joyce. Dr Cardew was rubbing his eyes.

'Tired already?' she asked in a low voice.

Dr Cardew winced. 'Anita has trouble sleeping' – he coughed – 'which means *I* have trouble sleeping.'

Clara suggested they stop off at the bakery on the way back for a rare treat of some broken biscuits. Joyce wasn't as pleased about it as Clara hoped. If it had been Alex or Rita or especially Evelyn, they would have been beaming. It was a waste of a half-shilling.

They passed Mrs Garrard, who was lugging in buckets of flowers. She sang out 'Lovely day.' Mr Garrard's dog Bertie licked Joyce's fingers, but even that couldn't put a smile on her sour face.

'Good news you're doing so well, hey?'

Joyce said nothing but clip-clopped in her heavy shoes.

Clara could imagine nothing worse than the iron lung, making you feel trapped and contained. What a lot the young girl had been through. And her family had abandoned her when she was most vulnerable. Clara knew that most of the children had been miserable at least for some parts of their early life, but something about this tale made her heart ache even more than usual.

Joyce looked haughty though and her proud mouth twitched.

'I bet you hated being in hospital. It must have been awful.'

Joyce began to cry.

'Joyce, sweetie, what is it?'

'It's...' Joyce couldn't get the words out for the tears. They ran into her half-biscuit. 'I loved it. Everyone asked after me. The doctors and nurses fussed around me. And the professors and even their students. Now, what is left of me? What's special about me?'

Clara was frozen. She hadn't anticipated this. She exchanged the crumbs in Evelyn's hands for a handkerchief, which gave her time to think of a reply.

'What is left of you? Wow, a lovely, strong and interesting young woman who has been through an awful lot—'

'I hurt everybody in the end.'

Clara immediately understood what this was about. 'Was it you who did it then? The comic?'

'I didn't tear it up. Stella ripped it. I would never have done *that*.'

'But you *did* take it?'

She nodded. 'I... I wanted it to go missing because I wanted to find it for him. I wanted you to notice me and thank me and think I was helpful.'

'But it was too messed-up to return?'

Joyce nodded again, then scowled at her feet.

Clara put her arm round her. 'We all make mistakes,' she crooned into Joyce's hair. 'The important thing is to learn from them.' She felt moved suddenly. 'Peter worked hard at that. And you, too, will find your thing and one day you can be whoever you like.'

'So you're not going to send me away?' Joyce asked. 'I can stay?'

'You're not going anywhere,' promised Clara, before quickly adding, 'unless the right family come along for you...'

And Clara was quietly confident that wasn't going to happen any time soon. The council worked at a snail's pace.

'And we still need to raise money?'

'We do...'

Joyce smiled shyly.

'Then can we do a second-hand sale?'

Each of the children collected things to sell, then put them on the wagon. The first thing Clara noticed were the three hand-knitted bears; she couldn't help feeling emotional about that. There were pencil sharpeners and marbles, chalk and books already on the wagon. Then they wheeled it down the street. Outside the flower shop, Mrs Garrard bought Maureen's beret. She couldn't believe what a bargain the sumptuous red quilt was.

'An Ivor?' she asked.

Clara winced, embarrassed. She had impulsively brought down Ivor's Christmas present to her from last year. She wished she hadn't – she realised now that she didn't particularly want to part with it – but already Mrs Garrard was handing over a note.

'All for a good cause.'

Local children rifled through the things with their palms outstretched and their coins in them. Doctor Cardew bought

Alex's magnifying glass – then generously gave it back to him. Anita Cardew bought some of Peter's comics and the postmistress did too. Clara thought if Ivor had been there he would have come and bought everything, but in the end they didn't need him. They sold to people they knew and other passers-by.

Peg displayed her collection of shells – there was no way she would sell any of them – but she charged for a look and Clara was astonished: people agreed to pay, *and* said they were excellent. The women said, 'She's adorable,' and when a couple of young men asked, 'What's wrong with her?' the older Grange boys intervened. Peter especially was protective of Peg.

Even Julian came out of his office and donated some money for one of Maureen's coconut ices. They were supposed to be treats for the workers, but never mind: a sale is a sale.

They made a tremendous £3 with some IOUs thrown in, but even better than the money, Clara thought, they were working together. It was true that 'Shilling Grange children stick together'. Alex said he would write it up in an article for the *Shilling Grange News* and Clara was proud of them and especially clever Joyce, whose idea it had been: the girl had a business brain, that was for sure.

One month to go until Christmas. Between them, they would save the Grange, she knew it.

13

Next Monday, Peg's teacher, Miss Howe, was so full of excitement she could hardly get the words out quick enough.

'The new teacher for Class One – she trained in the Hampstead nurseries in speech therapy! I thought of Peg right away.'

Miss Howe was expressive and she talked fast. Did Clara know the King had a stutter?

Clara did not.

'And he had a speech therapist.'

'This same one?'

Miss Howe's face fell. 'Not this *exact* person, but this one is good too.'

This was what Peg needed and it could be the result that Mr Sommersby wanted to achieve, but Clara knew that good usually meant expensive.

'I was thinking Peg and she could meet after school...'

Clara grimaced. She had to say it: 'I will have to make an application to the council. I don't know if we can afford it. To be honest, money and cutbacks is all we talk about now.'

It was all she dreamed about now too. Children in second-hand sales, in tug-of-wars, screaming at her to let them be still.

Evelyn's complaint: *eighteen schools, nineteen schools.* Joyce toppling over: *why do you keep moving things?* Just last night, Clara had dreamed about Peg dancing on Ivor's feet to 'Blue Danube', everyone squealing with laughter, and then Ivor shouted at Clara, 'You're not standing on *my* feet, you're an elephant – go stand on someone else's,' and she woke up confused. Had he actually said that?

'Oh no, Miss Newton,' Miss Howe squealed, 'This will be free. Peg will be her first student.'

The next day, Peg came out beaming from her after-school session with the therapist and showed Clara the cards and drawings she had done. There were a lot of Rita, some of her, none of Joyce or Evelyn.

Miss Howe hovered. 'They did cards, music, covering her ears, everything!'

Peg was grinning from ear to ear.

'You're lucky, Peg!' Miss Howe continued.

Clara didn't think you'd usually put Peg in the lucky category, but she'd take it.

'You can do it, Peg,' she said as they hurried back to the Grange together. The prospect of getting Peg to speak in front of Mr Sommersby was a sweet one.

Joyce had made some decisions too, since her appointment with Dr Cardew.

'I want to be a war correspondent,' she said. She had borrowed several copies of *LIFE* magazine from the library; the one she was looking at now was from July 1948. It said Betty Grable on the front, but it wasn't Betty Grable but a man in a cowboy hat.

'But there's not going to be another war,' said Clara,

although she was thinking that Joyce could hardly bear to walk more than the five hundred yards to school; how would she cope in the fields of war?

'That's what I want to do.'

'We all have dreams, I suppose.'

'You said I could be whatever I like,' said Joyce accusingly.

'Of course you can,' Clara said guiltily. 'And this is a marvellous plan.'

The thing about this ambition – achievable or not – was that it made Joyce determined to try to get her legs stronger.

Some weeks earlier, Billy had set up a horizontal wooden barre for her outside the shed. At first, Joyce had ignored it and only Peg had used it, for pretend ballet classes, but that afternoon, Joyce walked back and forth, back and forth, training her legs. Later, Joyce put her arm round Clara. It was the first time she'd done that and Clara had to blink back tears.

'I love my barre and my wagon. Thank you, Miss Newton.'

'I'm so pleased, Joyce,' Clara said, blinking back tears. The children never failed to amaze her.

Clara and Anita hadn't seen each other properly since the Jane Taylor Society meeting and Clara was looking forward to discussing Victor with her. And lunch – Anita always did a fine lunch. Clara wondered whether Victor would get the thumbs-up or not. Anita was unpredictable but surely Professor was right up there with Solicitor. And being widowed rather than married (Ivor) or perpetually single (Julian) or dead (Michael) must be a point in his favour too. No one could understand why, after the anguish with Laurie, Josephine March had settled for Professor Bhaer, but Clara thought she could. Jo March was tired of the drama and just wanted someone who appealed to her intellectual side. And according to the *Woman's Own* quiz, after all, Clara was 50 per cent Jo March.

They were eating venison schnitzel. Anita had already plated up some for Clara to take home for the children – Evelyn would go potty for it – when Clara told Anita that Victor was an academic.

'What is his subject?'

'Politics and international relations.'

'That's not a real subject, is it?'

Sometimes, Anita could be peculiar.

'Of course it's *real*. This is delicious, by the way.'

'Why not law or medicine? What do you have in common with this man?'

Last year, Anita had been pro-Julian, then she was pro-Ivor. Now she was inexplicably anti-Victor.

'Ha,' said Clara, trying to lighten the mood, 'I have quite the interest in international relations myself.'

Anita stared at her. 'Oh, you mean Michael?'

'Well, yes.' A joke spelled out is never funny.

'I don't think he sounds like your Michael,' continued Anita. 'Or Ivor.'

Anita could be excruciating sometimes. Clara cleared her plate and wished she hadn't selected such a modest portion.

'He's not. He's different.'

'How?'

'I don't know yet. I'll see,' said Clara, suddenly feeling fed up with the subject.

'When will you see him again?'

'Not until the New Year!'

Anita's face!

'He said he'll write!' *Which was more than Ivor did.*

'But still...' said Anita.

'Have you seen *Little Women*?' Clara asked suddenly.

'You?' Anita said. 'You're quite little.'

'I meant the film, or have you read the book?'

Anita had not and Clara felt downhearted; all the positive feelings about Victor, about lunch, about everything, squeezed out of her. Perhaps the world of grown-up relationships was not for her, she thought to herself wearily. She should stick to running Shilling Grange.

14

Billy and Barry's football matches were in Clara's diary every Sunday, like church. So far Clara had managed to go to none of them. Not a single one.

She tried to compensate, but it wasn't easy when there were so many other demands on her time. So many worries. She didn't dare take her eyes off Maureen for a moment – and Maureen was supposed to be one of the easy ones. As for the younger ones, they came with plenty of burdens, something Clara realised she had underestimated when she first came to the Grange.

If only she could be more like the latest comic-book character Peter was creating: *The Girl Who Could Be In Two Places at Once*. (The title was a work in progress, but Clara thought it was brilliant!)

Ivor would have gone to watch Billy and Barry's matches. Ivor would have been shouting praise from the sidelines and jumping in the air at the final whistle.

'I don't get why you have to play in winter,' Clara complained. Football would be a great game to play in the summer; she could bring the children along, a fuzzy picnic blanket, a sausage pie with a golden crust, a flask of lemon water. Instead, it was frozen fields, red fingers and blue lips. Barry said getting muddy and rolling around in icy puddles were the best things about it.

(*Good Housekeeping* quiz: What sport are you most suited to? Clara got mostly D's – Bowls.)

Their team, Lavenham Rovers, were playing against Bury St Edmunds Boys (A) and there was great excitement about it. Clara promised she would come for this one and she arranged for Sister Grace to look after the others. Sister Grace was employed by the council to clean and watch the children when Clara had her days off. A no-nonsense nun, she hummed while she scrubbed the oven and she loved to read stories. Clara liked her, and more importantly, the children liked her too.

Billy was particularly excited. He said, 'The other boys have a dad, grandad, or someone there,' and he wasn't saying it to make her guilty, that wasn't Billy's style, he was relating it as a fact.

Barry said, 'I'll score a goal for you, Miss Newton.'

'Just one?'

The November sky that day was a defiant dark grey. Enough blue to make a sailor's trousers? Nope, not even a teeny tiny sailor. Sister Grace arrived and Peg jumped onto her knee and Sister Grace read her *The Enchanted Wood* in her soft brogue before wandering off to clean the bathroom.

Clara wrapped up and was about to leave the Grange when the doorbell rang. A middle-aged woman peered in uncertainly.

'The council told me to come.'

Clara gulped. Was she a new inspector? Was this something to do with the sale?

'About?'

'The children... I am hoping to take one on,' the woman said, flushing deep red as though she didn't like how the words sounded.

Bother Miss Cooper. Trust her not to give Clara warning of prospective adopters. She was probably fussing about her trouser suits, Clara thought unkindly.

Mrs Smith was the visitor's name and she wore a patterned headscarf and a large overcoat that she wouldn't take off, even after she came through to the kitchen. She was much younger than she seemed on first impressions.

She said she and her husband wanted to make a home for a young girl.

'And where is your husband today?' Clara was used to both spouses coming along, even to the initial meeting.

'At work.' She tightened the belt of her coat, although there was no real room to tighten it. It was olive green, wintery, and Clara suspected that her dress underneath was summery or inappropriate somehow; her tights were thin and her tiny shoes had seen better days. Clara sympathised.

Mrs Smith was a nurse, she worked in a Glasgow hospital. 'Glasgow?' echoed Clara, thinking what a long way away that was.

'I had to stay the night in London.' She sighed. 'It took ten hours on the coach.' She was attractive with wavy, naturally blonde hair, but her figure was short and stumpy as though someone had put her under a flower press.

Clara could picture her better at work than she could sitting in the kitchen here, awkwardly, pulling tight and unpulling her belt.

'You didn't look at a children's homes in Glasgow?'

The woman looked at her oddly. 'No-oo...'

Clara realised she was going to miss the match. It was that or throw this woman out, and she couldn't do that, not after she'd travelled so far. She'd have to be extra-kind to the twins later. More cake. They didn't *really* want her there, she supposed. And she had at least saved the bus fare.

'Was it anyone in particular you have an interest in?'

'That's a strange question,' Mrs Smith said.

Clara supposed it was, but that was the way of it: like shopping for fruit. Just how bruised were those apples? You didn't want to talk about it in that way but there was no denying it. There was an element of weighing up the children, giving them a squeeze.

The children piled into the kitchen and stared. Clara wanted to say they didn't stare at everyone in this dopey way, but they did. They weren't great with visitors. 'Can we go to the park?' said Rita.

The park where the children played was less a park, more a shrubland with some abandoned swings. Rita had once made up a story about a ghostly girl who haunted them and it wasn't that much of a leap. The chains of the swings creaked miserably and the seats were the cause of many a splinter.

Clara sighed. She had probably missed most of the twins' match anyway.

Mrs Smith stood up. 'I'll watch them, shall I? I don't mind. I've finished my tea.'

Clara hesitated a moment. They didn't need watching. But perhaps this woman thought they did? And perhaps that was a good thing?

Mrs Smith misread Clara's apprehension and said, 'Fresh air will do me good too.'

'One hour,' Clara said decisively. 'No more.'

Soon after they'd left, Clara called the council. She had mostly stopped using the home telephone – the bill! – but at times like these, she appreciated it. Miss Cooper mustn't spring prospective parents on her like this. What if Clara had been out? What if no one had been there?

'Next time, would you please give me advance notice about visitors?'

She bet this Mrs Smith was one of those drawn in by that Donald Burton's *The Joys of Adoption* show on the wireless.

The programme had focused too much on the joy and too little on the hardship. Most of those who had applied, drawn in by the enchanting documentary, were completely unsuitable.

Clara didn't say, 'Miss Bridges always manages to' but she hoped her subtext did.

Miss Cooper coughed. 'I don't know what you mean.'

'You sent a woman? A nurse from Glasgow? A prospective adopter.'

'What are you talking about?'

Clara's heart nearly missed a beat. Oh Hell. She hung up immediately, jammed on her shoes and ran down the street, heart pounding. The council hadn't sent her. Who was she then – and what was she doing with the children from the Grange?

And at the back of her mind rattled another worry: if Mr Sommersby or anyone found out what she had done, then surely all hopes of staying would be over, finito, kaput.

Up to the playground and there they were, standing on the swings, two of them side by side! Ghostly girls! Rita and Peg with feet on the seats, Evelyn and Mrs Smith were pushing them. Rita was bellowing, 'Higher!'

Peg saw Clara and took her hand off the chain to wave.

'Noo!' Clara yelped. But Mrs Smith had already grabbed Peg round the waist from behind.

'I just...' Clara was breathless, 'came to see how you're getting on.'

'Higher,' Rita called again but Evelyn wouldn't. She said it was her turn.

'It's time to go,' snapped Clara. 'NOW...'

Mrs Smith looked as nervous as the children, who were unnerved by Clara's panicky appearance. Once they were back, when Clara told them, more sharply than usual, 'To your rooms,' they jumped to it without protesting.

Clara turned to face the woman: 'Now tell me who you really are.'

. . .

Mrs Smith made for the least comfortable armchair (Stella's favourite scratching post) and sat with her face in her hands. Her fingers were trembling – and Clara was glad to see it. She should have noticed that Mrs Smith wore no wedding ring either. Clara hadn't offered tea on their return to the house and this felt like a terrific breach of the social contract – a move that hopefully conveyed her anger.

'I was sixteen. I didn't even know what was happening, not 'til the end. Some people had families who talked about it. Mine didn't. We were at war. Everyone's minds were on different things.

'Eventually, a teacher asked me outright. I said no. I was in shock. I'd never even had a period. I'd never even been in love. But a few days later, I went back to her...'

Clara waited.

'And the... the father?'

'Back to America. He had no clue. Maybe my family would have helped me if she was properly white. Maybe. But when she wasn't, they were furious. And I was weak. I let them rule me, overrule me. I've been eight years a nurse. I progressed. They called me a natural but I'm not. I just remember what it's like to be afraid and my patients' knowledge and my patients' consent is important to me.

'I can do it now though. I've thought about my baby every day. I sent cards and everything.'

'What happened next?' Clara tried not to sound like a detective in a radio drama but it was difficult not to.

'I looked a few years ago. I tried to follow her.'

'Follow who?'

Mrs Smith went on like she hadn't heard her.

'Then I gave up. Then, I heard about this place. I heard

about you. How you were kinder than the others. You might understand.'

Clara did not understand. She thought of the swings, the way she thought the children would fall, smash head-first to the ground.

'What is it you want me to do?'

'Do something,' she said. 'Evelyn is my daughter.'

At first, Clara was concerned that Mrs Smith – or *Miss* Smith, as was her real title – had been turned down by Suffolk Council, but as it transpired, she hadn't approached them yet. She had a friend of a friend of a friend working at the Lavenham primary school. Evelyn Wyatt was an unusual enough name – and Miss Smith had been able to find out a few more details, including her middle name: *Margaret*. It had to be her.

And then Clara thought, what if it's not true? What if it's mistaken identity? It happened. But Miss Smith had the girl's birth certificate, which aligned with Clara's files – and even a photo: a scowling baby wearing a polka-dot bow.

Miss Smith said she had had thought about writing a letter, but she didn't know if it would get to Evelyn, 'or even if Evelyn could read, you know,' she said, dabbing her cheeks. 'I know that sounds daft but I had no idea about anything.' She had sipped her tea loudly, partly to cover up her sobs.

'I don't want to take Evelyn from somewhere she is happy,' she explained. 'She has to want to be with me. Does that sound strange?'

Clara paused. It did and it didn't.

'From the beginning, I was forced – into this and into that, things I didn't want. I don't want to... force her. Into anything. I want to build. I am happy to go slowly. I mean, we'll have to go slowly, won't we? What with the distance.'

She suddenly lowered herself onto the floor to stroke Stella. 'I always wanted a cat, but they are so skittish, aren't they?'

Clara sneezed. 'She's certainly something.'

Then Billy and Barry came home – trophies aloft – and chaos broke out. There was hugging and whooping and tales of victory snatched from the jaws of the defeat, of grown men rolling around in agony, and professional referees who were on someone's payroll, and Miss Smith watched and listened, then quietly left.

Clara didn't say anything about it to Evelyn that evening. There were other things going on – Sister Grace wanted to sing hymns, there was more football talk and an argument over lost shoes – all the while Clara was digesting the revelation. If it had been Rita's longed-for mama, it would be the opposite; there would be no dilemma, it would be the most welcome thing on earth. Evelyn though... Evelyn had never mentioned her mother, not once. The girl was not interested in family; the only things that got her going were cakes, crackers or, as she'd only recently learned, babies. Clara didn't know what to do. Her natural inclination was to tell Evelyn immediately, but that was still fraught – she had no idea how Evelyn would react.

In the morning, a letter came from Victor. He said he had been unsure whether to write but he found himself wanting to say hello. He talked about some of the things he had seen and the hotels he was staying in. 'They were better during the war – and they were diabolical then!' He said she wasn't to bother to reply (which was a relief – she wouldn't have known what to write) because he was not staying in one place for long enough. It was the final paragraph that stood out for her.

I am a philosopher, a man of thinking and words; what I admire is seeing someone do something, someone like you.

I hope you know you can lean on me.

Lean on me. She thought of their picnic and the sudden impression she had had of him as a brick wall. She would have leaned on him then given half the chance. This was progress. But should she be leaning on anyone?

The next afternoon, Evelyn was eating a cress sandwich in the kitchen, while the other children were upstairs measuring each other's latest heights. Somehow, they expected to grow like beanstalks. Clara had allowed them to mark the doorframe, distractedly thinking the pencil would rub out.

Now, she took a breath. 'I have some news for you, Evelyn.'

Be honest – she deserves that.

'Do you know who that woman you met yesterday was?'

Evelyn carried on chewing the crust. She didn't care that it was like putting your lip up a kerb.

'Miss Smith? Remember?'

Evelyn shrugged. Upstairs, Rita was shouting at Joyce: 'You're a liar – I've grown three centimetres since last week.'

'She is your mother.'

Evelyn patted her belly. 'Can I have an apple?'

She always wanted to have something in her mouth. It was a diversion tactic, perhaps. Clara decided not to go in too strong.

'She'd like to see you again.'

Evelyn didn't reply.

'It's up to you.'

The girl shrugged. It had felt monumental to Clara, but

now facing this non-reaction she wondered if she had overesti-
mated how important it would be to Evelyn.

'What do you think?'

'Or some milk?'

'Evelyn?'

Evelyn rolled her eyes. 'Fine.'

Clara went upstairs. They had used fountain pen on the
doorframe. It looked a smeary inky mess and she shouted at
them until Joyce stomped down to the parlour and Rita ran off
to the shed. Twenty minutes of scrubbing with Alex and Peg
later, you could hardly see it. Evelyn stayed at the kitchen table,
staring into space.

15

The children were, Clara told Miss Cooper at the December monthly check in the parlour of Shilling Grange, plodding along.

Perhaps better than plodding along: Joyce was walking more *and* seemed much happier. Evelyn had a possibility of reconciliation with her mother. Peg's therapist said that she was a delight to teach and making progress (although she still didn't say anything). Peter was drawing, and smoking out of the window, and seemed content. No news from the comic people yet. Billy and Barry were never home, Billy had hurt his wrist but it was a sprain not a break, then Barry had a quick trip to the hospital, but they sewed his head up and said approvingly he had a thick skull. Alex and best friend Bernard were determined to wear shorts all winter and Maureen, well, Maureen and Joe were never apart for long, but she was holding down her job and doing her schoolwork, so Clara could have no complaints there.

'Look at my accounts,' Clara said, because Miss Cooper didn't seem inclined to ask.

Miss Cooper confessed she was a dolt at maths, but nevertheless she admired the columns as though they were pretty as sunflowers. And then she said something alarming: 'Would it be the end of the world if you left here?'

'What? Why are you asking that?'

Clara had a sudden memory of sitting in a pub during the Blitz and a man from work who she didn't know well saying in the same tone, 'Would it be the end of the world if the Nazis won?'

Miss Cooper flicked her hair. 'Nothing, no, it's good to explore all avenues.'

Marilyn was whipping around the Highlands. She was having a whisky in a bar when she telephoned Clara. She said she had met a laird.

'I've never met a laird before.'

Clara could picture her, glass in hand, cigarette burning to a stub in the ashtray. The laird would be deliciously debonair and played by Dirk Bogarde.

'How about you, dear Clara?' Marilyn asked, which, stupidly, made tears come to Clara's eyes. 'Any news?'

Gosh, the only news was that she was lonely. This standing on your own two feet business could be seriously isolating. It made your body ache. What was it that Joyce said? *Everyone I like goes away...*

There was something so sincere in Marilyn's voice too.

'The children are working hard and behaving well,' Clara said.

'But...'

'I'm worried that we're going to have to leave here.'

'Still? I thought you were making the cutbacks and gathering the evidence, sweetheart.'

'I am,' said Clara in a little voice.

'Oh, hon. Can your Mrs Bridge help?'

'Miss Bridges? She's always busy.'

Miss Bridges always had some crisis or other at a cemetery recently. Clara felt like she was being fobbed off. And this was especially hurtful given how close they used to be.

'And the other, the blonde? The Blooper?'

'Cooper. She's...' Clara thought back to their unhelpful meeting. 'I'm not sure what she thinks.'

'Do you trust her?'

'On some things, yes.' *But not on this.*

'Even if they wanted to sell, who'd be interested in buying anyway?' Marilyn laughed. 'Clara, you overestimate the Grange's appeal. It's damp and it smells of children.'

The shelves bowed like sails and the low doorframes meant anyone tall – poor Peter – had to duck. There was nothing the council could do about that of course, but they could do something about the radiators.

'The thing is,' said Clara, somewhat hurt at Marilyn's stark summary, 'someone *might be* interested, unfortunately...'

'They could put you somewhere new! Where the doors close properly with hot running water!'

'Or they might put us somewhere worse,' Clara responded. Despite everything that had happened to her, her war, her terrible loss, Marilyn was essentially an optimist.

'Worse? Look, Clara, speak to someone. No point fretting about something that's not happened yet. A problem shared is a problem— Talking of which, my laird is waiting for me...'

In spite of herself, Clara laughed. 'Have a good time, Marilyn.'

∽

Julian probably wasn't the best person to speak to – but one thing he had going for him was the skill of knowing what was going on before anyone else. Forget the *Shilling Grange News*, Julian was the main source of gossip in Lavenham.

She collared him in the street one morning. 'I need to talk to you.' It was so cold, she could see his breath bunched up in the air.

'I will – but only over lunch.'

Typical Julian. Still, he usually provided a splendid lunch, and he would pay and he was company.

'I'll come by at midday?'

'Make it half past one, I have the children.'

'I'll be ravenous by then...' The way he said ravenous made her laugh.

'You always are.'

He smiled flirtatiously. 'You know me well.'

Don't get sucked in, Clara told herself. Julian was incorrigible.

At the pub, he was charming as ever, even if he held the doors massively wide as though she were a ten-ton tank coming through. She knew it was deliberate because he said on the way there, 'You're looking healthy,' and previously he had told her that meant 'chubby'.

He remembered her favourite drink – gin and lemon – and he told her that her hair looked 'better like that'. Julian always noticed things.

'I haven't had time...' she said, patting it, embarrassed.

'Suits you, it's more feminine.' He winked at her. 'I bet Mr Braithwaite likes it...'

Clara shook her head. *A couple of dates, a handful of letters and he already knew?*

'How's the rendezvousing?' he persisted.

'You are a gossip,' she said, slapping him on the hand. You couldn't be thin-skinned with Julian. Best to just play along, pretend everything was hunky-dory.

Victor wrote religiously and each time, it felt like his guard lowered and so did hers. He had started writing kisses after his name. Yes, he also went on lengthy digressions about the ruling classes and, 'Clara, I know you're not a member of the Labour Party yet', but still. Maybe the more you got to know someone, the more you liked them, she contemplated – and then peered at Julian. No, that was not always the case.

Julian leaned forward so she had the rare advantage of seeing the top of his head. He was thinning on top at a pace. She wondered if he knew. Or even cared. Probably not. She wondered: if women got this view of men more often, perhaps the world would be organised differently.

'What's he got that I haven't?' Julian continued, smouldering at her over his whisky.

Was he being serious? Hard to tell with him.

'Pass me the menu,' Clara said. The best way to deal with Julian was to deflate him ever so slowly.

'So... are you marrying him?'

'Who?'

'Victor Braithwaite,' he said with a flourish. 'I thought Ivor Delaney was next in line. Or are you planning on keeping a coterie? Or a harem of gentlemen at your service...'

'It's not like that, Julian. Victor and I are just getting to know each other.'

'I know what that means...' He winked.

Which, Clara thought, was probably more than she did.

There was no lobster; poor Julian had to console himself with liver and kidney. Clara ordered fish; she had an eye on the treacle tart for dessert. They talked about the children. Julian used to be negative about them and call them feral, bad blood, a pox on society or worse, but now he was more restrained. He confirmed that he rarely saw Maureen in the office, which was good, but Clara supposed this was because Maureen was always in with Browne, which was not so good. Still, Maureen was enjoying the extra income. And she wasn't mean with it either. She'd acquired a sketchpad for Peter and some sheet music for Rita.

This segued naturally into her questions.

'Go on then,' he said, sitting back with folded arms. 'Ask me anything.'

'Julian. I'm working hard to keep us at the Grange.'

'Don't we know it,' he said, chewing. 'Wagon sales, newspapers, jolly good show, Clara. I liked the article on the Bank of England.'

One of Alex's, of course. Clara looked at Julian closely. She could never tell if he was being sincere or not. 'Is Mr Browne interested in buying it?'

'Is he?' He tucked into his meat.

'Do you know anything about it?'

'It's complicated.'

'It's not complicated. We're not for sale.'

'Every man has his price. Every council does too.'

He twirled the pepper pot. She knew his face well enough to know what most of his expressions meant.

'I just need to know where we stand.'

She was surprised to see Julian's more sympathetic smile. His genuine one.

'You're not wrong, Clara.'

'Oh...'

'He wants the house. And he wants you gone.'

'B-bb-ut... Why?'

'Three reasons, I expect: one – a lot of people have never liked the home being in Lavenham in the first place. For years there has been a resistance. They just think it should be in—'

'Ipswich or Colchester. I know. Why?'

He shrugged. 'Property values. No one wants to live next to a children's home.'

'Why *exactly*?'

'They attract drunks. Or offenders.'

'Rubbish...'

'Or sexual impropriety.'

Clara blushed with a sudden memory of Julian and her tumbling around on his bed.

'They're children, Julian.'

'I know, but...'

Clara tackled the fish. It was too bony, too much effort for its worth, she thought, as she stripped off the flesh. Surprised at the skeleton there. Its tiny bones.

'You said there were three reasons?'

'Two: there are some people who are not that keen on you. I don't know why, darling. I think you're a diamond, you know that.'

'And three?'

'You're sitting on a goldmine, Clara, you must know that.'

'But the plan is, if I can prove that we save money, and if I can show that the children are flourishing, then the council said they won't sell. They said that, Julian, they did!'

At this, Julian leant back in his chair, 'If they said that, then fine.'

'The children are doing brilliantly,' she added. She sounded like she was trying to convince herself, but it was true and it astonished her every day that it was true.

'You probably know more than me.'

'I do,' she said firmly, flipping her fish to attack the flesh the other side. 'On this, I do.'

16

The next day, Clara was about to try Miss Bridges again – where was the woman hiding? – when she heard a kerfuffle outside the door. A man was shouting. He looked like a tramp. He *was* the tramp she and Marilyn had given Eccles cakes to. Long silver beard, long hair, goodness knows where he'd come from. Clara kept the door ajar. He was alternately muttering then shouting. The smell of him. Not just alcohol, layers and layers of it, but something else, pungent.

Eventually, she caught the words, 'Alex' and 'I know my rights'.

'What do you want with Alex?' Clara asked glacially. Her heart was beating fast.

'I'm his father.'

Oh Crikey. What a week for returning parents.

'Alex is not here.' Clara was relieved he wasn't. What would she do if he were?

She remembered Julian saying – was it only yesterday? – how the children's home attracted drunks and she had laughed.

'He lives here though, right?'

This wasn't good.

'He go to the local school? I'll find him there then.'

'No, no.'

How humiliating would this be for Alex if this *character* turned up at the school gate, among the blazers, the boaters and the hoity-toity parents? She'd have to bring him into the house and keep him here. Keep him out of trouble. Maybe he was all right, deep down. He'd probably had a hard life. 'You'd better come in...' Leading him into the kitchen, Clara tried not to inhale. Could you get drunk on someone else's fumes? Was bringing him in the right decision? Probably not. But rather this than have him make a fuss at the school. That would go down like a cup of cold sick if Mr Sommersby found out.

Stella bristled and ran away. Stella always listened to her instincts.

How did he know where Alex lived? What did he want? She tried to subdue him with politeness. 'I'm Clara,' she said. 'The housemother. Do take a seat.'

He laughed at that: said he was Mickey the Flea. Gave her his hand to shake.

Show him kindness.

He lifted his shirt so his white belly was showing. A dark line of insolent hair. Then he went to sit, but missed the chair and collapsed on the floor instead.

'Mickey!' She hauled him up.

'Shall I call the doctor?' she asked urgently, but he was laughing. No teeth, too much pink gum, less man, more animal. More enemy.

He didn't look like Alex, she thought, apart from in one moment when his expression showed a flicker of intelligence.

He eventually got into a chair and was drinking whatever it was out of his bottle. It smelled rank. It dribbled down his chin. He drained the bottle as though he expected more to reappear at any moment.

'I got medals, you know,' he said. 'You remember the war?'

'I remember the war,' Clara said. *Who did he think she was? A child?*

'Will Alex be back soon?'

'What is it you want with him?'

'Just want to see him... He's my boy.' He burped.

Don't be a snob, Clara reminded herself. There wasn't much that her parents had taught her that she kept in her heart, but the one phrase, 'There but for the grace of God go I,' was always there.

'How did you know he was here?' she asked.

He laughed again.

'Thought you'd keep it quiet, did you?'

Clara didn't think he would hurt her, but he was intimidating and he frightened her. She shouldn't have let him in.

'Got any beer?'

'I can make you some tea?'

'I don't want tea.'

They sat in silence for a few moments as he scratched his belly and yawned.

There was a knock on the door. *Oh no. If it was the council she would be done for.*

But it was Joe, coming in with a bundle of newspapers. Clara had never been so glad to see anyone in her life. He looked shocked too, at the sight of Mickey, but gathered himself quickly.

'This is... this is Alex's father,' she said. While Mickey fiddled with his bottle, she murmured to Joe, 'And I don't know what to do with him...'

'There's an outside tap, isn't there, Miss Newton?' he whispered.

'Ye-es, but...'

'I'm taking you out there, man, you reek.' Joe pulled at Alex's father's arms and then half-pushed, half-dragged him outside.

'Thank you,' Clara called after them, full of relief that, for the moment at least, that problem was solved.

From outside came the sound of water splashing on the ground – and then, what was that: was he singing now?

'What can you do with a drunken sailor?' drifted in through the open doorway.

And then he crawled onto the frosty grass and shut his eyes.

The children were back, Alex among them. Before Clara had time to say anything, Rita was squealing, 'There's a man asleep in the garden.'

Clara looked around helplessly. Was there a nice way of explaining this? Probably not.

She pulled Alex away from the others. She was squirming inside. She remembered her father coming up to school once and everyone saying, 'Newton, is that your father?' And her father wasn't half so unconforming as this man.

'Alex...' She didn't have to say anything else.

'That's my father, isn't it?'

'I think so, yes.'

Alex's shoulders slumped and he blew out of his mouth like he was blowing through a straw. Hard to tell what he was thinking. His tie was short and fat, rather like him, and his oversized school blazer was falling off his shoulders.

'Do you want to say hello then?'

'Can he come in?'

'I would rather he didn't.'

Together they walked outside.

'It's freezing,' Alex said.

'It's not freezing,' Clara muttered, but Alex was right, it was cold.

Mickey talked in his sleep. He looked ridiculous yet strangely peaceful there, among the tree roots, a serene expres-

sion on his face. One of his shoes had a heart-shaped hole in it.
Clara felt a mixture of despair at the sight of him and gratitude
that she wasn't in this state herself.

'I haven't seen him for five years,' Alex said.

'And was he... like this five years ago?'

'I think so.' His jaw moved from side to side.

'Will the council take care of it?' he asked matter-of-factly.

Her heart sank. The council mustn't know. Mr Sommersby
wouldn't like this. This was not *thriving*.

'*I'll* take care of it, Alex.'

He surveyed her, then nodded. He trusted her more than
she did herself. She put a thick blanket over his father then and
a cushion under him. When she went down to check a couple
of hours later, the cushion, the blanket – everything – had gone.

17

Mr Jenkins at the petrol station off the high road needed someone to fill up tanks. Walking past, Clara happened to see the sign stuck up on the door with brown tape, next to a photograph of Winston Churchill and his cigar.

The usual boy had gone to be an apprentice in Wales. Apparently, he found sleepy Lavenham too busy. Inhaling petrol smells, Clara and Mr Jenkins had had a lovely chat – Clara didn't often get nostalgic for London, but she did then.

As Clara made her way back home she felt a spring in her step for the first time since Alex's father's awful return the week before. Joe would be delighted to have extra cash in his pocket, especially with Christmas coming. He would still be able to do his paper rounds too. Clara didn't begrudge giving Joe his meals, and he contributed in many ways, but my goodness, in these straitened times, if he had a salary, things would be easier.

There was more: 'Potential to train as a mechanic,' Mr Jenkins had said, and tips too. 'It's the ones you least expect who are the most generous,' he'd advised. 'The rich don't get rich by giving their money away.'

Clara pictured Joe's face when she told him. Over the past

few weeks, she'd learned more about Joe and the many disad-
vantages he'd faced. That he was climbing out of the bleakness
of his background was to be admired. He was supportive not
only of Maureen but the other children too. It was a turnaround
from the sulky, whistling teen she had first met. Obviously,
looking out for Joe was not part of her role as housemother of
Shilling Grange, but looking out for him was no bother – in fact,
it was satisfying to do something that wasn't part of her role or
her duty; doing something voluntarily felt gratifying. He was
the icing on the top.

She was in such a cheerful mood that she decided to stop off
at the Cardews'. Anita was pleased about Joe's job, but more
curious about Victor and whether he had 'made his pass'. Anita
had learned much of her English from American films. Clara
supposed this was her version of Julian's 'rendezvousing'.

'Hardly, he's still in Germany,' she said.

Anita scowled. 'That's no excuse.'

'I've had some lovely letters though.'

Anita sniffed. She went on to talk about the nursery she was
preparing and the book she had, by Marie Stopes, which Dr
Cardew found irritating but she found 'life-changing'. Clara
tried to feign interest, but babies, stretch marks and the importance of giving baby lots of fresh air weren't her favourite
subjects and before long, she went back home.

Maureen was sitting in the garden, still wearing her school
uniform, Stella snuggled on her lap, when Clara bounded in.

'I'm looking for Joe.' Clara beamed, hoping Maureen would
ask why. It wasn't often she got to deliver good news.

Maureen yawned and stretched her arms over her head.
Sometimes, she was more catlike than the cat.

'Joe? Oh, Joe's gone.'

'What? When?'

'Today!' Maureen smiled brightly, fluffing up her hair.

Had Clara been too overwhelming? If Joe hadn't been loved before, was it too much? You had to tread so carefully. Had she stomped over him? She knew the road to hell was paved with good intentions but she couldn't think what she might have done wrong.

She thought of the conversation she'd had with Mr Jenkins, not two hours before.

'I need someone reliable, Miss Newton.'

'Joe won't let you down.'

Maureen pushed Stella off her and stood up, a mixture of pride and defiance.

'I told him to go.'

What had happened? Had Joe hurt Maureen?

'Oh?'

'We weren't getting on.' Maureen was poker-faced again.

Clara thought of how kind Joe was with the children. How in love he and Maureen looked: when they said their goodbyes; how even that morning, he had done his paper round then walked Maureen to school.

What was going on?

'Since when?'

Something didn't add up, yet it must. Or maybe it was not her business if it added up or not. There were limits on her involvement and Maureen was now fifteen. Who she 'rendezvoused' with was her business. Or was it? Clara didn't know.

'Always, I suppose. I tried to split up with him before. I've given him enough chances.'

'Okay.' Questions tugged at her. 'Is it to do with... what happened last year?'

At this reminder of her miscarriage, Maureen finally showed some emotion. Her lips quivered and her eyes filled with tears. 'We don't talk about that, Miss Newton, you promised me.'

Clara hated upsetting Maureen but she couldn't under-stand. And Maureen might want to pretend it never happened, but your history tended to come up and bite you when you least expect it.

It was hard to let go of Joe. And Mr Jenkins needed someone to help him Clara had enjoyed being the one who could fix it.

'I got him a job,' she said, more cautiously now. 'At the petrol station. He could go there tomorrow if he liked—'

'No,' Maureen said firmly. 'He's not coming back here, or to Lavenham.'

Heart in her boots, Clara went over to Ivor's workshop to see for herself. It was true, Joe had cleared out. And he had tidied up after himself too – all bits taken away or washed up. You wouldn't have known he had been there. And yet Joe hadn't come to say goodbye, and although she knew she shouldn't, Clara felt blindsided. She had put her hopes in him.

Goodness, she was being like one of *those* mothers. Fonder of the boyfriend than of the daughter – you read about them in the advice columns in *Woman's Own*. They weren't women with scruples. They preferred men. She wasn't going to be like that. She would remember to put her girl first.

No, it wasn't that. She just had a sense of dread for Maureen, like curtains coming down on one scene and opening up on another – and the other was one that she didn't feel Maureen was ready for.

For the first time ever, Clara was alone in Ivor's workshop. She slid her hand against some of the fabrics and pictured him sitting here, thoughtfully working. She did love this place. The materials and the threads, the boxes of buttons. There was something soothing and wholesome about it. Mending, making, restoring. It was so him.

Ivor had talked her through the history of upholstery once. He had a way with words. He stitched them together and made beautiful things with them too. Upholstery began with tents. Not camping tents but medieval battlegrounds. Pageantry, red and gold. And the tapestries hanging in country houses. He didn't know if it had always been in his family – Ivor, like Peg, was a foundling – but he imagined sometimes fathers, grand-mothers, other ancestors, sitting at a spinning wheel. Didn't these things pass down?

Sometimes Clara wondered what her parents had passed down to her. Tears came to her eyes and she wasn't sure who for: Ivor, Joe, Maureen, or herself.

Where on earth *was* Ivor? He didn't have any wider family to go to, Clara was fairly sure of that, so where might he have gone? And then she told herself that actually, she didn't care where he had gone – it had never been a question of that; the main thing was: were he and Ruby in love? The silence was cruel.

She knew she could cope without Ivor now – he wasn't indispensable – but whether she wanted to or not was a different thing.

At the back of the workshop, the telescope stood like a lone sentry. Again, she remembered Ivor holding her, so that she could admire the stars. It was probably that evening she had started to fall for him, although she hadn't admitted it at the time. She had always found him attractive, but that evening it had felt like there were possibilities. If only she had told him sooner, things might look different now.

She put the telescope to her eye, but she couldn't see anything. She remembered the cap, laughed at her stupidity and unscrewed it: once, twice, until it eased off; but even then she couldn't make it work. Something obvious was missing.

.   .   .

At the editorial meeting that evening for the *Shilling Grange News*, the children were already out of sorts and when Clara told them Joe had left, it only made them worse. They argued over whether Alex should take over as editor ('yes, but you're going to have to do what I say.') and if Alex's father's visit was newsworthy. (Fortunately, Alex overruled them so Clara didn't have to intervene. 'And I'm the editor now...') Alex wanted to put in something about Peter's comic contest, which made Peter seethe. 'I don't know the outcome yet! You've jinxed it!' while Rita wanted to put in something about her audition for the Festival of Britain –

'It's not for ages, Rita!' barked Alex. 'And it mightn't even happen...'

'But I will probably be the best person there,' retorted Rita.

Peg wanted to donate some pressed flowers. She ran away weeping when she was told that wouldn't work, which was unlike Peg. Joyce said if they were going to put any boring old rubbish in the newspaper, then she might as well do a piece about her stupid polio; she looked surprised when Alex said, 'Brilliant, Joyce, please do.'

Maureen arrived back late from Robinson, Browne and White. She swished into the cramped shed, whistling, '*O sole mio*.' She had done her hair in rolls and her skirt was swung round so that her petticoat peeked through. She looked cheerful, Clara thought, like a girl in an American film, the love interest in a screwball comedy.

She looked bemused at everyone's glum faces. 'What's the matter?'

'Joe's gone!' Billy said. The twins had loved the older boy, who'd taught them football chants.

'The paper will be rubbish without him,' Barry said.

'Mama,' whispered Rita.

'They all go in the end,' said Joyce fiercely. The children agreed. They were a dismal bunch.

'Oh, you'll be fine,' Maureen said, screwing up her nose, then she dropped some coins on the top of the piano. 'Here, for the saving-money fund.' A few coins fell to the floor and everyone jumped for them, shrieking.

Clara grabbed her arm but Maureen shook her off straight away. She smelled of perfume that Clara didn't recognise, perfume too old for her, musty and spicy. Clara stepped back. She mustn't lose her temper, she mustn't. 'What? How are you doing this?'

'You said we older ones needed to contribute more... "Best behaviour!"' Maureen added in an imitation of Clara.

'But how?'

'Mr Browne is generous.'

Clara stared at her. Maureen wouldn't meet her eye, but checked her hair rolls were in place.

'I look after his boy now, Martin.'

Clara felt her spikes retract. *O-kay.*

'If... *anything* else is going on, you'll have to stop working there.'

'What the hell? I'm only trying to help,' Maureen said, then left, the door swinging behind her.

18

Joe had left but the papers he was supposed to deliver were dumped by the kitchen door at six the next morning, four towers of them.

Clara and Stella looked at them. Stella seemed even less impressed than usual because they were in her favourite sunny spot.

'Someone needs to do it,' Clara said over breakfast.

Maureen said she already had a job, thank you very much. Joyce couldn't 'my leg!' and Evelyn had disappeared before the question was asked. Alex said he had too much going on, what with his homework and now his editorial responsibilities. Rita wasn't even there when Clara asked, she was in the shed. Peg put up her hand to volunteer but she was far too young. Peter screwed up his face and muttered, 'Comics take up my time,' which was probably true too.

It had to be Billy and Barry.

She picked up one of the newspapers. The headline was about the peanuts scheme in Africa. The British government had spent millions on a folly there. Clara folded it in half and then stacked the papers on Joyce's wagon. The twins watched her, uncertainly.

'Important to learn the value of hard work.' She studiously ignored Billy's expression. 'It'll help you become upstanding citizens and avoid follies.'

Barry rubbed his toe along the ground.

'If we do this, it's more likely we can keep living here!' she said.

They still looked unconvinced. *What on earth could she say?*

'It's good exercise, boys,' she tried finally. 'All the footballers do a paper round.'

The twins looked at each other open-mouthed, then chorused, 'Deal.'

They shook hands. Later, Clara wrote it down in her account log and her notes on how the children were thriving. Her files weren't looking too bad.

Now that Rita was preparing for her audition, she had lessons with Anita several times a week, mostly at Anita's house but sometimes in the shed. Anita would not take payment. If ever Clara suggested Rita was playing too much, they would both look alarmed and say actually she wasn't playing enough.

Anita came round with some pink roses. She proposed telling Rita about her pregnancy. Clara had wanted to put it off further – until a time when things were 'settled' – but how could she explain that to Anita, who thought they had waited long enough already? Understandably, her friend was excited and wanted to share her news. Clara carefully arranged the flowers in a china jug and wished she could feel excited about it too.

By the time Rita came into the kitchen Clara had worked herself into quite a state, but Anita was oblivious.

'I'm pregnant, Rita,' Anita announced, her eyes sparkling.

'What do you think about *that*, Rita?' Clara asked, trying not to see what she could already see in Rita's face.

Rita didn't reply.

'She's having a baby,' Clara added, uselessly.

Anita beamed. 'Due in March.'

'Spring!' said Clara, thinking, *Oh dear*.

Rita still said nothing.

'Ooh,' Anita said, even more animated. 'It's moving. Do you want to feel it kick?'

'I'll kick it,' Rita hissed.

There was a horrible silence. Then Clara shouted at Rita to go up to her room. 'No lesson today. And no tea either. How dare you!'

Rita tipped back from the table, flung out her arms and managed to knock the jug of flowers over. The water spread out so fast, it was like a large bloodstain. The collapsed flowers looked like people stunned. Rita ran off weeping.

While Clara hadn't anticipated it going well, she hadn't expected it to be a disaster. Anita was doing her best not to look horrified, but the worry was etched into her features.

'Why did she say that?' she asked, hand over her stomach. 'Is it about the lessons? Is she worried we'll have to stop?'

'I don't know what it is...'

Clara wiped up the puddle of water and restored the flowers but she couldn't seem to make them look half so lovely as they had looked first time round.

Later, Clara took up a slab of bread and butter to Rita's room. She knew rewarding the child after that demonstration would be frowned upon – *what would Miss Bridges say?* – but it seemed unfair to punish her without knowing exactly what was going on first. Besides, Clara had some sympathy with the girl. Evelyn might disagree but babies *weren't* the most interesting thing in the world. Clara had always thought part of Anita's appeal was how unmaternal she was.

Clara sat on the end of Rita's bed. 'I'm not leaving until I get some answers.'

'Why do things have to change?' Rita mumbled from under the blanket. 'Joe's gone, Marilyn's gone, Ivor's gone, Terry's gone. And now...'

The funny thing was, Clara thought, Rita never seemed to give a toss about any of them when they were there.

'Anita isn't going anywhere, darling. And Marilyn *is* coming back to visit. And Ivor will be back some day...' She paused. *Did she know that?* 'And maybe Joe too... some things change but other things stay the same.'

Clara stopped herself. If the house-sale happened, there would be even more change, of course.

'Will you look after me forever?' Rita asked. She came out from under the blanket and passed Clara her sodden Molly Mouse. She must have been chewing it.

'As long as I can.' Clara felt shaken suddenly. She remembered that sometimes her mother used to shiver and say, 'Someone is walking over my grave.'

'A lovely family might want to adopt you,' she suggested.

Rita wrinkled up her nose. Lovely families had never interested her.

'Do you want me to read to you?' asked Clara.

Clara's favourite poetry book fell open at the page of Ann Taylor's love poem 'My Mother.' In a split-second, Clara decided: not that one. They would both be in floods.

It must have been the shock, but not long after Clara started reading Jane Taylor's 'Poverty', Rita, thumb in mouth, fell asleep.

After school the next day, Clara took Rita over to the surgery to apologise. Anita stayed seated in her chair with her legs up on a footstool. Her ankles were swollen, she said (although they looked perfect to Clara; Anita never looked less than perfect) and her expression was wary. Clara felt worse. She hoped Rita would not come between the slightly precarious friendship between the two women. But Rita delivered her apologies with more sincerity than Clara had expected; her annoyance at the girl dwindled and Anita, graceful as ever, accepted them cordially, if not warmly.

'You'll be a special aunty, Rita.'

Rita hung back. 'Not that keen on babies, to be honest—'

'That's fine,' Clara interrupted, fearful of what Rita might come out with next. 'I'm sure you'll like it. And when baby is, say, six and you're sixteen, you'll be friends then, won't you?'

'If no one else is.'

That evening, Rita skipped of out the shed, a sheaf of papers in her hand. 'I wrote a song for the baby.'

'Can I read it?'

But it was music, not words, so Clara couldn't. It was for Anita to play on the violin.

'Anita is going to love it,' she said anyway.

'Thank you.' Rita paused. 'I like Anita but she's not my mama.'

'I know.'

'I mean, she's not the one.'

An important thing to realise, Clara thought. You can love people, but they might not be the one for you. Maybe that's how

Maureen felt about poor Joe. Maybe that's how she felt about Victor Braithwaite too, she pondered, but then decided that she *would* give him another chance. She had had three letters from him in three weeks – and after all, the professor had worked out for Josephine March.

19

The next afternoon Alex didn't come back straight from school and Clara was immediately concerned. It couldn't be a coincidence that Alex was missing just as his father was in town, could it? Clara stood in the street, willing him home. *I'll have to get help,* she thought, *if he's not back by five.* Then, *if he's not back by five thirty.* And who from? Council or police? Neither of them. Anita or Dr Cardew? Neither of them. Julian? No. Mrs Garrard? *Don't be so ridiculous.*

Why did she always miss Ivor at moments like these?

The school told her he wasn't there. She considered calling Bernard's home, but it didn't make sense Alex would be there; nor did she want to strike up a conversation with Victor's sister under these circumstances. The hours ticked past. The rest of the children didn't know anything, no matter how many times she asked.

'He was going on about the Industrial Revolution at breakfast,' said Rita, 'so I told him to boil his fat head.'

I can manage this, Clara told herself. There wasn't an alternative.

Just before seven o'clock she heard the front door and found him standing there: Alex; but not the usual Alex. A lopsided, uneven boy, who smelled of peppermint – and not just peppermint but something like cleaning fluid, and whose always wild hair was now forest-like.

He threw his blazer on the floor. It took her a few seconds to realise what it was: he was drunk. He rubbed his face and then mumbled, 'I'm going to be sick.' He bolted with that lopsided running gait he had. He didn't make it – he was sick on the stairs.

She put him on the sofa in the parlour, went to clean up. Stella came over to have a nose, the children shrieked and when Barry shouted it was vomit for tea, there was uproar. Clara shouted at them she had just about HAD ENOUGH. They scarpered quickly then.

What did you do? She thought she should call Dr Cardew but couldn't bring herself to. *Ivor would know what to do.*

He lay on the sofa and he was hardly her Alex at all. He coughed again and this time a red liquid spluttered out of his mouth into the chamberpot where Billy and Barry 2, the fish, used to live. Clara examined it until she was sure it wasn't blood. Next to her, Alex fell asleep.

The other children peered into the room. A sad-faced Peg helped Clara tug off Alex's shoes.

'What's wrong with him?' hissed Rita, looking appalled.

'Poorly tummy,' lied Clara.

'Shall we do a piece on this for the newspaper?' Barry tapped Clara's shoulder.

'Our readers have a right to know—' added Billy.

'Nooo!' snapped Clara. *Were they mad?*

Where was his father? It was he who had done this, Clara knew it. She checked out of the window. Was he out there, hiding among the trees, stepping between the cracks?

Later, biting his nails, Peter watched Alex while Clara sorted out the children, propelling them to bed. When she was

with them, they whirled around her and when she was absent,
even if she was only absent in spirit, they tended to go off
course.

The floor next to Alex in the parlour was hard and cold and
Clara couldn't get comfortable. Stella kept pawing at her. Alex
breathed loudly, then when he went quiet, she would sit up and
stare at him. She felt quite scared.

About midnight, Evelyn came down. She wasn't usually
one to ramble at night, so Clara was surprised to see her. She
offered to keep Clara company. Clara was about to tell her to go
back to bed, but thought better of it: she was rarely alone with
Evelyn.

The girl never mentioned her mother's visit. She seemed
profoundly unmoved by it. Miss Smith telephoned once a week
and if it was painful for Clara to listen to Evelyn's monosyllabic
responses, how much harder must it have been for Miss Smith
to hear them?

Now Evelyn said that she liked Miss Smith but she liked
living at the Grange too. 'I'm not sure what she wants,' she
explained uncertainly. 'I don't know why she is interested –
after all these years.'

Clara let the girl talk and then said, 'People make mistakes,'
and Evelyn yawned then went back upstairs.

When Alex woke at six the next morning, his hair was all
over the place and his eyes were on stalks.

'Miss Newton?' He looked around himself, shocked. 'Can I
go to bed now?' he asked, as though Clara had been the one
keeping him up.

'You've got school, Alex.'

'Oh.'

As he sat up, he made retching noises.

'Okay, to bed. I'll call them.'

Later that morning, she took a watery chicken soup up to him and sat by his feet, watching him awkwardly spoon it into his mouth and down Peter's old pyjama top.

'What happened yesterday then, Alex?'

'He took me to the White Horse. He introduced me to some of his friends. It wasn't his fault.' He looked at her with his massive eyes. 'He's my only family.'

'Is that what he says?' Clara felt confused. The contrast with Evelyn's attitude to her mother was stark.

'It's true, isn't it?'

'He's not good for you, Alex.' Clara stiffened. Alex shouldn't have to deal with this sort of malign influence in his life. No one should.

Alex shrugged. 'He's all I've got.'

'Not true,' she told him. 'You've got us.' But she could see it went in one sticky-out ear and out the other. For some reason, unfathomable to Clara, the boy was smitten.

20

Clara had mixed feelings about December. After Michael had died on that terrible Christmas Eve she had thought she would never enjoy Christmas again – but last Christmas at Shilling Grange had been her happiest ever and she wondered if she could make this Christmas just as special. Plus, Christmas was extra-important this year because she had all the work she had done to show Mr Sommersby.

She wrapped up her notes and her accounts and put them in a thick brown envelope that looked delightfully officious. On impulse, she added a drawing by Peg of them – 'the potato family,' Rita had titled it – and a copy of the *Shilling Grange News*. The second edition contained articles on the wagon sale and Marilyn's visit, and a coconut ice recipe.

She also put in the envelope a letter of commendation from Alex's headmaster: 'Alex shows a mastery of maths, history and Latin beyond his tender years.' A letter from Peg's therapist – 'we are confident that she is moving towards speech' – and one from Anita Cardew about Rita's bright future in music 'if she practises hard'.

She had a note from Billy and Barry's football coach: 'Great effort, Rovers, we're going to win the league!' and a rather drier one from the newsagent: 'The boys deliver newspapers and I have not had any written or verbal complaints.' She included a page (carefully selected) of one of Peter's comics. She also had Dr Cardew's signing-off note for Joyce. She hadn't been able to think what to do to show Evelyn's 'progress', but in a surprise move, Evelyn herself had come up with something – her report from school, in which the teacher called her an asset to the class and a joy to teach! This was surprising, especially since it was from Miss Fisher, a stern teacher Clara had never warmed to.

Clara felt pleased with the evidence she had amassed. Even if she had another few weeks, even if she had another few months, she probably couldn't have done much better to demonstrate that the children were thriving, and the books were balanced. She had done what Mr Sommersby wanted and more besides. As she sealed the envelope and gave it a superstitious kiss for luck, she felt optimistic. Even if she failed – and she didn't think she had – then at least there would be a resolution soon.

A Christmas card came from Ivor, but it was addressed to everyone. Clara didn't know what to make of it – Ruby wasn't mentioned which was good, but it was without a single clue to Ivor's whereabouts or his emotional state. The picture didn't give away anything about him either. It was of three dogs, Dalmatians leaping up at a Christmas tree. *Seasons Greetings*, it said. The postmark said Wales. She felt, as the detectives in the thrillers on the wireless would say, 'the trail had gone cold'.

Not that there was a trail. Of course not.

Clara placed his card on the mantelpiece next to a card of a nativity scene from Robinson, Browne and White. Their card said that they hoped next year would be healthy, prosperous and wise. It had rather obviously been written by Maureen in her childish scrawl.

As usual there was nothing from Clara's father: he was fervent about Christmas and goodwill to all men; but that didn't extend to his only child. Clara told herself she didn't mind but it was still painful. There was a card (a melting snowman) from her old boss Harris – written by his fragrant wife, no doubt – and a sweet note ('we are not sending cards this year – we hope you understand') from Judy's mother. Ex-resident Terry sent a lovely card too, with a drawing of her beaming adoptive parents surrounded by flowers which cheered Clara up.

A card – picture of a Christmas tree – came with no stamp. It must have been hand-delivered early one morning.

> *Dear Miss Newton, thank you for having faith in me. Yours sincerely, Joe.*

This one made tears come to Clara's eyes.

'Have you seen Joe at all?' she asked Maureen. Sometimes Clara thought she caught glimpses of him around town, but she never moved quickly enough to establish that it was him. She had no idea where he'd gone and the thought that he might be rough-sleeping in this weather was awful.

'Who? Joe? Nope,' Maureen said as she went upstairs to get ready for another party at Julian's. Clara tried not to think she was heartless, but she couldn't help it.

Victor sent a long descriptive letter, this time about German life, which also hinted that, in his case, absence had made the heart grow fonder. Clara was not sure that was the case for her. He sent a grainy photograph of himself with a group of similar-looking men outside the Bundeshaus in Bonn and she touched his craggy face and tried to remember what he was like in person.

She was surprised to get a card from the council – she didn't remember them sending cards before. Okay, it was an austere nativity scene, but it was signed 'the children's department at Suffolk council'. Miss Cooper dropped it round two days before Christmas, with a bottle of wine.

'Ooh, posh! This is a first,' Clara said, feeling very grown-up.

'French,' said Miss Cooper, like that explained it.

Anita and Dr Cardew were off to his father's place in Sussex and Mrs Garrard was going to stay with her parents only thirty minutes down the road. Miss Cooper said she was off to stay with her parents too. Her father was an accountant and her mother did the books for him. Clara, who loved to hear about normal families, asked what she was going to do there.

'Visit family and friends, and entertain all of the village – tedious.' Miss Cooper said, screwing up her nose.

Clara nodded sympathetically, but she couldn't think of anything less tedious. It sounded idyllic.

'Isn't Santa coming?' Rita said, 'Peg wants to know.'

Recently, the children had taken to planting questions and observations they didn't want to express into Peg's mouth. 'Peg wants to know if we can have seconds.' 'Peg says Billy just farted.' It was unfair, thought Clara as Peg scowled.

'Maybe we haven't been good enough?' suggested Joyce.

Clara knew she should have thought of something. Last year, Ivor had dressed up and now the children expected something. That was the unfortunate thing about doing entertaining things for the children – they expected you to do them over and over again.

'You've behaved well but Father Christmas has a lot of children to see.'

Rita pulled a face. Peg rolled her tongue, which may have
been an exercise from her therapist or may have been her being
rude; Clara didn't want to ask.

Maureen pulled at Clara's arm. 'You don't think they'll
believe that, Miss Newton?'

Clara looked over at the children. They seemed happy
enough. 'I don't know.'

'You should tell them the truth.' Maureen seemed to be
referring to something else. 'Always.'

They mightn't have a Santa but they did at least have a
Marilyn. She had sent elaborately wrapped parcels, cards and
strict instructions: nothing to be opened until the twenty-fifth.
Clara stuck the gifts under the tree in the parlour on Christmas
Eve – and they did make a heart-warming sight. The children
were over the moon. Peg thumped her heart with joy.

Marilyn had got Clara a bright red lipstick – one she had
seen advertised in *Woman's Own*. There were racing cars for
the twins, coloured pencils for Peter, Rive Gauche perfume for
Maureen that left the girl speechless, more sheet music for Rita,
a baby doll for Evelyn – Clara thought she would turn up her
nose but she adored it – and a skipping rope *and* a hula hoop
for Peg.

'Did she forget me?' asked Joyce timidly after the others had
opened theirs. It was Clara's fault; she hadn't realised Joyce's
present was still there, tucked away under a particularly bushy
branch. Clara apologised and handed Joyce the last lonely
parcel. Joyce unwrapped it ravenously.

'Ohhhh!' she said. It was a brownie camera, brand-new,
with a strap, a flashgun and an instruction manual and 'everything the beginner photographer needs'. For the first time since
Clara had known her, Joyce was gobsmacked.

Miss Bridges had been so distant that Clara hadn't expected

her to come this year, but just a few days before Christmas, she said, 'I'll bring a bottle of gin, shall I?'

She arrived early and helped with the dinner too, and made sure Clara didn't burn the potatoes or forget the stuffing. They agreed the chicken breast was a civilised choice and the Christmas crackers, like last year a present from the Cardews, were brilliant fun.

While they were eating Miss Bridges' pudding, Clara noticed that the bottle of wine, the French one from Miss Cooper, was no longer on the windowsill. She looked around the room but couldn't see it. Noticing Clara's expression, Miss Bridges asked what was wrong. Clara didn't want to spoil the day, so she claimed a touch of indigestion, nothing to worry about.

In the afternoon, they played What's the Time, Mr Wolf?, Chinese whispers and charades. Just as the charades were degenerating into a row over whether *Gone with the Wind* was a book or not, Clara walked Miss Bridges out to her car.

'It might be my last Christmas in this house...' said Clara. She couldn't help it; gin made her melancholy.

By contrast, gin made Miss Bridges gregarious. She was not usually physically affectionate, but now she slung a warm arm round Clara. 'Little birdy told me you did well.'

'Really?' gasped Clara, suddenly enlivened. 'Who said that?'

Miss Bridges tapped her nose. 'I cannot say!' Incredibly, she winked. 'But I think you might have cracked it, Clara.'

The bottle of wine had definitely gone.

Clara waited until the next day, when the children were having leftovers for breakfast, before she asked. Being older, Peter or Maureen were the obvious culprits, but it could easily just have been smashed (although Clara had hunted around for

a smell or stain – no child cleaned that efficiently, did they?).
She didn't think Alex would have drunk it; after the last time,
he had sworn off booze for life.

'Who took my wine?' Silence.

Should she punish them all? Miss Bridges might have, but
Clara instinctively found this unfair.

'What I'm going to do is sit in my room for the next hour
and I want the person who stole it to come and see me. And if
no one comes, there's no Kids' Club movie today.'

The children looked content to stay in their pyjamas and
play with their new things, so she upped the ante. 'And no
comics, no treats, nothing – for a week,' she added.

There was a collective sigh. 'I bet it was Joyce,' said Billy. 'It
was her last time with the comic,' Barry added. 'We know that.'

Joyce's chin dropped to her chest.

'I don't care who it is,' lied Clara, 'I just want to know.'

At fifty-nine minutes past, someone tapped on her bedroom
door. Heart in her boots, Clara called out, 'Come in.'

It *was* Alex.

'It's what my father wanted,' Alex said helplessly. He
crossed his arms. 'That's what he asked for. I tried to get some in
the shops, but they wouldn't serve me. I will pay you back.'

'Yes, you will,' said Clara 'but that's not the point.'

She was annoyed with herself for not working it out sooner.
Of course it was for Alex's father.

Alex was so brilliant yet so clueless when it came to him.

'Does he frighten you?'

'No.'

'What about if you don't do what he says?'

He shrugged.

Alex was changing in front of her eyes. It wasn't just that he
was growing broader, heavier, turning into a man, but he was
being put upon. He was being torn apart in this tug-of-war.
Something needed to be done, but what?

He shook his head and mumbled, 'He's my father.'

Those strange quiet days after Christmas, it was foggy, a true pea-souper, and you could hardly see the end of your nose. At first, the children were banned from going outside but soon Barry and Billy were thumping a ball at each other's heads so Clara relaxed the rule. Joyce was poring over her camera. Every so often, she'd look up, make a rectangle with her fingers and peer through it. Evelyn was on the hunt for the last of the plum pudding.

Maureen was out helping Martin Browne with his school-work. 'He gets so much homework!' she said wonderingly. (Martin attended a private school in Bury.) 'I help him with his maths and English.' It was on the tip of Clara's tongue to say, 'How is that possible?' but instead she asked, 'Do you like spending time with him?'

Maureen screwed up her nose. 'I prefer the office but as long as I get paid, I don't mind.' And she gave Clara her Christmas bonus money. 'I do want to help.'

'I know, sweetheart,' said Clara, trying not to look surprised. 'Thank you.'

Victor Braithwaite arrived back from his tour of Europe and on the afternoon of New Year's Eve, he dropped round like a creature from the mist. He had brought Clara the last book he had had published – this one was about the Russian Revolution – and inside he signed it: *To Clara. Love Victor.* He was embarrassed but proud at the same time.

'You don't have to read it,' he said, 'but I thought...' He paused, sweeping back his Beethoven hair, 'it's relevant. It's about some of the issues we face as a country. And I know that's something you care deeply about.'

Clara didn't know whether she should disabuse him of this notion. It seemed to be in a grey area, like pretending to believe in Father Christmas. She wondered what she had done to make him think so and if it counted as lying. Still, she nodded and said, 'I do,' which on reflection was perhaps not her best choice of words. He looked meaningfully into her eyes. He might have been leaning in to kiss her, but then something flashed. Victor blinked rapidly. Clara yelped.

'Joyce! Do not take our photo! Out!'

Joyce hurried away, the sound of one leg being dragged after the other echoing through the house.

'Sorry...' Clara apologised. 'Christmas present... Where were we?'

Talk about interrupting a moment.

This time last year Clara had been dressing up for a night out with Julian and they had ended up doing... rather more than rendezvousing. She tried to focus on Victor.

He had taken her hand. 'I'd like to take you out sometime once the fog has gone.' Clara smiled at him warmly. 'Perhaps with Alex and Bernard too,' he added. Clara kept up the smile but she was confused.

Was he interested in her romantically? She had thought so, but if so, why ask Alex too?

It was hard to tell – she was so out of practice.

The other question was equally simple and equally complicated: *Was she romantically interested in him?*

21

The mist cleared but there was still no news from the council, which apparently was to be expected, since the council leaders took long holidays over Christmas. Miss Bridges estimated Clara wouldn't hear anything until the middle of January at least. Miss Cooper had forgotten the whole affair, but when prompted said, 'Oh, it'll all come out in the wash!' She had got shingles at her parents' and wasn't feeling herself.

On New Year's Day, there was a meeting for the spring edition of the *Shilling Grange News*. 'Everyone should have finished their pieces over the holidays,' Alex insisted. 'If not, why not?'

He seemed to be enjoying the power of being editor too much. Billy and Barry were told off for they had produced nothing yet again. Alex might have anticipated that. Since when did Billy and Barry write anything down? But Alex, while being extraordinarily gifted academically, was not blessed with people skills. Clara thought that he was perhaps similar to Victor in that way.

'Rita, your article was far too long. You've got to cut it down.

You know, being succinct is an admirable quality and something too few people take seriously these days.'

Clara snorted.

'Shan't,' Rita snapped.

'And yours could have been longer, Maureen. Four lines? is that it?'

'I don't care,' said Maureen. 'I'm only here because I don't want to mop the bathroom.'

Alex looked beseechingly at Clara, who felt this was a battle best stayed out of and said nothing.

'Thank you for your poem, Peg,' he went on. 'I liked that you rhymed sister and whisper. Not many people would do that.'

Peg grinned and galloped outside.

'Shall we do a story on Anita having a baby?' Alex asked Clara.

'Perhaps you should wait until after the baby is born...' advised Clara.

'I'll do it,' said Evelyn, looking embarrassed. 'If you want.'

Alex looked at Clara, who said, 'Lovely idea, Evelyn!'

'I might do a feature on Ivor being missing,' mused Rita. 'Like a crime mystery feature. A whodunnit?'

Clara shot her a look. 'There's no need.'

At that moment, the doorbell rang, so Clara had a reason to hurry away. Miss Smith stood outside the house, all in black, under an umbrella, taut and unemotional. She reminded Clara of a beady-eyed crow.

'Don't want to intrude, Miss Newton, but I wonder if you'd give me five minutes of your time.'

You could say that for Miss Smith, thought Clara. She was mindful of boundaries. Miss Smith said that when she had been walking home from her visit she'd seen a notice at the doctor's surgery for a job. She had applied and would be starting next week. Clara stared at her.

A job at the doctor's surgery? Dr Cardew's surgery?

'It's so I will be able to get to know Evelyn,' Miss Smith continued. She knelt to stroke Stella, partly, Clara suspected, to avoid meeting Clara's eyes. Stella rubbed against Miss Smith's plump calves contentedly. 'And so Evelyn can get to know me.'

After the editorial meeting had finished, the children rushed into the kitchen and back outside.

'Evelyn, your mother's here,' Clara called.

'I'm going to play hopscotch.' Evelyn barely looked at Miss Smith.

'She just wants a quick word.'

Clara looked between Miss Smith and Evelyn. Evelyn was so clearly eager to go out to be with the others, it was painful.

'I'm going to move near here,' Miss Smith announced nervously.

'Oh?' said Evelyn, expert in haughty disdain.

'I'll be able to take you to the park sometimes after school, maybe. What do you think to that?'

Evelyn had a tiny grudge of a smile on her face. 'All right, I suppose.'

Miss Smith raised her eyebrows at Clara. She seemed to be saying, *I'll get there.*

Throughout January, Miss Smith was eager for more time with Evelyn. She had rented rooms in Ipswich. She was proud of the sofa-bed that she got from the nearby second-hand furniture shop.

'It's a sofa by day, bed at night,' she explained like it was the ninth wonder of the world.

Only once did Miss Smith let Evelyn down: the Saturday

she had a migraine. Evelyn shook her head, took to the kitchen and went searching for goodness knows what in the cupboards. Other than that, though, Miss Smith was reliable. She took Evelyn to the park and every fortnight they went out for a bun in Dedham, but if Evelyn had other plans, a friend from school or a detention, she bowed out graciously. Evelyn came back with gifts too – once an eraser for school and another time a pair of mittens that didn't fit.

Miss Smith started at the surgery and Anita was pleased with her. And since Anita was difficult to please, she *must* be good, Clara thought. Anita said she was like gold dirt. 'Do you mean dust?' corrected Clara but Anita ignored her. Miss Smith had great skills with the patients, apparently. *And* she remembered to feed the fish. Anita said Doctor Cardew was now less anxious about taking time away from the surgery.

Evelyn refused to go to see Miss Smith's home in Ipswich, and the miraculous sofa-bed, but Miss Smith said that was fine too.

'I do understand,' she told Clara one day on the doorstep. Clara always asked her in, but Miss Smith preferred to stroke Stella outside. And Clara didn't insist, for she was still awkward with her. 'It took me ten years to get here, it's going to take a while for her to get used to me.'

It seemed to Clara that Miss Smith was standing by her word. She had said knowledge and consent were integral to her; after her powerlessness as a young woman, she wouldn't inflict that on anyone else. And it moved Clara that Miss Smith was prepared to wait. But Evelyn didn't seem keen to see her much more. Clara wondered if it was because Joyce taunted her about it. One time, when Clara was tidying the upstairs hall, she heard the girls arguing in the dorm.

'You've got a mother who wants you. Mine hated me.'

'My mother's dead,' chipped in Maureen.

Clara pushed open the door. 'Girls,' she said firmly, not sure what to say next, '... girls, it's not a competition.'

'If it was, I'd win,' hissed Rita.

One day towards the end of January, when Miss Smith brought Evelyn back she hovered in the doorway, wringing her hands. Evelyn ran past her, fists full of fudge, eager to get to hopscotch.

'Miss Newton, is the Grange up for sale?' Miss Smith asked.

Immediately, Clara's senses were on high alert. It couldn't be true. The council were still mulling it over...

'Who did you hear that from?' she asked.

'A patient,' Miss Smith said. 'I need to know if you're moving away. It's not fair.'

'No, no... it's under control,' Clara told her – and she was telling herself that too. But Miss Smith still looked perturbed.

'I've upended my whole life to be here. I could have just stayed in Glasgow.'

Clara felt a surge of impatience. *What about the children?* 'So far as I know we're staying here. If anything changes I will let you know.'

Miss Smith's expression visibly relaxed but then she said, 'I'd like Evelyn to move in with me. Would you find out if that's possible?'

As she tucked Evelyn in that night, Clara asked her if she would consider moving in with her mother. She had expected Miss Smith to ask, but had not expected it to be so soon. She thought it might be a good idea, but it was important to go slowly, or at least at Evelyn's pace. The girl had had little control in her life and it would be good for her to be able to steer this.

'I have been moved eighteen times.'

'Nine,' Clara said. 'Which is too many,' she added quickly.

'I've got everything I need here. For now,' Evelyn said, rolling over on to her side, away from Clara. 'And I'm tired. I just want the chance to breathe.'

22

Miss Cooper called to say Billy and Barry's uncle and aunt would be visiting the next afternoon – with a view to taking the boys on.

Clara sighed. 'It's late notice.' She was more disappointed that there was still no news about the sale. What on earth was Mr Sommersby doing with her notes? He'd had them for over a month.

'Sorry,' said Miss Cooper breezily. 'You will be in though, won't you?'

Clara told herself not to be insulted. She would be in, it was true. She was in all the time. People came, people went, yet she stayed still. The prospect of the uncle and aunt's visit did not give Clara hope. After Peter's horrendous experience, even the word 'uncle' made her heart drop. Forgive her for being sceptical. *An uncle, huh? Where had this uncle been all these years?* And Billy and Barry had gone to an adoptive home already, last year, and that had not worked out.

. . .

The uncle, Stan, was blond, tanned and cleanly shaved. He had been overenthusiastic with the cologne. His hands were surprisingly rough and when she said, 'How do you do?' he said, 'Fine, great journey here.'

Clara had the impression he was trying hard and this endeared him to her a little.

The aunt, Ruth, wore long off-white gloves and she plucked them off her hands regally, but then looked at a loss as to where to put them. Finally, she dumped them in her handbag, but then her handbag wouldn't do up.

Cynically, Clara asked where they had magicked themselves from, but they explained it immediately.

'We were in Canada,' Uncle Stan said.

'Got back to Blighty last month.'

'Didn't like the weather there.'

'Cold as a witch's teat,' Aunt Ruth said. Clara spluttered.

'She didn't like the food either.'

'Nor did you,' Aunt Ruth said, adding apologetically, 'My ma is in England. She's not getting any younger.'

True of everyone, thought Clara, but she nodded in agreement.

'Canada is far away.'

Didn't they know that before they left?

Over tea, Aunt Ruth seemed to relax. She looked up at Clara with wide eyes.

'I was so homesick, I cried every day.'

'She did,' Uncle Stan said.

'We'd like to meet the boys before we make any rash decisions.'

'We've got two at home,' he added.

'Oh?' said Clara. They seemed awfully young.

'I made some money on the Premium Bonds,' Uncle Stan said.

'We thought we should share the good fortune,' Aunt Ruth said. 'I like kids. More the merrier.'

'I loved my brother.'

'It's what he would have wanted,' she said, taking Stan's hand and stroking it.

'Probably.'

Clara found herself warming to them. This wasn't Peter's uncle. It wasn't Alex's father. Every relative had to be judged on their own merits, she reminded herself, and these two seemed to have a lot of merits. But before she got carried away, she had to know Billy and Barry would like them. They didn't have to do so straight away, but there had to be potential there. A seed that would grow.

Billy and Barry stood to attention at the back door. They were both wet and muddy, ball under Barry's arm, blood on Billy's face. Not the best first impression.

'What happened?' Clara asked.

'Red card,' said Billy.

'You thumped him,' laughed Barry

'I didn't!' protested Billy.

'Boys... This is your Uncle Stan – your father's brother – and this is his wife, Aunt Ruth.'

The boys straightened up.

'Football or rugby?' Billy could not have been more serious. That question was everything.

Clara waited.

'We live just by the stadium at Highbury,' said Uncle Stan.

'On match days, he just leans out the window,' said Aunt Ruth. Uncle Stan put his arm round her. 'You can hear the cheering for miles and miles,' she went on.

'And when we get a goal, the table shakes!' He laughed.

'And when they win, I worry the house is going to collapse!' Aunt Ruth said, but she didn't seem worried, she seemed to think it was hilarious.

Billy's mouth fell open like he was catching flies. Barry spoke up first, his tone reverential, his question unequivocal.

'When can we come?'

23

Clara found that if she didn't go out for a walk regularly, she got ratty with the children. Even in winter – *especially* in winter – there was something about being trapped in the house all day on her own, and then trapped with them after school, that sucked the good mood out of her.

It was February and there had been nothing from the council. Perhaps the idea of selling was just a nonsense and it had been forgotten. One of those things no one would mention except in a few years' time as a funny reminiscence: 'Remember when they were going to move you?!' Clara crunched through the frosty fields, briefly conversed with Mr Garrard and his dog Bertie. She had grown to like Bertie; he did woof a lot, but at least he didn't make her sneeze.

As always, she marvelled at how she – an urban girl – had become a country girl. *People are capable of enormous transformations*, she decided.

'Watch out ahead,' Mr Garrard said then winked.

For an instant, Clara thought it was Victor Braithwaite's car parked out of place in the side clearing, it was with slight relief that she recognised it as Miss Bridges'. Miss Bridges had been difficult to get hold of recently. If Clara had thought their lovely Christmas Day together would herald a sea-change in their relationship, she had been wrong; Miss Bridges had become more distant than ever. Slippery as an eel, she wouldn't talk to Clara about either the children, the future of the home or anything.

The windows were misted up. As Clara approached the car, she could see the back of Miss Bridges' tidy head. Then she realised another person was with her. The person was leaning from the passenger seat into the driver seat – the heads joined again, they became one giant head, then disappeared from view. It was like they had bobbed underwater.

Someone was hurting Miss Bridges. Thoughts of Judy overwhelmed her. Thoughts of her best friend being killed and Clara being too damn polite and too damn English to intervene. She was too gullible last time to realise the truth. She wouldn't be this time.

What the hell was going on?

With one hand, Clara snatched at the cold door handle and with the other, she hammered on the glass.

Two figures went bolt upright. Miss Bridges and – Mr Horton?!

Miss Bridges' fingers were in her hair. She looked horrified. Mr Horton's tie was loosened and flapped slightly as a breeze rattled through the car door. There was something inexplicably funny about the sight. There was a blanket over both their knees.

Miss Bridges spoke first. 'Miss Newton, what on earth are you doing here?'

Clara stared between the two of them. *Horton and Bridges?* she thought. It sounded like an engineering agency. Horton was scarlet. Bridges was pulling down her off-white blouse.

'I saw the car.' Clara found she was speaking with her hands. 'I came over to say hello...' This felt redundant. Her head was trying to make sense of what was in front of her eyes. It was like she was late to something.

Miss Bridges pushed the blanket away and with that, she seemed to restore her dignity.

'We were about to have a picnic.'

And you were keeping the basket down his trousers? Clara did not say.

'I'll thank you not to mention this to anyone.' Miss Bridges spoke firmly.

'Very well, Miss Bridges,' Clara said. They were all red, but she might have outdone them. She clutched her shopping basket to her – she could smell the cauliflower.

'Good day to you both.'

Mr Horton? Of all the people to have this – whatever it was – with, Miss Bridges had chosen Mr Horton? Clara had never liked the officious bureaucrat. She had always thought him worse than Mr Sommersby, the poor man's version of him. He was the last man you'd want to rendezvous with.

But then she thought about his tie, his stricken expression and the pinkness of his gangly throat. *And if that's what makes her happy...* Clara hiccupped with laughter.

Who'd have thought it? Miss Bridges and Mr Horton smooching in the countryside. As the children would say: K-I-S-S-I-N-G.

Inexplicably, Clara felt a burst of joy. She wasn't feeling the cold any more. Love was in the air – it was sweet, wasn't it? Sweet and unexpected. She only wished she could tell someone about it – no, she wished she could tell Ivor about it. He would be the one who would best understand her surprise, who would sympathise, who would, like her, be shocked, and then like her, he too would laugh.

· · ·

The following day, Miss Bridges came round, looking sheepish, and Clara wished, almost as fervently as Miss Bridges probably wished, that she had not taken that particular path yesterday.

'I feel I should explain,' Miss Bridges muttered.

'There's no need,' Clara insisted, yet they automatically went into the parlour, the venue for serious talks, and Miss Bridges knotted herself up in a ball on the sofa.

'It was work or family for women in those days. One or the other – you couldn't have both. And then my brothers had died in the Great War, you see, I couldn't leave my parents. I liked my job, always did. So I broke off my engagement. I had to choose. You had to, back then.'

'But Mr Horton?'

'I've been alone for seventeen years,' Miss Bridges said, reddening again. 'Just me in my parents' house – baking for one, ironing for one.'

'I'm sorry—'

Miss Bridges flapped her arms. 'No need to be sorry. I enjoy my work, my life, the council. I just didn't meet anyone I wanted to be with – until now. I know you don't think much of him, Clara, but he's a respectable man and we have the same ideals. The urge for companionship has never gone away.'

Miss Bridges looked square at Clara.

'I know that wouldn't be enough for many women nowadays. Young women like you don't like to compromise, don't need to.'

Clara was reminded somehow of Jane Taylor, the unmarried sister, Ann Taylor the married one. Was Jane alone because she never compromised? Mr Dowsett had never said that but he did say that it was difficult for women back then, and that marriage was not just an expectation but the only way to be taken seriously in society. Perhaps not much had changed. Was Clara herself alone because she hadn't compromised?

'I get that.' Clara thought of Victor. *Was he a compromise?* The thought of him didn't make her heart flutter – although *sometimes* it did. How was a person to know?

It was the most confusing thing. Companionship, shared ideals – did Miss Bridges think those wouldn't be enough for Clara? Did she think Clara was holding out for an idea that didn't exist?

Victor was taking Clara to an art gallery. Clara had never been to one before and she couldn't help worrying that she would make a dreadful faux pas there. Victor wasn't in the best of moods, either, when she met him at St Pancras train station. He was unhappy with the election result. The Labour Party had won again but their majority had been cut. Victor thought this was disastrous. 'Everything we've achieved over the past few years could be in jeopardy. Children's services, the NHS, dentists...'

Clara wondered about the 'we'. The back seat of Miss Cooper's car had been full of Labour Party leaflets for Mrs Blowes, the local candidate, who'd talked about bonny babies, fair rationing and great health service. Clara knew that Miss Cooper was upset about the result too, she had cried when Clara telephoned to arrange the monthly check.

Julian though was cock-a-hoop as usual. When Clara'd seen him on the high road the day after the result, he'd said, 'Things will be back to normal soon.'

'But you didn't win, Julian.'

'Might as well have. Handicapped them.'

She hoped Victor wasn't going to fret about it too much.

There were still some posters in the streets of the candidates and if they walked past a Conservative one, Victor shook his

head and said, 'Shame.' Victor must have talked about it for over
half an hour before he turned to her and said, 'Forgive me, I've
been going on,' and politely she said that he hadn't, then
laughed and said, 'Oh you have, a little.' He made a strangled
sound.

The gallery was a compact building, a large house really, not
what she had expected. She had been going to tell Victor about the
only paintings she knew, by Sir Alfred Munnings, and why did
painters love ships, battles and horses so much? But she decided
not to say anything. She didn't want to give him further grounds
for thinking her daft. As they wandered around the house, she
admired the bright rooms and high ceilings while Victor admired
the paintings. It was warm too, much warmer than it was outside.

Victor was speaking. 'This is one I wanted to show you.'

He was looking at a painting called *Breakfast in Bed*. It was
of a young woman in bed and a child, looking lively, next to her.
It was incredibly modern somehow and seemed to convey the
exhaustion of looking after a little being. How tightly the
woman clasped her hands round the child. She took her responsibility seriously.

Victor said, 'The woman reminds me of you.' Clara gazed
again at the woman's gentle face, the flush of her cheeks, the
dark hair pulled back. It *was* a compliment, she thought,
although not an obvious one.

She had been about to say, 'I've never had breakfast in bed
in my life,' which wouldn't be true – she had once when she was
ill at school, after her mother's death, when even Matron was
worried about her. But she hadn't in her adult life – that was
true. She didn't say it though; she didn't want to say anything
wrong. Instead, she took his hand. She didn't overanalyse it,
maybe it was a reaction to the paintings. Victor coloured but let
her. His hands were surprisingly soft. If they had been in
private, she might have pressed one of them to her lips.

Later though, he mentioned that his Iris had introduced him to several great women artists. Clara nodded and wondered if it was related to the hand-holding.

He isn't ready to move on, she thought.

Then they talked about Bernard – and Alex – '*what an extraordinary boy.*'

Clara thought about confiding in Victor about Alex's father, but this was about getting to know each other and you don't have to dish it up at once. Best foot forward. She didn't think it would put him off her or Alex, but Alex's story was complex. The house had an equally lovely garden, with high hedges and winter flowers, and no one else was out there. This time, it was Victor who took Clara's hand, and it felt distinctly more than friendly, and he whispered, 'I haven't felt like this for a long time, Clara.'

And then they kissed. He leaned in and it was a proper kiss, open-mouthed and lusty. She had expected Victor to be uptight. She put her hand on the back of his hot neck. This was a turn-up for the books.

Goodness.

She shut her eyes and Ivor drifted into her vision. Ivor's mouth, Ivor's eyes, the way he said goodbye...

'That was nice,' Victor said.

Clara wiped her lips on her sleeve. What kind of word was nice?

Ridiculous to feel guilty about Ivor who was, lest she forget, somewhere – she didn't know where – with his *wife*. Mr and Mrs Delaney mooning around a hotel. Ivor would be commenting on the soft furnishings, Ruby would be doing whatever Ruby did.

She looked up at Victor again, Victor who was here and who was now. And who had just treated her to a lovely day out and shown her things she would never normally see. Victor, the

professor of politics and international relations, who had invited
her to visit him at his university.

'Very nice,' she said as she went in for some more.

Some days later, Miss Smith came to the doorstep. Stella rushed
out to brush against her legs. She said she wouldn't come in. She
said, 'Did you talk to Evelyn?'

'I did.'

Miss Smith's face lit up; she looked girlish. It was a sudden
reminder of how young she was.

'And? What did she say?'

'She's not sure if she wants to proceed just yet,' said Clara.
Evelyn's mother was so mild-mannered, nothing like, say, Alex's
father or Peter's uncle. Now she looked on the verge of tears.
'She probably will soon,' Clara went on gently, 'but for the
moment it's a no. She's sorry.'

Evelyn *wasn't* sorry, Clara thought. She didn't trust her
mother yet. She was happy at Shilling Grange and had settled
in at school. She got on with Maureen and Peg. She was tired of
moving.

Miss Smith blew her nose, then put her handkerchief back
in her bag. Her mannerisms were of a much older woman.

'I could insist on taking her. It is my right.'

'You could.'

'And the council couldn't stop me.'

'Probably... no.'

'I wouldn't want to do that though,' Miss Smith said, staring
down at Stella, who had balanced herself over her tiny patent
shoes.

'I didn't think you would.'

'I'll make it better,' Miss Smith said resolutely. 'One day, I'll
change her mind.'

Clara felt unexpectedly tearful. Poor Evelyn's mother. She was only a little older than Maureen when she had her baby. She had been bamboozled. She had been intimidated and now she was suffering again. But poor Evelyn too. Nine homes. Twelve schools. No wonder she wanted to get off the merry-go-round, just for a moment.

24

It was one of those wintery days when the air was warm but the sky was unpromising and Clara couldn't decide if it was worth hanging the sheets outside or not. After some chivvying, the children had gone off to their schools and Clara was upstairs scrubbing a stain on the floor when she heard someone – more than one person? – opening the front door. She heard two men's voices, then she ran down and she saw them in the hall: Mr Sommersby and Mr Horton.

They had their own key?

Clara froze at the bottom of the stairs.

'Did you let yourselves in?' she asked incredulously.

'We did,' said Mr Sommersby smoothly. 'No one answered, so...'

With his dark suit and his grim expression, Mr Horton looked like an undertaker and the way he clutched his briefcase was like he was fending off the dead. Clara couldn't help but think, *Really, Miss Bridges?*

Mr Sommersby continued, 'We had a full children's services meeting last night in Bury, where we looked at your submission. You did a thorough job, Miss Newton. Exceptional, you might say.'

'I would have come...' Clara began. She could have talked to them, explained what everything was. The thought that they would have passed around Peg's drawings or the Shilling Grange Newspaper, made her feel hot and silly. *What had she been thinking?*

'Mrs McCarthy sent her greetings. She remembered what a hard-working and likeable young woman you were.'

Likeable? thought Clara. Mrs McCarthy had also asked how was it possible Clara had made so many enemies in Lavenham in such a short space of time.

'We voted unanimously.'

Mr Horton was licking his lips. 'A majority is not unanimously,' he corrected quietly.

'What?' said Clara.

'We're selling up,' Mr Sommersby said. He turned to Mr Horton. 'A majority, yes, that's right.'

Mr Horton's face was inscrutable. 'You'll see it is for the best, Miss Newton.'

Clara felt dizzy. Her head was full of water suddenly. She hated them, especially Mr Horton. And then Mr Sommersby told Mr Horton to go out and wait in the car and she was pleased – horrible man fussing over the difference between unanimous and majority when there were so many more important things. She would have laid good money on which way he'd voted.

Mr Horton looked shocked to be dismissed, but he scuttled away like a dormouse. Clara wondered: what was it Mr Sommersby was going to say that couldn't be said in front of Mr Horton?

Once the front door had clicked shut, Mr Sommersby said, 'We didn't have much choice, Miss Newton. There were a lot of

factors to consider. We had a report from one of the girls' teachers. It seems you threw a child out of a car.'

'What? I nudged her!'

'Was the car moving?'

'Of course not! Anyway, it was months ago.'

'If you can't control the children...'

'I can.'

'The council feel this is a children's home, not some...' he
searched in the air for the word, 'asylum. I'm not saying that
was a major factor, but it paints a picture. Plus of course, the
tribunal last year.'

Clara breathed out. She was ready for a fight. She had gone
through the London Blitz, she told herself. Whatever the
Germans had dished up on those cloudless nights, she'd still get
up in the morning, she'd still be her in her body, looking for a
cup of tea.

'I think you're making a mistake,' she said. She thought of
the woman in *Breakfast in Bed*. What would she say?

'Maybe you're right,' he said. 'But that's what's happening.'

Clara stared at him, trying to think of what to say.

'But we'll stay together?' She had *told* the children they
would stay together – which perhaps was a premature thing
to do...

'I don't see why not.'

Clara felt her tension seep away. *This mightn't be so bad.*

'And in Lavenham?'

It was so important they stayed at their schools, stayed local.
They were settled: Alex at the grammar school. Rita and her
piano lessons. The twins and their football. Peg and her speech
therapist. Evelyn and her hatred of moving. Oh, and her
mother, of course. Everyone and everything was there. After so
much turmoil in their early lives, security was paramount. Joyce
and her photography. Peter and his comics. And she herself

could not move again, she couldn't... The need for familiar things felt overwhelming.

'Absolutely,' he said, then added, 'at least within five miles, I promise.'

Five miles. About an hour and a half's walk? Okay, that wasn't so terrible.

'And possibly in a purpose-built property,' Mr Sommersby continued.

Purpose-built? Even amid the unpredictability and fog, those words felt hopeful. A 'purpose-built property' sounded deliberate or intentional. It sounded like it was made expressly for them – would that be so bad?

She breathed. Bloodied, yes, but not defeated.

'Then there's nothing to worry about?'

'Nothing at all,' he said. He smiled at her and reflexively, she smiled back. She didn't have much choice but to trust him.

25

Clara started looking out for FOR SALE signs locally. She saw one outside a shop with a flat above and went off on a fantasy that she and the children could run a business. Home upstairs, a bookshop – no, a cake shop – no, a sweet shop downstairs. Staff numbers wouldn't be a problem.

There was another house up for sale, near the school, with a tangled secret garden. Nowhere would be as beautiful as where they were now, but it would be okay. Maybe renting would be better if it meant there was more money in the pot for plimsolls, blouses and hot water!

Sometimes, Clara let herself off the leash and daydreamed of a tall thin Regency house like the art gallery she had been to, or like Julian's home – each of the children having their own rooms, an airy living area with sash windows, the piano in the parlour and not in a shed (which, despite Ivor's insulating efforts last year, did sometimes leak). She imagined a dining room with brass candelabras and tablecloths, and children using the correct cutlery. She pictured shoes that fitted – and a place to put their shoes too, and perhaps one of those newfangled fridges you saw in the adverts, with a place for six eggs. Maybe they could have one of those hen-shaped teapots or flying ducks on the walls or even an electric fire. An ironing board that didn't catch your fingers and a shoe-scraper to get the mud off your football boots. Perhaps even – this was in the realms of impossibility – a rental television that they could sit around before bed. Could you imagine the children's faces lit up at the silver screen?

What would the council decide for them? It most probably would be somewhere better suited for children. Staying together was the important thing, she told herself. A house was nothing. A few miles up the road was nothing.

They were building whole cities – new towns – with playgrounds with more than rusty swings, with different equipment, slides and see-saws, and picnic tables, and everything a family could need. She could imagine them in a new town. There were a lot of positives to take from this. Miss Bridges had her back and Miss Cooper was more reliable than the aura she gave off suggested.

There were other positives too. They'd get away from Alex's father. They'd get away from Maureen's job, which meant getting away from creepy Mr Browne *and* smug Julian White. Clara also let herself indulge in the private and evil thought of leaving Stella behind with the house. Stella had taken to sitting on the eggs in the kitchen, like she was hatching six baby kittens. She also liked sleeping on the washing when it came in from the garden, which was why half of Clara's clothes were covered in hairs.

(No, knowing Stella, she would always be able to find her way to them.)

Marilyn was right. The council was right. A change of scene might do them the world of good. Now that everything was out in the open, Clara knew what she was dealing with and it proved her instincts had been spot on! The council would do their best for her and there was something exciting about a new challenge. Perhaps there were more possibilities in a new home.

She popped by the surgery to see Anita, who was baking and complaining about being fat. (She had not put on any weight as far as Clara could discern.) Anita asked Clara if the children knew about the proposed move yet and Clara said no and she was waiting to hear more herself.

'It's so up in the air.' She felt guilty not telling them, but she wanted to get it right. 'I hate to tell them plans before they're fully in place.'

Anita eyed her sceptically. 'There will never be the right moment...' she said, which prickled Clara, but she didn't say anything.

Anita was also looking at properties, although hers were even more ludicrous than Clara's.

'In Poland, there is an orphanage in a castle. In France, a lighthouse.'

'I don't think the council budget will stretch that far, Anita.'

'Why not? You need to insist.'

Clara could not picture going to the council and demanding a lighthouse.

'And we want to stay close by, for the schools – and,' she added, more to make Anita happy than through any deep-seated desire, 'so we can meet your little one.'

Anita placed her hand automatically on her stomach. 'I can't wait.'

But Anita worried too – and could you blame her after everything she'd gone through in the war? 'Are you sure they'll keep you together?' she kept asking.

'Absolutely,' said Clara, and it reassured her to say it aloud, 'that's what Mr Sommersby said. And actually, there's no reason for them not to.'

26

Dear Mr Downey

Smash, bang, wallop, pow and wow.

We were blown away by your comic, fantastic drawings and hard-hitting ideas.

We would love to meet you. Have a chat, get to know what you want from the future, and if all goes stupendously, we'd like to offer you that job!

PS. Don't fret about the last page, we know accidents happen.

Peter threw his arms round Clara – he hadn't hugged her for ages – and picked her up so her feet actually left the floor. She was flying like a girl in his comics!

'YESSSS!' he shouted. 'They liked it – even though it was smudgy!'

'Talent will out, Peter. Oh, I'm so proud of you!'

That evening, she let Maureen and Peter have a glass of beer at the table after the younger children had gone to bed. (She was secretly pleased when neither of them seemed to like the taste.) Maureen was complimentary to Peter, who blushed with pleasure. They did cheers and Peter thanked Maureen and Clara. And while Clara had some reservations about the venture, she also knew there could be few jobs in this world that would suit Peter more than this.

Unfortunately, with Peter, things were always complicated and it didn't end – or begin – there. A few days later, in the kitchen, he told Clara he had changed his mind: she stirred the stew. The onions were sticking to the pan. They did strange things when you didn't watch them.

That forlorn freckled face. He said he wouldn't go to the meeting: 'It's ridiculous. I've never done anything, and I'll never do anything. I'm a nothing.'

'Where is this coming from?'

'You can't make me.'

'I don't, I won't. I just can't understand.'

But Clara had a notion of what it was. A few days ago, she had seen Peter's uncle in town again. James Courtney. His car slowed down to go past the Grange before speeding away. An instinct told her that she wasn't the only one who'd noticed it.

'You saw your uncle, didn't you?'

Peter shook his head, but Clara knew. He was so flushed, like the onions she was sizzling. He gazed at his feet: the top of his head was that lovely impossibly carrot colour.

What had his uncle said to him? She could only imagine.

'You mustn't let him win, Peter. This job is a good idea. This is good.' She took her turnips out of the oven. They were burnt at the ends. 'These are bad,' she said, trying to get a laugh out of him. She didn't know what else she could do. Why did their families have to constantly reappear to prick their bubbles?

Alex and Peter were inexorably pulled backwards into their murky pasts like creatures being drawn back into a swamp.

She was the same though; she could empathise. You never get away, do you? A smell of lavender brings back your mother. A children's prayer brings back your father, so vividly as if he was in the room next to you. And the feelings come back multi-fold, good and bad. Clara with her mother: bewildered, loving, loved but afraid. Clara with her father: Bewildered, unwanted, disgusting, wrong.

She tried again to talk to Peter, but he wouldn't engage; he was an immoveable object and an irresistible force was pulling him back.

'No,' he said. 'I'm not doing it. It was a stupid idea.'

Although she had sworn not to, she wrote to Ivor again. They were still friends, weren't they? And he said he cared about the children.

Should she put 'love' at the end of the letter, or just 'from', or both? She hated herself for worrying about it – Ivor would have no such qualms – but she couldn't stop herself.

Dear Ivor,

I hope you are well. I am worried about Peter. Do you remember, you once said that in the short term Peter will need lots of help from us? It seems we are still in the short term and Peter still needs help.

He has been offered an amazing opportunity working with comics in London, only he doesn't think he is worthy of it.

I know you are busy but if you could get in touch that would be great.

Clara

27

The next editorial meeting of the *Shilling Grange News* was a bad-tempered affair. Alex had a collection of articles that he said he had edited (entirely rewritten, most likely) but he didn't have a front-page story, a story that shouted 'BUY ME!' He asked Joyce for her polio feature but she screwed up her nose. So then Peg proposed some drawings of seashells, which made Alex screw up his nose.

'I suppose I could do an article on the Boer War,' he mused. 'Everyone finds that interesting.'

Rita said it was about as interesting as Mahler.

Evelyn said she'd copy out a poem but only if he was desperate.

'I don't know if we are,' said Alex helplessly. 'Are we?'

'Why don't you do a piece on the sale of the Grange?' Maureen suggested.

Clara sighed. She should have known Maureen would come out with something like this.

Alex laughed. 'Not sure our regular readers appreciate idle speculation, do they, Miss Newton?'

'We have no *regular* readers, Alex,' Maureen snapped. 'It's not idle speculation anyway. It's going to happen whether you like it or not. The council decided last week, didn't they, Miss Newton? When were you planning to tell us?'

Alex looked up at Clara expectantly. Rita whispered, 'Mama.' Billy nudged Barry in the ribs.

Clara clapped her hands. Maureen had dropped her right in it. It wasn't *entirely* Maureen's fault – she knew she should have sorted it sooner. 'Grange meeting. In the parlour. Ten minutes.'

Some children sat on the chairs, others cross-legged on the floor and Billy lying on his back with his legs in the air. Clara had a sudden memory of being in this same place with Julian and announcing that she was getting married – that had come to nothing in the end too.

'Children, are you happy here?'

A poor start, ridiculously bad. The children stared at each other.

'*I'm* happy here,' Clara added hurriedly. 'But it's not the *here* that makes me happy, it's you. You make me happy. Yes, Evelyn?'

'Have we got pudding tonight?'

'No. You see, it's not the home that matters, it's where the heart is.'

Billy nudged Barry. 'Where the *fart* is.'

'It's the people that count.'

Peg held up her counting fingers.

'Very good, Peg. So what I'm saying is, the council have decided we might move from the Grange but we won't be going far – you'll stay at your schools, you'll stay with your friends.'

'And the shed?' Rita looked petrified.

'The piano should be able to come with us, but not the shed. We might have to change our... shape, but we'll still be us.'

Clara liked that phrasing.

The children were getting up. Billy threw a ball at Barry's head. Peter opened the window, lit a cigarette, leaned out. Maureen stood up straight like she had won something. 'I told you so,' she was telling everyone.

'And another thing,' Clara called as they piled out, 'is we might have more money to spend on ourselves – so that's...'

But they'd already gone.

~

Early March and Miss Bridges asked Clara to meet her at a cemetery that was badly in need of some care. There were bouquets of dead flowers tied with string strewn on the paths. Some of the graves were overgrown or had turned green and mildewy. There were fears that some of the older graves might collapse if there was a high wind. It was very different to the military graveyard where Michael was buried. Clara had often wondered how Miss Bridges balanced the two different sides of her job, children's services and cemeteries. Now she thought maybe there was something similar in the roles: taming, restoring, doing the groundwork.

Clara thought Miss Bridges had asked her there to find out how telling the children had gone. Without being prompted, she began, 'It went well – Peg didn't even wet the bed last night.'

But Miss Bridges scowled as she put on her gardening gloves. 'You didn't *actually* ask Evelyn if she wanted to live with her mother, did you?'

'Oh – I might have,' Clara responded nervously. Amid the worries about the house move and Peter's change of heart, she had forgotten about Evelyn. Miss Bridges' severe tone had also taken her by surprise.

'And Evelyn said no?'

'She suggested she's not ready.'

Clara thought of the unhappy girl, chopping and changing all the time. 'I'm tired,' she had said and Clara knew that feeling of being deep-down, bone-tired and just wanting some peace. Evelyn saw her mother regularly and she always went off and came back cheerful – of course Clara watched her closely, looking for signs of discontent. And Clara was sure Evelyn would want to live with her mother soon.

'You're the one with the experience. You're the one with the view. You can see what's on the ground, from the ground and up from the air, because you're older – so you need to make decisions not the children. If Evelyn wants sweets every night, or if Joyce won't do her exercises, then you need to be the one who says no. Children obey their elders.'

'Oh, come on.' It was astonishing that Miss Bridges would come out with this, Clara thought. Hadn't they moved on since those days?

Miss Bridges had got down on her knees and was pulling out the dandelions, daisies and other weeds. She threw every straggly one into a bucket. Hoping her stockings would last, Clara knelt to help.

'Evelyn should want to go to her mother. She shouldn't be that happy with you,' Miss Bridges continued, wiping her forehead with her arm.

'So I should be more like Sister Eunice and hit and whip them? Make them do chores all evening?' Clara's temper flared. 'Because if you want Sister Eunice back, you can have her.'

'What does Evelyn know about what's best for her? She's a child, Clara. Are you sure this is not about you? Are you wanting to keep the children instead of letting them move on?'

'What?'

'It happens sometimes. Housemothers getting over attached. You wouldn't be the first.'

Attached, thought Clara. An interesting word. Buttons. And ribbons. Children and their teddy bears.

Was she over attached to Evelyn? It seemed unlikely. The accusation might be fairly thrown at her over some of the children. But Evelyn? They didn't have a special bond. And was she motivated by anything else? Clara searched the dark corners of her heart and came up with nothing. She just sympathised with the girl and wanted her to feel like she had some control over her life.

'I think we're doing the right thing,' she said finally. She yanked a particularly stubborn weed from the path, but missed the bucket. Miss Bridges tsked and put it in.

'She has to go, Clara.'

'She *will* go,' Clara insisted. 'But this way, Evelyn will feel she has choices.'

'Choices?' yelped Miss Bridges. 'She must go whether you like it or not. Or I will tell the council.'

Clara knew Miss Bridges was making sense, but she also didn't want to hurry Evelyn's fragile journey. Angrily, she stood up, brushed herself down and parked herself on the nearest bench.

'That one's broken,' warned Miss Bridges, just as the wood began to crack.

28

The next day, Clara scrubbed her nails and dressed in a pleated skirt with a pintuck blouse to see Victor at the university; she didn't want to look a fool among the students. When she got there, she realised she need not have worried. She was not visible to the 18–22-year-olds who populated Oxford. No one gave her matronly self a second glance, which was both a relief and annoying. Had she become middle-aged in just a blink of an eye?

It seemed so.

There was a lot of cycling and people did ring their bells more than was strictly necessary. After a time, she got used to the jangling of wheels and the pomp of the 'Pardon me's'. She remembered to glance around her when crossing and she kept walking straight in case one of the more silent cyclists was about to overtake her. It was a quick and crowded world after the peace and quiet of cobbled Lavenham, but it was a pleasant change nevertheless. One day, she thought, Alex might come here, and she might visit him! How proud would she be?

Victor telephoned twice a week – Thursdays and Mondays

– and he didn't seem to mind when Clara had to run off to find
a thimble or to break up an argument about who Stella loved the
most.

She had told him about the council plan and he said that
Clara could be satisfied that she had done her utmost and she
thought that was a better way of looking at it. He said he would
look in his property papers for a likely home, which was also
kind.

She had grown partial to his low telephone voice, twirling
the cord round her fingers as he talked. Victor was clever and
concerned about fairness and justice. He still occasionally
wrote letters to her and it was in his letters that the more
passionate side of him came out, like a sleepy creature that is
transformed after dark.

She had to ask for directions to 'Professor Braithwaite's' study.
His name got a pleasant reaction too.

'Of course, I know him,' said the young man, who was
wearing a beret like a painter. 'He's my favourite prof.'

Clara told herself she needn't worry what these children on
bicycles thought, when she was there for the big cheese. Clara
thought about their kissing in the gallery gardens. It had been
more than nice. But now she was worried – where was the relationship going? There were things she needed to clear up.

Victor was in between classes.

'Oh?' said Clara, disappointed. 'I assumed you were free.'

But it was intentional. He'd *wanted* her to come to his
lecture. He thought she'd find it interesting. Clara thought, not
for the first time, *He thinks I'm cleverer than I am.*

His subject was the last days of the Tsar. Today's lecture
was 'Could Nicholas have averted the Revolution?'

'I don't know...' mused Clara and to her surprise, Victor
laughed.

'You don't have to know,' he said. 'You just have to decide one way or another and argue it.'

The lecture theatre was like she imagined the football. A men's zone. Where were all the women? During the war – her formative years – women had been everywhere, doing all the jobs. Here, it felt like they had been tucked away, like figures in a cuckoo clock.

She tried to concentrate on the Tsar. The family were lined up against the wall. The revolutionaries showed them no mercy and then it all went wrong. Clara thought perhaps it had kind of gone wrong *before* then, but Victor was talking about how the ideals, the dreams, were turned to ruin. Every time he talked like this, even if it was about communism or the Revolution, Clara thought perhaps he was talking about the trajectory of his own life – and her heart went out to him. Had the same happened to her? She didn't think so. Or at least, there were some wonderful things to be found in the ruins: she thought of Peg's seashell and Maureen's last round of Dundee cake and couldn't help but smile.

During the short break, Clara went to find a lav, but although the gentlemen's were everywhere, the ladies' were miles away – it was like women and their needs didn't figure here. By the time she got back, Victor was lecturing again, Trotsky – or was it Tolstoy? She wasn't sure. She decided to wait outside.

Back in his study, she told him she'd enjoyed what she'd heard and he said, 'But did you *learn* anything?' and she said, 'Definitely yes,' cringing at the thought that he might test her. He said it was his favourite subject on the curriculum and she said she could tell.

She wished they were on the telephone or writing letters. There was something so awkward about him, about *them*, in real life. It was hard to put her finger on why. It was because it was new for both of them, perhaps.

Clara told him how old the students made her feel and he
laughed and said, 'Me too.' Then, turning serious, he said, 'But,
Clara, you *are* young – you could marry and have children... If
that was your dream.'

He was blushing.

'The thing is – actually – I don't want children of my own,'
Clara said quietly. Acknowledging it to herself was refreshing.
But acknowledging it to others felt revolutionary.

He ran his fingers through his hair.

'I see...'

Clara proceeded. 'I just thought, if we are to... get into a
relationship (*had she overshot terribly here? How mortifying if
she had*), then it's only fair to let you know where I stand.'

She had wondered – showing her *Breakfast in Bed*, telling
her she looked like the woman in the painting, was it a coded
message perhaps? Was it – *I want you to look like the woman in
the painting?*

Victor paused for what felt like forever. Then he said, 'I feel
blessed to have Bernard. I would probably have liked more children ten years ago, but not now. I'm at a different stage in my
life and politically, I see it as wrong to bring children in the
world when so many are suffering. Better to do something for
those already here rather than reproduce. For me, I mean. Can't
speak for anyone else.'

He had taken her hand in his. 'So, if that's what you're
suggesting, it's no barrier to being in a relationship with you.'

Tears prickled Clara's eyes. It was a risk to be honest, but it
had paid off.

When he said, 'May I kiss you, Clara?' she nodded. She had
been waiting for this. Last time in the gallery garden had been a
brilliant taster – this time she was hoping for the main course.
She was leaned against the bookshelf and she felt quite knocked
out by his proximity and even more so by his lips on hers. It was
lovely. She decided to take the bull by the horns, as it were.

'I'm seeing a doctor next week.'

'What's wrong?'

'Nothing... birth control?'

He looked surprised, then flustered. Why did he have to look so surprised? It embarrassed her. Was she being too forward? Was she presuming the kisses would lead there when in fact they would not? Did he perhaps think she was a virgin? Or that she was an only-after-marriage girl? That ship had long sailed. She was twenty-seven now – she had lived through the Blitz! How did he think they'd got through those long terrible nights?

'Oh, I see,' he said, collecting himself. 'Splendid.'

Still, she wondered, as they kissed again, should she go back to the doctor who had seen to her before? She had travelled to a neighbouring town and given a false name. Now she would need *another* town and *another* name, which seemed excessive. She couldn't go to Dr Cardew though. He and Anita were lovely, but sometimes you had to draw a line between your friendship and your private things.

She was still figuring this out when Victor pulled back from her, saying, 'You have to go, don't you, Clara? Can we continue this another time? I need to pave the way for the Reichstag fire.'

She did have to go, but she had anticipated leaving at two, not one. It felt like she had been having a marvellous warm bath and now was being hauled out of the water. She felt let down – and then ashamed, because she had no right to be.

Victor didn't seem in a hurry to get to the next stage. Despite the kissing, he had kept his hands to himself both times. Maybe times had changed. Perhaps the frantic *can't-get-enough-of-you* days were over. Maybe urgency belonged in wartime.

On the train back to the Grange, Clara let out a sigh and unless the woman opposite had read her mind, she couldn't have known what Clara was thinking; *Clara* hardly knew what she was thinking! But still she looked up and chuckled and said, 'I know how you feel,' which made Clara laugh too.

It *would be* a shame, though, if they had to give up on all that.

29

A few days later, Clara managed another day out without the children: Peter had said yes to meeting the comic people.

'What changed your mind, Peter?'

It wasn't Ivor. After she'd sent the letter to the Wales address, Maureen had announced airily, 'Didn't I tell you? Ivor's moved again. No, I don't know where. Somewhere warmer, I expect.'

Clara decided Ivor and Ruby would have gone to the French Riviera. She couldn't get it out of her head. Ruby would have insisted on it. Ruby wasn't a two-up, two-down in Pembrokeshire, Ruby was St Tropez beaches. Ruby would be marching around in one of those two-piece swimsuits the girls wore nowadays that Clara would never dream of wearing.

It wasn't Clara who had changed Peter's mind either. Shamefully, she had been so full of worry about the sale, Evelyn's mother and Victor that she had hardly had a moment to think about Peter and his comics.

Peter shrugged. 'After you said we were going to have to leave the Grange, I realised that it's natural to move on and it's going to be okay.'

Clara blinked at him. *How grown-up*, she thought. She was glad now that she'd told the children. What was the use of telling them she was honest and then withholding things from them?

For the meeting, Peter was wearing long trousers and a tie that made him look older than he usually did. Clara feared she looked older too; she was wearing a pleated dress that Anita could no longer fit into. After her visit to Oxford, Clara had felt she needed to improve her image. The dress wasn't her usual style, but Rita, who noticed fashion, said she looked dreamy, Joyce said approvingly, 'Very modern, Miss Newton,' and Maureen said, in what might have been a jibe but it wasn't worth confronting her over, 'Wow, who's the lucky fella this time?'

On the train, Peter was monosyllabic – probably from nerves? – and stared at the comics in his lap, some he had read and some he had written. She looked at them over his shoulder. His work was wonderful; his drawings were similar to some of the published comics, but they were different too. Clara thought they were better!

'There are loads of cafes, restaurants, pubs and dance halls; it's a lively area where the office is,' Clara said, willing Peter to show some enthusiasm. He was too young for most of that but he nodded anyway.

They left the station and followed a map. It was a shame they didn't have someone who knew the city to show them around. Clara's father might have been in London, but there was no way he would have wanted to act as a guide for them and there was no way Clara would have asked. Peter told her off for holding the map upside down. They ate spam sandwiches on a bench in a square. Peter sat as far from her as possible. He had by now given up speaking entirely. And then it was time.

The office was full of bustle and hustle: Great posters hanging from steel frames, rows of ten, twenty people. Lots of laughter, lots of chat. A ceiling fan ineffectually blew cigar smoke around.

People dashing, yes, *dashing* over to study paints. Arguing about the colour of someone's shoes: 'They were black last week!' Admiring someone's drawing of a nose: 'You've captured the nostrils perfectly!' There was an urgency to the place; you would have thought you were in the emergency ward of a hospital and they were trying to save lives. As they stood there, amazed, a man in a shirt – no tie – raced over to them.

'The superhero twins – was that you?' He was grinning broadly. He had one eye missing, Clara noted. His moustache was thick and luscious, unlike the hair on his head.

'Y-yes,' stammered Peter. But he managed to shake the man's hand and introduce himself, as Clara had taught him. 'Peter Downey, Sir, pleased to meet you.'

A handsome man with his feet – with his actual shoes – on his desk, smoking a cigar, sat up. Next to him was an ashtray that needed emptying.

'Helllooo,' he called to Peter. 'You're younger than we thought.'

So are you, thought Clara.

'And blimey,' he continued, 'is this your sister?'

'And this,' interrupted the one-eyed man wryly, 'is the office Casanova.'

Clara, who hadn't been flirted with for some time (unless talking about Lenin was flirting), laughed before reminding herself, *This is Peter's circus.*

'I'm Clara Newton, a friend,' she said because she imagined Peter didn't want anyone to know he lived in a children's home. He hated anyone to feel sorry for him.

'Miss Newton is my housemother.' Peter surprised her. 'I live in a children's home.'

The men were surprised too. They looked at each other

with something unspoken and then one-eyed man said, 'That *is* impressive.'

And handsome man said, 'Extra-impressive; I mean – that's the kind of tale we love here... Overcoming adversity, triumph...'

'That's what many of our favourite stories are about.'

Clara didn't know how Peter would react to being called a story, but his face didn't betray anything. The men showed them round the office; some people jumped up, some called out hello. One man stayed seated, gaze glued to his paper, chewing manically, waving Churchill's two-fingered salute at them.

Peter was transfixed. 'I'd be doing this every day? All day long?'

'*Dandy, Beano.* Kids and teens. We're ambitious,' said the one-eyed man, who Clara had rapidly warmed to. He seemed gentle. 'We want to make a feature out of your cartoon strip. You've got fabulous ideas; I see them being as popular as Desperate Dan. You've certainly got your finger on the pulse.'

The handsome man looked at Clara. 'He's the age of most of our readers. That's a real positive here.' Clara would have pointed out that Peter wasn't much younger than him, but he made her rather tongue-tied.

The one-eyed man said, 'The woman with forty-eight hours in the day is funny. My wife loved it especially. And we adore Nathaniel the Spaniel.'

'Brilliant.' The handsome man was even more handsome when he smiled. He reminded her of Michael suddenly; the same even teeth.

Clara turned to see that Peter was looking shell-shocked.

'The incredible fish are delightful – need work, but we've never had fish characters before.'

'And the girl who lost her voice? How charming was that?'

Clara burst out laughing. *Pe-ter! Was she based on Peg?*

Peter shrugged. He was now tomato-red. She could feel the heat coming off him.

'This boy can draw.'

'It's rare,' said the one-eyed man. 'Usually people are proficient at one or the other, drawing or ideas. Peter here excels at both.'

The handsome man clapped. Clara was reminded again of Michael – he too had once been so full of enthusiasm and encouragement. Her heart ached.

'We definitely want you, Peter,' said the handsome man. 'But you'll be working on other strips too. For a start, before you get your own.'

'We've got accommodation blocks out the back. It's basic but you will have your own room.'

'Which is more than you have now,' interjected Clara, breaking her own rule of letting Peter speak.

'And you'll be in the heart of the city.'

Everyone looked at Peter.

Peter paused and then in a small voice, he said, 'I can't believe it!'

At Lavenham station, still euphoric, Peter and Clara went over it. After some negotiation, it was decided Peter would join at the end of October just after his sixteenth birthday.

'I'm afraid it's just a dream!'

Clara pinched him.

'Ow,' he said.

'There, you're not dreaming.'

Peter suddenly went red to the roots of his hair. Turning to see the source of his embarrassment, Clara saw the art assistant from Peter's school. She was wearing jean dungarees, her hair was in a knot, her lips were bright red – she had a look of Rosie the Riveter. *Peculiar,* thought Clara, or *cool?* The two often overlapped.

'Hi, Peter. Where've you been today?'

Six-foot-two Peter towered over her, but his body language said he was tiny. 'London, uh, I won the contest at the comic place. I'm going to work with them from when I'm sixteen... I've signed a contract and...'

'I told you!' The girl was gloriously excited; she squealed, patted him on the back. 'Oh Peter!' she said, 'You did it!'

'Yeah,' he said, flicking his hair. 'Unexpected, right?' He blushed over his blush. 'I wasn't sure whether to go for it, but...' His voice was deep when he said that.

Clara felt like saying, 'Aren't you going to introduce me?' but decided not to. That was probably another saying that was old hat.

'It's in Soho and there are loads of cafes nearby... it's really lively.'

The girl sighed in admiration. 'Oh, I'm jealous.'

Well, thought Clara. *well, well*.

Peter and the young woman were still staring at each other when the train rolled in.

'Your train...?' Clara reminded the girl eventually when she showed no sign of moving.

'Oh, thank you! See you later, Peter...'

'Definitely.' They watched the girl get on; Peter was beaming. She pulled down the grimy window and waved until she was out of sight.

'Good day, huh?' Clara said.

'Uh-huh.'

Peter would be okay.

30

There was a dead animal on the high road just outside the Grange. For a horrible moment Clara feared it was Stella, but thank goodness, it was a fox, a poor young fox, blood everywhere. Someone must have run it over and then just left it. The thought enraged Clara and made her sad too.

Who would have done that? Julian was careless and self-centred, but he didn't speed and he also cleared up his own messes, *generally*. Clara got out newspapers – it was fortunate, she had enough of them, towers of them – and wrapped up the blessed thing. The task brought tears to her eyes. *Be strong. Worse things happened in the war.* It was just so sudden, that painful salutary thought: one moment little fox was probably sniffing out some food; the next: all over.

She buried it in the garden. She had just come back into the house and was washing her hands when there was a knock on the door and there stood Victor, stern as a telegram boy.

'Clara, I need to talk to you.'

It wasn't a good time. Dead fox on her mind. Victor was from a different world and it felt like an interruption. She invited him in though. What else could she do?

They had spoken twice on the telephone since her university visit. She had already told him about the comic place and Peter's idea: the woman with forty-eight hours in a day – surely it was based on her? Victor had chortled and it was wonderful, the sound of his laughter: free as a bird. He said he was wiping his eyes, it was that funny, but then he said, 'Oh, Iris,' so Clara knew he wasn't thinking about her. But hadn't she done the same thing once, when she spoke Michael's name while in a clinch with Ivor?

She felt nervous that Victor might be going to ditch her; and that told her that although she was put out by this impromptu visit, she liked him more than she had thought she did. He pushed back his hair, even though it wasn't in his eyes.

'I am growing attached to you.'

Attached. There it was, that word again.

'Oh!' Despite herself, Clara smiled. *So this was good news?*

'I have to tell you – I'm moving to Oxford. The travel is too much.'

O-kay. So this is why he's been reading the property papers?

'What about Bernard?'

'I will probably take him out of school and put him in a grammar there.'

Poor Alex. He had never had a best friend before. He would miss Bernard awfully. The two were inseparable.

'I see.'

It wasn't this that Victor was worrying about though.

'I was wondering – is the distance too much... for us?'

'It's only up the road...' Clara felt flabbergasted. It was a couple of hours away. 'And Victor, as you know, we will be moving soon too. All of us. Not far, but...'

'I felt I should tell you before we... before you-know...'

Clara winced.

'What we discussed the other day?' he went on.

'I don't see how this changes anything, Victor? Unless you want it to.'

He leaned over and kissed her on the lips. 'I'm an idiot, aren't I?'

'Sssh.'

I am moving on, she told herself. *Just like Ivor did.* Ivor who was no longer in Wales but swanning around somewhere exotic, probably the South of France. Ivor-the-married.

She wished she hadn't just found the fox.

There was something else. Victor suddenly whipped open his briefcase and handed her his property paper.

'The other thing is, Clara, I came across this...'

Shilling Grange is a fine Tudor-style mansion set in the attractive high street in the pretty town of Lavenham.

Sitting on a large corner plot with well-established gardens, Shilling Grange boasts four upstairs rooms, including two large rooms currently used as dormitories, one bedroom and bathroom. Downstairs is a substantial kitchen and parlour, and multi-unit bathrooms.

Viewing Advised. Place of historical interest. While the property needs some attention, there is potential to convert into a hotel, restaurant, school, entertainment venue or other. Currently used as a council-run children's home.

Plans, views, deeds and price on application.

Clara was startled; she couldn't help it. This made it real. Nothing tangible had changed so far, so at times she could forget that the council had these plans. This showed that the

move was still on the horizon. Victor put his arm round her as
she read, but at that moment, she wanted him to take it away.

'Hoh,' she stuttered. Here it was. It was happening.

'Are there only four upstairs rooms?' Victor enquired.

'Ha,' she said. She remembered the quiz she had taken:
mostly D's, 'Home is where your heart is'.

'As long as we're together,' she said, and Victor looked
nervous again.

'The children, I mean – we could live in an igloo for all I
care!' She was trying to laugh but tears were rolling down her
cheeks now. It was the shock of the fox, she told herself. Little
unsuspecting fox, just trying to get home. 'An igloo might be
cold though.'

Victor was looking concernedly at her now, so she pulled
herself together, gave him a comforting squeeze: 'I'm fine.
Thank you for letting me know. See you next week.'

31

'Maureen's not in our room,' Rita announced early the next morning, but Clara knew she must be. She ran up. Usually Maureen was to be found shouting, slamming doors. She definitely hadn't slept in the bed last night though. Had she got back together with Joe? Clara found herself hoping that was the case. But Joe had handed back the key to Ivor's a long time ago, so where would they be?

Fretfully, Clara ran outside, but there was no sign, no clues there either.

She was cooking porridge, fretting, planning, when Maureen swung in just before six.

'Where *have* you been?'

'Out.'

'Where?'

Maureen had done this last year too, but she'd never stayed out all night. She used to hang around at the graveyards or in empty flats above shops.

'I didn't think you'd be up,' Maureen said.

Clara found she was pointing a wooden spoon at her. 'I asked you where?'

Maureen was the picture of laid-back insouciance.

'Mr Browne has a flat nearby, for when he's working late. He says I should stay there rather than disturb you. It's more comfortable too.'

Clara couldn't look at her.

'Alone?'

'Of course, alone! What do you think?'

'I don't think you should be spending so much time with Mr Browne.'

'He treats me well.'

Clara couldn't breathe. *Don't fly off the handle.* That sweaty man. That friend of Julian.

'He's fifty.'

Maureen yawned. 'Actually, he's only forty-eight.'

Only! Clara wanted to roar.

'People will talk.' (This was the least of her worries but it was the only one Clara seemed capable of putting into words right then.)

'I don't care.'

'What do you mean, you don't care?'

'I just said he treats me well, that's all. Miss Newton, the money helps. It's not like you don't have any male friends, is it?'

Clara saw Julian on the high road later that same morning and petted her old pal, Bandit, as Julian blethered on about his party the previous night. They'd had a band – the same band they'd had at the engagement, remember? Yes; Clara blushed, yes, she *did* remember – and the canapés were out of this world.

'Jimsy fell into the buffet table.'

Clara, who was already tense, stiffened further with disapproval. The fact that Julian was friends with Peter's uncle would never not be a sore point.

'I can't see how you can socialise with him. He's a disgusting person, Julian.'

'He drinks too much, I'll give you that. He had a hard war.'

Ivor was badly hurt in the war and he didn't drink too much. Nor, come to that, did Victor. Victor never talked about his experiences in France, but he alluded to them sometimes in his letters, and reading between the lines, he had an awful time.

'We're in the same club,' Julian continued. 'You know how it is—'

'No, I don't.'

'You had your chance.' Julian winked at Clara, oblivious to her mood. That's what he always said recently: 'You had your chance to have a say in my life. You had your chance to laugh about my hair.'

'Have you noticed anything going on with Browne and Maureen?' she asked.

'Maureen?' Julian raised an eyebrow.

'You know who Maureen is, Julian.' *Don't pretend.*

'It's not my business,' he chortled. 'Nor is it yours.'

'It absolutely IS my business,' Clara stuttered self-righteously. 'She's in my charge and she's underage.'

'Only just.'

Only just?!

'She's being used.' *Like an old sock.*

'Oh, Clara, just because you're not walking out with...' Julian looked at her face. 'Oh, you ARE now... Still with Victor Braithwaite, is it? Goodness, this *is* a long-running romance for you.'

'This is not about me.'

'We had a considerable age gap too, remember?'

Clara blushed. 'But we were at similar life stages. That's the difference.'

'Doesn't look like it from my perspective.'

'Maybe. That was wrong too, Julian. But this is even worse.'

She paused. Mr Browne was also a married man. Clara knew she couldn't say that though, she just couldn't. Julian would only respond with something hurtful about Ivor and he'd be right.

'I have responsibility for Maureen.'

'You're not responsible for her work though or her friendships.'

'Not officially, but morally, I am. There is no one else.'

'Morally...' Julian laughed like the idea was a joke. 'Clara Newton takes on the world.'

'Not the world, just...' she groped for a word, failed, 'men like Browne.'

'I'm serious, Clara. I know nothing. And even if I did, you must stop trying to fix everyone. Anyway, she's looking after his boy.'

Clara's shoulders slumped. 'Is that true?'

Julian laughed. 'Yes. Mrs Browne had an operation recently and Maureen is taking the boy out, helping with his schoolwork. God knows the little sod needs all the help he can get.'

Julian disappointed her every time she saw him. Not superficially; on the surface they could usually have an enjoyable time. It was a deep-down disappointment. He had always minimised what Peter went through. He said it was 'a fuss about nothing'. More fool her for having had high hopes of him.

And Clara, who had never been political before, felt a growing sense of injustice. It was not just that Julian entertained these men, but also that he had no qualms about it. Peter's uncle. Mr Browne. It was a giant men's club – and she and the children were just like toys to them.

She did talk to Miss Cooper; Clara went to her office in the council building. Miss Cooper was cramped on one side of the desk and if you were sat at the other side, you couldn't open the glass door. On the wall were hanging clipboards, and a map of Suffolk; it seemed ancient – Clara couldn't imagine it was helpful. The drawing pins denoted children's homes, but apart from that, it was mostly fields and churches. There was also a drawing of a cartoon bird with a massive beak, which seemed massively out of place. There were stacks and stacks of card folders on every surface and on one there was a photograph of Miss Cooper, her head thrown back in laughter.

Miss Cooper was a woman of such elan, in her closely fitting trouser suits – Clara knew no one else who wore them – so it was unexpected that she should care so little about the state of her workspace.

'Do you think Maureen is being exploited by this man?' asked Miss Cooper, her fountain pen poised over her clipboard.

'I don't know...' Clara tried not to think that Miss Bridges was better at things like this, but throughout the conversation, the way Miss Bridges would react seemed to haunt her.

'You could move her away?' suggested Miss Cooper.

Move her away?

'Maybe with nuns. I could see if there are any spaces up North?'

Send Maureen hundreds of miles away to live with nuns? Nuns who might be like the bullying Sister Eunice? *Whip them when they wet!* Clara felt sure the damage would outweigh the good. She knew she had given Maureen too much freedom, but she didn't want to imprison her now. She needed to know how she could roll it back – and of course, whatever she tried, Maureen would resist.

'Just keep an eye on her,' advised Miss Cooper.

Less than an hour later, as Clara was still digesting this unsatisfactory meeting, she walked by the not-very-good playground and there they were: Maureen pushing a whey-faced, spherical boy of about ten, who was standing up on the swing and shrieking.

'This is Martin Browne,' Maureen said pointedly.

Martin Browne! Clara could have squeezed the little pudding. So he *did* exist and Maureen *was* looking after him. It was a misunderstanding. She had grown paranoid, what with the Peter thing and the Judy thing.

'Hoh!' she said delightedly and Maureen rolled her eyes. 'What are you two doing next?'

'I have to go and make Martin his tea,' Maureen said, again with the pointed look: *see.*

'Not in the office?' Clara was feeling so jolly she would have offered tea herself, only it wouldn't stretch. The boy looked like he had an appetite that would put Evelyn to shame. He had chunky white legs under his grey shorts and chubby red cheeks. He ignored Clara and said to Maureen, 'Swing me again.'

'Not today,' said Maureen, 'tomorrow.'

'Good girl.' Clara patted her shoulder. *Lovely Maureen.* 'Pleased to meet you, Martin!'

As Clara walked away grinning like a cartoon character, she heard him say, 'She's mad!'

ARTICLE FOR THE *SHILLING GRANGE NEWS,* MARCH 1950

Best canapé recipe by Maureen

Cut bread into squares, diamonds and triangles. Put in the oven until golden. Put devilled ham on top followed by grated cheese and wait for it to melt. The smell is heavenly. Your party guests will love this.

32

Clara buried her precautions in her handbag under a handkerchief and Victor's book on communism. The thought of the children discovering them, while looking for her purse maybe, made her palms sweaty. It had been some time since Clara had been intimate with a man – was it like a bicycle? – hopefully it wasn't; Clara, unlike many of her contemporaries, was not a great one for cycling. She had her mother's weak calves.

Victor was taking her out for dinner and then on to a hotel. A hotel conveniently near to the restaurant. When he told her on the telephone she had nearly died. How embarrassing! Would he like her? She always dressed with care to see him but even so, she was no match for the winsome girls he must see every day at the university. She was fading. And she wasn't fading from a position of beauty either. She was fading from just being a nice-looking lass. There was something about looking after children that made you fade, she thought, before telling herself not to be silly: Michael had adored her. Ivor said she had the kindest eyes.

Clara was too nervous to eat breakfast on the morning of the

date, but Anita came over with macaroons. She said she had
been cooking like a demon all week. She looked paler than
usual but as exquisitely turned out as ever; her hair groomed,
her pearl beads at her throat. *You would have thought she was
the one going on a special date*, thought Clara despondently.

'I hate being fat,' Anita said as she lowered herself into a
kitchen chair.

'Fat!' scoffed Clara, as was expected. 'You look wonderful.'

Dr Cardew was at a conference in London for arthritis.
Anita said she didn't mind being alone. She couldn't sleep and
she was keeping him awake and feeling guilty about that and
'oh, it is only a few days'. Miss Smith was a wonder. Anita kept
saying it. 'I don't know how we'd manage without her. Honestly,
Clara, she's an angel, a godsend.' And then she thanked Clara,
even though Clara had nothing to do with it – and privately,
hadn't thought it was a good idea.

Joyce walked in with Peter and they both greeted Anita
warmly. They were better with guests than they used to be.
Especially guests who came bearing macaroons.

They were good at the weather questions Clara had drilled
them on.

'How was your journey?' Joyce smiled beatifically.

'I only live down the road, Joyce,' responded Anita,
bemused. 'As you know.'

Joyce whispered to Clara that she wanted to take a photograph. You could understand why; Anita Cardew looked glorious, that full round belly facing north like a snow globe in her
lap, her face full and dreamy. The Madonna in a church.

Anita overheard. 'Nooo,' she said firmly, 'not in this state,'
and Joyce went away disappointed, but she didn't kick up a fuss
and for that, Clara was grateful. Peter followed her away, he
was working on his comic strip.

'You do look beautiful though,' Clara said, once the children
had left. 'What's the word? "Blooming"?'

Anita shook her head, exasperated by this nonsense, then said she'd seen Maureen in the street with a child.

'That's the Browne boy,' Clara said confidently. 'She looks after him sometimes. Apparently, he's an affable child, considering.'

'I see.' Anita was not interested. 'I was worried he was a new one of yours. Right, tell me the latest about the house.'

'I told the children...'

'How did they take it?'

'Better than I thought they would. I reassured them and—'

'Have you seen some of the "purpose-builds?"' Anita pronounced purpose-builds like it was a mammal.

'They haven't shown me anywhere yet but maybe soon.'

Anita suddenly paled. Just as Clara was about to respond, *it's not that bad, they'll keep us together,* Anita got to her feet, then made a strange meowing sound.

Her beige skirt darkened suddenly. And she yelped, 'This is from Selfridges!'

Clara found she was too shocked to stand up. Stella came in, followed by Evelyn. As she saw Anita, Evelyn turned her attention away from the cat and said knowledgeably, 'Ooh! That's her waters breaking!'

Clara's stomach turned, but Evelyn was beaming. 'How many weeks are you, Missus?' she asked, and then she clapped her hands together and looked brightly at Clara. 'Looks like baby wants out!'

When neither Anita nor Clara replied, she continued in the same cheerful tone, 'Want me to fetch Dr Cardew?'

Gripping the table, Anita muttered, 'He's in London.' Her eyes were closed and she was breathing strangely. 'C-c-conference. Arthritis.'

'How can we get hold of him?' Clara was surprised at how collected she sounded. She had to, she supposed, for Anita's sake. Inside, though, she was petrified.

The table was beginning to shake. 'R-r-r-un to my house.' Anita fumbled in her massive bag for her keys. Her breaths were deep and ragged. 'The number is on my h-h-all table near the phone... Call the conference, tell him – come straight back.'

'I'll get Peter to do it,' Clara decided quietly, then went to the bottom of the stairs and bellowed. *Perhaps I should go*, she thought, but she couldn't leave Anita, not now.

'Hurry,' hissed Anita.

'Yes, go, Peter,' said Clara, once she'd explained his task. 'And get Miss Smith to come right away too,' she added. Today was the day when Evelyn's mother could prove to her daughter what a godsend she was.

'She's not there,' said Anita through gritted teeth. 'I gave her the d-d-ay off.'

For goodness' sake.

'There will be time,' Clara said confidently. Then looking at Anita, she thought, *will there?* 'Let's get you to the hospital.'

'No. Stay here.'

'Plenty of time,' repeated Clara.

'Ooh, I don't think there is,' chirruped Evelyn, eyes shining. 'Baby mightn't wait.'

Clara sneezed. 'I'll get the cat out,' she said. That was one thing she could do.

Peter ran back with the best news. 'Dr Cardew had already left,' he said. He was out of puff.

Clara felt she could punch the air. 'Brilliant!'

Even so, Evelyn was rolling up her sleeves, merry as a docker.

'I'll go up to the station in ten minutes,' Peter huffed, squinting at the clock, 'grab him and bring him straight here.'

Evelyn continued. 'Don't worry, I've done this before.' Clara gawped at her. She couldn't believe it – and yet somehow she did. Evelyn wasn't a liar – and one thing she always talked about was her affection for babies.

'Wait – done what?' Anita pulled herself up on her elbows.

'Delivered babies.'

'Aiiieee. How many?'

'Two.' Evelyn washed her hands at the kitchen sink, then disappeared. 'Just getting towels.'

'How old is she really?' Anita yelped at Clara. She was coming undone; her hair was falling away from the stern clips, her blouse had ridden up out of its waistband. Poor Anita.

Sometimes a lie is a kindness. Plus, Evelyn *did* look older, had done from day one. 'F-Fourteen.'

'She is NOT.'

Joyce peeped round the door, looking horrified. *How quickly the scene had transformed itself*, thought Clara. Just minutes ago, she was pulling up Joyce on her manners; now the kitchen had turned into a... a what? A maternity ward?

Evelyn bustled back with clean towels and a blanket; she was super-efficient, like the experienced matron of a busy hospital. She didn't even look nervous.

'Get on the floor, Mrs Cardew,' she commanded.

'I'm staying here,' Anita said angrily, but then, yelping, she did get on the floor; to Clara's astonishment, she got on all fours like an animal.

Evelyn ducked down alongside her. 'Nothing to worry about,' she said. Then she went to Anita's other end and shouted, 'I think I can see it, Miss Newton. Now breathe, that's it.'

Clara wanted to look but at the same time she didn't. She thought of Russian dolls and how she had lost her littlest one, her favourite one, that strange swaddled hourglass baby. The biggest was red and green, and Clara hadn't liked its expression. As for the others, she could barely remember them.

'What do you want me to do?' she asked Evelyn – the eleven-year-old.

Evelyn instructed her to dab Anita's forehead with a damp flannel. As soon as Clara tried to get near, though, Anita bellowed, 'Get away from me!'

Is that normal? wondered Clara. She thought briefly of Sister Eunice, and the nuns at school, and the first time she'd heard the facts of life and how, even back then, she had thought, *I don't think I want to do that.* She was sure she remembered them saying, 'The first baby can be slow. You might be in labour for some days.'

Clara knelt by Anita's head but made sure not to touch her. Anita called for her husband. 'Benjamin...!' Evelyn was in her element. 'That's it, Mrs Cardew, breathe, you're doing it.' And Clara was just petrified. What if there was a complication? Oh, please don't let there be.

Clara thought Evelyn's advice to breathe was superfluous, but Anita was now copying her, puffing away like she was playing an exotic instrument. Clara wanted to close her eyes as she'd seen the children do in moments of stress. She closed them for a moment but then Anita let out an especially disturbing roar.

The baby's head was out. It looked obscene. Good grief. Surely there must be a better way? There was Anita and between her legs, there was a head. And Anita, that impeccable self-contained woman, was now pure nature, animal instinct. Would she ever be prim, fashionable Anita again?

All of the baby was out. Should it be purple? Clara gaped. It was a squirmy fat fish of a thing, she thought of eels wriggling in a barrel. It was naked, obviously, with... with large privates.

Clara was frozen. Heavens. Evelyn didn't seem perturbed by any of it. In fact, she seemed delighted. She smacked the baby's bottom and it yelled out and Anita collapsed onto the floor. She wept a waterfall of tears. Evelyn deftly wrapped the baby up in a towel and when Anita was helped over to a chair, she laid it on Anita's chest. The baby – or it might have been Anita – mewled. Clara sank back into a chair. The back door was flung open and it wouldn't have surprised her if the Loch Ness Monster appeared and if Evelyn took control of that too

'Oh, my darling,' Dr Cardew cried. He dropped his bag where he stood. His coat was half off. His eyes were full of tears. Standing behind him were two breathless figures. One was Peter, peeping in nervously, his sweet, freckled face all hopeful. The other was dark-eyed Ivor.

Clara fainted.

33

When Clara came round, there was a tartan blanket, scratchy over her knees, a cup of lukewarm tea in front of her. Evelyn was stood at the kettle, making more tea and regaling everyone with stories. Joyce had her camera round her neck.

Oh no, thought Clara, *she hadn't, had she?*

Where were the grown-ups?

'We moved Mrs Cardew to the parlour,' Evelyn said brightly. 'She's more comfortable there. You were out sparko, Miss Newton.'

Clara gulped. She was not usually squeamish, but this had been something different entirely and— Was Ivor here? Had he ever been here? Had she hallucinated that – had any of it happened? Peter was mopping the floor. She shrugged the blanket off and stood up. She was still light-headed. She knocked on the parlour door – for the first time ever – and someone called out 'come in'. She was unsure what was real and what wasn't. Anita was on the sofa, her blouse undone, a great bald baby pressed to her. Doctor Cardew was fussing around them both.

He turned round when he saw her. His eyes were shining,

and she thought she had never seen him so human, and then she thought, insensibly, *is this what it is?* And somehow, she felt as terrified as she had when the baby was on its way.

'Sorry to be a nuisance, Clara.'

'Not at all.' She was still trembling. What was the matter with her? Anita was weary and radiant at the same time; she was the sun and the storm. Her cheeks were red and her eyes were shining.

'Have you met Howard Cardew? We're naming him after Anita's father.'

As Evelyn came in with a tray of tea, it seemed to Clara that she was no longer a child. She had skipped ten years.

'And we thought we'd ask the midwife for a middle name.'

The midwife?

Evelyn blushed. She considered for a moment and then announced that she had always thought the name Geoffrey was dreamy.

Clara eyed them. She couldn't decide if it was a joke. Or was it a dream? She'd wake up and she would be sitting in the kitchen, waiting for Anita to drop by with some plums.

'What do you think, Clara?' said Dr Cardew. 'Howard Geoffrey Cardew.'

'It suits him. He's a beautiful thing,' Clara said, as expected. In fact, she thought it was surprising that a couple as attractive as Anita and Dr Cardew could have produced this angry scarlet ball. He did have lovely eyelashes and sweet eyebrows – funny that a baby should have eyebrows, of all things! – but give him a cigar and – did they not realise it? – they might have been swaddling a teeny-tiny Winston Churchill.

It didn't seem right to ask if Ivor had been there or if she'd imagined him. She concentrated on the baby's tiny features, his gripping fists, his dark eyes.

She wanted to say, 'We will fight them on the beaches,' but

she guessed they would never forgive her. Instead she said, 'He looks like he's seen it all before.'

'He probably has,' said Evelyn, nodding sagely.

Sister Grace arrived and joined Evelyn in the bustling around and tea-making. Efficient Sister Grace was perfect on occasions like this. Then the newspapers that were waiting for delivery on Joyce's wagon were flung onto the pavement, Anita and Howard, wrapped in a blanket, were installed and taken off home.

It almost looked biblical. Clara *hadn't* imagined it, had she? The Three Wise Men appearing at the birth. She laughed to herself: *three stooges, more like.*

The workshop light was on. It *was* Ivor, wasn't it, this time?

Clara excused herself. Evelyn and Sister Grace were deep in conversation about the birth. There was no point tidying herself up – she had to know. She was still feeling shaky as she walked over to the workshop, although she told herself not to be so darn stupid. He was only a man.

Peg was on his lap. Rita had her arms round his neck, Maureen – when did she get here? – Peter and the twins, gathered excitedly around him, like ants on a picnic blanket. She wouldn't forgive him so quickly: Over six months without a word? More like seven months, in fact. How the hell do you explain that? Billy was telling him about the time he had fended off three attackers, two defenders and scored, top right, but he trailed off when he noticed Clara.

Everyone looked up.

'Ivor's here!' Rita squealed.

'I can see that!' Tears had sprung to her eyes and she wiped at them hastily: *good grief.*

Where was she then, his Ruby? That sophisticated woman

who Clara had only met once, briefly, but who was imprinted into her consciousness.

'Hello, Clara,' Ivor said softly.

No sign of her, the wife, no sign of anyone else either: Ivor was back on his own.

'What a day to return...' he said.

'Ah,' she said, then sneezed. She saw Stella sitting on a pile of cloth. Even the cat had come to pay homage. Ivor was like the Pied Piper.

'I saw Dr Cardew and Peter running from the station and I thought... one of you lot must be hurt. And now we have a new resident of Lavenham!'

What about Ruby, the other new resident? Clara thought miserably. *Where was she?*

The children talked over each other. Rita was boasting about the music she could play: 'Mrs Cardew says I'm better than her now. She says that I'll be the jewel in the Festival of Britain—'

'The Festival of Britain, eh?' Ivor repeated.

Clara patted her hair impatiently.

'What happened to your arm, Mister?' interrupted Joyce, who could never let Rita blow her trumpet. 'It's not there.'

'What?' Ivor patted his sleeve. 'It was there this morning!'

Joyce was uncertain at first, then grinned broadly. 'You're joking, aren't you, Mister? How did it happen?'

'Sssh, Joyce,' said Clara. 'That's not polite.'

'I'm afraid it got blown off,' said Ivor. He had always been as honest with kids as kids were to him. It was one of the reasons they liked him, thought Clara. She too tried to be honest, but she was often torn between that dreadful dilemma: be nice or be honest? He didn't have such qualms – maybe men didn't. They could say what they liked, and people didn't hate them for it, because men are men.

'In the war?'

'Exactly.'

Joyce nodded thoughtfully. 'I've got bad legs,' she told him. 'Not because of the war though. Because of the polio. I am supposed to exercise.'

'And do you?' he asked. It was a reminder of how caring he was. Clara couldn't help gazing at him; then, remembering herself, she looked away. *Did he have no idea how much she had missed him?*

Joyce wrinkled up her nose. 'Sometimes.' She looked at Clara. 'I want to take a photo of his arm.'

'Some other time, hey?' Ivor said diplomatically.

Lovely as it was to see him interacting with the children, Clara was desperate to get Ivor on his own. Where had he been all this time? Ruby might be down any moment: high-quality green coat, brooch, styled hair. She anticipated what she'd do. She'd have to hold out her hand. She should not curtsey. She'd say something casual like, 'Oh hi, we meet properly at last!'

Good grief, not that.

'Oh hello, we've been looking forward—'

No, not that either.

She'd just be nice. *Of course* she'd be nice. She'd be nice rather than honest.

'Hello, hope you had a pleasant journey.'

That was it, fine.

She looked around at them all. Peter, the opposite of Rita, had to be cajoled by Ivor to tell his story. And Peg just sat clinging onto him, like he was her shell.

Ivor looked up at Clara, and their eyes met, and it was boom, straight away, back to how it was. His eyes, that melting chocolate brown, locked into hers and she could have been anywhere. 'It's good to see you.'

For all her plans to give him no leeway, to punish him, she couldn't help but smile back.

'It's good to see you too.'

The workshop door swung open. Victor was at the entrance with Bernard and Alex, one on either side, each dangling from an arm. Oh gosh, she had forgotten! Today was the day. Their date, their *special* date in a restaurant near a hotel. It felt like they had planned it ages ago.

'Sorry to interrupt,' Victor said. He looked both puzzled and relieved to see her.

When Alex saw Ivor he ran over to him and jumped into his lap, shrieking, 'You're back. Why didn't you tell me? Can we go to the market again?'

'How's the little professor?' Ivor ruffled his hair. 'I missed you.'

'I'm top in maths, science and history. The teacher says I'm a born scholar. I'm bottom in music and art.'

'Someone's got to be.'

'And guess what? – I'm doing Latin!'

'*Ubi amor, ibi dolor*.'

'You know Latin?' Clara couldn't believe her ears.

'Only that. You all right, Clara?'

Clara was wobbling. She felt light-headed again. There was something about the two of them, Ivor and Victor, being in the same room that was hard to take in. It seemed wrong. Ivor shouldn't be here. She had got used to life without him. It was as if there was a show and if they were both, accidentally, on the stage at the same time, the illusion would crumble.

Victor shifted nervously from foot to foot. He swept back his hair, something Clara knew he also did when he was nervous.

'I'm sorry to interrupt this reunion, Clara. I'm ready when you are.'

'Thank you, Victor, yes. I'm almost ready.'

Clara could feel Ivor's eyes on them. She felt both torn and trapped. If only she'd been able to see him earlier. If only he'd written. She didn't know where she stood.

It was a shock, that was all. She could deal with it, it was just a shock.

She could see Ivor was thinking, *who is this man?*

This man is Victor. (And he was here when you weren't.)

She was still unsure on her feet.

'I'll... just pop back and get my bag.'

The bag – with its all-important contents.

Victor peered at his watch. Clara remembered that it was the last thing his late wife had given him. It was engraved with her name on the back. The man had experienced a lot of heartache. She must not add to it. He deserved better.

'You won't be long?' he said.

'Yes... No... of course, did you hear? Anita's baby was born today.'

'How wonderful. Tell me about it over dinner, darling. Nice to meet you, Mr...?'

'Delaney. Ivor.'

They shook hands. For too long. It was as though neither of them was prepared to let go.

34

Clara wanted to cancel. It was too much, wasn't it? – the baby, fainting, Ivor – she could see the headache coming from miles off. But she couldn't bring herself to cancel, she couldn't. In the car, Victor said, 'He seems a character,' and it seemed there was no room for her to say what she wanted to say and instead, stupidly, she blurted out, 'Who?'

Victor looked surprised. 'Your neighbour. Mr Delaney? Great workshop too.'

Clara had pushed the books from the passenger seat onto the floor. Her feet were resting on *1984* and her knees were shaking.

Victor didn't seem to register her turmoil and instead regaled her with stories about the university and his book. Faculties and vice chancellors – *was there ever a chancellor?* And the students. Victor was fond of the ones who had been to fight in the war. Less fond of those who had stayed at home. He didn't like the students who were Bolsheviks. It was something she hadn't thought about here in quiet Suffolk. He said, 'They're everywhere, Clara,' and she stared at his profile in surprise.

There was a lot of marble in the restaurant. She wondered what the Bolsheviks would think of that. Marble, mahogany tables and a polish smell. 'I like this place,' Victor said, and she lied and said she could see why.

This was meant to be their night. He said, 'You look lovely,' but she could only think about the precautions in her bag; she felt as if they were going off like a siren. Or like a wart on her nose. How could anyone not know they were there?

And after seeing dignified Anita like *that*, she was glad that they were there. She was going to have precautions in her bag until the end of days. It was like a superstitious thing to ward off the devil. But at the same time, it seemed wrong. And dirty. What would her mother say if she saw? And her father? Good grief!

Victor wanted to talk about the peanut scandal. He was disappointed in the government. Clara wondered if Victor had thought about what they should discuss at the restaurant, because she had, and peanuts had not featured highly. She certainly knew about the peanut scandal and she did agree with him, it was just, with the things in her bag, and the candles and... this was supposed to be a date, not a convention of the Anti-Bolshevik, Anti-peanut Front. Julian was rubbish but at least when they rendezvoused, they did rendezvous. And Ivor – well, with Ivor, they didn't need to think about talking.

They had just finished their orange juice starter when a man wearing a traditional suit came over and dived in, his hand out for a handshake. Clara thought he matched the room. He probably smelled of polish too. He gazed at Clara with interest, his eyes moving over her blouse.

'Who is this, Victor?'

'This is Miss Clara Newton,' said Victor smoothly.

'Are you one of our secretaries?'

'Miss Newton has an important role at Suffolk Council.'

Victor smiled at Clara and the affection in his eyes made her heart sink.

'Council worker?' he said. 'Well, well, well.'

Were three wells good or bad? Bad, Clara decided. Still the man lingered, his eyes roving over her.

'Glad to see you're moving on, Victor,' he said finally. 'About time.' He spoke to Clara's chest. 'This chap had such a broken heart, I thought he'd never pick himself up again.'

Once, he'd gone, Victor whispered, 'Don't worry about him, he's an idiot,' and Clara grinned back. That was one thing they could agree on.

Victor paid for dinner, although she protested. She had a growing feeling of dread. *What was going to happen next?* Before she had the chance to say she wasn't feeling up to it, though, Victor said in a low voice, 'I think I've overdone it.'

He put his hand over his stomach; it reminded her of Anita not eight hours earlier. She shook herself.

'Do you mind if we just um... a rain-check... I'll drive you back?'

Indigestion could sometimes be a blessing in disguise.

'Of course!' Clara said brightly before telling herself, *look sad, look sadder!*

He parked outside the Grange. Looking at it made her heart swell. *Home.* Inside, Sister Grace might be leafing through storybooks. Rita might be playing music in her head. Billy and Barry might be fast asleep. Alex would be researching Disraeli or Palmerston, 'discuss'. Joyce would be looking at the wounded soldiers and stoical nurses in her photography magazines. Evelyn would be revelling in her achievement today – *was it just this afternoon?* – or raiding the biscuit tin. Peg would be putting her shells in order. Peter would be plotting future stories.

And it would be over soon. But home wasn't in the building, it was in the children, it was her job.

She suddenly remembered Victor in the car next to her. He seemed lost in his own thoughts too: probably about the scourge of Bolshevism.

Clara grabbed her handbag.

What could you do? Victor was elusive. He was enigmatic. Was he still in love with his wife? Probably. There was a lot of that about.

She looked over at Ivor's workshop, where the yellow lights glowed, excluding her.

'I'm sorry...' It was hard to see Victor's eyes behind the grey hedge of his hair.

'It's all right. Honestly.'

And it was a relief, but even so, she would have liked him to be more disappointed. Perhaps he understood that, because he suddenly reached over and grabbed her hand.

'I'd like to arrange us a trip to Aldeburgh some time... It's a wonderful place, I'd love to show you around...'

'That sounds like a marvellous idea.'

'Iris loved it there,' he said, and then he bit his lip like he knew he shouldn't have said it.

'I'm looking forward to it already, Victor.'

Clara allowed herself to be effusive because it did sound like a marvellous idea – like walking on clouds or dancing on waves – only she had this funny feeling that it wasn't going to happen.

35

The next morning, Clara left the children at the school gate screeching about who had been most naughty and who knew their spellings. She had planned to go to see Anita and the new baby – she couldn't bring herself to call him Howard yet – but she would give them a little more time, she told herself – yes, she would go to welcome Ivor. That would be the *polite* thing to do.

Her heart was pounding as she returned on the familiar route. It felt like no coincidence that the sun was trying to shine. Flowers were reclaiming the roadside, trees were in bud and Ivor was back. But was Ruby here? She could be coming tomorrow. Or she could be with Ivor now, in a party dress and tiara like Grace Kelly, demanding his attention. One thing Clara did know was that people who expected to be treated well usually, unaccountably, were. Or she might be there, just wearing a bath towel, like the woman in the house where Joe used to deliver *The Times*. Clara gulped.

But by the time she got back and was standing in front of Ivor's workshop, it was locked up, the two padlocks positioned almost defiantly. Nevertheless, she tugged the door once, twice

– damn it – the postman was there, dismounting his bike, and he looked at her in surprise.

'He's not been here for months, Miss Newton! thought you knew.'

Rather than argue, Clara just muttered, 'Silly me.'

She should leave well alone – or, in other words, wait for Ivor to get in touch. Let him come to her. Wasn't that better – with men, as with cats and children?

He didn't get in touch. The workshop lights went on later that afternoon, but she was off to Anita's to see the baby and she warned herself not to be distracted.

Anita was both weary and elated and even Clara had to admit the baby was gorgeous – a sweet swaddle of milk and talc. He liked sleeping, but not for as long as the Marie Stopes book suggested he would; Anita was concerned, even though the midwife, the real midwife, had said it was normal. Anita insisted Clara hold him, so, heart in her mouth, she did. She dared not move a muscle; she sat rigid as an oak. The baby squirmed. For some reason he was wearing a pink woollen hat as if they wanted him to look like a flower.

Clara thought Anita would have forgotten or at least wouldn't want to talk about Ivor's reappearance, but she gripped Clara's arm: 'I can't believe Ivor turning up like that, out of the blue.'

It was excruciating.

'I know... a day of surprise arrivals, huh?' Clara stammered.

'So...'

'So?'

'Where is the Ruby?'

'I don't know. I don't care anyway,' Clara lied, before adding, 'I went out with Victor Braithwaite last night. My professor.'

She wished Anita had read *Little Women*. Perhaps she'd lend it to her. Not that Anita would have time for reading now.

Anita pulled a face, but before Clara could press her, the baby started grizzling so Clara handed him back. When her arms were free, she shook them – *phew* – and put her handbag back in her lap. That felt more natural.

'He smells fear,' Clara joked.

'He'll get used to it,' said Anita. 'And so will you when you have your own, one day.'

And then Dr Cardew bounded in, jubilant, the excited new father, and he thanked Clara again and when she protested she hadn't done anything, it was Evelyn, he said, 'Evelyn couldn't have done it without you,' which wasn't true at all. But then he said, 'It's two o'clock,' and Anita explained that it was feeding time. Anita held Howard to her, in his woolly hat, and Clara said she had to get back anyway.

In the afternoon, Clara busied herself with paperwork and cleaning. She could have knocked at Ivor's workshop but instead she took control of herself and decided the shed needed a tidy. She rarely went out there and when she did, she found sheet music on the floor, other papers and an awful drawing of her that must have been done by a child in a temper with the heading, 'Miss Newton smells.' (She suspected Joyce from the distinctive hard-pressed pencil strokes.)

Charming.

Over tea, Maureen said she'd dropped in on Ivor in his workshop. Peter said he'd seen him up by the station. Alex had seen him chatting with Mrs Garrard. *Was she the only person in Lavenham who hadn't had a look-in?*

'And has anyone seen his wife?' she asked casually. 'Ruby, is it?'

Perhaps no one had seen her because she was ill? Ruby was the type to have an *exotic* disease, one that only increases your beauty, making you wan and your cheekbones defined, instead of the kind that make you spotty and dull.

They pulled faces. 'Don't think so...'

That evening, as the children argued over chores and baths, she saw that the workshop lights were still on; but just when she thought she might go over, they went off. Bed or out? Perhaps he was going to fetch Ruby from the station? Perhaps she was there and they were having 'an early night'. That thought made her stomach turn. That was the trouble living so close: a girl could become obsessed. She knew too much and yet she knew nothing at all. That was another reason why moving might be the right thing, she told herself.

36

The van that pulled up the next morning had Surveyors & Valuers in swirly writing on the side. The letter Y formed a big and unnecessary loop. 'No property (another big loop) too big or too small. Est. 1945'.

Clara wondered why they bothered with the 'established in 1945'; it was so recent. Why were they blowing their trumpets about that? And then she wondered who they were going to see – it must be Ivor, it must be...

They were walking towards the Grange.

Clara opened the door curiously. Miss Cooper hadn't mentioned prospective adopters. There had been none for the last month. And prospective adopters didn't usually come in the morning anyway. The children were at school; three of the girls had a maths test and Peg was hoping to get moved up for writing. She wrote beautifully, but no one seemed to notice Peg's successes.

Two men in caps, 'Nothing to worry yourself about, Missus.'

'Come to take a few measurements.'

'Council sent us for the sale.'

'36-24-36,' the younger man said.

Clara blinked at him.

'Just a joke.'

Clara forced a smile, hoping he would stop.

'But if you need a bust measurement, I am your man.'

She would not offer them tea, she would not, under any circumstances.

The other man, the older one, stepped in. 'Ignore him. We've come for the house details.'

'I'm parched,' said the younger one.

Clara felt her determination wilt.

'Tea?' She put on the expected smile.

'Please.'

She followed them around the ground floor. They sighed, groaned and said, 'Oh dear, oh dear'. It sounded rehearsed.

'Are the windows that bad?' she asked.

'No,' the older one said, 'they can get asbestos put in everywhere. That'll sort it.'

'Asbestos?'

'Fantastic stuff,' he said, 'seals everything. Get your wall cavities, fire doors, cladding, pipe lagging, your windowsills. You name it. Get that shed out there done...'

She had just served them tea in the best china – *why was she concerned with doing the right thing?* – which they took upstairs when there was a knock on the back door. Ivor was standing there, white shirt, his habitual braces, five o'clock shadow. He should be in a movie, on a horse with flared nostrils. What would Sir Alfred, horse painter, think of that? She giggled nervously and said, 'Good afternoon!' in a bright voice, glad she wasn't in her apron and her hair looked tolerable. He said she had kind eyes. She fluttered her lashes, hoping he'd notice them.

'Who *are* those people?'

That wasn't the reunion she had imagined in her dreams.

'What the hell are they doing here?'

So *now* Ivor was interested.

Clara shook her head. He did look pale. If he *had* been mooching around the French Riviera, as in her imaginings, he had probably sat under a massive parasol. On a stripy towel.

'They're... it's not important.'

'Tea is a bit wet, Missus,' the younger one called down the stairs. 'Any chance of a biscuit?'

She turned back to Ivor. 'The council are putting us up for sale. These people are here to measure up.'

But Ivor's face was full of sudden fury. 'The council are?'

'Stay out of it, please, Ivor.'

But Ivor strode out to the hall. 'You've got no right to be here,' he shouted.

'Yes, we have,' said the older one. Tape measure in one hand, best china cup balancing in the other.

'No, you don't,' said Ivor, then he turned to Clara. 'They don't... you don't have to let them in.'

'We have permission from the current owner,' the younger one said. 'Not that it's any of your business.' Clara could hear them both laughing. She pulled Ivor back into the kitchen and shut the door behind her. 'They're only doing their job. It's not their fault.'

'You *knew* about this?'

She should have realised he'd be like this – grabbing the wrong end of the stick.

'You can't just charge in here like you... haven't been away all this time.'

'They're actually selling this place?'

'Maybe,' she said. 'Yes, they are.'

'And you knew about it?'

'I tried to convince them not to but it's too expensive and they decided to sell.'

She felt utterly weary suddenly. She had done her best and now she was being scolded like a child. Ivor squinted at her.

'And it's going to be fine.' She had a lump in her throat. 'They promised me.'

'They'll keep you together? You and the children?'

'Yes, definitely. They assured me. They *want* us to stay together. It's just the building. It's expensive. The damp, the everything – I can see their point of view.'

It was exasperating, yet embarrassing too. Ivor studied her. And she thought, *I'm not some curtain that you need to mend, thank you, Ivor.* She couldn't tell what he was thinking. He was wound up and part of her thought, *it's not your job. It's not your home, calm down*; but she also knew Shilling Grange had once been Ivor's home and how attached he was to it. How he helped. Even in the three days or so since he'd been back, the children's clothes were miraculously restored and they were in great spirits.

She put the kettle on again and as it came to the boil, they sat opposite each other at the table. Even though they were silent, it felt like they were still arguing. Then Ivor made some desultory comments about how green the garden looked (it didn't), it was clear his mind was elsewhere. She could hear the mens' footsteps on the stairs, trampling around up there, but she tried to ignore them.

'It's unlikely, isn't it, that you'll stay together?'

'Why do you say that?' She blew her nose on a handkerchief, waved her hand: 'Head cold, sorry.'

'They'll palm off the children all over the place. That's what they do.'

'Things have changed since you were a boy,' she said.

'Not that much.'

'I won't let that happen anyway,' Clara said, but rather than sounding defiant, she sounded petulant, like a toddler having a tantrum. She thought of the beautiful houses she had pictured in her head. Places where the children would thrive and be happy. Was she deluded?

'Is it because of that man?'

'What?'

'You haven't done anything about it because of your professor friend?'

She tried to see it from Ivor's perspective. He'd come back, heard the orphanage was going to be sold and decided that she was doing nothing about it. He'd put two and two together and come up with five hundred. And yet – it had nothing to do with him.

'It's not that. I haven't done anything because I don't need to. It will be fine. They've assured me of that repeatedly. It could be good, even. A fresh start.'

He gulped down his tea. Perhaps the phrase 'fresh start' had convinced him.

'A purpose-built property,' she added triumphantly.

He squinted at her.

She looked at him and he looked at her, and she could feel the same strength of feeling come over her. No, it hadn't gone away, it wouldn't go away, dammit.

'So is Ruby back?' she couldn't resist asking.

'She isn't here,' he said. And then, as if to leave her in no doubt added, 'I'm on my own, Clara.' He paused. He drank his tea, set it down, met her eyes. 'Unlike you.'

Flames of indignation. 'You expected me to wait?' The outrage of him.

'I don't expect anything from you.'

The tone was wrong. Everything was awkward and unease. His defences were up and so were hers.

Have we changed that much?

'Is she coming back?'

'Probably not.'

'Is she in France?'

'France? No!'

Clara hated the way he looked at her like she was a stranger, a stranger he didn't think he liked.

'Why would she be in France?' he went on.

'I just thought... I don't know.'

Going somewhere warmer. She had put two and two together and come up with St Tropez.

'She might go back to America, she's not sure yet. She's got some thinking to do. I support her in that, obviously.'

Why was it *obviously*? She was now boiling with rage: at herself, at Miss Bridges, at the men with their tape measures, at her irresistibly handsome and tone-deaf neighbour and at Ruby, who was clearly walking all over him. *Since when was Ivor a doormat?*

There was a tapping on the kitchen door. 'We're off now, Missus.' The men were both smirking like some comedy duo.

The younger one handed back the cups. 'We mean no h-*arm*. We'll leave you to your *handy*man.' The older one waggled his fingers at her, 'Ta-da!'

Clara didn't cotton on they were insulting Ivor at first. Then she was so flustered, she didn't know what to do with herself. Once they left, she took it out on Ivor.

'You've absolutely no idea how hard I've worked to stay here. I've cut the budgets, I've saved and saved, I've sold things – I've documented every single thing.'

As soon as it came out of her mouth, she knew that was the wrong thing to say.

'Documented?' he sneered. 'Ah yes, it's all about the paper-work with Miss Newton... *Get those files in order...*'

'I mean, I put together the evidence. I saved money. I did it all – but they decided, we'll be better off somewhere else. And that's okay. I'm not going to fight just for the sake of fighting.

You don't know anything about me anymore, Ivor. And I don't care about you anymore – you... betrayed me.'

She was crying now. Ivor got out of his chair first though, stormed towards the back door. Clara wished the ground would swallow her up.

37

**ARTICLE FOR THE *SHILLING GRANGE NEWS*,
MARCH 1950**

**THE   RETURN   OF   THE   PRODIGAL
UPHOLSTERER**

*The Ides of March proved to be nothing to beware of for the
children of Shilling Grange. A favourite, much-missed neighbour, Ivor Delaney, arrived back in Lavenham at the weekend
after an incredible six months away. Nobody knows where he's
been, nobody knows where he's going, but we are thrilled to
have him home.*

Welcome back, Ivor.

Clara felt like scrunching the paper into a ball and stuffing it in
her mouth.

'Alex, don't you think there are stories more newsworthy?'

Her voice was sickly sweet, to cover her rage.

Alex shook his head. 'Can't think of any, no.'

'Like, like... say, Anita's new baby. Or Peter winning the comic contest, or Billy and Barry's uncle and aunt applying to adopt them? That's going to happen soon.'

Alex clapped his hand over his mouth. 'I completely forgot. I'll do those later too. But is this okay for now?'

'I suppose if—'

'I wasn't sure about the analogy.'

'What's an analogy?' asked Rita.

'It's a comparison,' said Alex. 'I made the analogy of Ivor with Julius Caesar.'

'I don't...' began Clara.

'Sounds fair,' said Rita and shrugged; *little traitor.* 'Shame, I was going to do an article on him too.'

One week later, and it was the football match of the year: Arsenal versus Liverpool for the FA Cup Final. And Billy and Barry's Uncle Stan had tickets for everyone. Clara was glad of it; she could stop mooning over her neighbour. She could be sure Ivor wasn't spending his waking hours thinking about her.

Although it was April, the weather was filthier than it had been in February. Uncle Stan and Aunt Ruth came over in the morning, while the children were mucking about outside with umbrellas. Peter had asked if a friend could come with him and Clara was surprised to see that it wasn't another gangly fella from school but the attractive young woman from the train station. This time she was wearing a skirt that barely brushed her knees and a bow around her neck. Peter went red when she arrived, then said defensively, 'Mabel loves football, she does.'

Clara hadn't seen Ivor since their argument – or *her* argument, she thought dismally, since he had hardly said anything.

She had just been getting over him and now she needed to reset right back to the beginning of getting over him. She had an advantage over last time though, she realised. Last time he had gone missing, she had felt sorry for him – *poor Ivor, dragged away by his glamorous sweetheart*. This time, she felt a poker-hot fury, so... fiery that she wanted to punch him in the nose. She tried to locate the exact source of the fury, but couldn't. Never mind, she told herself, it was there. A *righteous* fury.

Whenever she tried to think kindly of him, six months came roaring back at her. No – it was more like seven. She would be a fool to let that go – perhaps she would have let it go if Ivor had come crawling back contrite with apologies, but he hadn't.

And then his suggestion that she had done nothing to protect the children. *Done nothing*, for cripes' sake! He had no idea how she worked her fingers to the bone for them, every single day.

But now Alex was missing. Uncle Stan was trying to herd everyone together and they couldn't find him. No one had seen him since breakfast. The rain was bucketing down – it just wasn't the type of day you'd go off for a wander. Not Alex anyway. Alex didn't wander.

'We've got to go.' Uncle Stan had been waiting for this chance for years.

'But Alex wanted to come.' Barry just wanted to get on with it, but Billy couldn't bear for Alex to miss out. 'He wanted to see the game.'

They waited ten more minutes, Uncle Stan glaring at his wristwatch. Alex wasn't particularly a football fan, but he loved an 'educational experience', more than any of them. And he had said it was just the story he needed for the sports pages of the *Shilling Grange News*.

'You go ahead,' decided Clara, for poor Stan was nearly having kittens. 'If Alex gets back soon, we'll hop on the train. If not, I'll listen on the wireless.'

.   .   .

Could he be with Ivor? It would be just like Alex to have holed up there, chatting and sewing, two dark heads together, putting the world to rights and losing track of time. They adored each other. But the workshop was locked up and presented a blank unwelcoming face to the world. Ivor was never there when she needed him most, she thought, before telling herself off – she didn't *need* him at all.

The street was full of puddles and the sky was slate grey. There was another possibility that Clara didn't like: *Alex might be with his father again.*

Surely hunger would bring him home. Time passed. She made herself an omelette for lunch, and it turned out surprisingly edible, but she couldn't eat much for worrying.

She put the match on the wireless and listened while peeling potatoes for dinner, nicking her ring finger in the process. She ran it under the tap. Blood in the sink. *Please let the children enjoy the game. Please let Alex come back soon.* They were two goals in when there was a knock on the door and she found Alex stood there. His hood was up and his collar was deliberately pushed high. At first she couldn't see what had happened.

'I'm c-c-cold,' he whimpered as the rain – or was it tears? – ran down his face, his teeth chattering. He was bruised, his coat was torn, his cheeks were grazed. He looked terrible.

Judy.

Clara grabbed her still-wet coat and steered Alex up the road towards Dr Cardew's surgery, firing questions all the way: 'Where've you been? Were you with your father? You were supposed to go to watch the football. What happened?'

'We went to the pub. He told me to wait outside. I fell off a wall and I saw stars. It wasn't his fault.'

'But he... helped you though? Alex, ALEX – he looked after you?'

Alex didn't speak.

'Did he help you?' She knew the answer. It was the same answer Judy would have given.

'He went back inside...' Alex said in a tiny voice. 'He left me.' And then he sobbed.

Miss Smith led them through. Dr Cardew – unexpectedly, a Liverpool fan – was also listening to the match, but when he saw them he leapt up so dramatically, it was frightening. But it was also a relief to know that Clara wasn't wasting his time.

He and Miss Smith worked efficiently together, whirring around Alex, somehow like insects around a light, moving in with this ointment or that bandage.

Judy, thought Clara. *My poor Judy.* She ran out to the lavatory, where she threw up her omelette lunch. 'He left me,' was echoing in the tiny room around her. Her forehead was drenched with sweat, her eyes on stalks. She looked panicky and bedraggled – but it seemed appropriate. She felt even worse than she looked. *Poor Alex.*

Dr Cardew told Alex to go and look at Billy and Barry 2 in the waiting room.

'Tell me if they sing,' he instructed as Alex stared at the patterns in the carpet.

'I'll go too,' volunteered Miss Smith kindly and Clara gave her a grateful look. 'It's feeding time. Alex, will you help me?'

Alex managed a half-smile at that.

Once they'd left the room, Dr Cardew wrote in his notes.

'I think he needs to get away from his father, Clara. He's not a good influence.'

'We're moving soon – it will be fine,' Clara couldn't help adding, 'They're thinking of purpose-builds.'

'I see,' Dr Cardew said gravely. 'Get Alex away from him sooner rather than later; can you do that, Clara?'

38

There was no Robinson, Browne or White at the spring meeting of the Jane Taylor Society, but the numbers were bolstered by two people who had got lost on their way to Ipswich and a student researching medieval architecture. Mr Dowsett had had a health scare in February and the meeting had been delayed. This afternoon he led an impassioned discussion on the effect of time – post Napoleonic-war era – and place – Lavenham, Colchester and Devon – on Jane's work.

When Clara arrived home, she found a man in the front garden digging a hole. He took one look at her shocked face and laughed.

'Nothing to worry about. I'm from the council.'

He sank a sign into the mud and there it stood, looking out into the road, bold as brass. It was about one metre high and the writing was neat:

FOR SALE:

INTERESTED PARTIES APPLY TO:

0749 390 (Suffolk County Council. Estates Department.)

The man threw mud back into the hole and patted it down as if he were playing pat-a-cake.

It really was happening.

When they got home from school, the children gathered around it as if it was an aeroplane that had crash-landed.

'What's it for?' asked Rita.

Peg was hanging off it. Clara pulled her off, afraid it would break.

'Who is for sale?' said Evelyn shocked.

'Why does it say interested parties?' Joyce asked.

Rita shouted back, 'You know what a party is, silly!'

Alex grimaced. 'Party has several meanings... In this case it means groups, isn't that right, Miss Newton?' Despite his bruising experience with his father, Alex was back to his correcting self. 'It means anyone who might be interested in buying the Grange.'

Maureen and Peter were looking at each other solemnly.

'Mama,' whispered Rita.

How important is time and place?

'Come away, children,' said Clara pertly. 'Everything is going to be FINE. Do you remember what I told you about moving – this is it! Exciting, right?'

Through the open workshop doors, she could just about make out Ivor at his sewing machine. He looked over; she wasn't sure if she could see, or if she was imagining his dark eyes on her. She pulled her cardigan tighter.

She remembered that when Maureen went missing last year, it was Ivor who went wobbling off on a bicycle for hours to look for her. She wouldn't shut him out. She had to remember he was a kind man (while trying not to remember how he made her feel).

He got up and closed the doors.

That evening, Peg wet the bed, twice. The second time, Clara felt so shattered she told the girl to pop in with her. Perhaps she was coming down with something? Peg returned, gripping her shell, which she hadn't done for a while.

'Peg,' Clara whispered. 'What's the matter, love?'

Peg used her fingers to sign. Clara tried to guess: 'Walking? Everyone is walking away?'

Peg traced tears down her cheeks.

'And you are sad? I see. Do you want to write it for me, Peg?'

Peg shook her head and showed her sign for 'sleepy'.

'Okay, but you can tell me. Yes?'

Peg did her fingers-together sign for speaking, like a duck quacking, then pointed at her chest.

'Tell me – yes, Peg. Tell you what?'

She clapped her hands together.

'Together – you want to know – if we will we stay together?'

Peg nodded vigorously.

'Oh yes, Peg, we will.'

Peg crossed her fingers, determined. Then pointed at Clara.

'Is it a promise? Yes, it's a promise.'

As soon as Clara said it, she knew she was breaking a cardinal housemother's rule: *Don't promise things you can't possibly know.*

ARTICLE FOR THE *SHILLING GRANGE NEWS*, APRIL 1950

'One day I Will Shout', a poem by Peg

One day I will sing
Songs by Vera Lynn
To an audience
Of ten.

One day I will shout
At football players out
In a crowd
Of 100

One day I will whisper
To my friend and my sister
That I love their dresses
And shoes

One day I will tell
The class before the bell
That 2 and 2 is four
And lots of stories more.

Until that day I have my hands
And my face
And my feet
And my dancing
And my family
And my friends
And my Miss Newton
And a place to call home.

39

When Marilyn eventually returned from her travels, it felt like the house went from ticking over steadily to racing around like a headless chicken – but in a good way. Clara was thrilled to find her on the doorstep.

The afternoon she arrived, Marilyn seemed more inclined to talk about Michael than before and Clara didn't mind. It was lovely collecting stories of the early Michael and the teenage Michael; some she knew – most, she didn't.

'Michael wasn't an ambitious kid,' Marilyn said over the shortbread biscuits she had bought in Scotland. 'He was like me. He liked chatting. He liked fishing and he liked an adventure. Did I tell you about the time he entered a pie-eating contest? He got home and said, "Ma, I came fifth," then threw up on the carpet.

'I thought he'd go into sales, or management maybe. But when war broke out, everything changed. Michael saw the boots, the flags and the Nazis – and he hated it. He used to say: "You don't have to be serious about everything—"'

'"Just be serious about one thing",' Clara said at the same time as Marilyn, and smiled remembering.

'And he joined up...'

'And he gave it his all,' Clara added.

'He gave it his *life*,' Marilyn said.

'He wouldn't have had it any other way,' Clara said.

Michael didn't want to die, but if he *had* to die, dying in his plane, fighting for good, would have made him proud – and this acknowledgement made her feel less devastated than it once did. Instead she felt that with Marilyn's help, she could remember with acceptance.

Marilyn cooed over Joyce's photographs: 'Your composition is perfection,' she said, kissing the tips of her fingers. Evelyn told Marilyn her baby-delivery story and if she exaggerated, slightly – 'Mrs Cardew was snorting like a camel,' – Clara did not say. 'Remarkable,' said Marilyn. 'She was lucky to have you there!'

When Evelyn left the room, Marilyn mouthed, 'She's not eating everything she sees any more,' and Clara startled before realising that, yes, it was true – she didn't know exactly when Evelyn had stopped scavenging but she had. She also went to see her mother regularly and came back without a complaint. She would agree to leave soon, Clara was certain, and the thought made her smile.

Alex said that it was a strain being the editor of a newspaper, especially when no one did what they were supposed to do. Everyone jeered, except for Marilyn, who patted his wrist and said, 'It's hard to be the boss.'

Billy and Barry said they were going to be professional footballers and Marilyn said, 'There's no money in that, you'll have to get proper jobs,' but when she saw their faces fall, she backtracked: 'It's a good ambition and ambitions are good.'

Peg skipped and everyone clapped and Clara whispered, 'The therapist says Peg is making progress,' and Marilyn didn't ask the obvious, like, 'What has Peg learned to say then?' She simply said, 'Fabulous,' and sent Peg to fish out some hard gums from her handbag.

Rita told Marilyn about the Festival of Britain and how they were going to perform at it next year. Her on the piano and some of the others, she hadn't decided who, singing along.

'You've not got through the audition yet,' chorused Evelyn and Joyce gleefully.

'If only I'd known about this,' Marilyn said, 'I'd have come next year. I'd love to see that.'

'Can't you come back then too?' suggested Rita.

'I am not made of money,' Marilyn said. Then a few minutes later, she said, 'Although if you are going to be in it, maybe I should.'

Marilyn asked where Maureen was and Clara explained she was sometimes in the office, sometimes looking after the Browne boy. When Marilyn asked, 'Are we happy with that?' Clara said, 'It could be worse...'

After the children had gone up to bed, Marilyn leaned over to Clara and in her earnest voice said, 'I couldn't help but notice the For Sale sign...'

Clara reassured her. 'It's fine. It's for the best, I think.'

And it probably was – Alex needed to get away, perhaps Maureen did too. The others? well – *as long as they were together*.

'And your special neighbour is back. The children told me...'

'Oh, him,' said Clara huffily. 'Turns out he's not so special.'

'He upset you?'

'Nooo. Oh, I suppose so.' Clara hadn't felt like telling Marilyn, but somehow it spilled out. 'Ivor doesn't trust me. He doesn't believe that the council will keep us together.'

'But you think they will?'

'Why wouldn't they?'

Marilyn took her hand. 'You told me he had a difficult time when he was young. You said he lived here. Maybe he has an attachment...'

There it was. That word again.

Clara thought for a moment, then said, 'And I can understand that, but he won't accept that I'm doing my best, just because he would do things differently.'

~

A London trip felt ambitious, even more so after Maureen refused to come – 'I've got Martin, remember?' and Peter didn't fancy it either. 'I've got work to do...' he said, although Clara wondered if he was instead, sneaking out to meet his friend. Still, seven children was more than enough.

Fortunately, it was one of those rare, blue-sky days, chilly but bright, and everything felt possible. The drilling, the scaffolding and the bombed-out streets were not irritating or horribly evocative for the children, but a bonus. The children were excited about visiting Madame Tussauds, especially since they had recently watched *Panic at Madame Tussaud's* at Saturday morning cinema club.

They played leapfrog while they were waiting in the queue. Marilyn told a tale about the time Michael went fishing and caught a boot. He told everyone he'd caught 'a big 'un'.

'That's just so Michael.' Clara laughed.

The family ahead of them kept looking round at the children. They were a sweet sight – mother, father, two children, on a special day out. The father had a camera round his neck – Joyce could offer to take their photograph, Clara thought.

Then the father suddenly yanked at one of his children's arms: 'If you don't behave, you'll end up like one of those kids.

Do you hear? I'll send you to the orphanage. They'll beat the hell out of you there.'

Clara wanted to confront him. Marilyn had also heard, but at least none of the children had. The best thing Clara could do, she thought, was make sure her children did not end up like 'those kids' of his imagination.

Inside, Rita and Barry rowed about who Abraham Lincoln was. (They swore he was that one from the Bible who built a boat.) Everyone liked the waxwork Churchill and the flags and the famous military commanders, and they bombarded her with questions. Clara was surprised that Alex came to her rescue, putting his hand in hers and leading her to another room.

'There will be a waxwork of you here one day!' he said.

'What a preposterous idea!' Clara laughed. 'What on earth for?'

'For looking after us, of course.' Then he ran off to stand next to Gene Kelly.

On a whim, Clara asked an attendant if there was a waxwork of Jane Taylor, 'You know, "Twinkle, Twinkle Little Star"?' but the attendant didn't know who she was talking about and Clara felt silly.

At the station, Marilyn, who had already paid for the train tickets, roasted chestnuts in the street and the entrance fees, insisted on buying them a puzzle book to share too. She was still thinking about the nasty father in the queue, Clara suspected. Clara couldn't forget him either. She turned her attention to the puzzles.

In one of them, one of her favourites, you had one word and then you had to change a letter each time to form another word before you got to the final word.

Change *Orphan* to *Family* in fewer than six moves, Clara thought. That would be impossible.

· · ·

As they walked back from Lavenham station, Clara asked each of them what the best thing about the day had been.

'The boot, I think,' said Evelyn.

'What?'

'The boot Michael caught and said, "it's a big 'un." That was funny.'

~

Julian had dashed over to Marilyn in the post office and invited her to one of his parties, declaring, 'A glamorous American will be the *pièce de résistance!*'

What was he celebrating this time? Clara thought resentfully. *Oh, to be that wealthy that you could throw a party every weekend.*

Clara calculated that what Julian spent each weekend on canapés and the band alone would probably be enough to support her household. And then she hated herself for thinking like that. *What was she becoming? A revolutionary? A socialist?*

'You don't mind, do you?' Marilyn said that evening, clipping on her ruby earrings and making faces in her pocket mirror. 'I can't turn down an occasion. It's my weakness.'

'Of course, I don't mind,' Clara lied. Marilyn's earlobes had gone red.

'He likes me. I can't understand why.'

'*I* like you,' Clara said. She couldn't help but feel sullen.

Marilyn pinched her cheek. 'I prefer you, girl.'

It hurt though. Was Julian sucking up to Marilyn on purpose? What purpose though? To annoy Clara? Julian did enjoy annoying Clara but he didn't usually go out of his way to do so.

'So how is Victor?' Marilyn said.

Clara was surprised she had waited so long to ask. 'We're both busy people,' she said.

Now Marilyn was filing her nails, something Clara had always thought one did in private. She looked up and pointed the file at her.

'That's it?'

'We had a wonderful meal out the other week.' Clara recited the menu defensively. She remembered it down to the choice of sorbet.

'You've talked more about the lemon sole than anything else. What about *your* soul?' Marilyn winked.

'Oh, I like Victor,' Clara said – and as she said it, she thought, *Victor is an honourable man. And he is not repulsive.* She should try to move things along.

Marilyn leaned over. Clara could smell her sweet perfume. 'Do you like him... in bed?'

'Marilyn!'

Marilyn let out a yelp of laughter.

'Oh, you English are uptight. Passion is important, Clara. You need something to see you through the lean times, believe me.'

Had Marilyn forgotten Clara had been engaged to her son?

Marilyn persisted. 'You haven't, have you?'

'We have not,' admitted Clara, thinking with some people you get embarrassed because you have, and with others you get embarrassed because you have not. Best thing was not to get embarrassed, she supposed. She thought of her protection. Seemed she hadn't needed to protect herself after all.

'Why not?' probed Marilyn. And at that moment Clara found herself longing for Miss Bridge's restraint or Anita's impeccable boundaries.

'It's none of your business,' she said defiantly, but Marilyn's skin was thick as hide. She just laughed, wrapped her fur throw around her and tucked her stockinged feet into her high heels: 'Please yourself.'

40

After lunch the next day, when the children had just gone back to school, Victor stood at the front door. Aware of Ivor probably skulking in the workshop opposite, and with Marilyn's exhortations ringing in her ears, Clara pulled him in enthusiastically. Ivor was nothing to her – she may have spent the last few months in cloud cuckoo land, but, no more – the cuckoos had come home to roost. Or something like that.

Victor crossed the threshold, let the front door slam behind him, but was reluctant to enter any further. Somehow Clara was reminded of What's the Time, Mr Wolf? Only she felt like she was the wolf – 'One o'clock, two o'clock...' – and he was the one running squealing away.

'It's all right,' she reassured him, 'no one's home.'

She was reminded that she should stop overthinking things. Ivor was married and anyway, he was not interested; he could not have made that clearer had he embroidered it into a tapestry and hung it on his outside wall. And it *had* been a long time since she had been intimate. *Good Housekeeping* said that 'Some women are still struggling with the hangover from the excitement of the war years...'

Clara would absolutely not have put it like that. But still...

Did Victor perhaps want to rendezvous with her now? She had decided to move the protection from her handbag to her desk drawer. The last thing she needed was Rita nosing around, then screeching about it. Or Billy and Barry kicking it about in the garden.

She put her arms round Victor's waist, only faintly aware that he was not reciprocating. Probably he was shy. He detached himself further. 'Clara, I dearly love being with you.' The *dearly* sounded like something you would say to your maiden aunt, but no matter.

'I think you know what I'm going to say...' he continued.

Clara jumped out of her reverie.

What was *he going to say?*

'Um?'

'I don't think we should go on as we were.'

Gathering herself, Clara said, 'Is this about moving again? I don't mind, Oxford is not the end of the world.' At least Victor was a driver – Ivor was not! Another point in the pro-Victor column – not that she had done *actual* columns. 'We can make it work.'

He moved his weight from one hip to the other. He was holding his briefcase. The tsar's face on the cover of a book peeped out from where it didn't shut properly. The tsar who was shot. Victor was so disappointed that the revolution had turned out that way. What should have been a new hope, a new way, had turned to dust. *Those* were the things that got this man going, not her.

'You're a remarkable woman...'

Which raises the obvious question, thought Clara, *why are you dumping me?* Because she realised that was what it was; she was not *totally* daft.

'I like that you are,' he gazed at his shoes, or the front doormat, hard to tell, 'so different to me – I talk about it – you do it – you are all actions, not theory.'

Clara thought that only Victor could think that about her. In fact, Ivor would have said the opposite. Ivor would have said she was obsessed with files and papers. Could they both be right? Perhaps she was a combination. Either way, it seemed a slight excuse to split up with her.

Victor blew his nose on a handkerchief as large as a tea towel. 'You're a woman of deeds, not words,' he continued.

This was getting silly.

'I am like the suffragettes?'

Victor nodded eagerly, licked his lower lip.

'Then why do you not think it could work?'

Do I not care enough about the fight against 1930s fascism? Is my world too small? Too domestic or too mundane?

He touched his chest and his face was so sad, it was heart-breaking.

'I'm sorry. It's just... I'm not in love with you.'

Oh for goodness' sake, she was snivelling. It was just so *insulting*: she had never been rejected like this before, at least, not by a suitor. She felt like a scarecrow, just dingle-dangling uselessly in someone else's clothes.

'Oh, I see.' She felt as though she had been underwater and was finally coming up for air. *I am devastated,* she told herself, but actually she was not: Victor was not the answer.

The thing was: she had always expected that she would be the one to let him down, not the other way round. It was a surprise, that's what it was – but it was *not* grief, she realised quickly. It was not much more than a feather-light disappointment.

'I am a terrible man,' Victor said. He looked like he was about to cry. 'I have misled you – you have done nothing wrong. I just liked the *idea* of us, I suppose. And Alex is so brilliant.

And you're like his mother. Two of you for the price of one. Alex and Bernard are so close and I thought...'

She was hurt, yes, she felt silly, like she was too old for this, but also her heart went out to him, he looked scared.

'I miss my Iris,' he breathed and then blew his nose loudly. 'And the thing is, I... I am not ready to not miss her. I am not ready to let her go.'

'I understand, Victor,' Clara said. 'Come in anyway,' she added brightly. 'I'll put the kettle on. I have gingerbread from Anita.'

He looked wary, but then he agreed.

As he walked past her, she patted that broad tweedy back of his. She wasn't for him. He wasn't for her. If she had paid more attention, she would have known that. She whispered, 'You're right, Victor, thank you.'

41

Victor had stayed for tea and had made himself at home. Rita had dragged him to listen to 'Moonlight Sonata' in the shed, Billy and Barry forced him to play a home-made game of worms and steps which he said was hilarious. He admired Peg's cue cards – *is this a drawing of an elephant?* – and chatted to Peter about the latest comic strip he was working on about a cat with ninety-nine lives and was based on Stella. Peter had given it the name 'Pusskin' and Victor thoroughly approved. Evelyn appraised him of the mechanics of delivering a baby and Victor grimaced before whispering to Clara, 'I think she knows more about it than me.' (Clara thought that was likely.) Evelyn also told him that she loved her school now – 'lucky number thirteen,' only Joyce insisted that she loved it *more* and then the two started squabbling.

Only when Victor went to say goodbye did it grow slightly awkward. Previously they might have kissed, or at least made plans for the next time. Holding his hat, Victor started up, 'I don't know what to say.' But Clara put her fingers to her lips, like she did with the children, and he managed a smile.

She wondered if Ivor was watching from his cocoon in the

workshop. There was nothing she could do about that and he probably didn't give a damn anyway.

Before school, Clara went looking for Stella. In the garden shed, to her shock, she saw there were piles of newspapers. Everywhere. On the piano stool, on the piano itself and over the floor. It was like they were reproducing. She charged into the kitchen, shouting, 'Billy, Barry! What the hell is going on?'

They came in sheepishly, Barry clutching his ears like he'd been deafened.

'Who has not been delivering their newspapers and why?!'

The twins looked guiltily at each other.

'Billy's not doing it.'

'No, Barry's not doing it!'

'Whoever's not doing it, simply must do it!' Clara said, exasperated. Instinct told her to go up to their room and there in the wardrobe, under the beds, under the mattresses, under the pillows even, were more undelivered papers, stacks of them. Clara was outraged. She took her eye off them for one moment – and this happened.

Barry sighed. 'The news is rubbish anyway. It's peanuts, peanuts and more peanuts.'

'Who wants to read that?' Billy argued. 'No one cares.'

Clara rolled her sleeves up. 'All those people waiting for their papers – you've let them down!'

Uncharacteristically, Billy had burst into tears. He was dressing rapidly. 'We'll do it now...'

'You've got school now!' she bellowed. 'But if you ever get this behind again, there will be hell to pay.'

So now, even though she had *plenty* of other chores to be getting on with, Clara found herself delivering days-old newspapers along the high road and beyond. Not what she wanted to be doing; she would have liked a cry over Victor or Ivor or whoever. And she was racking her brains too – were the twins being affected by anything in particular? Was not delivering the papers a cry for help? She didn't think so, but she couldn't be sure. Maybe they didn't want to go and live with Uncle Stan and Aunt Ruth – but what could she do then? This adoption was taking ages, as they all did, but according to Miss Cooper, it would happen 'any day now.'

As she was dragging the wagon along, Marilyn came after her.

'I'll help if you like.'

Once again, Clara marvelled at the older woman's willingness to join in. And once again, she wondered what life would have been like if she and Michael had married and got to America. She struggled to imagine it in any other way than lovely – she did try to picture it in a different way, a negative way, say; Marilyn being overbearing, Marilyn being distant – but she couldn't. Marilyn was none of those things.

Damn war.

You have to play the hand you're dealt, she reminded herself; but was it wrong to sometimes want an almighty shuffle?

They went along the houses, Clara warning Marilyn about unexpectedly-fierce-dog or the unexpectedly-in-lingerie-lady. Marilyn laughed, but not so much as usual. Clara had a feeling something was on her mind; Marilyn had been so busy touring and partying, maybe she was tired.

They chatted about Victor. Marilyn didn't say, 'I told you so,' because she wasn't that type, but she did say, 'If it's *for* you, it won't pass you by.'

Then Marilyn said, 'Clara, I overheard something at the party last night.'

Marilyn did love a tittle-tattle. As she continued though, Clara realised she was more serious than usual. Her nose was glistening, droplets under her powder.

'Have you heard anything about Australia?'

'In what way?' Clara didn't doubt that Marilyn would be planning to go there next. Get those Australians into hobbies or day trips. She was indomitable.

'In connection with your children?'

'Alex will know about it,' Clara said brightly. 'I'll get him to get his maps out.'

She delivered the next paper. She could feel Marilyn's eyes on her. She almost got her fingers caught in the letter box. Some of them were as sharp as crocodile's teeth.

She returned. 'Clara!' Marilyn's tone was serious. 'They were talking about it regarding the sale of this place.'

'Oh?'

Who were? People at the party?

She folded the paper ready for the next house. Number 13, lucky for some.

'They even knew the name of a ship, something about Largo Bay?'

'Largo Bay?' *It sounded more like a coastal town...*

'Do you know it?'

'I've never—'

'Clara, I might be mistaken, I hope I'm mistaken, but they were talking about – once this place has gone – sending the children there.'

Clara remembered hearing about Australia when she was little. Her parents were world travellers. They'd always talked about it with a reverential tone in their voices. Other adults liked to stay at home, but hers liked nothing more than a ship or a jungle trek.

More recently, Clara's view of Australia was formed by the news reports that they showed before the feature films at the cinema, with the posh voiceover making superior jokes.

Australia was like England but newer or fresher. Or like England but less developed, greener. English-speaking but foreign. Foreign but not *that* foreign. Hot. They grew oranges and bananas. Or was that the Caribbean? Less formal. More friendly. Too friendly? She felt uncomfortable saying the word 'Oz'. Oz was too intimate, like they were old friends or great pals. They were *not* old friends.

She knew sheep outnumbered people in Oz. She didn't know if that was supposed to be a good thing.

'They were talking about sending the children there.' What was this? No one, but no one had mentioned that. As far as she knew, the council were looking for a Suffolk property fit for eight or nine of them. A purpose-build not far from Lavenham. When she last spoke to Mr Sommersby, on the telephone, he had reassured her, 'There are plenty of towns to choose from, some quaint properties too.' And, 'Oh yes, they'll stay at the same schools although I hope you don't mind, Miss Newton, they might need to get a bus.'

A bus? Was there a bus from the other side of the world?

Miss Cooper said Miss Bridges was out all morning, working in the cemeteries.

'Tell her I need her as soon as possible, it's an emergency.' Clara slammed down the telephone and the picture of a water-fall over the hall table trembled.

To her credit, Miss Bridges telephoned back shortly after lunch, but she sounded cross.

'Miss Cooper is your main contact now. You know that.'

'I know, but you always promised to tell it to me straight.'

Now Miss Bridges sounded hesitant. She cleared her throat. 'Always. Is this about Evelyn? You need to get her to her mother. We can't wait—'

'It's not that.'

Clara had a sudden feeling that once this question was out there, everything would change. There would be no going back. Depending on the answer, there would have to be action of some kind.

'There's talk about putting the children on a ship called the *Largo Bay*?'

Miss Bridges laughed. 'Is this coming from Ivor? Is he winding you up?'

'No, it isn't.'

'It sounds like one of his crazy ideas. You need to trust us, Clara. We're keeping you together.'

'You originally said no sale – and you were wrong. They'd kept you out of the loop. Maybe you're wrong about this one too? Have you really not heard anything about Australia?'

There was a long pause and for a moment, Clara wondered if Miss Bridges had hung up on her. Marilyn wandered into the hall, then backed out apologetically.

'I'll look into it,' Miss Bridges said finally. It was like something had just occurred to her.

'What does that mean? You'll ask Mr Horton?'

'For a start, yes.'

'How do I know he'll tell you?' *How do I know you'll tell me the truth?*

'I'm sure it's a storm in a teacup, whatever it is. Could people have misheard or got confused? Australia and...' Miss Bridges searched for a similar word, found none. 'Somewhere else? I'll find out more and I'll let you know. Just hold fire, Clara.'

Clara slammed down the phone. She had no fire to hold.

In fury, Clara unpegged the washing. She'd been calm with Marilyn, cool with Miss Cooper, icy with Miss Bridges; now, alone, the rage bubbled up as she plucked the clothes from the

line, folded them into the basket. If only you could fold up this
nonsense like you could a school shirt. Stella, the blighter, sat on
the clean washing and Clara yelled at her to get off.

*How could she have believed they would keep them together
in Lavenham?*

She had though, she really had. She had put her faith in the
council. She had poo-pooed the far more cynical Ivor. She had
dismissed him. She pictured him saying, *they'll palm off the
children all over the place.* And yet she saw it now – it was deliberate naivety, a deliberate failure to shine the glass. The other
side was blurry, and she had not made the effort to see it clearly.

Had she been in denial?

She remembered Chamberlain and his white paper. The
photographs of his success in the newspapers. And as they cele-
brated with him, there was a thumping sensation around the
ears; you knew it wasn't going to stick, you knew it was a tempo-
rary thing, but you were just so grateful that nothing was going
to change right away that you allowed yourself to be swept up
in it.

And now, they were planning to disperse the children like
seeds of the dandelions that Peg liked to blow.

Clara remembered her mother telling her that they were
going to Africa, the way she'd tried to hide it, like putting
vegetables in your shepherd's pie. 'We won't be back for the
holidays, Clara, do you know why? Because we'll be making a
difference. And you'll continue the progress you've made at
school and you have the Lord on your side – these poor children
don't.'

She couldn't remember the last time she saw her mother; it
was probably at the school, but it might have been in the school
grounds, it might have been in the hall, or in her dormitory. She
didn't know because she didn't know it was her last time – or
maybe she didn't know because she was just a bad daughter.

Her mother with her orangey-brown hair. Her mother was

taller than her; they used to say women outgrow their mothers, but Clara never did. She wished she could remember other things about her, not height, not hair colour, but the things that were far more revealing, her interior life; but she could not and so she was left with these reductive labels: orangey-brown hair. Five foot six. Almost the same height as Clara's father.

Why had they never had the conversations, the important conversations?

Marilyn came out to give her a hand, Stella followed warily behind her. Clara sneezed.

'I hope I haven't set the cat among the pigeons,' Marilyn said.

'Not at all,' Clara said quietly. 'Or if you have, it's a good thing.'

42

The next morning, Miss Bridges was on the doorstep before Clara had had time to clear up the breakfast things; she had been busy dispatching nine children to school, Evelyn had forgotten her ruler and Clara was sure Barry hadn't brushed his teeth; his toothbrush was bone dry. Peg wanted to practise her spellings and Joyce's hair had freed itself from its bobble before she'd even left the house.

'It IS Australia, but it's not what you think.'

'What the?'

'I won't talk to you unless you calm down, Clara. Shall we go in the parlour?'

'The kitchen is fine,' Clara said mutinously. Somehow, in the past forty-eight hours, she had convinced herself it wasn't Australia, it wasn't bad, and that anyway, all would be well – and here she was, back at square one. Yes, they blooming would stay in the kitchen.

'Firstly, it's not *all* the children.'

'What?' Clara sprang up. This was ridiculous. 'Who then... why?'

'Please, I haven't seen a finalised list yet. I'll find out more but, Clara, I have to tell you: this is a wonderful opportunity for some of them.'

Clara put a fake smile on her face. For once, she didn't believe Miss Bridges and this was as painful a feeling as any.

'You said,' she hissed through gritted teeth, 'we would stay together. The council have always said that.'

It was the one thing they were consistent about.

Miss Bridges paused.

'Okay, I was wrong. But it's a great chance for the children. Don't you see?'

Clara starfished her fingers over her face. She couldn't believe it. It felt like an absurd game of Chinese whispers.

'What did Mr Horton say about it?'

Miss Bridges looked meek suddenly. She got up to put the kettle on and with her back to Clara said, 'Mr Horton said it might be a wonderful opportunity.'

'Separating them is a wonderful opportunity?'

A wonderful opportunity was what her parents had said when they were planning to go to Africa and leave her at a boarding school she didn't like. The phrase should come with a warning.

'They're not brothers and sisters, Clara, so it's perfectly acceptable.'

Acceptable?

'And me, separating them from me, that's acceptable too?'

All that talk at her interview and her tribunal about how she should be reliable, consistent, long-term, yet when it suited them it was *bye, bye, lemon pie!* Disposable people.

'You're *house*mother, Clara, not their actual mother.'

That was Mr Horton's language she was parroting, Clara was sure of it. Was Miss Bridges that suggestible? Last year, they had threatened to separate her from the children. Now they were separating the children from each other and their home.

Miss Bridges sat down abruptly, exhaustion all over her face. Clara suddenly felt sorry for her – it wasn't her fault. *Don't shoot the messenger.* But she couldn't stop.

'The children don't want to be moved again.'

'Don't they?'

'They *shouldn't* be moved again,' Clara insisted.

'What is it you're most afraid of?' Miss Bridges asked softly.

Impossible to put into words. Clara watched Stella make her way to the window. The cat who followed the children to school and back. 'I'm afraid they won't find their way.'

After Miss Bridges had left, Clara set about her chores. At lunchtime, she thought about visiting Anita, but Anita was so wrapped up in the baby lately – naturally – she didn't want to burden her. She took a spam sandwich into the garden and chomped it, feeling sorry for herself.

Once the children came back, there was no time for melancholy. Peter wanted compliments on his latest cartoon. Joyce's leg needed looking at. Alex needed some reassurance about his essay on *The Turn of the Screw.* Maureen was complaining about the dunderhead Martin Browne. Rita was in despair over her latest piece – Anita wasn't overseeing her practice because of the baby. They'd tried leaving Howard out in the garden (like the Marie Stopes book advised) but on this, Anita was surprisingly soft and wouldn't even give it ten minutes. 'I can't concentrate when he's squawking,' complained Rita (which annoyed Evelyn, who got upset if someone slighted *her* baby).

Clara got the twins into the parlour after tea – she hadn't forgotten the newspapers, although it felt like weeks ago – and said, 'Boys, is there anything I need to know? Something troubling you, maybe?'

Maybe the twins didn't want to go to live with their Aunt Ruth and Uncle Stan. Maybe this was a cry for help.

But Barry and Billy didn't know what she was talking about. They just hadn't bothered with the papers. 'Sometimes,' Barry said, screwing up his nose, 'you just want a lie-in, don't you, Miss Newton?'

'I do,' said Clara primly. 'But if you make a commitment, you keep to it...'

They apologised again and Clara decided there was no deep-seated anguish here. Sometimes an undelivered news-paper is just an undelivered newspaper. She was glad to move on, for she had more vexing things to worry about.

'Do you know anything about Australia?' Clara asked Alex at bedtime. She wasn't sure what she was asking or what she was hoping to hear, but Alex spun out of bed, thrilled to be of help, to show off his encyclopaedia; Clara gazed at helpless joeys in their mothers' pockets and bug-eyed koalas clutching at trees. That didn't help.

43

The day before Billy and Barry were due to go and live with their Uncle Stan and Aunt Ruth the Lavenham Rovers were playing against Leicester Blues. If the Rovers won this match, they would win the league, but Leicester Blues had a reputation for being cheats.

Marilyn promised to keep an eye on the children and so, for the first time, Clara went to the ground to watch the twins play. If nothing else, it was one way to get her mind off Australia and Ivor.

It was warmer, almost summer; the breeze was pleasant. She followed the sounds of children shouting. A grey-haired man handed her a cigarette: 'You look like you'll need this, love...'

She told him she was supporting the Lavenham Ravers – no, the Rovers – and he laughed.

'That's your lot over there.' He pointed to a gaggle of people who looked much the same as them.

'Does it matter?' asked Clara timidly.

'Not to me,' he said. 'You might feel more at home there, though.'

'Oh, I'm fine,' she said.

He told her he was the grandfather of a Leicester Blues boy, said he never missed a match.

The boys were doing funny walks and exercises. Barry waved and his teammate asked him who he was waving at: 'That's our house mum,' Billy said loudly.

'What's that?' asked another of the boys doing up his laces. Doing up laces took an inordinate amount of time and effort.

'It's like a special aunty,' Barry explained. 'Who looks after you if you haven't got a real mum or dad.'

Billy blew a kiss. Overhearing, the man next to her muttered, 'Well done,' and she said bashfully, 'I do get paid,' and he said: 'Not enough, I bet.'

Barry was a defender; he was a meaty man on a mission. Billy was a dart, moving around – full of the tricks that Clara had seen him do in the garden, but never before when twelve stone of sixteen-year-old was hurtling towards him.

There was a beauty here in this game, Clara realised, but how lovely that Billy and Barry were going to be with people who would recognise it and revere it more than she ever could.

'Is there an intermission?' she said to the man next to her.

He laughed. 'It's not the cinema.' He looked at his watch. 'Half-time in twenty minutes.'

As the other team were haring towards Billy, Clara couldn't help but shriek, 'He's behind you.'

'It's not the pantomime either.' Her neighbour winked.

Clara said it was like that though and he laughed. 'Great stress relief, isn't it?'

And it was. The tension of the last few days, of the Australia issue, came out in a terrific release. Clara bellowed like a warthog until she saw Barry – or was it Billy? – fall to the ground, clutching his leg – agony.

My boy, thought Clara, still unsure which of them it was, but knowing it was one of hers.

'Barry!' guessed Clara racing onto the pitch, only dimly aware that her neighbour was telling her not to. 'What's going on here?'

Everyone was laughing.

'Missus... Are you with him?'

'I am.' Clara started proudly, but the referee had marched towards her and he blew his whistle in her face.

'Out. OUT!'

Clara was sent behind a wire fence, feeling like a naughty schoolgirl. She couldn't see a lot; the pitch was round the corner, and when she dared poke her head around for a better view, the ref pointed his finger at her and made a stern face.

The final score was 3–2 to the Lavenham Rovers. Billy ran over and clutched her and Clara was relieved that they weren't embarrassed by her – or if they had been, she was forgiven. She apologised, but Billy thought it was hilarious and Barry said, 'It happens.'

She asked how his leg was and Barry said cheerfully, 'Oh, I wasn't hurt.'

'What?'

'He was trying to get a free kick,' Billy explained.

Clara couldn't believe this. 'You were pretending? What? Nooo!'

Billy and Barry were laughing so much, they nearly toppled over.

'I don't believe it.'

'Miss Newton,' they chorused, 'you know nothing about football.'

'Never said I did,' Clara said, collecting herself.

On the train home, the boys took up the whole bench, with their muddy legs and their filthy shorts. Clara hoped no one else would come in. She still felt this pressure, in public, for the children to look clean at all times. She knew it wasn't fair – all children get mucky playing football – and she knew many children got judged, not just the Grange children – but hers would be judged *more* for it. She knew that.

And Clara also felt so guilty, for hadn't she always praised Peter's comics, Rita's recitals, Maureen's cakes? And she had encouraged Alex with his schoolwork and his exams, Joyce's photography, Evelyn's interest in babies, Peg's everything. By contrast, with these two, she had just waved them off gaily, glad they weren't roaming around bothering bullocks or breaking glasshouses. Anything could have happened.

'Do you wish I'd come to see you play more often?' she asked. It had been easier with the others – their interests were based in Shilling Grange. Billy and Barry's passion was outside.

Billy nudged her. 'No way. I heard you yelling when I had the ball.'

Barry creased over, laughing. 'And you ran on to the pitch...'

'It's all right,' Billy said kindly, offering her a mint. 'We understood. The little kids needed you more than us. And we've got each other.'

'And our extraordinary talent. Don't forget that.'

Laughing, Clara took the mint and gazed out of the window at the leaves coming into bloom. The branches dipped with the glorious weight of the blossoms. The spring sky was never more beautiful. The clouds, fine wispy things, like young boys' moustaches, came into view, then in seconds had disappeared.

Peter's uncle was still tearing around town. Sometimes his Jaguar screeched down the high road, making you wince for the tyres. Other times, the car was parked outside Robinson, Browne and White. Clara had learned to avoid him – to look away and not meet his eye. Peter was so wrapped up in his comics and his new 'friend' that Clara knew it was stupid to get offended on his behalf. Nevertheless, she dreamed about sliding a sharp object along the side of that expensive car, or putting nails down in front of the tyres, under cover of darkness. Not that she ever would. It was just a fantasy. *Revenge is living well*, she told herself. Peter might be living well, she thought, but she was living on a hair trigger.

As she and the twins walked down the high road after the match, Peter's uncle gave her a mocking salute.

'Who *is* that?' asked Barry and she told him it was no one.

Idly, she wondered if the sale of the house had anything to do with him. He would have loved to get his revenge on her and he was friends with some influential people.

She sent the boys ahead and popped into the library, where she found Mr Dowsett up a ladder that was alarmingly high and wobbly for his advanced years. He descended precariously and Clara hovered uselessly underneath, her arms out to catch him if he fell, although she doubted she could.

'Mr Dowsett, do *you* know anything about sending English children to Australia?'

There were few things in this world that Mr Dowsett did not know about, but at this he looked puzzled and felt his wizardy beard.

'Not a thing, but I can look into it if you like.'

Clara thanked him, 'It's probably nothing,' she said.

44

ARTICLE FOR THE *SHILLING GRANGE NEWS*, MAY 1950

We are the champions

by Billy

On a warm wet day in May, the Lavenham Rovers thrashed the bejeezus out of the idiot Leicester Blues. Billy scored loads. They were cheats. They played dirty, we played dirtier.

'You wanted me to reserve three pages of the sports section for this?' Alex's voice was high with incredulity.

'Uh-huh!'

'Couldn't you make it any longer?'

'Ninety minutes not long enough for you?'

'I meant the article.'

'Not really.'

Alex had his head in his hands.

Barry shrugged at Clara. 'I thought it was all right.'

The next morning, packing their bags, Billy said, 'I feel like we've done this before.'

Clara held up football socks caked in mud that had been squidged behind the side of the bed.

'You have. I hope it works out better than last time.'

'Can we come back if it goes wrong?'

'Yes, but no hitching this time.' Clara gave them some emergency money and the Grange phone number, which they memorised, just in case. 'It's going to be football, football and more football. What can possibly go wrong?'

Aunt Ruth had telephoned. *What meals do they like? What's their favourite pudding?* Clara had typed up and posted a copy of the twins' files to them. They'd only be an hour away. Easy to keep in contact. It wasn't a goodbye, she told them, but a see-you-later.

Just before she hung up, Aunt Ruth had said, 'The rumours weren't true then.'

'What rumours?'

'That the council were slow. We thought we'd be stuck on a list for years!'

It was a school day and the others had gone off, crying into their sleeves. Even Maureen said she'd miss the boys, although she also jabbed their elbows and said it meant more fruitcake to go round.

'Do you remember the ghost that first day?' Clara asked the twins now.

'I do,' Barry said.

'I said from the start that Miss Newton is a good sort,' said Billy.

'No, you never! I said it to you.'

'BOYS!' Clara laughed.

They came out with their bags. They didn't have much to show for all their years at the Grange and that made Clara's heart ache too. Miss Cooper, looking more glamorous than ever in her sunglasses and pedal-pushers, was taking them. Leaning against the car, she yawned. Clara wondered about Miss Cooper's exotic life and her freedom, but right then she wouldn't have changed her own life for the world. Forget the sale, forget the Australia thing, this was what the job was about – helping children get to appropriate permanent homes. She didn't doubt that Uncle Stan and Aunty Ruth were right for the twins.

'Will everything be okay here?' Billy asked.

That was the question.

'Of course. Don't make a nuisance of yourselves.'

'You too, Miss Newton.'

The boys bundled into the back of the car and Clara waved, and kept waving even after she could no longer see them. And then she ran to the newsagents to tell them that no, they wouldn't be delivering newspapers anymore.

45

Miss Bridges drove Clara to London, where they were going to meet a Miss Holdsworth to find out more about Australia. Miss Holdsworth was in charge of travel arrangements: visas, tickets and placements. It was exactly one week – or seven sleepless nights – since Australia had entered Clara's consciousness and she was struggling to think of anything else.

'I know you're annoyed but try to keep an open mind—' Miss Bridges started.

'I'm not annoyed,' said Clara. The word 'annoyed' seemed inadequate to encompass the range of emotions she was experiencing.

That morning, Alex – who had a sixth sense when it came to Clara's emotional state – had asked, 'What are you doing today?'

'Meetings!' she had told him. 'With Miss Bridges.'

At that, he'd looked worried. 'I don't want to see my father ever again, Miss Newton' he said and took a breath. 'But I don't want to lose you all...'

'I'm going to sort something out.'

Now she wondered if she had the wit or the wherewithal to do any such thing.

If she had been avoiding Ivor before, now she was taking even greater pains not to see him. He had been right; the council were going to palm them off. She had been duped but she couldn't bear to admit that to him. Ivor was a darn know-it-all at the best of times.

Sometimes, she would see his workshop lights turn on and off and wonder if it was a sign, a code for her. If he were perhaps saying, 'Please come over, let's make up.' If only those smoke signals were clearer. The temptation to run to him, to throw her arms round him and say *I can't stop thinking about you* remained as strong as ever, but she wouldn't do that, she couldn't do that, especially not now. There was such a thing as burnt bridges and she had truly decimated theirs.

She held her handbag and her paperwork so tightly her knuckles were white. Miss Bridges smoked as she drove; the car had an ashtray that was full, not only of cigarette ends but cigar ends too, Mr Horton making his presence felt. Miss Bridges gave her a full-beam smile as if she expected Clare to do the same back, then when she didn't, she patted her hand.

'I hate it when you fret, Clara.'

'I can't help it – it's a mess.'

'We always put the children first, Clara. Remember that.'

When they arrived, Clara said, 'I can go in by myself,' but Miss Bridges wasn't having any of it and bustled them towards a slim red brick building with a sign next to the door that said CHILD MIGRANT PROGRAMME.

Inside, the room was full of mostly empty bookshelves and smelled of paint. Miss Holdsworth was an older, thin-faced woman with her hair in a net. She seemed both flattered and bewildered by their visit.

'You're from Suffolk Council, is it? Lovely part of the world. I'm not sure how I can help you though.'

Miss Bridges said, 'As I said on the telephone, we've just got a few questions about the children going to Australia.'

'Not sure I can help,' she repeated. 'They just send us the list and we arrange the details – the bookings, the allocations, that sort of thing.'

'That's all we want to know – the details,' Miss Bridges continued smoothly and Clara thought to herself, not for the first time, that Bridges was a suitable name for her – she built bridges everywhere she went.

Miss Holdsworth apologised that everything had been packed for redecorating – she gestured around her – but she had managed to find an up-to-date photo album they might be interested in. This was a positive, thought Clara. On the front, there was a yellow sticker: DAVENPORT DOWNS 1948.

There were four children in the photos. They did look happy. On a seesaw, a girl laughing, legs outstretched. Shades of Peg. A boy sitting in a rubber tyre hanging from a tree. The same children on a blanket having a tea party, squinting open-mouthed into the camera, shafts of light making patterns across their clothes. Two boys pushing out their skinny chests and flexing their tiny arms; they could have been Billy and Barry five years back. 'Wonderful isn't it? Sheer joy,' Miss Holdsworth said.

'It's so far away though,' Clara mumbled to herself.

There was a map of Australia on the desk. Upside down, it looked like those meteorites they thought would hit Planet Earth in 2020.

'How many have gone so far?' Miss Bridges asked.

'Not sure.'

'How about an approximate figure?' she persisted.

'Oh er, several thousand.' This seemed a large number, but Clara didn't know if, in these circumstances, it was or not, and Miss Bridges didn't ask.

'And this is... have you more photo albums?' She thought, that's what Mr Dowsett might ask.

'You've seen one, you've seen them all,' Miss Holdsworth said.

Miss Bridges took the photo album from Clara's knees and smiled indulgently at the pictures. 'Oh, look, Clara,' she said. 'This child is playing with a hose – I bet the children would love that.'

A hose, thought Clara. *Big deal.*

Clara's stomach was churning now. If this visit was meant to reassure her, it was not working. She felt a powerful yearning to be back at Shilling Grange. She wanted to hang on to the children for dear life. Miss Bridges perhaps caught some of Clara's uneasiness, for she closed the album.

'So do you have the names of those going?' said Clara.

'I don't decide,' said Miss Holdsworth quickly. 'I told you, I just get sent the lists.'

'Do you have the Suffolk list here?' Miss Bridges sounded like she was pleading.

'I have three from Suffolk children's homes.'

'Lavenham then?'

Miss Holdsworth searched among the paperwork on her desk, then handed over a paper to Miss Bridges with a toothy smile. Clara's heart was racing.

- Billy and Barry Coulson, 14 years.
- Rita Jane Withers, 11 years.
- Alexander David Nichols, 12 years.
- James Peter Downey, 15 years.
- Maureen Amy Keaton, 15 years.

'Six,' Miss Bridges said.

'Six,' repeated Clara, open-mouthed.

'That's not many,' said Miss Holdsworth. 'I've sent more from one establishment before. Far more.'

'B-but two of them – Billy and Barry Coulson – have already left.'

If they couldn't get this right, what else were they getting wrong? Or were they saying they'd go and get Billy and Barry from their new home?

'Shame,' Miss Holdsworth said. She didn't hesitate, just drew a line through the twins' names as though they had never existed. 'Fourteen? They sound just right for it.'

'How do you mean?'

Miss Holdsworth ignored that. 'Just four then.'

Clara was shaking her head. 'Why not Joyce or Evelyn? Why not Peg? Why those and not the others? It seems so arbitrary to leave some children out, especially if it's – as you say – sheer joy for them.'

Miss Holdsworth's expression was vacant. Clara felt like doing what the children did to her sometimes: waving a hand in front of her eyes and going, 'Cooee, is anyone home?'

'I don't know...'

'Is it because Peg doesn't speak?'

'I really don't know. If I did—'

'Maybe they haven't got the facilities for Peg?' suggested Miss Bridges, ever the moderator.

'What facilities does Joyce need then, or Evelyn?' Clara asked.

'They chose the ones who will benefit the most,' Miss Holdsworth said stirringly. 'There's no point sending ones who won't. The idea is a clean break. A fresh start.'

'What happens to the ones not on the list?' Clara asked.

'Wouldn't we all want that, someday?' Miss Holdsworth said, chuckling. She had an extraordinary knack of avoiding a question. 'I know I would.'

'How do they decide which children will benefit most?' Clara asked.

Miss Holdsworth took the album and slipped it onto a shelf. She sat down again. 'But you say it's perfect for them...' Clara persisted. 'How can it be an idyll for some but not all of the children?'

No one spoke. Clara could hear faint footsteps and distant voices from the offices above.

'Miss Holdsworth?'

Miss Holdsworth scowled. 'I don't do the selection, I told you.'

Selection?

'And is the selection final?' chimed in Miss Bridges.

Miss Holdsworth didn't sound as composed as she had earlier. 'We've never had any issues before.'

Clara imagined stowing away on this great ship – *Largo Bay*, was it? and surprising them on arrival. Was that the answer? That she should go with them to Australia? That would give Ivor something to think about! She would be in desert boots and long crusty scout shorts; they would march down dusty roads to the sound of a didgeridoo. Didgeridoo. The word pleased her. It had funny sounds. She imagined saying it to Peg, and Peg laughing.

'And what happens to those not on the list? They'll stay with me, right?' she asked.

Peg. Evelyn. Joyce.

'That's not my department.' On this, Miss Holdsworth was clear.

Maybe they'd *want* to be in Australia – maybe this was the answer, a wonderful opportunity for them.

But it wouldn't be for Peter, who was counting the days until he started his dream job in London.

Nor for Maureen, who hated leaving Lavenham even for just one day.

Not Rita, whose every waking thought was of the Festival of Britain and impressing her mama.

Maybe Alex, who would enjoy anything if you put the word 'educational' in front of it – but none of the others– well, maybe Joyce would rise to the challenge. She was the only one of them who wanted to travel, she wanted to see the world. But she wasn't even on the list...

Trust your instincts, Clara tried telling herself. What did they say now?

'I think, no thank you,' she said finally. 'It's not for them. Not my children.'

Miss Holdsworth laughed, then stopped abruptly. She bowed her head and Clara could see the hairnet and it was like something dark and monstrous was trapped in there.

'You don't seem to be understanding, dear, they're on the list.'

'Then take them off the list,' snapped Clara, losing patience. Miss Bridges whispered, 'Clara,' and stretched out her hands, palms down.

Miss Holdsworth had clearly had enough too. She stood up, nearly banging her head on one of the shelves. 'We're proud of the Child Migrant Programme. It's changing lives.'

'*Changing* them is one way of putting it.'

'The children will go to Australia if they are on my list,' Miss Holdsworth retorted. 'It's for their own well-being. There is no reason, no case, not to.'

'Then why not *all* of them? It doesn't make any sense.'

'Evelyn has a mother here, perhaps that's why...' Miss Bridges tried.

'And Alex has a father here, and Rita *believes* she has a mother here, so it's something else and I want to know what—'

'If you don't want to send them, I can only conclude the reason is that you're xenophobic.'

Clara peered at Miss Holdsworth. She didn't recognise the

word but she didn't like it. Miss Bridges' expression was incredulous; she gulped like Billy and Barry 2 listening to classical music.

'I mean it. What have you got against Australia?'

Clara shook her head, lost for words.

It had begun to rain while they were in the office. Just on the short walk from there to the car, Clara's hat, her hair and coat got drenched.

They were silent for most of the journey home. It would have been hard to speak over the windscreen wipers, which made a screeching noise like Stella if you trod on her paw but Clara didn't want to talk anyway. What was there to say? The wipers didn't work fast enough, either, and the windscreen was a blur of water. Miss Bridges' face was almost pressed to the glass, her bottom at the edge of her seat. A car screeched by on a roundabout, far too fast for the conditions, and Clara thought it might be Peter's uncle.

A clean break. A fresh start.

Australia equalled beaches. She knew the children loved Lyme Regis. Digging, building castles in the sand. Less of a class system too, not like here where the top jobs were held by Lords or Sirs. They were good in the war as well, Australia; better than good, they were heroes.

The rain continued. They had more sunshine over there. The temperature was consistently ten or fifteen degrees higher than it was in Suffolk. Clara had looked. (Indoorsy Alex wouldn't like that. Sunny Peg might. But Peg wasn't even on the list.)

One hour later, the car skidded to a halt outside the Grange. The lights were on in Ivor's workshop. What would he say about this? What *could* he say? Other than 'I told you so!'

Miss Bridges looked worn out. The home-bound journey

had taken a long time. The list, the damn list of selected children, slid across the dashboard towards Clara. She read it again:

- Rita Jane Withers, 11 years.
- Alexander David Nichols, 12 years.
- James Peter Downey, 15 years.
- Maureen Amy Keaton, 15 years.

Not Evelyn, not Joyce, not Peg.

Clara and Miss Bridges both started to speak at the same
time:

'Over my dead body—'

'They're not going—'

The two women looked at each other and then – it began as
a nervous chuckle, a reaction to the meeting and the tense drive,
but then they were both properly side-splitting laughing from
the guts like comic-book characters.

'That's settled then,' said Miss Bridges. She grabbed Clara's
hand. 'We're going to fight this, girl. All of it. They're not going
to Australia. Not like this. Over my dead body. That's not children first. I don't know what the hell this is, but it's not
happening on my watch.'

46

'Okay, so what are we going to do?' Miss Cooper said two days later, in her office. Although Clara knew space in the office was tight, she was always surprised how grubby it was. Still, she was grateful that Miss Cooper had been persuaded to join the battle.

Miss Bridges let out a large breath. 'The obvious thing to do is try to stop the sale.'

'We've got more hope of flying a man to the moon,' said Clara.

'Couldn't we just persuade Mr Browne not to buy?' said Miss Cooper. 'There must be someone he'd listen to.'

Clara could feel her heart thud-thudding out of her ribs. If Maureen would help, maybe. But she knew Maureen wouldn't help.

'Clara?' asked Miss Bridges.

Clara felt hot. She fiddled with the button of her collar. 'I doubt it. What other ideas are there? We must have some other ideas!'

Miss Bridges was always a fan of a plan B. And she didn't disappoint now.

'I suggest the main thing we focus on is working out alternative places for the children so that they avoid going to the other side of the world,' she said.

'Some of them,' she looked at her notes, 'already are in process, which is promising – we need to treat these with great urgency and get some more through.'

'I've already managed to poach a couple,' Miss Cooper said, 'from Sussex.'

'Poach?' Clara's mind went to eggs.

'Prospective adopters. There's a man in children's services there who,' she hesitated, to readjust her hairclip, 'shall we say, has grown fond of me?'

Clara could imagine. Miss Cooper was the kind of woman men made drooling fools of themselves over.

'The Woodwards have gone through the checks already – so if they matched with one of the Grange children, it could be quick.'

Clara would not allow herself to think about the child in Sussex who was ready to be paired and had had it snatched from them. She had to get her children good homes.

'They've been working in Africa.'

'Missionaries?'

'Mrs Woodward is a teacher, her husband is an engineer.'

'O-kay.'

Miss Cooper sifted through her notes: 'I think they'd be an excellent choice for Rita – if you're in favour, we'll push ahead with that.'

Clara's heart sank. Not Rita, not her Rita who curled up like a comma at night and whispered 'Mama' when she opened the lid of her piano. Not Rita who swore she spoke cat language and who tried to blink at Stella to make her go to sleep. But rather that than have her sent away to goodness knows where.

'Fine,' she said. The word hung in the air for ages and it seemed to say, *not fine*.

'I think I'll be able to arrange something for Peter...' Clara added eventually. The comic people in London were keen on Peter, she knew it in her bones. And the job came with accommodation. They would have taken him on straight away, it was Clara who had proposed he wait until he was sixteen. Peter, Peter was safe.

'How about Maureen?'

Clara breathed out. 'Last year there were some people interested in her. I remember a family.'

Miss Bridges shook her head. 'The mum's dead,' she said. 'Cancer.'

'Oh.'

'And Alex?'

'I might have an idea for Alex...' said Clara. Something had occurred to her just a few days ago. At the time, she had dismissed it as ridiculous – but now seemed a time for ridiculous ideas.

'Not his father, Clara,' warned Miss Bridges. 'He's entirely unsuitable.'

'No, not him...' Clara responded, annoyed. *Did Miss Bridges think she was completely dopey?*

'He won't be happy with anything we do...'

'I've thought of a way round that,' Clara said.

Be more Mama Bear, Clara thought. While she had loved her mother, and felt her loss acutely, no one could ever have accused Mrs Newton of being Mama Grizzly. She was, in no particular order, church, husband, prayer. Clara was a cub who had to make her own way in the world. She wasn't having that for Alex – or any of the Shilling Grange children.

'We give the impression Alex has gone missing—'

'Missing?'

'Yes,' Clara continued uncertainly. It wasn't a great plan. 'Just to get his father off the scent.'

'Isn't that cruel?' Miss Cooper said, after a while.

'Yes. No. Well, it's the answer to a problem.'

'And Evelyn?' Miss Bridges said. 'She'll be going to her mother, I presume.'

'Any time soon,' Clara said, crossing her fingers. 'That will be happening.'

'The other thing I want to say is,' Miss Bridges went on, 'we must keep this absolutely between ourselves. No telling anyone, Clara, not even Victor or Ivor.'

'Victor and I are no longer together,' said Clara, flushing.

'Excellent,' Miss Bridges said, then she gave a sad smile to Clara, 'I mean, sorry.'

Clara was going to say, 'and Ivor is not talking to me anyway', but Miss Cooper was flapping her papers, meaning the meeting was over.

Miss Smith's campaign to win over her daughter had not yet fully succeeded, but she did not falter. They went for walks and to tea rooms. (More tea rooms than walks, but still.) Sometimes, Evelyn went to the surgery to meet her mother after-school (and to check on Billy and Barry 2). And they often went to the park together. Evelyn swung on the rusty swing and Miss Smith pushed. Miss Smith was canny enough to understand that the way to Evelyn's heart was her stomach and she always kept a liquorice or a penny chew in her handbag.

That weekend, for the first time, Evelyn had consented to a night away with her mother. The pair went to Southwold and stayed overnight in Miss Smith's friend's house. Out of all the things – the sea, the amusements – Evelyn seemed most impressed by the rock garden. Evelyn brought back a shell for Peg's collection and a toad ornament for Joyce, who had once expressed a passing interest in frogs.

'Did you have a lovely time?' Clara had asked her.

'The best,' she'd said. She was so exhausted she could barely get up the stairs. 'We had scones on Saturday and an English breakfast today. Ooh and candyfloss and a stick of rock.'

Usually, Miss Smith didn't stop to chat with Clara. She was still defensive or antagonistic with her. Maybe she blamed Clara for the delay. Clara thought that might be fair enough. But after this night away, she did and as they chatted, for the first time, Clara liked the woman. *We might grow to be friends,* she thought suddenly, 'She held my hand,' Miss Smith whispered to Clara as she left the doorstep. 'All day long.'

She couldn't have been prouder.

47

Clara went back to the library first thing the next morning. This time Mr Dowsett was deep in the newspaper section.

'Any luck?'

'Maybe...'

Mr Dowsett had found some articles about the journey to Australia. Some of the accounts were glowing. He read aloud: 'There was a pool and my sister won a dance contest.' Others were less so: 'We slept in dormitories; the drunks carousing kept me up all night.' Or, 'The sound of people vomiting over the side will never leave me.'

'Oh, this is interesting,' Clara said.

Some of the stories he quoted were amusing: 'Six weeks on board for some was party party party; my mate got together with a sailor, imagine her surprise when we disembarked and a woman came running over to him shouting, "he's my husband".'

'I was going to work in construction. I met Peggy Sue and we now have three little Aussies. Fred hates boats and Pip hates trains.'

Clara laughed.

'So, have you got anything about what happened after they

arrived? Or,' she scanned the article she was holding, 'anything on orphans in particular?'

'Not a thing.'

'Ho,' Clara said, feeling discouraged. 'That's useless, isn't it?'

Mr Dowsett was stroking his beard. 'There should be though, shouldn't there? If, as you say, thousands have already gone, and there are plans for thousands more, where are these children disappearing to? It should be logged. It should be followed through.'

If anyone loved record-keeping, Clara did. She sat up straight. 'You mean there's nothing anywhere?'

'Nothing, in the newspapers. I'm drawing a complete blank.'

'So what does it mean?'

He shrugged. 'It could just be incompetence or...'

'Or?'

'I'll keep looking.'

48

When Victor Braithwaite saw Clara standing outside his lecture theatre, he threw his arms in the air and shook his head from side to side, which, thought Clara, was not an entirely auspicious start.

He was carrying *How Communism Works* and he placed it over his heart.

'Five minutes,' Clara said, holding up her fingers for emphasis. 'That's all.'

Victor led them out to a sloped lawn. There were students everywhere, shouting, laughing, pontificating. The young men wore waistcoats and had rolled up their sleeves like they were performing manual labour. The young women wore the New Look jackets nipped in at the waist and didn't look awkward or down-at-heel. And they didn't sink into the grass like she did.

'Remember you said you'd love one more in the family?'

The fear in Victor's eyes!

'Clara,' he said in a sterner voice than she'd ever heard, 'did I not make myself clear?'

She almost laughed. 'I don't mean me, Victor!'

He stuttered and she would have told him about the King's speech impediment, but he probably already knew that; Victor knew everything, or at least it felt like he did.

'I am pleased to see you,' he said, 'I'm just concerned you've got the wrong idea.'

Don't flatter yourself, she thought, but she couldn't say that; she had to be pleasant if she was going to win him over. This wasn't Miss Cooper-level poaching, it was scrambling, maybe. Or boiling.

'I have got an idea,' she said. 'It's for you to decide if it's the wrong one.'

Some students said, 'Hello Professor Braithwaite,' as they walked by. When the students had moved out of earshot and were playing a game of French cricket with tennis rackets, Clara turned to him again.

'Alex needs a permanent home. It has become important now, more than ever. I wondered if you would consider adopting him?'

Alex was only twelve years old. His skin was less clear than it was and his hair had grown longer – no bad thing perhaps because it disguised his jug-ears. He was still short and perhaps heavier than he should be. He adored reading and quoting impossible quotes. Bernard was his favourite person in the world, probably followed by Peg, Ivor and Peter.

And he had his drunken father stalking him and a place on a boat to Australia.

'I know this may come as a shock.'

Victor grimaced. 'I wouldn't say shock exactly.'

Clara thought how much she liked this burly man, not loved but liked. Perhaps it would have turned into love one day, if they had given it time. Or perhaps you didn't need to get involved with every eligible man you met. Friendships were important too.

'What would you say?'

She remembered he had praised communal living. He thought there were too many uncared-for children in the world to have one's own. But was he one of those men who was all talk no trousers? He wanted kindness – but he didn't want to be kind. Clara had a bad feeling about this. Was Victor a communist in theory, yet a capitalist in practice – like so many men? He would be agreeable when it was no skin off his nose – yet when it was...

She knew her parents might have said, *it's God's duty*, but Victor had no God. Did he have citizen's duty?

'I thought single people couldn't adopt...'

'That's right, but your sister lives with you and she always wanted to have a family, didn't she?'

'She does. Eliza did, yes.'

He lit a cigarette.

'I didn't know you smoked.'

'I don't usually,' he said, inhaling deeply. 'Only when I'm... what's the word... *confuddled*?'

He was so right for Alex!

'So what are you saying here, Clara? You think it's my duty to take on Alex?'

'It's not what *I* think that's important here,' Clara lied. 'It's what *you* think.' She watched the smoke curl up to the sky. 'And Alex is a lovely boy.'

Alex. Alex and his jug-ears. Alex and his vocabulary. Alex and the way he laughed. He could be destined for great things – and even if not, he was destined for loveliness.

Victor was still deep in thought.

Clara felt a sudden bolt of despair. She should have known; when it came to people like Victor, he was for the good of the people, *the social contract*, but not *these* people... He had theories about how other people should live but he didn't want to put himself out. There was always going to be an excuse.

'I have a heart, Clara,' he said finally. 'You might not think so—'

'I know—'

'I'm not unfeeling, I didn't want to lead you up the garden path.'

'There are no hard feelings.' Clara felt like his students might feel in his lessons – waiting gloomily for their marks to be returned.

'Will the council be able to expedite the process?' he asked. He picked up a daisy and narrowed his eyes at it.

Clara's hopes unexpectedly lifted. Was he coming round to the idea?

'Apparently so. It won't be official immediately – he'll just be a visitor – but it shouldn't take long if you and Eliza consent.'

'But, Clara, if the father finds out, he'll trace him to us, no?'

'Yes, which is why we'll cover up where he's gone. The father, he is... I don't think he's got the means or the will to push too hard.'

Out on the water, on that soft, muzzy river, students were punting. It was beautiful and timeless. It could have been 1849, thought Clara, or the year 2000. It wasn't the most efficient way to get around, but sometimes aesthetics are important. And sometimes taking the long way round was the best way to go.

'And you've thought of a way to cover up, in case his father does come after him?'

'Nearly – you'll have to leave that to us. Obviously, the fewer people who know the better.'

She thought of Ivor again. He would have to be kept out of this; and the children would tell their teachers or their friends, so they mustn't know either. No, awkward as it might be, it was best it was just between them.

'During the war,' Victor said, 'I had to get a man out of occupied France – one of our own, a pilot, he was in hiding. There was a Jewish boy there, also in hiding – he was ill, very ill, but they couldn't get him any medicine and there was hardly enough food. We were under instructions to get our man out, only our man. "Don't go inviting trouble," they said. Of course, I ignored it. I wanted to take the boy with us. But our man was badly injured, he couldn't walk, and I couldn't carry him and the boy didn't want to leave either. And that was it. I don't know if he survived. I like to think he did. But deep down, I don't think he made it...' Victor's head was so low, it was almost on his knees. 'I wasn't able to help him. I'll always regret that.'

Clara couldn't think what to say. Poor Victor. The things people lived with. The memories they carried around with them. You couldn't tell from the outside either. It made her heart ache. She patted his hand. Finally, she said, 'War is terrible,' and he looked at her with his sad, craggy face and nodded. A few minutes passed before he said, 'I'll have to ask Bernard for his agreement, of course.'

'Of course!' Clara agreed. He was going to say yes, she thought, he really was.

Students were looking over at them. She didn't care. She felt heady. She might have kissed him then.

Just ahead of them, a punter, a beginner perhaps, got stuck, and the boat moved on without him. He clung to the pole, cuddling it like a koala in Alex's encyclopaedia, and then – it seemed like slow motion – fell into the river, to applause and laughter. He came up smiling, his hair slicked back, living in the moment. It was planned, suspected Clara, but that took nothing from it.

'And Eliza...'

'Definitely.'

She imagined Eliza, that kind woman who had been so horribly bereaved. Would this make her life better or worse? Clara believed strongly it would be better. Alex was irresistible. And she thought for a moment of her dear departed Judy, her best friend, who had wanted Alex so much, and how that could have turned out differently too.

Then Victor grinned broadly, and it was as refreshing as a splash into water. 'I think we both know what they'll say...'

49

The Woodwards reminded Clara of the people who had adopted little Terry last year – the Lewises. Slightly older, weathered, beautifully patient people. The notes said they had lost a child too; there was no special word for those.

Clara called Rita in to the parlour, where they were waiting, but she insisted she was going to the shed.

'Can we come out there?' Clara suggested, but Rita walked off, 'Not today.'

Clara grabbed hold of her in the kitchen and whispered, 'What's going on?'

But Rita looked incredulous before shaking her off. 'There's no way I'm going to live with them.'

Clara began her rehearsed speech: 'Your mama would have wanted you to—' But Rita tossed this aside: 'I've got the audition for the Festival of Britain soon.'

'Is that all you're thinking about?'

Rita screwed up her nose. 'I've been practising so much.'

'You'll be able to play and perform wherever you go, Rita.'

'I don't want to do it somewhere else, I want to represent Shilling Grange and Suffolk next year. Tell them to go away.'

'Rita!' Clara found herself almost hysterical. *Australia*, she thought. *Australia is coming for you*. She imagined the ship at the dock with its portholes and plimsoll lines. The party, party, parties every night. Little girls getting lost. No one looking after them. Crying into their bunks. Drowning in the pools. She shuddered.

She knelt down by Rita.

'Now you listen to me. You have to—'

'No, I don't.' Rita skipped outside. Clara could go out and drag her back, or...

Shame-faced, she went back in to the parlour: 'Slight problem...'

～

Exactly one week after Clara's conversation with Victor, on an overcast goose-pimply morning, the clouds intimating rain, Marilyn left. 'No fanfares,' she said firmly, 'we've done that. And who knows, I might have to come over next year too.'

That they had done it already didn't stop Clara feeling tearful.

She did love having Marilyn nearby. Even if she was unpredictable and too friendly with Julian's crowd. Even if she kept going on unlikely coach trips to places Clara had never heard of, even if she came from a world far away and a culture absurdly different. Marilyn made Clara feel safe. The children loved it when she was here. And Clara thought they behaved better when she was around too. Marilyn had that ingredient Clara felt she lacked: authority. She could be silly, but one look from her could make you swap your knife and fork over or give your shoes that extra shine.

Marilyn said she had one request before she left.

'Anything!'

'I want you to meet up with your special neighbour.'

'Ivor?' Clara's voice cracked. 'Why?'

'He's worried about the children. Very worried.'

Clara turned away from her. Marilyn managed to stick her nose into everything.

Clara had been avoiding Ivor – well, he had been avoiding her. But she couldn't see him, because of the stupid things she had said to him. And also because she had these secret plans going on, which Ivor wasn't to know about. The fewer people who knew the better; Miss Bridges would kill her if she told anyone.

Marilyn steamrollered on. 'And you, Clara, dear, Ivor worries about *you*.'

Clara made a harumphing sound. 'If he worried about me, he would have behaved differently when he came back.'

'I know what I see.' Marilyn buttoned her coat. There were so many buttons, like little black coins; it took her ages. Clara puffed out her cheeks and waited.

Marilyn's voice was low when she said, 'Michael would have liked Ivor.'

'Don't say that,' Clara said, a sudden lump in her throat, but this only made Marilyn more ardent.

'He would have, sweetheart. I know it. He wouldn't have wanted you to be sad or lonely. What would he have said? *My best girl deserves a good life...* You know he would.'

There wasn't time for speeches with Alex, or perhaps it was that neither of them wanted to. He sneaked into Clara's room early in the morning though, his hair dishevelled and his pyjamas askew.

'Who is to take over the newspaper?' he whispered.

It had been getting harder to get the children to contribute. Rita – who used to want to be a writer – had decided she was too busy with her piano. Peg would only do poems. Joyce and

Evelyn copied half-heartedly from books. Alex was the only one who bothered.

'Perhaps you can still do it from Oxford?' she suggested but he shrugged.

Alex had never been a cuddly boy and he wasn't about to change. He said, 'Thank you for getting rid of my nits – my hair has been a veritable extermination ground.'

'Pleasure.'

'And helping me pass the eleven-plus exam.'

'You're welcome.'

'And finding me a new home,' he rubbed his eyes. 'I think it's a sensible idea to get away from—' he paused, 'my father, I do.'

Clara told him to stop now, he was making her cry.

He climbed into her lap and kissed her cheek. 'I'll always love you, Miss Newton.'

Clara had prepared for this. '*Te amimas*,' she said in Latin.

He looked her deep in the eyes. 'That doesn't work.'

Marilyn and Alex went everywhere together that morning and spoke to everyone. Marilyn pulled her enormous trunk. Alex also had a large bag, a suspiciously large bag.

'Where are you two off to then?' asked the Garrards.

'Going anywhere special?' the postmistress wanted to know.

They stopped to stroke Julian's dog, they saw a teacher from Alex's old school, they returned some books at the library and Mr Dowsett told them the books Alex had reserved on the Archbishop of Canterbury were in, but Alex had refused to take them, which was odd. Then they went to the station and took the train to London. The ticket-master was sure he'd heard them say they were heading for an airport. Mrs Garrard said they may have said Heathrow but she might have imagined it.

The postmistress thought she heard New York. No one knew what was going on and that was exactly the point.

Clara sat the children down that evening and explained: 'Alex has gone. I want to reassure you that he has gone somewhere he is going to be very happy – his permanent home. He's going to write to you as soon as he is settled but for the moment I can't tell you any more.'

The children seemed to take the news with equanimity – perhaps since Clara was so positive about it – but later, Peter knocked on her bedroom door.

'What's happening to us?' he asked, for once looking her directly in the eye.

'How do you mean?'

'I overheard you talking about ships with Marilyn.'

'It won't affect you, Peter.'

She had telephoned the comic people and spoken to the handsome man from the interview. She had asked for 'flexibility with the starting date. That is, can we bring it forward?' Often turning sixteen could be a disaster for children in care; in this case, however, Peter's age was going to save him – he would have accommodation and an income; and what's more, Clara would be able to visit him. Without hesitating, the handsome man said absolutely yes. He also said that he'd like to take Clara out for a date one day and she had giggled, not only at his audacity but because it was ridiculous. Handsome man hadn't looked much older than fifteen himself. No dates would be happening. But then he had turned unexpectedly serious: 'I want you to know, Peter has great talent. We'll nurture him and take care of him, don't worry.'

'But what about the others?' Peter said, his freckly face still concerned. 'Is it true they are going to be sent away?'

'Not if I can help it.'

. . .

For the next few days, Clara worried that Alex's father would come for him. She dreamed about him putting his foot in the door, forcing his way in. She pictured him rampaging through the house, petrifying Stella. She thought of the words she would say to him, to try to calm him down, to help him make a retreat without feeling like he'd made a retreat: 'The council have rehoused Alex. If you make an application, they'll give you a contact – if,' she would add querulously, 'they deem it appropriate. Does it seem appropriate to you?'

She identified what she might use as weapons – umbrella, iron, doorstop and, if the worst came to the worst, the bread-knife – and decided to keep them to hand.

Or perhaps he might come sober or contrite and they would sit nice and civilised and talk of the weather. She would tell him Alex had been taken in by a family who would look after him, educate and encourage him, and he would sigh, and say, 'For the best, isn't it?'

The one thing she didn't anticipate was that he wouldn't come by at all – but he didn't. Maybe he didn't care that much. Maybe it had grown too complicated for him. After about two weeks of jumping every time the doorbell went, Clara began to forget about him.

50

On Sunday evening, even though it was their day off, Miss Cooper and Miss Bridges came round. Miss Cooper was in her louche weekend clothes and when her white-blonde hair caught the light, she looked like someone from one of the photography magazines Joyce borrowed from the library. Clara scolded herself. There was no need to be jealous.

Miss Bridges launched in: 'Things are turning desperate. We need to stop Browne getting his hands on the Grange. That would buy us some more time at least.'

Peter was sorted. Alex was gone. It was just Maureen and Rita left on the Australia list. Clara was shocked at Miss Bridges' urgency; she had thought they were on top of things.

'Why? What's happened?' she asked. The women looked at each other.

'Tickets for the *Largo Bay* have been sent. We've got less than three weeks before they're off,' said Miss Cooper.

Three weeks?!

'So, any ideas?' she went on. 'Have we got anything we could do about Browne?'

They both stared at Clara, whose head was reeling. *Focus,*

she told herself. She knew suddenly what they were thinking and she shook her head.

'I don't want Maureen involved.'

'But she *is* involved, isn't she?'

'No,' snapped Clara. She remembered seeing Maureen and the puddingish boy, Martin. Clara couldn't go around making accusations about Browne. That would be disastrous for everyone.

There was a clattering from behind the door.

'Uh-oh, we've got a peeping Tom,' said Miss Cooper, standing up. She flung open the door to reveal Joyce standing there. 'Shoo, shoo, shouldn't you be in bed?'

But instead of turning on her heel, Joyce tentatively approached them. She looked frail in her nightdress, her feet bright white on the rug.

'I've got something that might help...'

'No, Joyce,' said Miss Bridges. 'This is for adults... Clara, she shouldn't be—'

'Photographs,' Joyce said softly.

Everyone paused.

'Photographs? What have they got to do with anything?' asked Clara after a moment.

'Of Mr Browne and—'

Miss Cooper caught on the quickest: 'Go and get them then.'

Joyce went upstairs, then came back with a large brown envelope that Clara hadn't seen before. She tipped it upside down and the contents dropped out onto the coffee table. The women raised their eyebrows at each other. Clara moved closer to the table. The others followed. Joyce spread out the pictures, making sure they were face up and evenly spaced. Miss Bridges had put on her reading glasses. She knelt on the floor.

'Oh my giddy aunt!' she whispered.

They were photos of Maureen and Mr Browne, in various

settings. Clara picked up one taken in early-morning light. The sun bleaching an embrace on the steps of Robinson, Browne and White. How could they have been so incautious? This one alone was incriminating enough.

'Oh crikey,' said Clara, turning pale as the moon.

She wanted to turn the photos over so she wouldn't have to look. She knew she would never forget them now. They were imprinted on her memory. For shame. She had asked Maureen, she had interrogated her, but she must have asked the wrong questions. She had never asked directly. And she had been conned.

Maureen was fifteen years old.

'Brilliant. We'll tell him that if he tries to buy the place, we'll destroy him,' said Miss Cooper cheerfully.

'Imagine the headlines: *Man in a relationship with an orphan buys orphanage,*' Miss Bridges said. She too sounded thrilled.

Clara stared at the picture in her hand. She felt as though the room was spinning.

'Maureen will never agree.'

She wondered, though; some of these appeared so staged: Maureen's raised leg, her eyes closed, long lashes. Were they posed? Had Maureen suspected she was being photographed?

'Why did you do this, love?' Miss Bridges was asking Joyce. Clara forced herself to turn her attention away from the devastating photos to the young girl who took them.

'You can't go round spying on people, Joyce.'

'That's what they do, the masters like Henri Cartier-Bresson... they wait and they wait.'

One picture stood out. It was of them under the lamppost outside the Grange. Everything about it was familiar but with them standing there, unfamiliar too.

Unbelievable.

'I had to wait for two hours for that one,' Joyce said.

Canoodling, right outside the Grange. In the open. It was almost as if they wanted to be seen. Clara reconsidered: it was as if *Maureen* wanted to be seen.

Joyce continued. 'And Robert Doisneau, he took *The Kiss* in front of the Hôtel du Ville – not many people know it was staged.'

Clara picked up one of Maureen and Mr Browne kissing in the park, framed by a tree in blossom that arched over them like a wedding arch and confetti.

It was extraordinary. *Joyce* was extraordinary.

'Robert Capa and his girlfriend Gerda Taro set up the Magnum Photo Agency and they said, "If your pictures aren't good enough, you aren't close enough," so I got closer...'

Joyce stood uncertainly, awaiting further instructions. Looking at Miss Bridges, Clara stacked them carefully into a pile.

'These will be useful, thank you.' Then she went over to the girl. 'I don't know how you did it.'

'It's actually *because* I can't walk far,' Joyce explained. 'My legs get sore, so I rest and wait and wait and then I see something...'

Clara stared at her. The girl had used her limitations and created something that others could not. Her disability had forced her to try things differently; she couldn't do the norm or the ordinary, so she had done things in her own way – and the result was something out of the ordinary.

'Back to bed,' Clara whispered. She couldn't think of anything else to say.

Miss Bridges was talking. 'Of course, there's always the issue that even if he steps down, someone else will just step into his place...'

'You think the council will still want to sell?'

'Not necessarily. The impetus has definitely come from Browne. It wasn't on the cards before, I'm sure of that. He made it easy for the council. He made them an offer they couldn't refuse. I feel that if they have to go through the open market, they mightn't bother. And if they do, at least we'll have bought ourselves some time.'

'They'll still ship out Rita and Maureen,' Clara muttered.

'Maybe,' said Miss Bridges, 'but you'll still have the Grange.'

Clara leaned back in her chair, still trying to get her head around this. *Was it bad? Was it that bad? Yes. And Yes.*

She had failed.

She needed to get away from them both, just for a moment, just to take it in: Maureen's predicament, Joyce's talent, the home. In the kitchen, the kettle whistled as she blinked back tears. She could say it was just steam.

Peg was clutching her shell in the doorway. She gave Clara a fright.

'Couldn't you sleep?'

Peg shook her head sadly. Clara rubbed her bony back. Sometimes, Peg was assailed by black thoughts and dark memories. *At least she wasn't on the Australia list*, thought Clara. *Thank goodness for small mercies.*

In the parlour, Miss Cooper was saying, 'I wouldn't be surprised if Joyce has photographs of all of us,' and Miss Bridges was agreeing: 'I doubt anyone's escaped her beady lens.'

'There's none of me with my hand up someone's shirt on a park bench, thank you!' Clara responded snottily, placing down the tray of cups with a clatter. Yet as she said it, she remembered Miss Bridges in a car with steamed-up windows and for the first time since she'd seen the photographs, she wanted to laugh.

Miss Cooper *did* laugh. 'It's always the quiet ones.'

Clara picked up the photo on the top of the pile. Although it was dark, slightly fuzzy, it was unambiguously Browne with his tongue down an unambiguous Maureen's throat. It was like a gorilla mauling its keeper.

She should have known. Now she saw it, it was so obvious. Martin Browne was a cover – Clara should have done something.

'Use it,' said Miss Bridges and her voice was husky. 'Don't let that scoundrel get away with this.'

'But Maureen will kill us...'

'I'll do it if you won't,' Miss Cooper said firmly.

'No, *I'll* do it,' insisted Clara. She thought of Billy and Barry rolling around on the ground when they played football. What was it they said? *'They* played dirty. So we play dirtier.'

51

The next morning was the first real suggestion that summer was on its way. The sun bathed the kitchen in a golden, syrupy light. The children were in fine spirits. Even Stella was in an improved mood, hanging around expecting treats. Rita picked her up and nuzzled into her, and Peg hopped. *Keep faith*, Clara told herself, *she could do this*.

They were just about to leave for school when Evelyn tapped Clara's shoulder. Clara spun round to find the girl looking serious.

'Miss Newton, I think I'm ready.'

'You'd better be, we're leaving in five...'

'Not that – to go and live with my mum.'

Was it possible that all the noise quietened? The singing, the clatter, the birds, the cars in the street. The milkman on his round?

Evelyn had come to the decision by herself. And the timing could not have been better. Evelyn would have a fine life with her mother, Miss Smith. There was no reason to think that she wouldn't.

'Will you tell her, Miss Newton?'

'It'll be my pleasure, Evelyn – and for what it's worth, I think it's the right decision, love.'

Evelyn paused, then asked uncertainly, 'Do you think she'll be happy?' and Clara laughed since, surely, Evelyn must know that her mother would do anything for her: then, just as quickly, the thought subsided and Clara realised – that need for reassurance from a mother never goes away.

What would she have done for one more minute with hers?

She patted Evelyn's hand. Ever since Evelyn had helped deliver Anita's baby, Clara had found a new respect for her. She was a girl with many skills and potentials – Clara just hadn't seen them at first.

'She'll be over the moon, Evelyn.'

The girl nodded, inhaled. 'Just checking.'

There was no time to feel proud, but Clara was. She had done it her way and she had been proved right. Some children did get their happy endings.

Now was the time to ensure that the others got a fair shot at theirs.

Mr Browne's office couldn't have been much more of a contrast to Miss Cooper's. His was a large, bright and airy room, with huge sash windows overlooking a sunny courtyard. A mahogany desk formed a centrepiece. Paintings of horses on one wall, Sir Alfred's she presumed, and countryside scenes on another. She remembered Julian once saying that Mr Browne was a collector of 'pretty things'.

There were the filing cabinets where Maureen must have opened the drawers under his lecherous eye.

On the corner of his desk, next to the dark green ink-pad and the ink bottle, was a photograph of his wife, a stern-looking woman with a downturned mouth. There was another one of the children, Martin and a daughter. Interesting – he used photographs to convey to the world an image of a family man; well, Clara would use photographs to convey another.

She was nervous but resolved. She hadn't spoken to Maureen; she still needed to figure out what her approach should be with her.

She remembered when she was at boarding school. Her friends went home for the weekend. It didn't hurt when they went off – one teacher had lent Clara her typewriter, another asked her to do some chores for her. Clara kept herself busy and the time flew by. But it hurt when they came back, flushed and weary, with their tins of fruit cake and tales of shopping, cinema trips. *That* was the moment she used to think, *I am not like them*. *That* was the moment when, if there had been a Mr Browne, she too would have been vulnerable.

'I can't imagine you're here for probate...' he began.

'It's about your proposed purchase of the Grange,' Clara said. She would not be intimidated. Outside in the street, a truck had pulled up and was delivering flowers to Mrs Garrard. She could hear Mrs Garrard exclaiming, 'Nothing better than a geranium.'

'Thought it might be.'

'We're not selling to you.'

He paused. She had thought he might laugh but he didn't. He was, she supposed, too careful for that.

'It's not down to you though, is it?' Cocky smile, what *did* Maureen see in him?

Clara agreed. 'Oh absolutely – it's up to you.'

She pushed the photos across the desk. They looked quite something altogether like that. You might think they were promotion for a romantic film – unless you knew the backstory; then it was more like a horror.

'You might find these interesting.'

Was *interesting* the word? She found them repulsive now.

Browne's expression was still mocking as he put on reading spectacles to look at them. Then he gazed and gazed and then the sneer, imperceptibly at first, turned into something else. The snark turned into shock. She could tell he was working out how to react. He picked one up: not the kiss, which Clara privately thought of as 'Fred and Ginger', but the one with Maureen on the bench and him standing behind her with his hands on her shoulders. There was something sweet or tender about this one; you might think it was a father–daughter photo – an affection-ate-before-you-go-away shot.

'You can keep them if you like,' Clara suggested coolly. 'Per-haps your wife might take a look? Or even young Martin?'

His cheeks coloured from the collar up but his voice didn't change tone. 'The council will still sell, but they won't get as good a price. All it means is that there will be less money for your *waifs and strays*.'

Joyce deserved a reward for this. A massive reward. Clara scooped up the pictures.

'I'll see myself out.'

52

Two days later, Clara came back from the shops, basket handles digging into her suffering palms, to find Mr Sommersby in the kitchen, drinking a cup of tea out of her cup and sitting in her chair like he owned the place.

Which in a way, she supposed, he did.

'Most ingenious, Miss Newton.'

'Good afternoon, Mr Sommersby,' she murmured. The cheek of the man. She could smell his cologne: *eau de pompous*, she thought.

'I've had irate Sussex Council and furious Sussex families on the phone all week: *stealing* their adopters, hey?'

'Poaching,' she corrected. She thought maybe he didn't know about Browne and the photographs after all.

He gave her another smile. You'd think he liked her. Miss Bridges *and* Julian said he admired her.

'Don't think I don't know who is behind Mr Browne dropping out from buying the Grange.'

Ah. Clara stared at her red hands. What did he expect her to say? He didn't seem annoyed though; he took another sip of tea and laughed.

'You have my respect, Miss Newton, but you won't be able to stop the sale forever. It has been decided. Mr Browne or no, the house *will* be sold. We're putting it to auction next month – and four of your children *will* be on the *Largo Bay*.'

Clara shuddered.

'Only two...' she corrected him. 'Alex has gone – and Peter is going too. It's only Maureen and Rita.'

'Two,' he repeated, raising his eyebrows. It gave her some satisfaction to see that he hadn't known this. 'Better than none.'

Rage sparked inside her. 'How can you send children into the unknown?'

'Is that what you're up in arms about?!'

The way he said 'up in arms' like her fears were inconsequential!

'Miss Newton, we've been doing it for many years.'

'So? That doesn't make it right. We don't know anything about where they go or what they do. Nothing!'

He pulled at his collar, less at ease now than when he was telling her off.

'It's working. I would have heard otherwise. Australia is beautiful, Miss Newton. Full of opportunities. If I didn't have commitments here, I would think of it myself.'

Clara gazed at him; he didn't seem to be joking.

'Some of the children ride horses to school, imagine that!'

She tried to imagine Rita on a horse. Or Maureen.

'Wait, wait.' The idea just came to her. 'Maybe *I* could apply to adopt them?'

He winced. 'There are several reasons that's not a good idea: The tickets have been organised, plans made. Anyway, single women can't adopt, you know that. And you don't have any money to support yourself, never mind a handful of orphans. And, this is more sentimental – *all* the children need you, Miss Newton, not just one or two. You're a fine house-mother. Don't give up on us.'

Mr Sommersby had never said such nice things to her. He tilted his head sympathetically again.

'And Miss Newton, I swear there is nothing to fear – Australia is a good option. Wouldn't you like to be where the orange trees grow?'

'What about the other children?' she asked finally.

He pulled a note from his pocket and read from it.

'Peg, Joyce and Evelyn will go to the Home for Disabled Children in Walthamstow.'

'Why will Evelyn go to a home for disabled children? I don't understand.'

'She can't go to Australia.'

'Why not?' Clara had a suspicion it was to do with the colour of her skin. Someone didn't want Evelyn there. What else could it be? Mr Sommersby was suddenly flushed around the gills. He knew. 'It's what has been decided... Walthamstow will suit her better.'

'Well, she's not going there either,' Clara said triumphantly. 'Her mother is taking her on. Just a few checks and it will be arranged.'

'Oh.' He smoothed down his tie. 'That's excellent. Best for everyone. So just the two girls then. I will let the Home know. Rest assured, we don't do this lightly – it's ideal for Peg and Joyce.'

'I don't see why Joyce needs to be there. She is progressing at school and at home. She could stay—'

'I'm not debating this with you, it's decided.'

'And Peg's not even disabled,' Clara snapped.

Mr Sommersby smirked. 'Miss Newton, you know as well as I do, Peg does not communicate.'

'She does,' Clara said firmly. 'Just not with speech. She's one of the most brilliant communicators I know.' She took a breath. 'Would it have made a difference if she could speak? Would you have let us stay?'

'Who knows?' He rolled his eyes, then grinned. For a brief moment, she could imagine the younger Mr Sommersby. Smug schoolboy, a rugby player, the boy with his hand balled up in a fist, first up in the air in class. She didn't even know his first name – P. Peter? Patrick? Perigrew?

'I'd better be getting along.' And then Mr Sommersby was the leader of the council again, suited and booted, the man with the power. She remembered Victor's words about the revolutions in France and Russia and the Treaty of Versailles: *They could have made a brave new world but they just screwed it up again.*

'I imagine you've been wondering what we've got planned for you...' he said when he was at the door.

Everything he said sounded like a trick-question.

'We've got a few places in mind.' For once he looked at her like he was seeing her properly. 'Miss Newton, you understand this isn't spite or anything, it's purely logistics and budget.'

'If I say no?'

'If you say no, it will be worse for everyone. And I doubt you could blackmail every buyer who comes along. A fair number though maybe.' He winked.

As he left the Grange, he gave her the paper with the girls' names on it. There was also a telephone number. He said, 'It's easy to put the children first when it suits you, but let's see if you can put the children first when it doesn't...'

Clara felt like her children were being attacked from every angle. She didn't trust Mr Sommersby an inch. She wished she had taken Ivor's side long ago. Damn her pride and damn her trusting the wrong people. Right now, she needed to turn the house into a fortress. She needed a moat and a drawbridge. She needed to get the children to the right places. She telephoned Miss Cooper.

'I need help. Have you still got those people you poached?'

53

The Woodwards couldn't come until later the following evening. Clara explained to Joyce that they were coming to see her with a view to adopting her and Joyce stayed up excitedly. She wanted this. No qualms. Before they'd even taken off their coats, Joyce had told them about her polio and her lessons and her friends, but mostly she talked about photography. Mr Woodward scratched his stubbly cheek thoughtfully.

'I've got an old Leica from before the war – wonder if it would still work?'

Mrs Woodward nodded at everything that was said.

When Clara eventually told Joyce to go up to her room, 'school tomorrow,' the couple looked disappointed. Joyce had won them over. Clara excused herself for a moment and when she went upstairs, she found that the younger girls were asleep but Joyce was sitting in her nightie at the edge of her bed. She looked like an old man ruminating on life's mistakes.

'How would you feel?' Clara said softly. She would never not be emotional about these questions. 'About living with them?'

'But what about everyone here?'

'You have to follow your own path.'

Joyce thought about this. 'They've got a dog,' she said as Clara tucked her in, 'named Bailey. I don't mind Stella but I always preferred dogs.'

Downstairs, the Woodwards were pacing the parlour. Mrs Woodward's hands were clasped together as if in prayer. They both spun around 180 degrees when Clara came in.

'It was the presenter Donald Burton who swayed us.'

'Pardon?'

'*The Joys of Adoption*, the radio show? Lovely, it was. We'd been thinking about it for a while, but that's what pushed us over the edge,' Mrs Woodward said.

'Poor choice of words,' Mr Woodward said dryly.

Clara laughed. 'It kind of works...'

They both took deep breaths.

'What did Joyce say then?' asked Mrs Woodward.

'Does she like us?' asked Mr Woodward at the same time. They looked at her with worried eyes. Clara realised she had the power here and it felt scary. She couldn't speak for a moment, but then she nodded. 'I think it's a yes.'

'Over the edge we go,' said Mr Woodward and they shook hands and laughed.

ARTICLE FOR THE *SHILLING GRANGE NEWS*, MAY 1950

My time with Polio by Joyce, aged 11

I remember they carried me in, and I had a fever. I was fright-ened because I had seen it happen to other people and I didn't want it to happen to me. Our beds were separated by glass and the people wore masks to speak to me. I liked the doctors and nurses. They tried to make me laugh to distract me from the pain. We weren't allowed visitors at the beds but through a glass window, but my mummy didn't come. The girl in the bed next to me had people waving at her all day long but no one came for me. Her mummy had finger puppets. They did Red Riding Hood and Goldilocks. My favourite doctor said it happens sometimes: 'Families can't handle it.' He said, 'It doesn't mean anything,' but he was wrong. The boy opposite went to the iron lung and his mother read to him Shakespeare plays. The girl in the bed next to me – the girl who liked Red Riding Hood – died. They brought in another girl and her mummy came in the morning and her daddy came after work still in his overalls. I got tired of people waving not at me. They said I would struggle to walk but I practise and I try and I am not too terrible at it. One doctor said Franklin D. Roosevelt had polio and look at him! Matron said we are all born in the gutter but some of us are looking at the stars, and that someone famous said that but she couldn't remember who. I want to be the first woman war correspondent and the first who has had polio.

54

Maureen was crying on a bench outside Lavenham station. The more she attempted to stifle her weeping, the more anguished she sounded. When Clara sat next to her, Maureen shuffled away from her, then cried some more. Handing over a handkerchief, Clara told her she was listening. Behind them, a train noisily pulled away and rumbled down the tracks.

'Everything is falling apart,' Maureen said.

What would she say if she knew about the photos? It didn't bear thinking about.

'He doesn't want to know me any more.'

Clara gulped. *Here it came.*

'Who doesn't want to know you?'

'No one...'

Maureen had a strange look on her face. She crossed and uncrossed her legs as she sobbed. She had a run in her stocking and a scab on her knuckle.

'I wish you'd tell me what was wrong – maybe I could—'

'I went to see Joe.'

She was talking about Joe? Clara hadn't expected that. *Okay, ask about Joe.*

'What happened?'

'He's at the garage – where you got him that job.'

Clara thought of that sweet-tempered lad who she had disliked at first and then had grown so fond of. How Joe loved making things and getting things done. She thought he'd led Maureen astray: it hadn't turned out like that.

'And? Maureen?'

'He's got a new girl. He said he loves me but we're no good for each other. He saw a fortune teller on Southwold pier and she told him to let me go.'

Maureen sobbed. Clara clasped her hand tightly. Opposite, a woman was holding the hand of a tiny girl with pigtails and looking in the window of the bank. How much easier the younger ones were, thought Clara. Looking after Maureen felt like walking through a minefield sometimes. She daren't put a foot wrong.

Maureen wiped her eyes. She had her own handkerchief. (Here was one habit Clara could be proud of instilling.)

'Shall we head back?' Clara asked, hoping the storm was over.

'And I've lost my job at Robinson, Browne and White's.'

'Oh,' said Clara, careful not to give anything away. 'That's... hard.' She couldn't help herself. 'Any idea why?'

Maureen shook her head no, then burst into hot fresh tears.

A train pulled into the station and there were shouts and smoke and doors slamming. People poured out from the station. The mother and the little girl were waiting – 'Daddy!' she cried out. The man picked her up and spun her round. Family. The thing her children were looking for. But sometimes going without what everyone else had meant you might rise in other, astonishing ways.

Clara knew she had to say something to Maureen.

'Mr Browne was taking advantage of you. It's not fair.'

Maureen snuffled.

'You don't know what men are like, Maureen; not all men, obviously, but some.'

Clara paused. She remembered that Maureen was the tiny girl who had discovered her mother murdered by her father. That she had laid tissues over her mother's body. The problem was not that she didn't know what some men were like.

'Finished?' said Maureen. She stood up.

'Uh-huh.'

'I'm going to see Ivor. He wants me to do some work for him.'

'Oh?' said Clara. She couldn't think what to say. She felt ridiculously, insanely jealous and that made her ashamed.

Miss Cooper had wanted the photographs of Maureen and Mr Browne to come out.

'You can't have him go unpunished!' she said. 'Take them to the newspapers if not the police. It's not right!'

Clara thought how people went unpunished all the time – look at Peter's uncle careening around the town, careless and carefree as Edward the Sixth. Look at the Nazi war criminals living it up in South America or developing nuclear bombs or merrily fixing wonky teeth in New Jersey.

Good Housekeeping *Quiz – What is your worst character trait?*

Mostly D's – Naivety

'I'm not doing it,' Clara had told Miss Cooper. The important thing was to protect Maureen, even if that meant letting Mr

Browne get away with it. Because everyone knew there was
only one person whose reputation would be ruined here, one
person who would have the labels attached to their name, one
person who would be treated with suspicion by those around
them, one person who would be the worst person in the world,
sent to Coventry. And it wouldn't be Mr Browne. The
photographs were damning but, in isolation, they couldn't
change the world.

Miss Cooper didn't agree with her, but for once, she pursed
her lips and said, 'Whatever you think is best, Clara.'

55

It was Miss Cooper who said, 'You can't keep it from the children any more. There's only two weeks to go – they need to know.' Miss Bridges had taken the opposite position: 'Why tell them if there is still a possibility of it not happening? Why make them worry for nothing?'

But as the date of the auction came closer, Miss Bridges changed her mind.

'It mightn't be so bad. They were fine when you said you were moving,' she reminded Clara.

'That was different, we were staying together then.'

'Children are resilient—'

Clara knew it was time to get it over with though. The children had sniffed the change in the air, of course they had; and she had promised to tell them the truth. As she took Rita and Maureen to the parlour, her heart was beating fast.

She said, 'You already know about the house sale – so I have some more news: you two... might be going to Australia.'

Maureen spluttered. 'What about the others?' She narrowed her eyes at Clara. 'Is that why you've been racing around like a headless chicken getting everyone into new homes?'

'Kind of,' admitted Clara. Maureen was always so adversarial.

'Is it definitely happening?'

Clara thought of the tickets she had seen: Southampton to Freemantle. Single. Child Migrant Programme.

'I am trying to figure out if there is a way you won't have to go.'

'I'll go,' Maureen said, jumping up. 'Might as well. Nothing to keep me here any more.'

Clara's blood ran cold. The temptation was to say, *but there's us!* but then she remembered there was no 'us' any more. Now, when they needed stability the most, they were being dispersed like tiny, shattered fragments of something broken.

'Are you sure?'

She half wanted Maureen to say 'No, I want to stay with you, Miss Newton,' but the other half knew it was best to accept it with equanimity. Maureen begging to stay was not Maureen. True to form, she looked at Clara and scowled. 'Why not?'

Then Maureen turned to Rita and said, 'It'll be fun, yes?'

Rita asked to go out into the shed. Clara didn't know what to say – had the implications sunk in? She wanted to say more but Rita followed Maureen out of the room. Clara was over-whelmed with tenderness as she watched. Her retreating back was slender and straight. Her hair smoothly slicked back into its neat ponytail. While the others always came home from school with their hairstyles undone, Rita's hair never dared disobey her; she was always tidy and clean. May the country of oranges suit her as well as Lavenham did.

Clara had never hoped for anything so much in her life.

At bedtime, Peg signed, 'Am I going too?'

'Not to Australia. You, my darling, are going to a beautiful home in Walthamstow where you will make lots of friends and they will look after you and cook tastier food than I do here. And I will visit you lots, I promise.'

That was what Clara had prepared to say, that was probably what she *should* have said. But instead she said, 'I'm doing my best to keep us together, Peg.'

Peg puckered up for a kiss and then rested her head on Clara's collarbone.

'How did they react to Australia??' Miss Bridges said on the telephone later that night.

Clara was determined not to cry. 'I don't think they understood.'

'Maybe they understand better than you, Clara?'

'Maybe...' Clara hoped that was true.

'And Peg?' asked Miss Bridges. 'How did she take the news of the home?'

'I couldn't tell Peg,' Clara admitted. 'I just couldn't.'

She thought Miss Bridges might scold her but she was surprisingly kind. She said that things had worked out in the end with Evelyn and her mother because of Clara and she should have faith that they would work out with the other children too.

At her desk, Clara tried to update her files, but found herself stupidly writing the word 'Ivor' over again. She missed him more than ever, more now that he was just over the road again than when he was hundreds of miles away. Why had their reconciliation turned so sour? She watched him come and go to his workshop: he always looked pensive and she didn't know why. The children spent time with him. Why couldn't she? She wondered if she was destined to be alone or if she would always muck up her chances. *Good Housekeeping* magazine now had a column by a woman 'left on the shelf'. Clara was never sure if she pitied her or admired her.

The next day, Rita asked Clara if Australia was near Exeter. She'd heard some children at school talking about Exeter and they said there was plenty to do there.

Clara's heart skipped a beat. Slowly, she said, 'Rita, Australia is the other side of the world.'

'I'll still do the Festival of Britain next year,' mused Rita, then laughed. 'If I get through the audition. Which I will, obviously.'

56

Saturday, and on the way home from the razzle-dazzle of the local market, Clara was called over to the flower shop. Mrs Garrard wanted to know about the sale of the house. She had seen it was going to auction now – was it true and if so, why? And how much would it go for?

Clara said it was but she didn't know why, and as for the price, this was not her area of expertise. She thought about confiding in Mrs Garrard about Australia but decided not to – Mrs Garrard lived a perfumed life. She'd never understand what it was like to live with insecurity, when even things that had seemed certain could start undulating under your toes.

Peter's uncle's car zipped past; he was showboating as usual.

'He drives too fast,' Mrs Garrard pointed out and, in a rare moment of accord, Clara agreed.

'I saw Ivor this morning,' Mrs Garrard went on. 'He looks sad recently, don't you think? Like he carries the world on his shoulders...'

Clara looked at her. Was this a pointed remark or just passing the time of day? Hard to tell with Mrs Garrard. She made a non-committal expression.

'That Ruby has him wrapped around her little finger,' the other woman said.

It was Rita that Clara noticed across the road first and then Stella, tail up, fur up, chasing something invisible to the human eye dashing into the road just as Peter's uncle's car went roaring down it.

Where did Miss Smith come from? Miss Smith who had always loved that cat. There she went – she galloped forward – Clara had never seen her move so quickly – and shouted at Stella, who had frozen, back arched, tail ahoy. Miss Smith ran to save her. The brakes screeched: they sounded like a banshee, with the terror of an air-raid siren thrown in.

Where the hell was Rita?

Oh, thank heavens – Clara could see Rita standing on the kerb, she hadn't gone into the road. Rita was safe. Stella was safe. She remembered the fox she had had to bury all by herself. *I bet it was him*, she thought. *Peter's uncle.* She was going to say that to Mrs Garrard, but Mrs Garrard was transfixed by something in the road. What was it? It was Miss Smith, flat out on the ground. Then a middle-aged woman appeared from nowhere and threw her arm round Rita. The woman clamped her palm first over Rita's mouth, then over her eyes – she didn't seem to know which one she wanted to cover most. *What was she doing to Rita? How dare she?* thought Clara, but she was unable to move. Next to her, she was aware of Mrs Garrard holding a bunch of flowers, the distinct smell of roses, the texture of thistle, perhaps, brushing against her arm. Mrs Garrard's shocked voice.

'Who is that?'

Peter's uncle's car was taking up the centre of the road but he just sat, hands on the wheel, unmoving in the driver's seat like a waxwork from Madame Tussauds in the 'magnificent men and their flying machines' room.

Silence for a moment and then hustle and bustle. Clara

blinked, gulped. Miss Smith was still on the road, but she didn't look like Miss Smith and it was only because she had seen her just seconds before that Clara would have known it was her. Nurse's outfit; but whereas before her hair was hidden beneath her nurse's hat, now it was spread out on the cobblestones, and now it was in a dark red puddle. Clara thought of the word 'splattered'. She shook herself. Two people were now crouched by Miss Smith. Were they friends? Did anyone know her here?

Peter's uncle had got out of the car now – his arms were outstretched like someone at the football, like he was protesting a referee's decision; then he stuck his hands on his head, elbows out, you could see through the two triangles of space he made, like a frame. One woman, looking undignified, knelt on the ground, her skirt hoicked up so her garter was showing, slamming her hands on Miss Smith's chest. *Not so hard*, thought Clara, *what are you doing? You'll break her.* Poor Miss Smith. She still had not moved.

Mrs Garrard had thrown down her flowers and was running flat-footed away from the shop – did she want Clara to watch it for her? – she was away in the direction of the surgery; others were heading that way too. They hammered at the door. Clara heard their raised voices: 'Dr Cardew! Emergency – come quick!'

Clara looked back to the crowd by the car. A massive fur coat had been wrapped around Rita and still someone was shielding her eyes like there was an eclipse and she might be blinded.

And Clara was unable to move. She was frozen. She should move towards Rita at least, she knew that; her brain told her that, and she should move towards Miss Smith. But all those shapes, the triangles of Peter's uncle's arms, the circle of blood, the horseshoe of people were immobilising her.

Anita, with the baby, and Evelyn too – what was she doing there? – appeared, looking startled, on the surgery steps. A conversation. Mrs Garrard pointing. Anita shouting. Evelyn running down the stairs. Down the street. Plimsolls pounding. Evelyn getting there before Dr Cardew.

Evelyn. Evelyn.

Then Peter's uncle was running suddenly, legs splayed, through the crowd. There was shouting. Maybe Clara shouted too. 'Stop him. Stop!'

He was brought back between Julian and a policeman. As Clara found she could move, finally, she made her way to Rita. Rita was moaning 'Mama'. Thank goodness for Anita, she had her arm round Evelyn and was whispering something to her, trying to pull her away.

Peter's uncle was crying. 'It was an accident, Julian,' he pleaded, 'you know me. I'd never hurt anyone on purpose.'

But Julian was shaking his head, white-faced and bug-eyed. 'I'm not getting you out of this one,' he spluttered. 'You bloody idiot.'

Julian looked over at Clara and mouthed something. She didn't think it was his usual 'you've had your chance' but something else, maybe it was: 'I'll see to this.' Maybe that's what it was.

That evening, Clara kept replaying it: the terrible vision of the car careening towards the cat. Did she hear the impact or did she just imagine she did? Then the eerie silence before the commotion.

Miss Bridges and Miss Cooper came over to the Grange and made sweet tea that she couldn't drink. Rita was in shock and had fallen asleep on the sofa.

Evelyn had gone back with the Cardews. They'd had to tear her away from her mother in the end.

Stella wandered in, went to her food, probably wondering what the fuss was about.

'I just stood there.' Clara swallowed. 'It was like I was in the cinema in front of a horrendous film.' She wept softly. It wasn't just the images, it was her own role in them; that made it worse. People had run towards the calamity; others had taken off their coats to use as blankets or made pillows of them. There was that woman, whoever she was, trying to thump some life into Miss Smith, while Clara had stared from a distance like a seagull watching fish but deciding not to swoop.

'Clara!' Miss Bridges startled her.

'What?'

Miss Bridges' voice was also choked. 'Miss Smith died immediately. There was nothing you could have done.'

'If only I—'

'No,' Miss Bridges said firmly. 'Don't think like that.'

It was about two o'clock in the morning and Clara still could not sleep. She should have sent Evelyn to her mother sooner, then none of this would have happened. She had found no relief looking out of the window since Ivor had come home, but she did so anyway, and she saw the moon and how in its changing it was somehow unchanging, and she tried to remember the science but could not. There were the stars, the constants, they too, unchanging in their changing, and she knew she would wake up the next morning, she would stir the porridge, she would curse the too-hard butter, she would shout at one child for not being ready, she would tell Rita yes, her hair was beautiful, but everything had changed.

As she lay in bed, a piece of paper appeared underneath the door and mystified, she padded over to pick it up. It was a page of drawings, Peter's, but nothing like his usual ones. It showed not his usual meticulous style, not his fine use of colour, but his rage. There was a character, maybe Peter himself, and he was laughing; but the main pictures were of a man being hand-cuffed, then thrown in jail, and then sat head in hands in prison outfit.

'I am glad,' it said along the top. 'I am so sorry about Miss Smith but I am happy he is going to jail. I hate him.'

And in the morning, Clara would tell Peter that she hated his uncle too.

57

Evelyn's face was drawn and her eyes massive. She slept later than usual, had to be shaken up out of bed in the morning and was first to go to bed at night. She managed to go to school every day – she *wanted* to go to school; one home time, her teacher, Miss Fisher, said in a low voice to Clara, 'She's so normal – you wouldn't know anything had happened.'

Evelyn said, 'I know it wasn't my fault, I know she loved me, I'm going in the hammock.' When she wasn't in the hammock, she was rifling through the bread bin again. She frequently asked if she could see baby Howard. Clara tried to steer her away – surely it was too much for Anita to handle a traumatised child alongside a baby and Howard was teething, his cheeks like fire engines – but Anita said, 'She must come over any time.'

Miss Bridges suggested that maybe they shouldn't ever talk about Miss Smith again, saying, 'Maybe bringing it up puts her in a bad mood.'

But Clara overruled her. 'It's her mother!' she argued.

And Anita retorted, 'She's already in a bad mood.' Anita felt even more strongly about it than Clara.

Miss Bridges was so thoughtful on some things, thought Clara, yet could be quite obtuse on others.

The auction was only days away and once the house was sold, now her situation had changed once again, Clara assumed Evelyn would have to go with Peg to the Home for Disabled Children in Walthamstow. But no one was clear on this.

'A decision will be made,' promised Mr Sommersby cheerfully. 'We are in communication all the time.'

In communication with whom? wondered Clara. Miss Holdsworth from the Child Migrant's Programme maybe? But she didn't ask. She felt like she was not quite drowning but not doing much more than keeping her head above the surface. She could not cope with extra details. Even if those details were good – even if it were a lifeboat on the far horizon, she would not be able to swim there. She could tread water but do little more.

She lit a candle for Evelyn's mother and Evelyn said she liked it and that she had written something for their newspaper that she would send to Alex.

Rita sat on Clara's lap and tucked her head under Clara's chin, even though she was getting too big. When had her legs grown?

'What are you thinking?' Clara asked her.

Rita cleared her throat. 'At least she knows where her mama is...' she said.

'*Oh, Rita!*' Clara stroked her hair.

Might Evelyn be sent to Australia with Rita and Maureen? Which was better? Which was worse? Heads or tails? What if both options were wonderful? What if both options were dire? Clara wondered if her head might explode.

What would Michael have said about her now?

Anita and Dr Cardew said they would take Evelyn to the funeral, if Clara could look after the baby. Dr Cardew was going to give a speech about what an excellent nurse Miss Smith was. He would talk about her sweet nature, her patient skills and her attention to detail. Clara was filled with shameful relief that she didn't have to go. She still hadn't got over Judy's terrible funeral last year. However, she didn't relish the idea of looking after Howard for long either.

On the morning of the funeral, Anita wheeled Howard round in the pram and gave Clara a piece of paper.

'I'd be grateful it you stick to this, Clara.'

It was an hour-by-hour set of instructions.

'No problem,' Clara lied.

Evelyn skipped out of the house. She didn't seem to be struggling. Her hair was pulled back and she had the polka-dot bow in it that she had worn on her first day at the Grange. She was wearing her school uniform because it was the only smart thing she had. Anita gave Clara a disapproving look and turned to Evelyn: 'We'll pop to mine and see if we can put together something else, shall we?'

Baby Howard was in a woollen hat that Clara thought made him look like a turnip and layers of jumpers and cardigans. Even though it was warm, almost hot, Anita always worried about Howard catching a chill. Clara told Joyce and Rita to take him for a walk up the high road in his pram but was then spooked by thoughts of car accidents, so she joined them and walked closest to the road. Each car that went past made her tremble and imagine collisions. It's a normal response, Clara reminded herself. It was like that during the war. You'd walk past a shop and you would imagine a bomb annihilating it and then two days later, it would actually happen.

After they'd walked up and down the high road for ten

minutes, Joyce asked if they could go back – her leg was tired. And Rita complained that Howard didn't do anything anyway.

When Clara asked her what she expected him to do, Rita pulled a face.

Howard *was* a sweet fella though. Clara could see Dr Cardew in his features – she looked hard but could see little of Anita yet, except maybe his elfin ears.

When she was nearly back at the Grange, she saw the doors to Ivor's workshop open for once. So much had happened since their argument, she wondered how they would ever catch up and be on the same page again – Joyce's incriminating photographs, Mr Browne pulling out of the sale, Evelyn's mother...

Ivor waved to her and she thought, *why not?* and waved back. *We're adults. Why wouldn't we speak to each other?*

He rose to his feet and came out. 'So Anita's got you looking after Howard now, has she?'

'It's the least I could do,' Clara said honestly. Face to face with Ivor, after all this time, she thought she was going to cry again. 'After the last few days.'

He gave her that reassuring look he had, the one that always made her heart beat faster.

'I'm so sorry, Clara. It must have been awful.'

She nodded. It was a tragedy and so terrible for Evelyn; to witness her stoicism broke Clara's heart. It was like Evelyn expected everything to go wrong, she believed things were too good to be true – and it seemed she had now been proved right. And Clara had to constantly stave off the feeling that if only she'd let Miss Smith take Evelyn earlier, none of this would have happened. If only she'd kept to the council rules, rather than her own sensibilities, then Miss Smith might still be alive.

Meanwhile, Peter could barely disguise his happiness at his uncle getting his comeuppance and seemed to realise that he was on the cusp of a better life, putting his orphanage years behind him, moving on to a brighter future. At the same time there were so many practical things to do: packing up the Grange, getting the children ready to move on – those going to Australia especially. And she missed Billy, Barry and Alex too and she couldn't talk about that because it probably wasn't allowed. They would say she was 'too attached' or something. There was so much happening that the full range of emotions had deserted her and she was left with just one thing that wasn't even an emotion – the need to get on with it.

'I was just about to take a break – fancy a walk to see the bluebells?'

'What? Where...?'

I haven't time...

'It's not far.' He grabbed his jacket and shrugged it on. Clara couldn't bear to see even that minor struggle and she looked away. 'It's been a while since we talked,' he added.

She would not say anything snide, she would not.

'With the baby?' she asked, gesturing to the pram.

'Is this the baby? I thought it was a turnip.'

'Ha! So can I bring the pram?' she said doubtfully.

'Sure, there's a path.' He took the handle. 'I'll help.'

'But Anita has given me a strict schedule...'

He grinned. 'I'll bet she has.'

It *wasn't* far. They walked around the back of the Grange along one of the footpaths, but then took another footpath away from her usual walk. The pram wheels made shushing noises through the reeds and bumped up and down on some of the stonier parts. Nevertheless, Howard slept on.

Clara tried not to think of the bleakest of funerals that would be starting right about now. The funeral for poor Miss Smith who had just about managed to turn her life around, who had been so proud that Evelyn had taken her hand, so elated that Evelyn would finally be coming to live with her on that magical sofa-bed. And Evelyn, although she had taken her time, had finally been ready for that new life. All gone now. And what of Evelyn? Stuffing breadcrusts in her mouth to keep herself from crying. She was probably destined to have move upon move upon move. She'd be lucky to keep it under thirty schools.

And then suddenly ahead of Clara was an extraordinary blue, violet blue, a large square of it, trees either side of it, framing it somehow: a tiny square of bluebell wood. Far-stretching, knee-high, a colour so vivid she had to blink to readjust. And it was so unexpected that she let out a gasp and Howard's eyes sprang open, then shut again; it was too bright for him maybe, what with the sun pouring down in the gaps between the branches.

'Like it?' said Ivor and she smiled up at him. She had forgotten how glorious nature could be.

'Love it.'

'Thought you might.'

They stood there, gazing into the sea of blue, for five, ten minutes, in silence. At first it was an uneasy kind of silence – they were not as familiar with each other as they once were – and then they got used to one another and it became companionable again. The annoyance that she had at Ivor seemed to fly out of her and she couldn't name it any more, or remember why she had felt so hurt. Her body didn't seem able to hold on to her anger with Ivor: it was a strange thing like her heart was dragging her towards him, to forgiveness.

'It was difficult without you,' she said eventually. Being here in this wonderful, unexpected setting made her want to be honest with him, to take a risk. 'I missed you. You've always been a champion of the children.'

Her heart was racing.

'I missed you too,' he said.

She could hear him gulping, see his Adam's apple travel up and down.

'The children mean a lot to me. The Grange is an important place for me.'

'Yes,' her voice seemed to come from far away and she wasn't sure what she would say next. 'I know that.'

'I let you down,' he said.

She swallowed. 'Perhaps I shouldn't expect so much.'

'I'm sorry—'

Then Howard started flapping his arms, then rocking his head from side to side, as though he were having a bad dream.

'Guess we should go back,' said Clara, feeling guilty about Anita's optimistic schedule. But Ivor rocked the pram the way Anita did – but with only one hand, of course – and making shushing noises. It felt odd to be there with just him and a baby: like they were play-acting at being a family or trying out an alternative existence.

Good Housekeeping Quiz: What kind of mother would you be? Three times she had taken that quiz and three times it came back: Mostly A's. Soft as butter.

'You're good at that,' she ventured. The intensity of the last few moments had evaporated. She felt she could breathe again.

'I'm sure you are too.'

'I'm not!' She laughed. 'Howard's lovely but I'll prefer him when he's about ten. I'm not interested in looking after babies.' Ivor was tucking Howard's blanket around him and didn't look as if he was listening, but he must have been because over his shoulder he asked, 'Why's that, Clara?'

'Oh, it's what I'm used to, I suppose. I understand children...' She laughed self-consciously. 'I can *remember* being a child, but I can't remember a thing about being a baby. I'm not a natural with them, some people are.' She thought of Evelyn again. Sweet, *capable* girl. 'Which is fine because I don't have to do it, thank goodness.'

'Mm,' he said. They had walked to the edge of the fields, back to the more familiar path. The smell was less woody there. 'What do you think the hardest thing about looking after babies – I mean, children – is?'

'Everything.' She laughed again but he seemed serious, so she tried her best to articulate it.

'Children equal compromise. And that can be hard.'

'Is that what you do? Compromise?'

'I try,' she said wryly. 'I try and put the children first. Think what's best for them. It was hard for me, last year – as you know – but I hope I'm better at it now. Some days, I'm not too bad. Other days, I'm awful.'

She turned her attention to the baby. 'Especially with babies, that's one thing Rita and I agree on – they don't do much' – she laughed – 'although I don't mind you, do I, Howie?' She looked up at Ivor; his expression was tight. 'Anita goes mad when I call him that.'

They had walked in a circle all the way back to the Grange.

Ivor, who had gone quiet, asked, 'Would you like me to come to the auction next week? It's going to be – emotional, I imagine.'

Clara took a deep breath. The thought of him being there, the two of them united against the world, was wonderful. The thought that she didn't have to do this alone any more.

And yet she couldn't let go of that last remaining shard of hurt.

'No.' She shook her head resolutely. 'I can stand on my own two feet, thank you. I've had to.'

She didn't mean for it to come out so spikey. Fortunately, he didn't take it that way.

'I don't doubt that,' he said, 'I just... let me know if you change your mind. You know how I feel, Clara.'

'Do I?'

Ivor was about to say something else, but a black car pulled up in front of them, its exhaust pumping out fumes. They both stared at it; Howard yawned.

It was Victor. He tooted the horn, waved. He was in a great mood but his timing stank.

'It's not what you think,' Clara began. Ivor, next to her, had grown tense. She could almost feel him bristling. 'There's nothing going on with me and Victor...'

Ivor shook his head – 'Fine' – but it was as though the something between them that had been delicately restored by the trip to the bluebells had just been scratched or tarnished again.

Victor bounded out of the car and clasped Ivor's hand like they were best friends. He had had his hair cut; he looked less like Beethoven now and more like any other middle-aged man.

'Nice to see you again, Mr Delaney.'

'I've got to attend to some business,' Ivor said. 'Please excuse me.'

Was Clara imagining it, or did Ivor have tears in his dark eyes? A few minutes later she saw him striding purposefully down the street towards the station and he kept his eyes fixed ahead.

Victor had brought a letter from Alex. They had decided that the boy shouldn't come back for a while, not while his father may still be on the prowl. Clara was so excited to see Alex's writing, she could have inhaled it.

Dear Miss Newton,

Hope you are well and enjoying the mild weather.

As per your last request, I'm going to give you a written illustration of life at the Braithwaites'.

We are a family of four. Bernard's aunt is called Eliza; I call her Aunt Eliza. She is helping me with Latin. She thinks I have the makings of a scholar. They have more dictionaries in the house than they have in Lavenham library.

We also play chess. Bernard is better than I. But I will have my vengeance. It is a sport I excel at. Do you remember, I used to lie down when we played cricket and rounders in the back? Now, I lay down the king. (That is a chess-joke!)

I may have hung up my editorial hat for now, but I hope the Shilling Grange News *lives on. I asked Bernard about setting up a Tankerville Drive newspaper. Regrettably, he was not keen.*

As you know, Victor Braithwaite is a congenial man. He misses Bernard's mother. There are pictures of her everywhere and he has Iris *(her name) delivered once a month. Bernard and I agree it's time Victor moved on, so if you do have any suitable friends, Miss Newton, send them our way! We believe he's what they call an eligible bachelor and will make someone happy one day. Bernard said why not you, but I told him that was impossible!*

I have also written to Peter. Please give Ivor my love.

PS Please send the magnifying glass that I lent Barry to look at his spots.

'Have you read this, Victor?'

'Of course not!' Victor looked appalled. 'Alex deserves his privacy, as do you. Why?'

Clara smiled, thinking of Alex's call for single friends. 'No reason.' She wondered why he thought the idea of her and Victor was impossible. Mostly, she felt content that Alex sounded so at home at the Braithwaites'.

'We're happy with Alex,' Victor was saying. 'All of us. Bernard, Eliza and me. I want you to know how grateful we are.'

And then Victor left, and Clara waited, nervously, for the Cardews to take the baby away and to deliver Evelyn home. The poor mite would be full of distress, she was sure of it. Clara remembered when her own mother died, the numbness that had surrounded her for weeks, the feeling of cotton wool in her ears, everything being muzzy or fuzzy. How people paid attention in those first grim days of adjustment, but how it was later, when everyone else had moved on, when you needed them most.

A short while later, Dr Cardew came and said Evelyn had fallen asleep there – it had been a long day – and he'd just take Howard, now asleep in his pram, and send Evelyn back in the morning.

'She was so brave,' he said. 'She showed such maturity.'

It felt like a rebuke. Clara knew she should have been there at the funeral, by Evelyn's side, but when she said that to Dr Cardew he looked surprised.

He said, 'When you first came to the Grange, I said that we needed someone with consistency, reliability and commitment – do you remember?'

Clara remembered. She gathered Howard's many cardigans, his bottles and his nappies, sniffing back tears again.

'We got that in spades with you. And, Clara, do you remember I said it would be good news not just for the children but for the whole town?'

Clara handed everything over to Dr Cardew and stifled a sob. *What was the matter with her?*

'You do so much – don't think it goes unnoticed,' he said, 'but sometimes you need to let others help you too. We are all responsible for looking after children – it is *all* of our jobs.'

ARTICLE FOR THE *SHILLING GRANGE NEWS*, JUNE 1950

Miss Susan Smith

Susan Smith was born on 4 July 1924 in Govanhill, Glasgow. After she left school, she trained to be a nurse. She worked as a nurse for over ten years before she came to Lavenham to work in Dr Cardew's surgery. He was pleased with her and the patients liked her too. She sometimes saved people's lives. She also took care of the fish.

She was my mama. I didn't know her well but she liked the park, the seaside and would always chose chocolate cake over a Victoria sponge. She taught me the words to 'Home on the Range' and she liked Donald Burton on the wireless. She said my papa was a kind man from America with a big smile like me. I was going to live with her in Ipswich. She had been waiting a long time for me. We were going to choose curtain material and she was going to sew them. Now we won't get the chance. But she did tell me she loved me. And she did come back for me and she wanted me. I know that. She waited for me and she listened to me too – she listened like what I said was important, like what I thought mattered.

I will always remember that.

From Evelyn, her proud daughter.

58

It was a windy afternoon. The clothes were flapping on the line, the milk bottles were rolling down the paths and Clara's hair was flying everywhere. Judy used to say that children behaved worse on windy afternoons and Clara thought so too: Billy and Barry always used to fight when it was blowy, even Alex would get uppity.

Before school, Peter said he would be late home – he and Mabel – the football-loving girl from the train station – were going out for tea with her parents.

'Are you really just friends?' Clara asked.

'Ha,' Peter said enigmatically and she knew better than to press him further.

That afternoon, Clara and Anita were in the living room next to the surgery. Baby Howard was squirming on a wool blanket on the carpet – Clara worried his fingers would get caught in the knots.

Joyce was going to live with the Woodwards soon. All

paperwork present and correct. Clara didn't know what would happen with Evelyn though. Mr Sommersby seemed to think it would be the Home for Disabled Children in Walthamstow. 'I'm not sure Australia is the right fit for her,' he kept repeating, yet infuriatingly failing to give a reason why. Maureen and Rita, however, were definitely on the Child Migrant Programme and Clara had been surprised to be given a voucher to buy some clothes for them.

Peg was going to the Home for Disabled Children. People took against the others, but it would be hard to have anything against sweet-natured Peg, the baby of the family. Peg could melt the coldest of hearts. This was an advantage in life, surely and it made Clara feel more optimistic than she might have otherwise.

Clara had presumed she and Anita were going to talk about the auction, only two days away, but then Anita dropped her bombshell.

'We're going to apply to adopt. Obviously, I want your blessing first.'

Adopt?!

'I don't want to go through pregnancy and childbirth again, but I want Howard to have a...' – she looked up at Clara – 'sister.' Anita smoothed her hair. She looked so immaculate. Clara still found it hard to believe the dishevelled woman growling on the kitchen floor was the same person.

A sister? Clara couldn't say it. The word froze on her lips. What would the girl say? Rita didn't like change. Wouldn't she love to be with her piano teacher though? No, not particularly. Theirs was a singular relationship. It met a need. Would Rita cope with the upheaval of another move? She didn't want another mama – she had always been clear that although Clara was the nearest thing, her mama was the only one she wanted. But this was it – she needed a miracle to rescue her from the *Largo Bay*, and here it was.

And Anita? Anita wanted two children; really? Was this some kind of post-partum madness?

'And we'd like to make an application...'

Rita wouldn't have to go on the ship. She wouldn't have to wear a sunhat with an elastic knot under her chin. She could play piano all day long – and not in a shed. The Festival of Britain was occupying every crevice in Rita's cluttered mind; she would be—

'For Evelyn.'

'*Evelyn*?' yelped Clara. She couldn't help sounding shocked. She *was* shocked. Anita Cardew wanted to adopt Evelyn?

Where had this come from?

Anita continued, oblivious to Clara's turmoil.

'It's not just because of the sale of the Grange – although of course that's made us think about it sooner. We'd want to do it anyway, while Howard is still little. Evelyn's so sweet with him. Although her poor mother was only with us for a few months, I got to know her. And she loved her daughter dearly. And so it's kind of a thank-you to her. Evelyn is like Miss Smith in many ways. Caring for babies, looking after the sick – it's in her blood.'

Evelyn and the Cardews? It was a weird proposition – a bolt from the blue. Clara peered at Anita. Maybe it wasn't just children who behaved oddly on a windy afternoon.

The baby let out a yelp and put his chubby fist in his mouth as though silencing himself. Anita knelt by his side and showed him a bear.

'You're my lovely boy.'

She looked up at Clara. 'You're quiet.'

Clara covered her mouth with her coffee cup. 'Just a surprise, that's all. Have you asked Evelyn what she thinks?'

'Oh yes,' said Anita, her eyes still on Howard, 'she jumped at the idea.'

'Then...' Clara still felt stunned. 'That's marvellous.'

Joyce had taken a photo of Evelyn's mother the morning they'd gone to Southwold. Miss Smith was in the garden while Evelyn slowly ate her breakfast. Clara remembered wondering if Evelyn was deliberately making her wait. Miss Smith had been flicking through a magazine, but then had set it on her knees and was staring into the distance.

The light coming through the trees was perfect. It was so vivid it sliced the picture with bright diagonal lines. And there was Miss Smith immortalised in her beige spring raincoat, her umbrella at her side. Her patience and her gentleness captured in an instant. She probably hadn't even known the picture had been taken.

The Cardews had done up the loft room for Evelyn – 'Whether she comes to live with us or not' – admitted Anita, embarrassed, 'she will always have somewhere to stay.' It had stripy curtains and a brand-new continental quilt. They put the picture of Miss Smith in a silver frame over her bed.

'I'm not surprised,' Miss Bridges said when Clara consulted her. 'Anita and Evelyn have become thick as thieves.'

Thick as thieves? Was there a worse phrase? Clara thought. But perhaps it wasn't the phrase that annoyed her, it was the fact that she had missed the development of this relationship, when she prided herself on being attuned to what was going on in the children's lives.

'Were *you* surprised, Clara?'

Clara lied, 'No! It makes sense. But is there time?'

Miss Bridges thought so. 'Everything is in place. The Cardews already know Evelyn; they're married, they have a regular income, a stable home, their references will be excellent. It should be simple.'

Clara found she had tears in her eyes as she remembered Evelyn's first day: her subdued card-playing; her hunger and her resignation. Finally, one last time, it would be worth her while unpacking.

59

Clara was mindful that while Evelyn might be relieved at the prospect of this adoption, Rita might feel hurt or excluded.

'You know Evelyn is not coming with you to Australia?' she said to the girl.

'Yes.' Rita skipped around the dorm, a picture of glee. She had done about three circuits when Clara held up her hands. 'Enough, Rita!'

'Is she going to the Home for Disabled Children in Walthamstow then?'

Brace yourself.

'She's not going there either. Dr and Mrs Cardew have applied to adopt her.'

'Mama.' Rita climbed into Clara's lap. Her forehead was sticky and she smelled of sweat. She popped her thumb in her mouth and sucked noisily. She was eleven rewound to three again. Clara stroked her hair.

'Do you mind awfully?'

Rita popped her thumb out like a cork.

'Mama first. Second Miss Newton.'

Her eyes were owl-like in her sallow face.

'I don't want to go to Mrs Cardew,' she said. 'Always. Here. This is my home.'

Clara felt sick.

'Rita, don't you remember what I told you: this place is being sold and you're going to Australia?'

'Going to Australia. Oranges and lemons.'

'And bananas.'

'And pianos.'

Clara kept her fingers crossed. 'I hope so. I'm going to put a letter in your bag telling them about you and how you must have access to a piano and a brilliant teacher who must encourage you to play.'

Stella came into the room and Rita clutched her.

'Stella is coming with me.'

Oh no.

'I don't think she'd like the journey, sweetheart. What about if I look after her until... until some day?'

Rita scowled. 'I think I'll stay with Stella.'

'We'll see,' whispered Clara. She couldn't face it now, and she hated that she couldn't, but she felt completely defeated. She didn't know what would happen to Stella either, and whereas before Stella's fate had barely troubled her, since the cat's near-miss, Clara found herself worrying about her too.

Rita fell asleep, and maybe Clara dozed off too, for a few minutes later. Maureen, Peg and Evelyn rushed in and startled her.

'We need you in the kitchen right now,' they demanded.

Not another incident, Clara thought. Any more shocks and she might just burst. She and a sleepy Rita gathered themselves up. Rita was surprisingly compliant but Clara didn't think anything of it.

Downstairs in the kitchen, on the table was a clean white tablecloth and in the middle was a fruit cake with two lit candles. Next to it were cards and drawings.

'Happy Birthday,' the children shouted and then Evelyn asked uncertainly, 'It is today, isn't it?'

'It is.' Clara glanced around, overwhelmed. 'I don't tell anyone though, because I don't like a fuss.' Even though she was touched, she couldn't help scolding them. 'How on earth did you find out?'

'Marilyn told us,' yelped Rita and everyone told her to shush. Joyce sighed. 'She also told us not to tell you.'

Maureen had made the cake at Anita's so that it was a surprise. 'You didn't guess?'

'I had no idea,' Clara said. The effort they had gone to! She picked up Peg's card. It was a picture of the night sky with bold six-pointed stars. Inside it said, *I love you, Miss Newton.*

Clara's hands were shaking as she tried to stand it on the table. This was too much.

'You're only two years old, Miss Newton,' Evelyn called out.

'Ha...'

'It's a symbol of your second year with us,' Maureen explained. 'Make a wish then!'

Clara shut her eyes and wished to hang on to this moment forever. She felt like she didn't have the energy to see what life was going to throw at her next.

'I know what you wished,' shouted Joyce.

'You wished they don't sell the Grange,' said Rita and everyone yelped. Even Maureen was annoyed: 'You've jinxed it now!'

Peter sidled over to Clara and said that, if she didn't mind, he was going to slip out.

'Where to?'

'To see his *girlfriend*,' said Joyce, sticking out her tongue at him.

'She's not my girlfriend,' he snapped.

Maureen said, 'Ooh la la!'

But then Peter gave Clara a kiss on the cheek – he'd never done that before – and said, 'Happy birthday, housemother.'

After the cake, there were shoes to polish, clothes and toys to put away, in boxes now, instead of drawers. An empty trunk was sitting hungry in her room. Back upstairs, Clara tucked in Evelyn, who still had crumbs around her mouth. Evelyn said, 'I'm sorry I was mean when I first came here...'

'You were fine,' said Clara. *She was*, she thought, *she really was*.

'You were too nice,' Evelyn said. 'I just thought I could never live up to you and I would always let you down.'

'What changed?'

'You make mistakes too. I realised you're normal actually,' Evelyn said. 'You just hide it.'

Clara thought that was probably one of the sweetest things the girl could have said.

She went over to Joyce, who was wide awake – she always was after having sugar. Late-night cake was a bad idea.

'I've another plan, Miss Newton,' she said.

Joyce's scheming put Clara, Miss Bridges and Miss Cooper combined in the shade. Maybe she *would* be a war correspondent one day. She definitely seemed to have all sorts of ways of disrupting an enemy.

'Do you know what barricades are? We put our furniture against the door and wait.' She paused. 'It's better if we have cake.'

'Then I'm not sure we'd last long, Joyce. Especially not if I made the cake.'

'I could last for days, Miss Newton.'

Clara thought for a moment.

'Did you do that, Joyce?'

The time she was due to come, and all the time she hadn't come, last September. And Miss Bridges saying, 'Don't ask' when Clara questioned the delay. Was that Joyce's last stand?

'I may have done *something* like that, Miss Newton,' Joyce admitted.

Clara shook her head, laughing. 'That's a last resort. Let's see what happens at the auction first.'

Clara's bedroom with its faded mustard flowery walls was nearly empty. The packed trunk in the middle of the room was sated. It was all change. The kitchen had been almost entirely depleted. Julian would be collecting the piano – or sending some men to collect it – from the shed soon. They were nearly ready for their next steps. She tried not to think of Ivor and their time together in the bluebell woods, yet she couldn't stop replaying it. There was so much more she wished they had said to each other.

Someone knocked at the door.

'Can I have a word?' It was Peter, back from seeing his friend. 'Are the girls still going to Australia?'

'The house might not sell.'

'It is going to though, isn't it?'

'I think so... And yes, I think they are.'

'And I don't have to go?'

'You don't. You've got a job – with a place to live.'

It had turned out that Peter had the best prospects of them all, thought Clara, remembering the kind one-eyed man and the handsome man and the lively atmosphere of the comic place. Peter sat down on the bed. His long legs took over the room.

'Rita doesn't get it. She thinks you're going too.'

Clara sighed. 'I suspected that.'

'She said she's going to smuggle Stella in a trunk.' He chewed his lip. 'And I doubt Maureen will like it once she's there either.'

'You could be right.'

Peter said quietly, 'Last year, I just wanted to die.'

Poor Peter. 'But then everything changed. I got on with my drawing, my job and Mabel...'

'You've done so well—'

'I shouldn't be, but I'm so pleased he's going to jail. It makes me happy.'

'I can understand that.'

'I've decided – I'm going with them,' he said abruptly.

'What?'

'To Australia. I can't have them go out there on their own.'

'Peter, no! Your job, your... *friend.*'

'I know,' he said and his voice was soft. 'But Maureen and Rita are my sisters, I need to look after them.'

'You don't have to. There's no obligation and—'

'I know... just... I think I should. We Shilling Grange kids stick together.'

He slipped out the room before she even had the chance to hug him.

Darling, darling boy.

Clara slept badly. Abandonment and failure were at the centre of her dreams. She had stood on her own two feet yet look what a mess she had made of everything. The cries of a fox or something else wild out in the street mingled with her dreams.

60

The auction was in Dedham at midday. If Clara left at ten, it would give her plenty of time to get there. Hard to explain why she had to be there, but she had this compulsion to see it. Not from a sense of completion; more like ambulance-watching, to see the disaster unfold. Or perhaps she wanted the autopsy of it. She still felt uneasy about not going to Miss Smith's funeral.

She would prefer the Grange not to sell but had accepted that the chances of that were slim to non-existent now. Mr Sommersby had called, not only to check the packing was done, but also to thank her. She would have a 'challenging' new position soon – no files yet but hey-ho. Probably a medium-sized home in Rutland Water. Five children. Or maybe seven. Some finer details to iron out, but she'd know soon enough. He hoped she would bring her 'verve and vitality' to the role. That was flattering and she felt herself warming towards him. Maybe it wasn't so bad. She was a woman used to new starts. But then Miss Bridges called and chanted, 'It's for the best,' so many times that Clara feel unnerved again. Miss Cooper was going to drive the 'Australia' children to the docks on Saturday morning. Miss Bridges advised Clara not to go. 'Unsettling,' she said. Or 'Upsetting' – (the line wasn't great).

Mr Dowsett, who had never visited the Grange before, tapped on the front door as she was having one last cup of tea before setting off.

'So this is where the forgotten Jane Taylor lived?'

'And the ne'er-do-well children,' said Clara pointedly and he laughed until he had a coughing fit. She showed him around and he was awestruck and grateful. 'Can you imagine her here?' he kept saying and 'I think you would have been great friends, Miss Newton. She loved children too.'

Clara rummaged through her trunk and then pulled out her first edition book of Jane Taylor poems that Julian had given her. She could picture it in the library. The Jane Taylor Society would probably value it more than she could. She loved the book but the fact it was from Julian tainted it somewhat.

'Would you like it?' she asked. She knew it was the right thing to do – but at the same time, it was painful.

But Mr Dowsett declined. 'You keep it. It's lucky, I think.'

She laughed. It wasn't lucky. 'Lucky' would be keeping the home, keeping the children together. Still, his visit was making her feel relaxed, confident even on this strange morning. The children, bless them, were coping with the changes being flung at them, and if they could, she had no excuses.

Mr Dowsett was just about to leave. His hand was on the door handle when he said, 'The wife said not to bother you, but I said, I know Miss Newton, she likes to know everything.' He unfolded a copy of the *Melbourne Advertiser*, then guided Clara to a column on the third page. There was a dead fly on it, which they both ignored.

Boy missing in the bush. He walked for fifty miles and survived on rainwater and some sweets. The boy attempted to shoot a squirrel and tried some leaves. The police found him on the third day looking for him. Constable Mulroney said that it was remarkable. 'The boy was in great condition. He didn't panic and he managed to build a den to keep him warm at night. Great initiative for a nine-year-old!'

'I don't get it.' Clara looked up.
'Have you got to the last paragraph?'
'Not yet.' She continued.

The boy is a resident at Fairbridge Farm. He claims that he is from England: that his father died in the war, his mother died when he was three and he was told he was going 'on a day trip'. He claimed that the Christian Order make him, and several other orphaned children from England, milk cows, pick oranges and mend farm buildings all day long without breaks. He said they are beaten if they are too slow or too noisy, or tired. He showed his cuts and bruises, but the Order assert that they must have been acquired on his three-day walkabout.

She thought of Maureen and Rita. And Peter. Rita and Maureen. *Oh help.*
'Is this... what it is?'
Mr Dowsett's eyes looked worried. 'I think it might be. For some.'
She read on.

The boy was returned to Fairbridge Farm on July 1st. All allegations have been strenuously denied.

After Mr Dowsett had gone and she was alone in the hall, on a whim Clara grabbed the paper Mr Sommersby had left.
'Home for Disabled Children in Walthamstow.'

There was a phone number on it and Clara dialled it. She felt like an idiot for not thinking of it before. *This was for Peg. Dear loveable Peg. Everyone adored Peg.*

At first no one answered, so now she felt like even more of an idiot – she was wasting her own time, this was a dead end – but just as she was about to hang up, someone picked up the phone, said the number.

'Hello, I wonder if you could help. I would like to speak to the person in charge.' *Peg would be fine.* A woman's voice came back, she sounded uneasy, like she wasn't used to using the telephone. 'I'm afraid Sister Eunice is busy right now,' she said nervously. 'Would you like to leave a message?'

Clara hung up.

61

There was ivy, obscuring the red-brick walls, climbing all the way to the roof. The auction house was a friendly, welcoming building. The only thing that gave it away was the brass knocker on the shiny black door: that meant business.

People were moving purposefully towards it from the car park and from the street, and Clara followed them. Inside, the seats filled up quickly, with most people leaving a space next to them and laying down a coat or a bag. Some seats were reserved, but eventually these started filling up too.

There was a programme on each seat. Clara balanced it on her knees. She knew the Shilling Grange listing by heart:

Place of Historical Interest. Needs some attention.

Clara folded and unfolded it. Marilyn had called paper folding origano? or origam-y? and had tried to get the children to do it. They had failed miserably except for Alex, the boy who was usually a clumsy clot; he had made a sailing boat, which he wore as a hat, and everyone had laughed.

She wondered if Ivor would come. She wished she hadn't told him not to. Everything was falling apart and she was frightened for the children now. How would Rita, Maureen and

Peter cope if they were sent to a place like Fairbridge Farm? And who was to say they wouldn't? No one seemed to know anything about where they'd be going or what they would be doing there. Where were the details?

The boy 'showed his bruises'? For goodness' sake. The whole thing was utterly shameless.

Her children: Maureen, who needed to be looked after as much as a girl ten years her junior, maybe not when it came to cleaning and cooking, but certainly when it came to affairs of the heart.

Peter, who was only months away from his first job – and teetering on the edge of his first love affair – was going to be ripped from his dreams.

And Rita, oh Rita. It didn't bear thinking about. The girl working so hard on her Festival of Britain audition wrenched away from all that she loved.

And how would Peg cope at the Home for Disabled Children? Was it the same Sister Eunice as before? It couldn't be – and yet Clara feared what would happen to Peg if it was. Peg couldn't go there, she couldn't.

Don't sell. Don't sell. Clara was shaking. *Please don't sell. Of course that was what she had wished on her birthday.*

Resentfully, she looked around the room at the men in posh suits and the women with fashionable hairdos and bone structure, and thought it was a bugger not to be born into wealth. If she had money, she could have bought all the properties in the brochure – turned them into homes for the poor. She thought for a moment. Julian wouldn't like that. Victor would probably approve. She didn't know what Ivor would think.

You have to get over the unfairness of life, otherwise, you'll be stuck feeling bitter about it forever – which is no way to live – but it's still unfair, whether you get over it or not. Most of the people in the room were just handed down stolen money. Lords living off the land.

Goodness, Clara supposed, she was thinking like Miss Cooper now. Shouting about revolution and workers' rights. She was becoming one of those people the establishment were afraid of, the reds who were under the beds; but the thing was, she thought, the reds weren't *entirely* wrong. There *was* so much that was unfair. So much was unjust. And here she was fighting for her cubs because the rest of the world wanted to turf them out their homes, because somewhere else would be more convenient, cheaper, easier to manage.

There were so many people here too! She had imagined the auction room would be a room like a shop, but it was the size of the cinema at Ipswich. And the people here were just as excited. She remembered how her old boss Mr Harris used to go to the car auctions to catch a bargain. Always knock-down prices. She remembered him saying, *They can't give them away.*

She had to hope the Grange didn't reach the asking price. £300 sounded like an awful lot. Surely no one would want to pay that? Not when the toilets leaked and the bedrooms were icy, or as Marilyn said, 'It smelled of children.'

But Clara loved Shilling Grange, the garden, the parlour with the fire going, the expansive bedrooms. She'd pay £300 – she'd pay twice that – if she could.

And even if it didn't sell today, even if they fended them off here, what was to stop the council selling in three months or in six months now the finger was out of the dam? Shilling Grange was a lost cause. Yes, Browne had been defeated, but there would be another buyer. The only hope she had now was that someone had discovered a terrible fault, subsidence or bad drains, and no one would buy it – but that wouldn't hold them off for long either and the council would still kick them out. But at least if they moved later, if they had just one month, two months more, they could work out a way to be together; she could fight Australia and she could fight Walthamstow. She could insist they were kept together; she didn't know how, but somehow she would.

The auctioneer spoke fast and with authority, like a thin Churchill. He had proper bags under his eyes and gaunt cheeks. There was something about him that just screamed 'war'. You just knew with some people. Years and years of it had taken its toll.

There was no preamble, just bustle and papers flashing and rules. Over to the right of the room, there were telephones and cables. To the left was a table stacked with more programmes.

The bidding on the first property, Tyrell House ('*A fine house in mint condition with its own private woods*') began. Ivor still had not come. He had believed her when she had told him not to. Damn it.

Clara sat stony still – any movement could be misconstrued. There were people whispering, but it was mostly the auctioneer's voice that was heard.

'£250? Anyone. Over there in the hat, yes, you, Sir? Do I have... yes.'

It sold for £410 to the man in the hat.

Was this a good sign or a bad sign? Clara didn't know.

Shilling Grange was next up. Bidding started at £150.

Nothing happened at first and Clara felt a sudden burst of hope: *it's not going to sell. No one wants it!*

But someone's hand, two rows in front, was already up like they knew the answer in maths class. And there was the back of a head she knew well. It was Julian, of course. He looked neat and self-possessed from behind and probably from the front too.

Julian? Of course; they worked together. Browne had got him in to do the dirty work – or maybe Julian had got Browne in to do the dirty work. Who knew? Either way, Julian turned around, saw that Clara saw him and gave her a wink. *Pig.*

Someone else, a man towards the back, Clara had to twist to see, in a grey suit, silver thready moustache – she didn't recognise him – was bidding. He was in the £5s, Julian was in the £10s, incrementally, step by step, pushing the price up, pushing the children out.

The council are going to sell anyway, what does it matter who it goes to?

It did, and it didn't.

At £285 and it was Julian's turn, and he didn't bid. He didn't bid and then he did, he was raising his hand – but Clara knew him, and he was doing it grudgingly now.

He'd committed to £290.

Mr grey-suit still looked confident.

'£295?' said the auctioneer and grey-suit man signalled his assent. '£300 – Do I have—'

Over by the telephones at the side of the room, someone shouted, 'Here!'

Clara swivelled round to see who'd shouted. It was a woman, auction staff probably, her whole arm raised in salute while she talked to the person on the phone.

Moustached man looked torn; he must have thought he had it.

Clara's heart sank: anything over £300 and they were lost.

With just the tip of his index finger, moustached man agreed to £305.

They were sunk, realised Clara. Now, not in three months, not in six months; now. It was over. She'd pack up the house and the children would be dispersed all over again. Even while she was anticipating that, the price was climbing again.

She was not going to cry.

'Sold to our overseas investor for £320. That's Shilling Grange.' The hammer came down like a guillotine. 'Thanks to Mrs Hartley on the telephone.'

Sob. Oh yes, she was.

She sat through the sale of Saffron Manor ('*boasts own duckpond and stables*') and the sale of Cottesmore House ('*a delight for fans of Edwardian architecture*').

It was happening.

Rita and Maureen were lost now, although Peter would do his best to take care of them. But she could still probably fight for Peg.

Was she too attached?

She would have to start again. Return to go, like in a game of Monopoly. She should have understood this was how it was. She was alone and she would stay alone.

Everything was selling today. She was surprised when she saw Julian bid on Saffron Manor too, but he hadn't won; it had gone to a man sitting just in front of them. The woman next to him had patted his knee and said, '*Now* can we go?' as if he'd just bought a pair of shoes.

Cottesmore House had sold for £601 in a contest between one person in the room and two people on the telephones. Even Clara, caught up in her grief, was spellbound.

And then there was a fifteen-minute break, said the auctioneer, who had been losing his voice and was in vain chucking back glasses of water, and it was her chance to leave.

She picked up her coat and, although the room was warm, put it on for something to do. The hall was musty with other people's breath. There were money conversations going on everywhere. Privilege in the air. There was no need to sit through the next three houses. Clara wanted to avoid Julian too. One good thing – the person the other end of the telephone, whoever that was, had wiped the smug smile off his face.

62

He was there, in the street. Ivor. The sight of him, in his Sunday best and an apologetic look on his kind face, was exactly what she needed. Emotions churning, Clara threw herself at him. She could feel his shock and then he switched into action.

'Clara, it's okay.'

He was so warm and lovely, holding her up. He smelled great too and she felt safe for once.

'Am I too late? What happened?'

After a few more moments of sobbing, she had calmed enough to get the words out. 'It's gone. It's over.'

'Oh no,' he said. 'Really? Oh no.'

He stroked her back. His lips were in her hair and it felt wonderful. Were they not made for each other? This was who *she* was purpose-built for.

He held her away slightly and peered into her face. 'What about you? Where do they want you to go, Clara?'

'Rutland Water,' she sniffed. 'I've never even heard of it!'

She'd probably never see Ivor again after this. Neither of them drove. Would he feel motivated enough to get on a train to visit her? She glanced at him, his set lips, his dark eyes fixed on the pavement. Probably not. He had a lot going on here, after all. Which meant... if she was never going to see Ivor again, she might as well tell him how she felt. She felt both undone by him and restored by him. And she knew, with a thunderbolt of certainty, that he was exactly the chap she was looking for. *Mostly B's. Homely.*

He smiled at that. '*I* have.'

'What's it like then?'

He shrugged. 'It's no Lavenham, but then not many places are.'

'Will you come and visit me?'

He took her hand and she thought it was going to be a no, but he said, hesitantly, 'If you want me to, Clara.'

She was sobbing again. 'Maureen and Rita are going to have to go away, and poor Peter, to the other side of... I can't help them any more. I screwed up. And Peg, little Peg.'

'Ssssh.' He pulled her to his chest. 'It wasn't your fault.'

It wasn't her fault. She had been lied to, again and again. But it *was* her fault too. Why had she been so willing to put her faith in Mr Sommersby? Why had she trusted the men in suits more than her own instincts? She remembered Mr Horton's uneasiness with her – he knew, she decided. Mr Sommersby and Mr Horton both knew she was never going to keep the Grange, but they had let her jump through hoops, let her scrimp and save and hope when this had been the plan all along.

'They mustn't go to Australia. It won't work.' She was crying again. 'I've heard the most terrible things, Ivor, brutal things. And Peg can't go to the Walthamstow home, she mustn't.'

'Clara... CLARA. It'll be all right.'

'I must be able to do something – I must...' She paused. The panic was rising inside her, she was filled up with it. 'Maybe I can adopt them.'

He grimaced at her. He looked so sad. 'But where would you live? How could you possibly support yourself?'

'I don't know... I don't know.'

A partner, a home, a job. She could do this.

She stared into his dark eyes. *Tell him you want to be with him,* she thought. *Do it. Do it now.* She fumbled to find his hand again. But he must have guessed what she was about to say because he backed off, just a tiny step but it felt like a mile, and then in one breath, he said, 'Clara, God knows I am crazy about you, but this isn't the— Hello?' His tone had changed entirely. 'Can I help you?'

A woman was standing in front of them, waiting for the chance to speak. Clara glared. She had something in her hand that was shaped like a cigar but white. Clara realised it was one of the women who'd been on the telephones in the hall.

'Pardon me, it's Miss Newton, isn't it?' she said. 'They told me you were here.'

Clara stared at her. She didn't know this woman, so how did she know her name? The woman was sweating and smiling, one ear, the one that had been pressing against the receiver presumably, was redder than the other. She pulled her shawl around her. The day was cooler than it looked.

'It is... Miss Newton,' said Ivor helpfully.

Clara scowled at him, sniffed. *She must look a terrible state.*

Wiping her nose, she said, 'I... *am,*' while Ivor gave her a look that said *what took you so long?*

'I'm Mrs Hartley—'

'Yes,' said Clara, more aggravated. Chatting with a stranger in the car park wasn't a priority right now. 'I mean, pleased to meet you.'

'I have a message for you.'

'Oh?'

The 'cigar' was a rolled-up paper that the woman now unravelled dramatically. She had two-tone hair; the top was grey while the bottom was red. There was something compelling about it.

'The buyer of Shilling Grange wants to communicate something to you.'

Clara didn't want to hear some daft homily; she needed to get back to the house to regroup, to take it in. But Ivor put out his hand – *wait*.

'Go ahead...'

Mrs Hartley was clearly a patient woman and in a fantastic mood. She grinned at Clara.

'They want you to know that they are loaning it to the seller for an initial set period of ten years under the following conditions: that the house continues to be run as a children's home and that the children maintain their links with the local community and that the housemother of said home is—'

'Clara!' yelped Ivor.

'A Miss Newton.' She grinned. She was just as breathless as Ivor. 'For as long as she desires.'

Loaning it to the seller? They're loaning it to the council?

'And has the seller agreed with the conditions?' Ivor butted in.

Clara thumped him on the arm.

'I don't get it... What does this mean?' she said and her voice was squeaky.

'It's still under negotiation...' Mrs Hartley paused, but then she looked Clara right in the eye, 'but as I understand it, it's a fantastic offer – so once the details are ironed out over the next couple of days, I imagine they'll snap it up. It's unusual – but it's extremely exciting!'

She beamed again. Clara was finding it difficult to order her thoughts. She was vaguely aware that Ivor was clutching her again and saying, 'This is amazing, Clara, don't you see?'

'It is.' Mrs Hartley was nodding. 'It's quite a thing!'

Clara wasn't sure. After the hope and the agony she had been through, was this some kind of joke?

'So... so who is the buyer then?'

'She's an American,' Mrs Hartley said.

A woman?

Mrs Hartley continued, 'She goes by the name of Marilyn Adams. Mrs. She's a property investor. It's our first time dealing with her. She's a fan of Lavenham, apparently.'

Once Mrs Hartley had gone, Clara squealed, then covered her face with her hands.

Unbelievable. They had been saved.

Ivor slapped her on the back. 'I don't believe it!'

Marilyn had always been a support and she was certainly generous, but never in a billion years could Clara have suspected this.

'Oh, Clara,' Ivor said, and she couldn't help it; the way he said it was sexy, there was no getting away from it. 'I'm so pleased for you and the children. For all of us.'

They were safe. They were home. Rita. Maureen. Peter. Peg. The children would stay with her for as long as they needed. They would be able to keep their home and they would be able to leave their home when the time was right for them – like most other children do.

No strange ship, no Sister Eunice, no fear, no guilt. The children still had a place to call home.

And then Clara and Ivor were drawn into each other's arms again. And quickly, Clara's feelings went from relief and celebration to something else. She knew they oughtn't, it was hardly the time or the place, but she couldn't help herself. He had said it, hadn't he? She had heard it. '*God knows I am crazy about you.*' It was said with sincerity, and even if he hadn't said it aloud, perhaps deep down she had known it all along – he was in love with her. As she was with him.

He pulled away; she couldn't read his expression.

'Go and tell the kids that you're all staying in the house. They've been worried. And it's wonderful. Everyone will want to celebrate.'

'But, Ivor...' She felt stupid now. Flushed and totally wrong-footed.

'I need to get back too,' he said throatily. *Why was he being so distant?* 'I shouldn't be here... It's not fair.'

Did he know what she felt about him? Was he toying with her?

One look at his face told her he wasn't. He looked distraught and she couldn't work out why.

63

It was morning in America. Clara found time zones more confusing the more she thought about them but she worked out that this should be an acceptable time to call and Marilyn answered as soon as the operator put her through, like she had been waiting for the telephone to ring. Clara was almost lost for words; she kept repeating 'thank you so much,' and 'You've saved us.' Then, when she asked, 'How can I ever thank you?', Marilyn responded, 'I do have one request, darling. Could we change the name of Shilling Grange?'

'Anything, Marilyn, of course.'

Michael – Marilyn... this. In one way, it didn't make sense – it certainly hadn't made sense at the time when she'd lost him – but in another way, it made perfect sense. Clara hated the phrase 'everything happens for a reason' – it was just someone looking back and trying to make sense out of the senseless. However, sometimes you can meet someone and it can make a major difference to the rest of your life. If you let it. If you let *them*. Tomorrow, she would write Marilyn a long letter, and perhaps send some of the local fudge Marilyn had liked. Although nothing she could give her would ever be enough.

'You're not alone, Clara,' Marilyn said. 'Remember that.' Then she asked if Clara was okay. 'It sounds like you're crying?'

'I am crying,' admitted Clara, 'but I am okay.'

The children couldn't believe it. Peter took himself off to his room, choked up. 'I know I won't be here for long anyway,' he said, 'but I love that this is a place I can come back to... this is my home.'

Joyce was disappointed that there would be no barricades with cake. 'I was looking forward to a battle,' she admitted.

'You're going anyway,' Rita snapped at her. 'To your forever home with the Woodwards.'

Was Rita annoyed about that too? Probably.

'Yes, but still – it would have been fun.'

Rita insisted everyone came out to the shed and listen to her play a piece she had composed herself. Joyce muttered that Rita was making it all about her. Clara thought it was going to turn into an argument, but Rita laughed it off: 'It is *mostly* about me.'

It was a brilliant but sombre piece and after she'd finished, Rita spun round and said, 'I'm going to write a happy one next.'

Peg slipped her hand into Clara's and squeezed so tightly that Clara winced.

'We're staying, Peg,' she whispered, and Peg lifted her hem and danced a jig. She whirled around then she collapsed onto the floor giggling. And a tremor went through Clara at the thought of Peg having to go to a place run by Sister Eunice again. Peg was safe but those poor, poor children in Walthamstow—

'So I just heard – we're staying?' Maureen bounded into the kitchen. Clara realised she didn't know where she'd been; Maureen had stopped telling her.

'Yes.'

'I would have liked Australia...'

Clara sighed. She couldn't do anything right with Maureen. 'You can still go – just when you're older.'

Maureen shrugged. 'I think I will. Ivor came to the auction then?'

'He came afterwards, yes.'

'So now you know?' Maureen went on.

'Know what?'

Maureen went slack-jawed. She held the table to steady herself.

'Nothing.'

'Maureen?' How high-pitched Clara's voice was, how squeaky.

Maureen was as pink as a ribbon. 'I've got to find the... the others...'

'It's Ruby, isn't it?' Clara asked quickly. 'She's back?' Watching Maureen's face for answers, she racked her brains. 'Or... Or someone else?'

Maureen was shaking her head fearfully. 'No, she's not back. It's not *her*.'

And then Clara knew. She just felt it. How had she ever not known? There had been a reason Ruby had come back, and then they had gone away together. She remembered the way, in the bluebell woods, Ivor had been rocking Howard's pram and she'd said, 'You're good at that.'

And he'd said, 'I'm sure you are too.'

She had told him she didn't want a baby and now she remembered his strange expression – she couldn't work out what it was: uncertainty, surprise, disappointment? She should have known it then.

'Is it... Has Ivor got a baby, Maureen?'

'I can't say,' Maureen said. But she didn't need to say; it was written over her face.

And there it was, her explanation.

Clara sank back down on to the kitchen chair as though someone was crushing her. She put her face in her hands. She couldn't believe it.

64

Soon the kitchen was full of celebration. Clara had washed her puffy face and with the help of some powder and an eyebrow pencil, looked reasonably presentable. 'Best behaviour,' she told herself.

Miss Bridges thought she had been crying with relief.

'It's over now,' she said comfortingly.

'Yes,' said Clara. 'It is.'

Miss Bridges said, 'Once again you've been a trooper.'

Clara was going to do the usual denial, the expected, *oh no, I haven't*, but this time she agreed. She said, 'I suppose, I have.'

Anita and Dr Cardew came over with baby Howard in another of his funny hats. Dr Cardew was yawning again. Anita looked like she'd walked off the set of *A Streetcar Named Desire*. Mr and Mrs Woodward also came, with a collection of cigarette cards for Joyce that included a series of dogs, one of which was the exact same type as their dog, Bailey. Anita and Mrs Woodward telephoned each other sometimes to give each other advice about eleven-year-olds – 'or eleven-year-olds going on twenty,' as Mrs Woodward liked to say.

Anita was relieved that no one would be moving, but Clara

thought Anita was especially pleased because of the festival auditions, which were coming up soon. The event meant a great deal to her. Rita would play the piano, Rita, Maureen, and Evelyn would sing and Peg would be involved too. (Anita took care not to leave out Peg, thought Clara, although she wondered how exactly Peg would contribute. The speech therapist was lovely, but she was not a miracle-worker.)

Anita barked with laughter about something, which woke up Howard who squealed in dismay. It was Evelyn who ran over, plucked him out of the Silver Cross pram and patted his back.

'Wind,' she pronounced authoritatively. 'Get that gripe water from my bag.'

The adults snapped to attention, Dr Cardew followed the instructions and went looking for the bag.

Clara slipped into the hall to telephone Billy and Barry. She wanted to hear those carefree, sunny voices. The boys were out – playing football, naturally – but Aunt Ruth said that she would pass the message on and that it was going great guns except they ate *everything*. 'I know,' sympathised Clara, leaning against the wall. She felt exhausted. *Ivor*, she thought. *What happened?* It was difficult to arrange a visit – the twins had so many matches and training and friendlies – but they put a date in the diary for the following month. She wanted to say, 'tell them I miss them,' but thought Aunt Ruth might think that was too much. As a housemother, she was meant to fade away like a shadow.

Peter turned up with the girl 'who is not my girlfriend', but they certainly seemed fond of each other. Clara admired her clothes and her hair, and the not-girlfriend, Mabel, said she'd go shopping with her if she liked. Clara couldn't imagine it, but said, 'yes, please' and 'how lovely'. Peter took up position at the kettle and both served up the hot drinks, and they were somehow more adult than most of the adults.

He had an idea for a comic-strip, he said, something about 'a home with nine lives.' Clara laughed and squeezed his arm. She would never forget what he had offered to give up for them, never.

It would have been lovely to have Joe there too, Clara thought guiltily. She had liked Joe.

Maureen was agitated that she had let the cat out of the bag – self-righteous too. Once she'd said hello to everyone, she prowled after Clara, who wanted just to sit upstairs among the mustardy flowery wallpaper with her head in her hands.

'It's just a baby,' Maureen hissed. 'It's not Ruby, she's not coming back.'

'I-I... okay...'

'You had someone in the past anyway, didn't you?' Maureen said, almost aggressively.

'Ye-es.'

'Lots of people.'

Not that many, thought Clara.

'And you've got us to look after...'

'Yes.'

'So how is this any different from Ivor having a—'

'It just *is*, Maureen, you don't understand.'

The door went. It was Mr Horton lugging a gramophone. Stella zipped past him, out into the garden, which was Clara's first reaction too.

Peter asked if they could roll back the carpet in the parlour; they wanted to do the hokey-cokey. Clara's heart fell – she wanted everyone to go home now, so she could collect her thoughts – but she managed a smile and said, she didn't think the new landlady, Marilyn, would object. And it *was* lovely to see shy Peter twirl Mabel around and everybody clapping.

They hadn't been dancing long when Miss Cooper's car

rolled up. She stepped in, in a trouser suit like Marlene Dietrich. Although they saw her regularly, the children still stared in awe. Clara wished she had dressed for an occasion too.

'I want to be Miss Cooper when I grow up,' Rita said and Clara tried to joke, 'So do I.' But Rita looked confused, so Clara clarified, 'I mean, she's an inspiring person.'

'So are you,' said Rita defensively. Clara tugged one of the girl's plaits. 'Thank you.'

Surely in a few minutes she could sneak off upstairs to be alone?

But then the doorbell rang again. This time it was Julian, slick as usual, lingering his lips on her cheek like a snail leaving a slimy trail.

He flicked her chin – 'Well done, you' – then squinted. 'You look done in. I thought you'd be having a ball.'

It was disconcerting how well Julian knew her.

'I'm just worn out... Enjoy the auction, did you?' she snapped.

'Could have gone better, frankly.'

'Who were you bidding for, Julian?'

She thought if he said Mr Browne she might as well just kill him there and then.

'Myself!' he said. 'And I also would have come to a deal with the council for you.'

'Huh, right,' said Clara. He was grinning at her, and she couldn't tell if he was telling the truth or not.

'I'm trying to build up a portfolio of properties. Do I remember correctly you used to like Monopoly? Maybe we'll do it together some day.'

Same old Julian. She realised he was slightly drunk again.

He pulled her into the kitchen – somehow it always felt like he took over a place – and showed her a silver chest about the size of a shoebox. It was ornate, beautiful and unlike anything she'd seen before.

'What *is* this?' Clara asked, meaning *why are you showing me this?*

'It's Romanov, antique – it's lovely, right?'

'I mean, what's it here for?'

'It's for your Joyce.' Julian grinned.

'I don't...'

'I hear she's been taking *the most extraordinary* photographs.' He arched one eyebrow at Clara, who flushed. 'I thought she might need somewhere equally extraordinary to put them. She's off soon, isn't she? Call it a goodbye gift...' His face softened. 'I used to think these children were...'

'A "pox on society"?'

He shrugged. 'I've realised they might not be – in the right hands.' He grinned, more pleased with himself than ever.

Clara felt speechless, but she managed to thank him just as he strutted off to 'teach those ingrates how to dance. Coming?'

'I'll be in later.'

He winked at her. 'You had your chance.'

Clara exhaled. Searching for that elusive quiet moment, she snuck out to the shed. It had never been so tidy, everything packed up and ready; but on the floor was a puzzle book, lying open. One of Peg's, perhaps, or Evelyn's. It was open at a page of those puzzles where you have to get your dog to its kennel, there are three possible routes, three black lines leading from the START to the FINISH, and you have to follow the swirly contortions to the right place. You'd always get there in the end, even if you didn't choose it first or second, as long as you didn't give up.

She looked up and Miss Bridges and Anita were at the door, studying her. Both looked worried.

Would they stop following her around? They were as bad as Stella.

'What are you doing out here all alone?' Anita asked.

'I don't know.' Clara smiled weakly. She felt wobbly on her

feet. The last thing she wanted was to faint again. 'I'll come back in...'

'There will be files soon on the new children,' said Miss Bridges, smiling. 'And this time you'll get to see them in advance. Change in policy, Clara. Another thing that's thanks to you.'

'Good, good...' but Clara didn't feel good. It was amazing and a triumph, but she also felt hollowed out and confused. Was this what victory felt like? Because without Ivor to share it, this victory didn't feel half as amazing as she had thought it would.

'Ivor not here?'

Clara hated having to answer that. She looked around herself dramatically, then pretended to be shocked.

'Doesn't look like it, does it?'

'Go and get him then...' Anita said, jiggling baby Howard, who had cheered up since being liberated from his hat. He held out a gift of damp bread to her.

'I want to meet the infamous Ivor Delaney,' joined in Mr Horton, who had crept up from nowhere. Clara cringed. He might think they were friends now, but in her book, they were not.

'If he wanted to be here, he'd come...'

'Go and see him then,' Anita said and baby Howard dropped his bread in agreement.

'I don't think—'

'You know you want to.'

'I don't.'

'Go-ooo,' they insisted. It was hard to argue with all of them at once and Clara felt so tired and so in need of a break from them that she agreed.

Soon Clara was out of the Grange, with a plate of cakes in one hand and a bottle of beer in the other. She felt untethered and full of doubts. And yet the relief of the home being saved propelled her forwards. She had got through that, hadn't she? She was stronger than she thought. Time and time again, she proved that was the case. And what was this but another hurdle to overcome?

Stella followed her out and Clara told her to go home, please, and Stella stalked off to sit in the wagon next to some newspapers.

At the workshop, Clara called hello, and Ivor yelled back, 'Come in!'

She didn't have a hand free to open the door. By the time she had set the cakes and beer down on the ground, the door had opened and he was in its frame. He peered cautiously out.

'Don't worry, I didn't make them,' Clara said pretend-brightly about the cakes. 'They're Anita's doing.'

Ivor chewed his lip.

'They said I should come and see you.'

Warily, Ivor grinned at her, and then, as though remembering himself, he said, 'Better come in, then.'

His workshop was full of things yet it was tidy and organised, and as inviting as ever. The materials, draped and piled around, made Clara want to run her fingers across them or wrap them around herself. He led her to the back, away from the street, where it was even quieter. There was a dark, dark window there and, in front of it, two armchairs with a small round table between them and a glass of whisky or something on it. The telescope was still there, stood close to the window too, watchful, like a crow. Or a sentry saluting the night sky. She couldn't help thinking this was a magical place. She couldn't help remembering the evening – that felt so long ago now – they looked through the telescope together, and the way his arms had felt around her, and his breath on her hair.

She had to say something. He didn't seem about to. 'I hope we are okay.'

He swallowed loudly. 'You'll always be my friend, Clara,'

he said, and at that word, that word that could be so full yet also be so empty, Clara's heart sank. So. Friend. That's what she was. That's *all* she was. And she knew as he said it, knew unequivocally, that she wanted more.

A whimpering sound came from upstairs.

So, it was true.

Ivor sprang up, half apologetic, half resolved. He rubbed his forehead. 'I'd better...'

He was only gone a minute, maybe less. He came back with a swaddled package like a tiny mummy from one of Alex's pharaohs and pyramids book series.

'Who's this then?' Her voice was steadier than she thought it would be. She *could* do this.

'This is Patricia Kate Delaney.' His dark eyes were full of questions too. 'I collected her the day before last. Maureen's been marvellous.'

Clara stood up awkwardly, her cardigan catching on the chair.

'That's a lovely name.'

'Do you want to...'

Ivor held the baby out to her, and then there was an awkward too much touching/I'm trying not to touch exchange as she took the baby out of his arms and into hers.

She sat down. The baby was a darling thing. Clara remembered saying that babies could smell fear. She remembered how nervous she was when she first met the children. *Eight children!* Right now, she felt afraid of everything. Ivor was looking encouragingly at her, with his approving smile.

Strains of singing from the Grange, and the piano. Rita was off again.

She held the baby, who stared up at her with those baby blue eyes. It was like little Patricia Kate was weighing her up, making decisions, evaluating whether she was friend or foe. It was spooky. Was she going to cry? Clara thought to herself, *I'm*

*Miss Newton, the housemother of Shilling Grange, and I'm here
to get the best for you.*

And it wasn't so bad. She had managed to stand on her own
two feet for a long time; but then – a sob rose in her – she had
found she didn't have to. She had friends, she had people to
support her and people she would support. And Patricia Kate
would too.

'How old is she?' she asked. The baby had pink, curved
cheeks and a pouty mouth and her hair was wispy, like it had
been sketched on. She was considerably tinier than baby
Howard, who, in Clara's mind's eye, now appeared huge.

'Four weeks tomorrow,' Ivor said tensely. Why was he so
nervous? She wasn't going to drop the baby. 'I meant to tell you,
Clara – I was waiting to find out, and then for the right
moment... and then there was the worry of losing the Grange
and the auction and...'

'And Ruby?'

'Back to America,' he said with less emotion. 'She's Ruby's
daughter. Not mine but...' He sighed. 'She didn't know what to
do. She never wanted to be a mother. It's a complex situation –
she had already left her American when she found out she was
pregnant, and I made a promise a long time ago that I would
always be there for her.' He paused. He was watching Clara
carefully. 'She had a difficult pregnancy, and her state of mind
was – I didn't feel comfortable leaving her; and then she went
into a nursing home in London and gave birth. She recovered
there for a while, and now she's gone. We agreed Patricia is
going to stay here in England with me. It's for the best – and...'
His upper teeth chewed his lower lip, 'I didn't know how it
would be – but already I adore her.'

Patricia Kate Delaney gripped Clara's finger and blinked
slowly. Wide glassy eyes like marbles, lashes like tiny feathers.
Clara looked between her and Ivor. He was standing over them
now, so awkward he didn't know what to do with himself.

'Hello, baby,' she crooned as Ivor edged away, saying he'd make tea. 'This is a special place; lots of people are going to look after you and love you here.' She paused. 'I'm going to sing "Twinkle, twinkle, little star" to you and with any luck, your papa is going to knit you a turnip hat.'

The kettle was whistling loudly, and Patricia was sweetly cooing, so Clara could hardly make out what Ivor said next, but it was something like, 'Thank you for being here, Clara.' The tenderness in his voice was unmistakable.

Back at the house, the party was in full swing. Clara picked up Peg and the girl clasped her scrawny legs around her, nuzzling her neck. Peter, Mabel, Evelyn and Miss Bridges were dancing to Peggy Lee's 'The Way You Look Tonight' – while Maureen was animatedly talking films with Mr and Mrs Garrard. Baby Howard was asleep in Anita's arms and Dr Cardew was fussing around them both. Clara swallowed. Leaving Ivor had been hard, but it was important to be here now. She and Ivor had time. They would find a new shape for their relationship, a new way of being, she didn't doubt that. It might not be what she had envisaged but then nothing ever was.

And then Joyce was shouting, 'I want to take a photo of you all!'

Everyone groaned, except for Dr Cardew, who said, 'Excellent idea, you could send it to Mrs Adams, couldn't you?', which meant they had no choice but to oblige. They made the younger children sit in a row in front, cross-legged – 'Pull your skirt down, Peg' – then the older children knelt up behind them: 'I'm not a child,' huffed Maureen. In the back row, Miss Bridges was standing so close to Mr Horton they took up the space of only one person, while Miss Cooper did a sultry pout and a pose straight from the magazines. The Cardews and baby Howard, who still had his eyes shut despite the kerfuffle, joined one end.

Julian, with uncharacteristic delicacy – 'We won't all fit in, will we?' – managed to manoeuvre himself, the Garrards and the Woodwards out of shot.

'Where do you want me?' asked Clara hesitantly. She picked up Stella, partly as a defence, then sneezed. Damn cat.

'In the middle, of course!' instructed Joyce.

Clara clambered between the standing and the kneeling rows and squeezed behind Peter and Mabel, who were, she noted, holding hands. The parlour was warmer than usual and smelled of orange squash and biscuits.

Joyce stood in front of them. She had the authority, with her camera, the strap wound round her fingers, reminding Clara of that piece of string round her thumb all those months ago.

'Ready? – say cheese!' she said.

'I prefer to say cheesecake,' interrupted Anita Cardew.

'Do we have any cheese?' Evelyn called out.

'I know,' suggested Clara, enjoying herself. She was back home, back in the middle of her family, and everything was going to be all right. 'Let's say: The Michael Adams Children's Home.'

'That's a bit long.' Joyce scowled, ever defiant.

'No, it's perfect,' said Miss Bridges, smiling broadly, despite, or perhaps *because* of Mr Horton's heavy arm around her. 'After three, everybody. One two three: *The Michael Adams Children's Home!*'

'Let me straighten my plaits first,' Rita shouted just as Miss Bridges was saying two.

But it was too late. The flash had gone off, the camera shutter had been pressed and Stella had leapt out of Clara's arms and was scrambling onto an unsuspecting Maureen's shoulders: 'What the hell!' she yelped.

'Don't swear!' cautioned Clara automatically, as everyone laughed.

A LETTER FROM LIZZIE

Hello, hello,

Thank you so much for returning with me to Lavenham and the (formerly known as) Shilling Grange Orphanage – I hope you have enjoyed this, the second book in the series. If you enjoyed *A Place to Call Home* and want to keep up to date with my latest releases, just sign up at the following link. Your email address will never be shared and you can unsubscribe at any time.

www.bookouture.com/lizzie-page

I've been working hard to bring you Book Three. I've never written a series before and it's been a real journey of discovery for me. Now I know that I should have made more detailed notes at the beginning; alas I did not. Lack of organisational skills plus a perimenopausal memory have slowed me down. However, I have a well-thumbed copy of *The Orphanage* next to me, full of Post-its, so if I need reminding of someone's surname, someone's age, someone's eye colour, I can, hopefully, find it. Some people use spreadsheets for such things – I wish I had!

There is a restriction on things I can write about now: restrictions built by me! A number of times, I've embarked on writing a new storyline before going, 'Wait a minute! Didn't I say that she was from such and such a place? – oh blow, yes, I did.' But, and here's the big but, writing a series is so enjoyable too; there is a challenge and excitement in finding a way through those restrictions. I do think limitations can often be the mother of creativity (something I tried to show with Joyce and her photographs).

I have loved writing Clara and Ivor's relationship. Rest assured, I do know where I'm going with this one – this road is paved with good intentions 😊 We'll just have to see how they get on. I do love having a large cast of characters; I hope it's not been too confusing – they feel different and individual to me. I love how in a series you can stretch out a storyline, so it's more like real life, where things come in and out of sharp focus. In Book One Peter was in despair, in Book Two he was wobbling but on the up – where will he be in Book Three? You'll just have to... oh, you know.

All of us who write historical fiction are affected by contemporary concerns to some extent – impossible not to be – and some of my concerns are interwoven here: children's safeguarding, decisions made by bureaucrats, the English class system, etc. However, I also try hard to be guided by the conventions of the time – which can be difficult because there are always, in any era, those who defy conventions...

I love to hear from readers. Do feel free to get in touch through social media.

And if you have enjoyed *A Place to Call Home*, do please consider putting a review up on Goodreads or Amazon, or your favourite bookish platform. Every little bit helps to bring my lovely Clara and the children to new audiences.

facebook.com/LizziePage
twitter.com/LizziePagewrite
instagram.com/lizziepagewriter

ACKNOWLEDGEMENTS

There are so many people to thank for keeping me and my writing afloat. 😊

Firstly, the magnificent Bookouture – a responsive, forward-thinking publishing company, with a great team who have helped bring out this book – including Rhianna Louise, Alexandra Holmes, Celine Kelly and Jacqui Lewis. (I hope I haven't forgotten anyone.)

Kathryn Taussig, my usual editor, is enjoying maternity leave right now but if it weren't for her, there would be no Shilling Grange Orphanage series, so massive thanks to you, Kathryn.

I wouldn't be with Bookouture if it weren't for my brilliant agent, Thérèse Coen from Hardman & Swainson. She picked me up out of the slush pile and I haven't looked back since. Thank you again, Thérèse.

Readers sometimes ask writers: 'Where do you get your ideas from?' Sadly, there isn't a lovely ideas shop next to Ikea: however, storylines can be informed by radio-documentaries, newspaper articles, overheard conversations and discussions with friends – if that is you, THANK YOU.

I teach creative writing with Richard Kurti at Create98 – it's a fantastic programme for students, and sssh, it's a fantastic programme for me too. It's like having professional ongoing development every week. Some of the brilliant guests we have learned from include: Taika Bellamy, Jackdaw Editorial, Ed Wood, Meera Dattani and fellow Bookouture authors S.E.

Lynes, Emma Robinson and Beth Miller. Our students are fantastic too. Thanks so much, guys, for keeping me on my toes.

To family and friends, to all the dogs I know and love, thank you.

Readers – I need to thank you most of all. Thank you for your kind comments, your lovely messages, your photographs and your reviews. It feels so wonderful when a story finds a home in someone's heart. Do let me know if this one does.

And to anyone who is still reading this, thank you for your perseverance!

Made in United States
Orlando, FL
04 April 2024

45465235R00246